WHAT A TRIP

"Amid the turmoil of the 1960s in America, a young woman and her circle of friends find meaning in the power of friendships, romance, and many unexpected adventures. It's a wild ride!"

— Vivian Fransen, author of *The Straight Spouse: A Memoir*

"Wow—this is a trip! Anyone who remembers those days will find themselves in a familiar world, rich with detail and lyrics of the times, including a song playlist at the end. The author's protagonist has an authentic voice and her worries were our youthful worries."

— Linda Moore, author of *Attribution*

"The cusp of adulthood is both scary and hopeful, and it was particularly fraught in the late '60s and early '70s. *What a Trip* skillfully evokes the era as well as the poignant personal lives of nineteen-year-old art student Fiona O'Brien and her best friend, Melissa. My fingers were crossed all along the way for Fiona to figure out who she is and what she wants, and have the courage to take a chance on her future. A novel that feels deeply honest and true."

— Heidi Hackford, author of *Folly Park*

"An engaging trip through the social and political upheaval of life in the '60s through the eyes of a young woman looking for love and meaning in life. Sex, drugs, and the Vietnam War provide the backdrop for a story that dramatically illustrates the complexity of the times and the changing values from one generation to the next. Despite the clamor all around them, attempting to pull them apart, the characters in this entertaining and heartfelt novel admirably demonstrate the importance of human connection."

— Debra Green, author of *The Convention of Wives*

"*What a Trip* by Susen Edwards is like entering a time machine back to the 1960s. Many of the themes in this book—abortion choice, drugs, government corruption—are as relevant today as they were then. Whether you lived the '60s or only heard about that transformative time from your parents, this book will take you on a journey you will not regret."

—Patricia Grayhall, author of *Making the Rounds*

"Susen Edwards takes us on a '70s, wild, generational jailbreak ride in her novel *What A Trip*. Vietnam, the draft lottery, Woodstock, witchcraft, protests, acid . . . it's all here! Told through the eyes of the wide-eyed Fiona O'Brien, the story is a sensorial immersion in the unhinged explosion of consciousness of the times; I could almost taste the iceberg lettuce salads with fluorescent French dressing, hear the lyrics of a Creedence Clearwater Revival tune, and smell the home-grown weed."

—J. Dylan Yates, author of *The Belief in Angels*

WHAT
A
TRIP

WHAT

A TRIP

A Novel

Susen Edwards

SHE WRITES PRESS

Published 2022
Printed in the United States of America
Print ISBN: 978-1-64742-285-1
E-ISBN: 978-1-64742-286-8
Library of Congress Control Number: 2022907314

For information, address:
She Writes Press
1569 Solano Ave #546
Berkeley, CA 94707

She Writes Press is a division of SparkPoint Studio, LLC.

Book design by Stacey Aaronson

For Cecelia

PART ONE

Fiona cringed as she watched Melissa dump the contents of her purse onto the unmade bed. Gum and candy wrappers, lifeless raisins, tobacco shards, and torn matchbooks blended with the crumbs already littering the sheets.

How long has it been since you changed the sheets? Fiona wondered. *Weeks? Months?*

Melissa brushed the trash to the floor and kicked it under the bed, where it joined an army of decomposing debris. By her pillow lay an errant Marlboro, cast from the pack, only slightly damaged. She reached under the bed for a matchbook, lit the cigarette, took a deep drag, and turned to Fiona. "I need money, Fee."

"What about your job at Bella's Gift Shop?"

"Bella pays shit," Melissa said. "And she's around all the time now, so I can't borrow as much from the cash register."

Fiona snorted. "Borrowing means you're gonna pay her back."

"Bella owes me. I'm just taking what's mine."

Fiona shook her head at Melissa's rationalization.

"If I had more money, I could take these sheets to the laundromat. I could buy a carton of cigarettes instead of scrounging through my purse. Me and Mickey could move into our own apartment and get away from Rick and Chana."

"I don't know how you can stand to live with Rick and Chana," Fiona said. "They get on my nerves, and I'm away at school most of the time."

"There's another reason I need more money, Fee. I—I'm—"

"Hey, Mel, open up!" Mickey banged on the bedroom door.

Mickey, Melissa's boyfriend since high school, was one of Fiona's least favorite people. She checked him out as he stood in the doorway. His jeans, frayed at the ankles and pockets, had a gray pallor from ground-in joint and cigarette ash. His T-shirt, once navy, had faded to match his pants. At least his hair, hanging over his eyes in an attempt to model Paul McCartney, was still black.

A whiff of burned hair brought Fiona's attention back to Melissa, who sat with her head bowed, her white-blond hair covering her face. A plume of smoke drifted up between the long strands.

"Hey, Mel, your hair's on fire!" Mickey shouted.

Melissa, unfazed, brushed her hair from her face, exhaled the final fumes from her lungs, and put out what was left of her cigarette. "What's up, Mickey?"

"Rick has some opiated hash. Where's the pipe?"

"In a minute. First, can we talk?"

Mickey sat on the bed and brushed off a stray raisin.

"I've got some big news," Melissa said. "Got a cigarette?"

"Do you want me to leave?" Fiona asked, feeling a little uncomfortable.

"You're my best friend, Fee. Stay."

Mickey handed Melissa a Marlboro. Fiona grabbed a cigarette from her purse. The three lit up.

Melissa's blue eyes opened wide. "I'm gonna have a baby!"

Fiona felt a tightening in her stomach. No young woman wanted to hear those words from an unmarried friend. She focused on Mickey's face, waiting to see his reaction.

"Holy fuck. You gotta be shittin' me. I thought, I mean, what the fuck?" Mickey stood up, kicked the door, started to leave the room, then turned back to Melissa. "I'm sorry," he said, regaining self-control. "I just never expected. What are you gonna do?"

"What are *we* gonna do," Melissa corrected him. "I guess I'm gonna have the baby. What else?"

Mickey recoiled. "I can't be a father. What about college? What about my parents? What about your mother? Everybody's gonna be really pissed. How did this happen? I thought you were taking the pill."

"I am—I was—but I think I missed that time we dropped acid in the park with Peach," Melissa said.

"Fuckin' Peach," Mickey said. "It's all her fault."

"That's not how it happened," Fiona mumbled.

"You keep outta this," Mickey warned her.

You're the one who should've kept out of Lissie's life.

"You can't have this baby," Mickey said. "You gotta get an abortion. Talk to Chana. I think she knows someplace you can go. Now where's the pipe?"

"No way," Melissa said. "I don't like her friends. Maybe I'll have the baby and give it up."

"Do what you want, Mel, but if you have this baby, don't look to me for help. I'll say it's not mine. I'm goin' to Boston University in the fall, and I'm not goin' with a baby or a pregnant girlfriend. End of story. Rick's waitin' downstairs. If you wanna smoke, come with me. Otherwise, see ya later."

Melissa crushed her cigarette on the floor and kicked it under the bed. "Don't say anything to anybody until I figure this out, okay?" she asked, her eyes welling with tears.

"Okay, sure." Mickey planted a kiss on her forehead and pulled her to her feet. He looked into her tear-filled eyes. "I love you, Mel."

"You do, really?"

"Of course. Come on, let's go." Mickey grabbed the pipe and left the room.

The moment he was gone, Melissa turned to her friend. "What am I gonna do, Fee?"

"I don't know, Lissie." Fiona sighed. "But you sure as shit don't want to bleed to death in some filthy alley after a backroom abortion."

"Mickey will figure something out," Melissa said. "He always does."

"I wouldn't count on it this time," Fiona said. "Let's find Peach; maybe she'll have some ideas."

The Friday night party was in full swing downstairs. Rick and Chana, home from their day jobs, played king and queen to the usual collection of burnouts and hero worshipers. Rick, it seemed, had some excellent stash: two pipes were being passed around and a third was being loaded.

Fiona and Melissa stood on the stairs until they saw Peach in the corner, waving them over. They made their way to her through plumes of smoke.

"What's happening, Peachie?" Fiona asked.

Peach shrugged. "Ready to try this stuff Rick got. But I gotta work at the hospital tonight, so I can't get too messed up." Peach had enrolled in a nursing program right out of high school. In a few months she'd have her LPN and be on her way to earning a decent living—a far cry from the rest of the crowd.

Mickey and Rick had sunk into the couch on the other side of the room. Mickey looked up at his girlfriend for a moment, then turned away as Rick passed the pipe to him.

The pipe came to the girls. They each took a hit, held their breath, and then blew out in unison, creating a giant cloud of smoke.

Peach coughed. "Whoa, this is some good shit!"

Melissa put her arm around Peach. "I need to talk to you," she whispered. "Can we go outside?"

"Sure."

The three girls stood and walked to the front door. As they did, Mickey glanced at them and cocked his head, as if to say, "What's up?"

Melissa shook her head.

He immediately went back to his conversation with Rick.

The girls brushed dead leaves and unidentified trash from the front step and sat.

"You look serious, Lissie." Peach scowled. "Is that bastard cheating on you again?"

"I don't think Mickey would ever cheat on me," Melissa replied. "He just told me he loves me."

Everybody knows he's cheating except you, Lissie.

"What do you want to talk about?" Peach asked.

Melissa came right out with it. "I'm pregnant, Peachie. Mickey wants me to have an abortion, but I'm scared. Remember that girl Chana sent into the city? She almost died. Mickey said if I have the baby, he'll say it's not his."

Peach exhaled sharply. "How pregnant are you?"

"Maybe seven weeks, maybe more."

"You're only eighteen. Are you ready to be a mom?" Peach asked. "You can't have a kid and live here. How would you support yourself? Your mother sure ain't gonna help. Hell, she'll probably never speak to you again."

"I thought I'd go to Boston with Mickey and have the baby," Melissa said. "His parents are rich. We could live on what they send him. They don't have to know about me."

"Are you for real? After Mickey said he wants nothing to do with the kid?" Fiona stared at her friend. "And what if his parents find out? Think this through. Are you dead set on having it?"

Melissa thought for a moment. "Maybe I could take something and have a miscarriage, or maybe I could accidentally fall down the stairs."

Fiona could see Peach was getting as frustrated as she was.

"Come on, Peachie," Melissa pleaded. "You're the nurse. Help me."

"I didn't want to say anything," Peach said slowly, "but since I've been working at the hospital, a few women have come in for abortions. If you or the baby are at risk, they'll do it."

"So, it's settled," Melissa said. "I'll have some kind of accident and they'll have to give me an abortion."

"No, Lissie, don't be stupid," Peach said. "But there *is* one other thing that might work. If they think you're unfit to be a mother—"

"Yes! I'll tell them I don't have any money and Mickey doesn't want to be a father."

Peach shook her head. "That won't work. They'd tell you to have the baby and give it up. But a chick came in a while back who was really fucked up—a nervous breakdown or something. She was talking all sorts of crazy shit, and they gave her an abortion, no problem."

"Do you think they'd do that for me?" Melissa asked. "Do you think I could convince the doctor I'm nuts?"

Fiona was too good a friend to tell Melissa no acting was necessary.

"Let me check things out," Peach said. "I'll ask about that chick, talk to the nurses, and get the name of the doctor." She put a hand on Melissa's knee. "Hang tight, trust me, and I'll take care of you."

The girls finished their cigarettes, threw the butts in the bushes, and went back inside to join the party.

Later that night Fiona lay in bed staring at the ceiling, thinking about Melissa's pregnancy. It was after three o'clock before she fell asleep.

After what seemed like minutes, her mom knocked on her door. "Fiona, you have a phone call."

Fiona shook herself awake. "Be right there, Mom."

"It's after ten, Fiona. Half the day is gone."

Fiona ignored the comment, stepped into the hallway, and picked up the phone. "Hello?"

"Fee, fi, fo, fuck. How are you, Fee?" This was Melissa's standard greeting and had been since they became best friends during their junior year in high school.

Melissa's upbeat mood was in sharp contrast to her tears from the night before.

"What's happening?" Fiona asked.

"I'm feeling a lot better this morning. Mickey's been really sweet. I think things might work out," Melissa said.

Fiona had her doubts but said nothing.

"Can you get your mom's car tonight?" Melissa asked. "We can go riding around."

Fiona's mom never used her metallic blue Corvair on the weekends. "Sure. I'll pick you up after dinner."

Fiona ate a quick dinner with her parents and politely asked to borrow the car. As expected, there was no problem. Before leaving, she made a detour past the family's well-stocked liquor cabinet and grabbed a fifth of Southern Comfort. It wouldn't be missed.

Fiona checked her appearance in the mirror. Her best feature, fiery red hair, hung in soft ringlets around her face. Her mom had instructed her at an early age never to leave the house without being fully made up. This was about the only lesson she took to heart, probably because it helped conceal her white skin and accentuate her green eyes.

She tucked her poor boy sweater into her tight jeans, pulled on her boots, and for a second wondered why she went to so much effort when she and Melissa would probably end up at the diner after they ran out of liquor and joints.

Hey, you never know when Mr. Wonderful might walk into my life. Maybe I'll be lucky and get laid tonight.

She smiled into the mirror and winked at herself. It was time to go.

Melissa looked more fragile than ever as she got into the Corvair. "Man, am I glad to get away from that shit shack," she said to Fiona. "Chana is such an asshole. I know she's stealing from me."

Fiona wondered what Melissa owned that was worth stealing. "Maybe if you got a full-time job, you and Peach could get a place together. Might take some of the pressure off you and Mickey."

"I can't leave Mickey with those guys. He'd forget about me in a heartbeat, plus I want to be free to move with him in the fall." Melissa passed a joint and bedraggled pack of matches to Fiona.

"Hang on, Lissie. I want to put towels over the seats in case we drop the roach. My mom would kill me for sure." Fiona reached for the old towels she kept behind the back seat.

"You're always so fucking prepared," Melissa said. "I wish I was half as prepared as you."

Fiona laughed it off. "God made me that way. Look what else I brought." She pulled the bottle of Southern Comfort from under the front seat.

"Cool. Just like Janis!"

Melissa and Fiona were smitten with Janis Joplin. They had stumbled onto a *Big Brother and the Holding Company* album the summer before and immediately fell under Janis's spell of blues and booze.

Fiona started the engine. "Let's get out of here. One of these days they're gonna raid your house. I hope I'm not here when they do."

The girls passed the bottle and joint and headed for the country roads. "I want to go to Billy Brown's Road. We can park and talk. The cops never go there," Melissa suggested.

Fiona turned onto Billy Brown's Road. Was there really a ghost named Billy Brown who haunted the deserted house at the end of the road, or was it simply a stoner legend?

They pulled into the dirt cul-de-sac, parked behind a stand

of trees, then cut the engine and headlights. It was a moonless, overcast night. The only illumination came from the tips of their cigarettes. Fiona smoked Kools, not socially hip like Marlboros, but she liked the menthol rush. Tonight, Melissa smoked Kools.

Even in near darkness, Fiona could see Melissa hadn't washed her hair. Her clothes, too, had seen cleaner days.

"I've been thinking about Peach's idea and how to convince the doctor I'm unfit to be a mother. Any ideas on what I could say?"

"You mean besides not having a decent job, a husband, or a place to raise a kid?" Fiona asked.

"Maybe I could tell them I believe in fairies." Melissa took a hit of Southern Comfort and passed it to Fiona. "There's something else I haven't told anybody yet."

Fiona took a drink and a deep breath. "What?"

"Well, I didn't get pregnant by accident. There's more going on than you know. I think it's Denise's fault."

Denise was a year younger than the girls, a senior in high school. She was about to graduate at the head of her class and head to Boston University in the fall.

"What are you talking about?" Fiona lit another Kool and passed the pack to her friend.

"She's got a thing for Mickey. I know he goes to her house sometimes when I'm working. I think she put a spell on me, and that's why I got pregnant."

"This whole witchcraft thing is a fad," Fiona said. "You should never have gone to see *Rosemary's Baby*."

"It's not a fad. Black magic is real and so is the Devil," Melissa said.

"It was a movie, Lissie."

"That's what you think. I know the truth."

Fiona knew better than to argue with her friend.

"Denise is trying to break us up and ruin my life. That's why everything's in the toilet."

"Are you telling me this 'cause you believe it or because that's what you're gonna tell the doctor?" Fiona asked.

A sob burst from Melissa's throat, exploding into a gush of tears. Once freed, they wouldn't stop.

"C'mere, Lissie." Fiona opened her arms to her friend. She held her until her sobs quieted, making sure Melissa's face was away from her body so no mascara would melt onto her sweater.

What kind of friend am I who cares more about a sweater than my best friend? No need to question her motives. Fiona knew the answer.

"What am I gonna do, Fee? What if she goes to Boston with Mickey and I'm here? What if we can't break the spell?" More sobs waiting in her heart worked themselves up and out. Melissa raised her head. Ribbons of mascara dripped from eyes to chin. "I can't go to the diner looking like this, okay?"

"Sure. Let's hang out for a while, then we can go home." Fiona got a tissue from her purse and wiped her friend's cheeks.

"I love you, Fee." Melissa planted a kiss on Fiona's lips.

Is that your tongue, Lissie? Fiona pulled away slowly and pretended nothing had happened.

Another cigarette, another drink, and it was time to go.

Melissa had an idea. "Let's drive by Denise's house. See if she's home. Maybe catch Mickey with her."

A drive-by was always fun, checking who was home, who was watching TV with their parents, who was visiting whom.

It was nearly midnight by the time they arrived. All the windows were dark. Denise's car sat quietly in the driveway. Was she sleeping soundly or casting a spell under her bed covers?

"Hey, let's park around the corner and sneak up to the house," Melissa suggested.

"Okay." Fiona had enough Southern Comfort in her belly to not give a shit.

The windows of the ranch house were a little too high to look into. The back door was locked. All was quiet.

"I have to pee," Melissa announced.

"Can you hold it till you get home?"

"No, c'mon, let's pee in Denise's backyard. I'm gonna do it right in front of their barbecue."

"I can't. I'll wait till I get home."

"It'll break the curse. If you love me, you'll do it. Please?"

"Okay, but I'm going behind the barbecue."

The two desecrated Denise's yard. *This better work.*

They rode in silence the rest of the way home, then kissed good night. This time there were no tongues.

Fiona's head was spinning but not from Southern Comfort. The events in Denise's backyard had washed away any remnants of drunkenness. She sat in the driveway after Melissa went inside the house, thinking, *She's crazy. I need to get away from her, start a new life. Get some new friends. But how can I leave her now?*

More than anything Fiona craved peace and simplicity—a sunny Victorian shaded by ancient trees, a coffee house that sold her artwork, and a writer or musician boyfriend who adored her. Instead, she found herself moving further and further from her dream.

She was startled by a knock on her window. Was that Jack,

the boy she'd had a crush on since her sophomore year in high school? What was he doing here? She rolled down the window.

"Hey, Fiona! Open the door."

Fiona felt a lurch in her stomach. *Don't get sick now*, she thought as she reached over and unlocked the passenger door.

Jack was even cuter than she remembered. His blond hair was longer, and he'd added a mustache, both neatly trimmed and combed. He wore blue jeans, a faded T-shirt, and a denim jacket. Fiona got a whiff of Dr. Bronner's peppermint soap, her favorite.

"I didn't know you hung with these people," Jack said as he plopped into the passenger seat.

Fiona's palms were sweaty, and her heart was pounding. "Melissa's my best friend. I don't really know Rick and Chana. What are you doing here?"

"Not much else to do on a Saturday night. I should be home studying for finals, but what the fuck, there's always tomorrow." Jack attended the local community college. "Hey, you look great. What'cha doin' now?"

"I don't know. I thought I'd head home."

Jack stretched and let his left arm rest on Fiona's shoulder. "I heard you and Andy broke up."

Fiona didn't want to be reminded of Andy, her high school boyfriend, and their breakup. "That's ancient history."

"I've always liked you, Fiona. How come we never got together?" He inched closer to her on the bench seat.

"I thought you had a girlfriend." Fiona had heard the rumor about a gorgeous girlfriend who attended private school.

"Oh, that," Jack spat. "That's been over since last summer. Anyway, we were never exclusive. I'm a free agent." He gently lifted her hair, blew into her ear, then turned her face toward him and placed a soft kiss next to her eye.

Fiona thought she would melt into the vinyl. She moved closer. Lips met. Tongues touched. Hands clasped. Things were moving way too fast. She needed to get hold of herself, or this could turn into a one-night stand.

She had a history of passion winning over reason and hated herself each time. Tonight had to be different. As she pulled away, she saw how quickly they had steamed up the windows. Thinking fast, she wrote *next weekend?* on the windshield.

Jack smiled and sat back. "Next weekend it is. I'll call you during the week."

Fiona smiled her sexiest smile. They exchanged numbers and kissed once more.

She put the Corvair in gear and backed out of the driveway. It had been quite a night.

Chapter 3

Back at college, Fiona could think of nothing but her upcoming date with Jack and her friend's pregnancy. Days stretched into infinity until Friday rolled around.

Fiona sat on her bed packing an overnight bag. She had only one class on Friday and was free to head home by eleven o'clock. Before leaving, she glanced at her freshman roommate's side of the dorm room. The girl had been missing in action most of the semester.

All that remained of her was an unmade bed piled high with dirty clothes and forgotten textbooks. Fiona did her best to stay away from that half of the room. By contrast, she kept her half spotless. Her clothes were organized by color and style. She changed her sheets weekly and made sure her Indian import bedspread, which Melissa had pilfered from Bella's Gift Shop, lay without a wrinkle.

Bill, her ride home, pulled up to the dorm in his '55 Chevy Bel Air. He had piled his books and suitcase on the front seat, so she'd have to sit in the back.

"You goin' to the Spring Fling Dance next weekend?" Bill asked.

I wouldn't be caught dead with those assholes. Ever polite, she replied, "No. Too much studying for finals. Are you going?"

"I was thinkin' about it. That would mean I'd be stayin' up here for the weekend. Would you wanna go with me? You'd have the rest of the weekend to study."

"I'll have to let you know on Sunday, okay?" Fiona would never allow herself to be seen in public with a creep like Bill.

"Sure thing," Bill said.

They rode in silence the rest of the way home.

Back home, Fiona made herself a tuna sandwich and spent Friday afternoon going through her closet, deciding what to wear on her date. Jack had invited her to a Saturday evening concert at the community college. The band, Devil's Triangle, had cut their first album and were playing the East Coast college circuit. Jack had scored last-minute seats at the back of the auditorium, not great for music but far enough away from the sound system so they could talk.

She settled on a bell-sleeved white cotton dress she had hand-embroidered. It was short enough to show off her legs, but not so short her mom would freak out. What she needed was a pair of silver hoop earrings. Bella's Gift Shop was open for another hour and had just the pair. Fiona took some money with her in case Melissa's boss was around and she'd have to pay for them.

No need for money. The shop was empty except for Melissa and Peach. They were deep in conversation as Fiona made her way to the back counter.

"How's it goin'?" Fiona asked.

"Cool, Fee," Peach said. "Lissie and I've been talkin', and we made some decisions."

"Peachie convinced me to see the doctor at the hospital and get the abortion. I'll get rid of the problem, and Mickey won't be pissed at me anymore." Melissa's tears from the previous weekend were a distant memory.

"Not so fast, Lissie," Peach said. "You have to convince them you're unfit and then come up with the money. You also need to tell your mother."

Melissa's mood went from elation to gloom in a matter of seconds. "But I'm eighteen."

"Yeah, but when you're considered unfit, you need somebody to sign for you. Go see your mother tonight after work. And take Mickey," Peach said.

Melissa hung her head. "Okay, I guess."

Fiona pretended to act concerned, but all she could think about was her date with Jack and the earrings that called to her from the jewelry counter.

Conversation stopped as two customers came into the shop. Fiona used Peach as a shield and cupped the earrings into her palm.

"Hey, you're good, Fee. Cop me a pair too."

Fiona was only too happy to comply. The earrings slipped into Peach's back pocket.

She knew the shop had no security mirrors and the owner didn't track her inventory. *If she's dumb enough to run her store this way, then she deserves to get ripped off.*

"Store's closing," Peach said, looking at her watch. "Time for us to split."

What a Trip

"Fee, can you give me a ride home?" Melissa asked. "I just have to lock up."

"No problem."

Chapter 4

"**R**ick and Chana's car isn't here," Melissa said as Fiona pulled into the driveway. "That means I can talk to Mickey without anybody butting in."

You mean besides me?

"Mickey!" Melissa yelled as she walked into the kitchen. No answer. "Mickey?"

The girls went upstairs to the bedroom. No Mickey. Fiona heard a scuffling across the hall and a door opening. The scent of hashish floated into her nostrils. Mickey, his hair mussed and clothes more rumpled than usual, slid into the room.

"You're early, Mel," he said, ignoring Fiona.

"Not really. It's five thirty, same as always. Can we talk?"

"Now? Rick and I are listenin' to the Stones." He didn't look happy.

"Now, Mickey." Melissa took his hand and led him to their bed. "I talked to Peach today. She's gonna get me in to see the abortion doctor next week."

Mickey's expression changed to one of relief. "Now you're talkin'."

"There's only one thing," Melissa said, "I have to tell my

mother. I'm gonna do it tonight before I chicken out. I want you to go with me."

"No fucking way!" Mickey pulled his hand away and stood. "This is your mess. Your mother. You know how she feels about me. Take Fiona or another one of your asshole friends. I'm outta here."

"But, Mickey—" Melissa's tears were back.

Fiona wondered how many times her friend had cried in the last week. She jumped when she heard Rick's door slam.

"Please," Melissa whispered.

Fiona heard laughter followed by the Rolling Stones *Beggars Banquet* at full volume.

"This is wrong. It's his baby too." Melissa stomped across the hall and knocked on the door. No answer. She made a fist and hit the wood as hard as she could. "Open the fucking door!"

The music faded as the door opened a few inches. Mickey stuck his head out. "What? I thought we were done."

"I know you don't want to go with me tonight, and I know you're upset," Melissa said, "but I just want to know you're gonna be there for me once this is over."

Mickey stepped into the hallway. He wiped her tears away and hugged her. "Sure, Mel, don't worry. Now be a good girl and go see your mother."

He opened Rick's door. Before going inside, Mickey turned to Melissa. "Everything'll be okay. You've just gotta get through the next couple of weeks. See you later."

Mickey disappeared. The Stones returned, louder than before.

What a piece of shit, Fiona wanted to say, but knew her words would cause Melissa more pain.

"Fee, I can't face my mother alone."

"I'll come with you," Fiona said. "Maybe Peach should come too. She's the one with the plan. And let's bring a pizza. It'll put your mother in a good mood."

"Good idea." Melissa wiped her eyes, took a few deep breaths, and went downstairs to call Peach.

"Missy, you should talk to Peach about a job at the hospital," Mrs. Patten, Melissa's mother, said. "If you're not going to college, you need to start thinking about a career. This past year has been a complete waste."

"I have a job, Mommy, and I like what I do," Melissa replied.

"There's no future at that silly store. The ladies at work say it's about to close. Peach, maybe you can talk to her."

"Actually, Mrs. P, the hospital is the reason we're here." Peach didn't waste any time.

Melissa put down her plate. She glared at Peach.

Everyone's plate was now on the table. Mrs. Patten leaned back into the sofa. In her yellow pantsuit, she nearly disappeared into the gold-and-brown flowered cushions that served as her living room, dining room, and bedroom. "Are you sick? I knew you'd catch something living in that run-down house. I don't know why you had to move. You have a perfectly good bedroom here."

"I'm pregnant, Mommy." Melissa's words tumbled out before she could take them back.

"*No!* You're not still seeing that good-for-nothing Mickey, are you? Or is it some other boy?"

Melissa was crying again. "I-I'm gonna be sick." She ran into the bathroom.

"Peach, what are we going to do with her?" Mrs. Patten asked.

"Mickey and Lissie are in love, but they can't have a baby now. Mickey's leaving for college in the fall, and Lissie has her whole life ahead of her. I think I have an idea." Peach was doing her best to act mature and take command of the situation.

"You mean give the baby up for adoption? How could I live knowing I had a grandchild living with a strange family?" Mrs. Patten said.

"Well, there's a program at the hospital that will give girls an abortion if they think they're unfit to be mothers. I thought we could get Lissie in to see the doctor next week, but we need you to help convince them."

"We're Catholic, Peach. Abortion is a sin, and it's illegal." Mrs. Patten sat straight up on the couch and crossed her arms over her chest.

They sat without speaking. The uneaten pizza stared up at them from the coffee table. In the background, Melissa's retching broke the silence.

"Please, Mrs. P, Lissie can't have this baby," Fiona pleaded.

After an uncomfortable minute, Mrs. Patten said, "I agree that Missy isn't ready to be a mother. Maybe we could look into it."

The toilet flushed, the water ran, the bathroom door opened, and Melissa walked back into the living room. Against her white skin, her eyes appeared red and sunken. She sat with her head bowed, peeking through a maze of blond tendrils.

Mrs. Patten picked up her pack of Parliaments. "Peach told me about the program at the hospital. I'm not making any promises. No matter what we decide, you need to see a doctor. We'll make an appointment for one day next week."

"Thanks, Mommy. Peach and I will call on Monday. I'll let you know when they'll take us," Melissa said.

"Try to make it during my lunch break so I don't miss work." Mrs. Patten took a last drag from her cigarette and doused it in her uneaten pizza.

The girls let the screen door slam behind them.

"Holy shit, she went for it!" Melissa practically jumped out of her jeans.

Fiona was more subdued. "She didn't say she'd go for it. Let's have a smoke and sit in the park." The girls lit up, inhaled deeply, and walked across the street from the apartment to the town park.

"But at least she's willing to talk to the doctor," Melissa said.

"Lissie, you've got one chance to make this work," Peach said. "Here's what you need to tell them—"

"I know, I know, tell them I believe in fairies," Melissa interrupted.

"That's not enough. You need to tell them your mom has no money, and she can't help you. You also need to tell them what a deadbeat Mickey is."

"Mickey's not a deadbeat. He's scared shitless like I am. He loves me!"

Fiona was getting frustrated. "If he loves you so much, why didn't he come with you tonight?"

"He's afraid of my mother."

That's not all he's afraid of.

"Listen, Lissie. For this, you need to make them think he's a loser. It's gonna make the story look better. And that business about Denise being a witch. Tell them that too," Peach said.

Melissa fidgeted, lit another cigarette, and said, "I can't say that in front of my mother. She'll think I'm crazy."

"That's the idea," Peach reminded her.

"Denise will find out I told them, and she'll make my life even worse. She'll really go after Mickey and put a bigger spell on me."

"You've got one chance. Don't mention Denise's name. Tell them about the curse and how scared you are. And whatever you do, don't mention tripping or any of the other shit you've been taking. The last thing you need is to get your house and the rest of us busted," Peach warned.

"I wish I was dead." Melissa lost her balance and stumbled over an invisible crack in the sidewalk. She collapsed in a heap on the ground, lay on her side, and began hyperventilating.

Fiona and Peach watched her, helpless. Two middle-aged women were coming toward them. "Lissie, get up before those women get here," Fiona commanded. "Let's go for a ride and smoke a joint. You'll feel better, I promise."

The girls grabbed Melissa around the waist, pulled her until her legs straightened, and practically dragged her out of the park.

An hour later, Peach pulled into the parking lot outside Melissa's apartment.

"I gotta get ready for work. Will you guys be okay?" Peach asked.

Fiona doubted anything would be okay with her friend.

Melissa rolled out of the passenger door. Fiona helped her straighten up.

"C'mon, Lissie, let's get you upstairs."

"Shh, maybe my mother's sleeping and we can sneak in," Melissa whispered.

They quietly opened the screen door and could hear Mrs. Patten on the phone.

"Missy's losing her grip on reality," Mrs. Patten said. "She was fine till Marty left us. It's all his fault."

"Who's Marty?" Fiona whispered.

"My father. He walked out on us five years ago."

"Marge, I'm telling you, Melissa's not fit to be a mother. But abortion?" Mrs. Patten said.

"She's talking to my aunt Marge," Melissa whispered.

"No, I stopped going to church. Sundays are sometimes my best day at Sears."

Mrs. Patten paused. "Of course, I'm still a Catholic. The Pope tells us life begins at conception."

"How would he know?" Fiona whispered.

Melissa's eyes filled with tears. She pressed her face into Fiona's shoulder so her mother wouldn't hear her crying.

Mrs. Patten was silent for several minutes. "Maybe you're right, Marge. Let's leave it up to the doctor."

Melissa lifted her head and smiled for the first time in hours. "That sounds hopeful. Let's go back outside till we see her lights go out."

The girls tiptoed downstairs, stood at the curb, and stared at Melissa's living room window.

"How long before she goes to bed?" Fiona asked.

What a Trip

"Once she gets off the phone, she'll wash up, make up the couch, pop a Seconal, and be asleep in no time."

Half an hour later the apartment lights dimmed.

"All clear," Melissa said. "I'll call you tomorrow."

Chapter 5

Fiona's new silver earrings sparkled under her copper curls. Putting them in her ears the next evening, Fiona shivered as she remembered how Jack's tongue had caressed her earlobe. Where would his tongue explore tonight? She didn't have much time to fantasize. She heard Jack downstairs introducing himself to her parents. The voices sounded upbeat, a change from her parents' usual reaction to her friends. Score one for Jack.

Fiona enjoyed making an entrance. Her background in dance gave her grace and poise that she used to her advantage as she descended the stairs. Her dad's eyebrows raised ever so slightly.

"I'll have your daughter home at a reasonable hour, Mr. and Mrs. O'Brien. The concert should be over around eleven o'clock. We'll probably get a bite to eat and spend some time chatting, since it'll be loud in the concert." Jack was laying it on thick, and her parents were eating it up.

"We like her home by one. Two at the latest," her dad said.

"No problem, sir." Turning to Fiona, he said, "Shall we go?"

Holy shit! Is this guy for real? "I'm ready. G'night, Mom and Dad."

Fiona's mood took a sharp dive as she checked out Jack's

ride. A decades-old bomb of a car sat in front of the house. "Is this your car?" she asked.

"It's my nana's car. I know it looks weird, but I promise you'll change your mind after tonight."

"Um, what is it?"

"Nash Airflyte. I call it the living room or the bedroom, depending on who I'm with. Check it out."

Jack opened the passenger door, and Fiona climbed inside. The seats were like sofas. Fiona began keeping score. Jack had scored two points for chatting up her parents and two more points for opening her car door. He would lose those points if he couldn't show her what the car could do.

He started the engine and carefully backed out the driveway. Fiona's parents watched from the window. She waved as they turned the corner. Once out of sight, Jack pulled to the curb and put the car in neutral.

"This is the living room. Now for the bedroom." He flipped a lever, and his seat reclined until it lay flat. "Now for yours. Find the lever on the side and lift." Her seat fell back and she with it.

Jack added four more points to his score.

After the show-and-tell demo, he returned the seats to living room mode and made small talk on the way to the concert. Fiona learned Jack had grown up in Virginia. His parents died in a car accident when he was in eighth grade. His aunt had legal custody of him and his sister. She only had room for one child in her home, so she sent him to New Jersey to live with his grandmother and start high school. Because his grandmother wasn't in the best of health, Jack decided to stay at home and attend community college.

Fiona couldn't remember the last time she had connected

with a guy at this level. They were either ready to jump into her pants or eager to impress her with their intellect. Jack seemed like he really wanted to get to know her. She wondered what she was doing with a guy like him. How soon would he realize that she was a worthless piece of shit and dump her?

She decided to put her negative thoughts aside and focus on the present moment.

They arrived at the auditorium in plenty of time to get decent parking. Instead, Jack parked at the back of the lot, away from the rest of the cars. "Can't be too careful with Nana's car," he said as he cut the engine. "Slide into my living room, Fee." Jack put his arm around Fiona and pulled her to him. He kissed her softly at first, then more urgently. Before she knew what was happening, he lowered his seat. "Welcome to my bedroom!"

"Now, Jack? What about the show?"

"We're plenty early. We've got time for a quick one." He slid his hand under Fiona's dress and gave her panties a gentle tug.

"But it's our first time. Why rush?" Fiona's protests fell on deaf ears.

"I promise there'll be more later. Lots more."

Fiona couldn't stop now even if she wanted to. She let her body take her where she'd wanted to be for three years.

It felt like it was over in a flash, but when Jack checked his watch, twenty minutes had passed.

"That was great. We better get going or we'll miss the show," Jack said as he stuffed himself back into his jeans.

Fiona could care less about the concert, but it was a first date. She returned her white lace panties to their rightful home, smoothed her hair and dress, and gave Jack a final kiss. "Let's go."

They were two of the last people to get seated.

"I know it's the nosebleed section, but it's the best I could do at the last minute," Jack apologized.

Fiona's mind was still back in the Nash. She was having a tough time with the reality of the auditorium. Hundreds of people surrounded them. None knew what she and Jack had just done. A bit of an exhibitionist, she almost wished somebody had stood outside the car and watched them.

Jack reached for her hand and whispered, "That was the best sex I ever had."

The music drowned out his voice. "What?" asked Fiona.

"That was the best sex I ever had!" A few people turned to look at them. Fiona felt the color rising in her cheeks. She loved every stare.

"Me too!"

They kissed, then kissed some more. The music wailed. The crowd roared. Jack and Fiona stayed wrapped in their own universe. More than anything, she wanted to leave, to return to their private world. Finally, it was intermission.

"Let's blow this joint." Jack pulled her from her seat and maneuvered their way through the crowd. Fresh air hit them as they ran from the exit. Fiona had never felt so free.

The Nash was still in bedroom mode. They climbed in, practically tearing off their clothes before closing the door.

"Hang on a sec, Fee." Jack reached into the glove box and pulled out a small carved wooden box. Inside lay a brass pipe and something wrapped in foil. "I got some of that opiated hash from Rick. Let's have a couple of tokes. Not too much. It's powerful shit."

He lit the pipe, inhaled deeply, and handed it to Fiona. She followed his lead. One hit was all they needed. She lay back and raised her arms toward Jack. He rolled on top of her. "We have at least an hour before the show's over. Let's make it count."

Voices were coming closer. The show was over. *That had to be the best hour of my life*, Fiona thought as they got dressed. True to his word, they stopped at the diner and shared a piece of cherry cheesecake. At 12:55 a.m., they pulled into Fiona's driveway.

"How 'bout I drive up to see you at college next weekend? We can study for finals together." Jack gave her a last kiss on the cheek, not lingering too long in case her parents were watching.

"That would be great." Fiona slid across the seat. As she opened the door, Jack gave her behind a tiny pinch. She turned and smiled at him. "I can't wait!"

Chapter 6

"**F**iona, wake up. It's time for church." Fiona's mother knocked softly on her door, and then more urgently. "It's after nine o'clock. Church is at ten thirty."

Fiona lay in bed, reliving last night. Church was the one thing she hated about coming home. All she wanted to do was sleep in. Once she got her own car, she could make up an excuse and head back to school Sunday morning.

"*Fiona!*"

"Okay, Mom, I'm awake."

Breck shampoo and Dove soap washed away the faint scent of peppermint on her skin. She vowed to get a bottle of Dr. Bronner's for her dorm room and one for home. It was one more way to keep Jack in her life.

"That Jack seems like an okay guy," her dad said at the breakfast table. "Sure is polite. How was the concert?"

"Okay. Loud. Hot," Fiona mumbled as she stared into her cornflakes.

"Did he ask you out again?" her mom asked. "He's a nice-looking boy. I just don't like you staying out so late on a Saturday night. You don't want to miss church."

"I probably won't see him till I come home for the summer," Fiona lied.

Mrs. O'Brien was religious to a fault. She and her husband sang in the choir. She was the church treasurer, attended Bible study on Tuesday evenings, went to the Ladies' Aid Society on Thursday mornings, and took her turn running the fellowship hour after Sunday services. A belief in Jesus was her answer to everything. Fiona was sure her mom had earned enough points to secure a one-way, first-class ticket to heaven.

As always, her parents left half an hour early for church. Fiona promised to get there on time. The less time she spent in church, the better. After all, she didn't need a front-row seat.

At 10:25, she put on her best Christian smile and slid into a back pew. A few church ladies turned and smiled at her. Nothing had changed for these women since the 1940s: tight gray curls, flowered shirtwaists draping ample hips, sensible shoes. They dreamed of coffee and cake after the service.

From the choir loft, Mrs. O'Brien nodded her head at her daughter. Her dad chatted up one of the other tenors. Pastor Ritchey took his place at the podium, signaling an end to squirms and whispers. *Here we go, the longest hour.*

Over the years, she'd become an expert at tuning out, turning in, and entertaining herself with her week in review. She relived last night's lovemaking moment by moment, Jack's fingers traveling from the nape of her neck to—

Did Pastor Ritchey mention the war in Vietnam? She snapped out of her reverie and focused her attention on the sermon.

"War creates suffering. War is against God's teachings and violates the sixth commandment, 'Thou shalt not kill.'" He continued his sermon, contradicting everything Fiona had heard from her parents, who supported the current political agenda.

What a Trip

Fiona was a pacifist and had been long before she knew the meaning of the word. She avoided killing even the tiniest ant and cringed when her dad swatted spiders and flies. As a child, she rescued baby birds and mice and took on the role of mom for all the family pets.

"So today, in memory of the Vietnamese who are living in such adversity, I ask you to forgo your Sunday dinner for a bowl of rice. This simple gesture won't stop the war, but it will make you think about your brothers and sisters on the other side of the world. Let us pray." Pastor Ritchey bowed his head. The congregation followed.

Maybe there was something to get out of church. Maybe she had been looking at religion all wrong. Fiona tuned in to the prayer.

After the service, Fiona joined the congregation for the fellowship hour. The coffee was weak and the cookies stale, but perhaps she could engage someone in a discussion about the sermon. She approached Mrs. Watowski and Mrs. Miller, two fixtures of the congregation.

"I can't stay too long," Mrs. Watowski said to her friend. "I've got a huge roast to cook. You know how Mr. W gets when his Sunday dinner is late."

"You don't have to tell me," Mrs. Miller replied. "We're going out for a late brunch at the Log Cabin. They make delicious omelets. No cooking for me today. I'm off the hook."

"Enjoy your meal, Marge," Mrs. Watowski said.

"Believe me, I will. It's all you can eat and no dishes to wash."

The two women headed toward the exit and grabbed a few stale cookies on their way out.

Fiona was speechless. What about the rice? What about the starving Vietnamese? She wanted to say something. But what and to whom? Everyone was stuffing their face, oblivious to the pastor's message.

Bill, her ride back to college, was due at two o'clock, which meant she had time to boil some rice for the family before heading out. As she poured the dry grains into a pot of boiling water, her mom walked into the kitchen.

"What are you doing, Fiona? You know I made macaroni and cheese for today." Her mom turned off the burner and lit the oven.

"What about the sermon? I thought we were supposed to eat rice today." Fiona couldn't believe her mom would defy the pastor's request.

"Come on, kiddo. I know what he said, but that's just a metaphor. Something to get us thinking." Mrs. O'Brien placed several slices of Wonder bread and a stick of Imperial margarine on the table, then reached for a head of iceberg lettuce and an orange bottle of Kraft French dressing, her excuse for a salad. "Dinner's at one."

"Sorry, Mom, no dinner for me today unless it's rice."

"Suit yourself. *George*! Dinner at one. Don't get too involved in anything."

"Yes, dear." Her dad's standard response shot up from the basement.

What a Trip

Stifling a sob, Fiona ran up the stairs and slammed her bedroom door. "That's it for me," she said. "This religion shit is over!" She packed up her things and sat at the window, waiting for Bill. For the first time, she looked forward to the ride back to school.

Chapter 7

Between preparing for finals, an art project, and a term paper, Fiona had little time to think about her near conversion to religion. As she headed toward the Art Department, she passed through the student center packed with students drinking Cokes, smoking cigarettes, and playing cards. A table of casual acquaintances waved to her to join them.

What a waste of time, she thought as she waved back and shook her head. They would be up all night studying while she would be dreaming of Jack and next weekend.

Fiona's final project for Basic Drawing was a still-life charcoal sketch. She found it boring and simplistic, nothing like an assignment she would have been given if she had gone to a first-rate art school instead of a mediocre state college.

She resisted the urge to destroy the simplistic piece. Instead, she added fine lines with pen and ink, bringing the drawing to life.

That's better, she thought as she sprayed fixative on her finished work and laid it on her instructor's desk.

For her Contemporary English Lit class, Fiona handed in a paper analyzing *One Hand Clapping* by Anthony Burgess. She'd read the novel early in the semester and wrote most of her analysis a month ago. All that remained was to edit and proofread.

Her first final exam was scheduled for Wednesday, which left only two exams the following week. Then three months of freedom.

Freedom was a relative term. A summer job teaching art at the Methodist summer camp waited for her at the end of June. If she was destined to be an art teacher and follow her parents' wishes, she thought it best to get some experience.

Back in her dorm room, Fiona was lying on the bed daydreaming when she heard her name called.

"Fiona O'Brien! Phone call!"

Two pay phones hung by the elevators. Fiona jumped to attention. Incoming calls were rare. She worried someone had died, or worse yet, Jack might be canceling. She bolted out of her room and down the hall.

Breathless and shaking, she answered the phone. "Hello?"

"Fee, it's Lissie. I need to see you. Can you come home?" Melissa's voice was barely audible.

"I can't. It's finals, and I've got no way to get there." Fiona failed to mention Jack's upcoming visit.

"I saw the doctor yesterday with my mother. It was horrible. She started crying and screaming at me right in his office. It got so bad the nurse had to take her out so the doctor could talk to me.

"I talked to him for a long time. I told him everything. He examined me, took some blood, and told me to wait while he talked to my mother. After that, he brought me back in and said he would operate on me as long as the shrink approved."

Melissa took a deep breath and continued. "My mother cried

all the way home. She never went back to work, so I know she was upset. I stayed with her last night."

"I'm sure that made your mother feel better," Fiona said.

"I think so too," Melissa went on. "Today, I saw the shrink. She was really nice and easy to talk to. And you know what's weird? Neither the doctor nor the shrink asked to see Mickey. It's like he's not even part of this whole thing. They care more about my mother than him. And guess what? They approved the operation!"

"Far out, Lissie." Fiona noticed Melissa was now calling it an operation, not an abortion.

"Friday they'll do some tests, and Monday they'll operate. My mother talked to the shrink after I did, and now she's even okay about it. Can you come home this weekend? I need you."

Fiona wanted to cry. "There's no way. I'm so sorry."

Melissa stifled a sob on the other end of the phone.

"Finals are over on Wednesday. I'll be home for good on Thursday. I promise to come see you as soon as I can. We'll hang out, and you can tell me all about it," Fiona said.

"I have to stay in the hospital for a few days. Peach will know where I am."

"I love you, Lissie," Fiona said sincerely.

Walking back to her room, Fiona nearly collided with one of her dormmates. She excused herself, opened her door, collapsed on her bed, and lit a cigarette. She wondered how life had gotten so complicated. She vowed never to forget to take her birth control pills.

Chapter 8

Saturday appeared after one of the longest weeks of Fiona's life. Jack planned to arrive around noon and stay until the following day. Twenty-four hours would make or break their new relationship. What would they talk about? Where would they go? What would they do? Would she be able to entertain him, or would he get bored with her after a few hours? Anxiety overcame anticipation.

Her room was spotless except for the mess on her missing roommate's bed. She showered, fixed her hair, applied her makeup, and chose her best jeans and a sexy green top to match her eyes. While she waited, she sketched Jack's face from all directions, then quickly hid her drawings so he wouldn't think her obsessed. The closer to noon, the more restless she became. Some yoga perhaps? Some slow breathing to calm her nerves?

Then, over the loudspeaker: "Fiona O'Brien. Visitor in the lobby."

For a second, she thought she would vomit. Once the feeling passed, she took one last slow breath and made her way to the elevator, knowing she would make a better entrance from there than the stairwell. The door opened. Fiona paused for a moment, then approached Jack.

"You're even more beautiful than I remember," Jack said as he hugged her.

Fiona relaxed in his embrace.

"Let's get you signed in," she said, walking him to the reception desk. "Boys can visit until eight o'clock."

"But—"

"Come on, Jack, let me show you my room." She escorted him to the elevator.

Once the doors closed, she continued. "Don't worry. The rules say we can have guys in our room on the weekends from noon till eight. We're supposed to keep our doors open, but nobody does. This is the last weekend before summer, so no one's paying attention. We'll sign you out, then sneak you back upstairs. As long as we don't make too much noise—"

"So no loud screams like in Nana's Nash?" He pulled her close and nibbled on her earlobe.

"Only if my record player is turned way up." She smiled and kissed him on the cheek.

Fiona opened the door to her room and tried to imagine it through Jack's eyes. It didn't take long to get a reaction.

"Interesting decor, Fee. I especially like the crap on the bed. Are you making a statement on the futility of life?" Jack laughed.

"That's one way to look at it," Fiona replied. "It could be a reflection on the futility of my missing roommate's college education. She's gonna have to come back one of these days and pack up, unless she decides to hitchhike to San Francisco to hang with the hippies in Haight-Ashbury."

"Enough about her. C'mere, sweet thing." In one move, Jack pushed the door closed and drew Fiona toward him. "Just think, twenty-four hours. No place to be. No one to disturb us."

They moved as one onto her neatly made bed and picked up where they had left off the previous weekend.

"One second, Jack. I've got a couple things to do." Fiona rolled away from him and walked toward the window. She dropped the blinds and then dropped her jeans to the floor.

"Nice ass," Jack remarked.

She turned and smiled, a faint blush crossing her cheeks.

"One more thing. Just in case," she said as she flipped the lever on her record player. *Days of Future Passed* by the Moody Blues dropped onto the turntable.

She dropped back onto the bed and into Jack's arms.

Several more albums made their way onto the turntable before the lovers returned to reality. They lay tangled together, about all they could do considering the size of Fiona's bed.

"That was great, Fee. I really like you," Jack said.

"I like you too, Jack. I'm glad you came to visit."

Jack was quick to change the subject. "I sure worked up an appetite. Got anything to eat?"

"How about some Oreos? Or maybe Ritz crackers and peanut butter? That's all I've got."

"Either one should go with the wine I brought. Sorry, it's not cold." Jack reached into his bag and pulled out a bottle of Boone's Farm apple wine.

Fiona hated cheap wine, especially room temperature cheap wine. Jack was losing points. Not wanting to appear rude, she politely replied, "Sure, why not?"

They straightened the bed. Fiona grabbed a towel to use as a tablecloth, two coffee cups, and a roll of paper towels. Not exactly fine dining, but it was the best she could do.

Jack passed his pack of Marlboros to Fiona. "No thanks," she said. "I've got my own." She reached for her Kools.

"How can you smoke those? They taste like a chemical yard."

"I like the menthol. Kinda like going outside after it snows."

"You watch too many commercials. So what are your plans for the summer?"

"My dad got me a job teaching art at the Methodist summer camp for July and August. He said I need to think about my future. He wants me to be an art teacher after I graduate."

"How boring is that gonna be?" Jack said. "I'm going to Richmond to visit my aunt and sister in a couple of weeks."

An Oreo stopped midway down Fiona's throat as she envisioned a summer without her new boyfriend. "For the whole summer?"

"Hell, no. Then I'd never get to see you. I'll just be gone two weeks." He gave her a peck on the cheek.

The Oreo slid the rest of the way to her stomach.

"I'm gonna cut some lawns and do some gardening for Nana's old lady friends. Turn on the charm. Speaking of charm, d'ya think your parents liked me?"

Fiona thought back to last Saturday and Jack's performance at her house. Jack had charmed the pants off her dad.

"My dad really liked you. My mom, who knows. She doesn't like anybody under thirty, especially boys who could steal my virginity."

"Guilty as charged, Your Honor," Jack said with a smile, "though I think somebody stole that long before I came along."

Fiona ignored his comment.

"Tell me more about your parents," Jack said.

"My parents got married in 1947. My mom went right from high school to marriage. She was valedictorian of her class. She could have done anything, but instead, she gave it all up to be a fucking housewife."

"Yeah, but then you wouldn't have been born, and where would I be now?"

She blushed. "My dad's nine years older than my mom. I can't imagine marrying somebody that old. I can't figure out what he saw in her other than her looks. I used to think they never did it for the first couple of years they were married."

"Nah, everybody gets laid. Did you ever catch them?"

"No way," Fiona said. "I doubt they do it anymore. What about your parents?"

"I hardly ever saw my dad. Never really knew him. He was in the navy and away a lotta the time. When he got home, my parents spent most of their time in the bedroom. When I was little, I thought he was tired, but then I figured out what was going on. I used to try and look through the keyhole. I never saw anything, so I just sat by their door and listened. Sometimes it got pretty loud."

"That's gross," she said. "How come you guys didn't travel with your dad? I thought that's how it worked."

"My dad was in Naval Intelligence. He enlisted right after Pearl Harbor. Dropped outta college and everything. After the war, he was stationed in Norfolk, where he met my mom. She worked at the base."

You're losing points, Jack. The military? Both your parents? "Was your mom in the navy?"

"Nah, civilian job, but her father was a navy man, just like my dad's father. That's how she coped with Dad being gone so much. I don't know how true it was, but Mom told us Dad's work was top secret and we weren't allowed to know where he went or what he was doing. When you're a kid, you believe everything. More wine?"

"Sure. And another cigarette." Her tastebuds had become numb to the battery acid that Jack called wine.

Jack lit Fiona's cigarette and one for himself. "What about your dad? What branch was he in?" he asked.

"He never made it into the service. It's kind of a sad story. My grandfather was a stockbroker on Wall Street. They lived in a penthouse apartment with maids, a nanny, everything. My dad and his brothers went to private school. When my dad was nine, the stock market crashed. They lost it all. They had to move to a smaller apartment with relatives, and the kids left private school.

"I don't know what they lived on, but one night a couple of years later, my dad heard a loud noise from the fire escape. He went to see what happened and saw my grandfather lying there, dead. He'd shot himself in the head. I guess he couldn't take it anymore."

"Holy shit!" Jack interrupted.

"They moved to my grandmother's farm here in New Jersey. My dad was a big football star in high school and went to college to play football. He hurt his back and knee in 1940, so he couldn't play anymore. The army wouldn't take him 'cause of the injury, so he went back to work on the farm."

"I wonder how he coped when all the men came home from the war," Jack said.

"I think he was glad he didn't have to fight after what he went through as a kid. He didn't have an easy life."

"Man, that's so different from my dad. That's all I heard from him and my grandfather. War stories. Made me want to join up as soon as I could."

I knew Jack was too good to be true. How could she be with someone who supported the military? She suspected he backed the war effort, but hesitated to bring it up.

"What happened?" she asked. "How come you're here instead of the navy?"

"Promise you won't think bad of me if I tell you?"

For the first time, Fiona saw a chink in Jack's armor.

"I promise."

"I wanted to go to Annapolis, but I fucked up my SATs. My scores were too low. I know I'm smart enough to get in, plus I know I coulda got a recommendation. I don't know what happened. Then I kinda lost interest and decided to go to community college."

"I'm glad you didn't go." Fiona reached for Jack and nudged him down onto the bed. "Let me show you how glad I am," she said as she climbed on top of him.

"We worked up a hell of an appetite," Jack said. "Where can we go for dinner?"

"There's a diner not too far from here. I feel safer there than on campus. Somebody might wonder who you are and where you're staying," Fiona replied.

"You sure you're not hiding me from your other boyfriends?"

"I'll never tell," Fiona teased him.

Jack ordered a double cheeseburger, fries, and two chocolate milkshakes. Fiona stuck with her usual tuna salad platter and a Coke. Worry had killed her ravenous appetite of an hour ago. What if they caught Jack in her room and threw her out of school? What would she tell her parents?

She could hear her mom. *I knew from the time you were a baby that you were no good. I wasted eighteen years of my life trying to save you.*

"You're a million miles away, babe." Jack snapped his fingers and brought her back to reality.

"Sorry. I was thinking about how to sneak you back into the dorm. They're having this stupid Spring Fling Dance tonight. Kind of a farewell thing. Most of the girls who stayed on campus are going, so we should wait till after eight when that starts."

"That's about an hour from now. We could cruise in the Nash and smoke a J," Jack said.

"Great idea! Let's go."

Getting caught was only part of Fiona's concern. Tonight would be the first time she would spend an entire night in bed with a boy. She'd been to parties where everyone was too messed up to leave and had woken up on the floor in the arms of someone she barely knew. Those nights were better off forgotten.

She wondered how they would fit into her tiny bed. What if Jack snored? What if he farted in the night? What if she did?

How did her parents manage to sleep in the same room? Is that why her mother insisted on twin beds? Everyone had bad breath in the morning, but was hers worse than most? Jack would see her without makeup. No boy had ever seen her that way.

She knew she needed to get good and wasted; otherwise, she'd never be able to sleep.

What a Trip

Worry never did anyone a bit of good, and Fiona was no exception. They left the Nash in a public parking lot and walked halfway across campus to the dorm. Jack went to the back of the building and waited behind the dumpsters. Fiona signed in, took the elevator to the third floor, unlocked her room, and quietly made her way to the service stairs. She counted to ten before opening the door and letting Jack in. Her paranoia was unfounded. The dorm was as good as empty.

They stifled their giggles until Jack was safely behind her locked door. They broke out into a tickling frenzy and fell on the bed.

"We made it!" she cried.

"Let's celebrate. I just happen to have another bottle of Boone's Farm," Jack said.

Two hours later, they were fast asleep. Neither of them snored or farted.

Fiona woke before Jack. She wiggled out of bed and tiptoed into the bathroom. What was the correct protocol? A shower? Wash and dry her hair? Makeup? She wanted to look natural, like she woke up beautiful. She washed just where necessary, brushed her teeth, smoothed out her hair, and applied a dab of mascara.

It'll have to do, she thought, checking herself in the mirror.

After nearly twenty-four hours, Fiona was experiencing mixed feelings about Jack. It was the longest time she'd spent with a guy, and it wasn't over yet. She was bored and expected he felt the same about her. She wanted him gone.

Jack rolled over, opened his eyes, and caught Fiona staring at him. "Hey, babe," he said sleepily. "What's happenin'?"

It's gonna be okay, she thought for the umpteenth time that weekend.

"Morning, Jack. How'd you sleep?"

"Great! How 'bout some breakfast?"

They washed and played in Fiona's tiny stall shower, dressed, and sneaked out the back door of the dorm. Brunch would take them until noon, when she could sign Jack in as an official visitor.

Back in the room, Jack spun her around and ran his fingers through her auburn curls. "One more time before I go?"

"I thought you'd never ask," Fiona said as she slid her hand inside the back of his jeans.

They were lost in their lovemaking when they heard a click in the doorknob. Fiona felt her body stiffen. She felt Jack stiffen inside her.

The door opened. Her missing roommate, Elaine, stood there, not knowing what to do. "Oh" was all she said.

"Oh," Fiona echoed.

"Ooohhh," Jack moaned as he collapsed on top of Fiona.

Elaine stepped back into the hallway and closed the door.

Chapter 9

$\mathcal{M}$ r. O'Brien took a day off from work to bring his daughter home from college.

"How were exams?" he asked.

"Good, Dad. I don't think I'll make a 4.0 this semester, but it'll be close. My art teacher loved my final project."

"That's my girl. Any idea what you'll do for the month of June before camp starts?"

"There are some drop-in classes at the art center that I'd like to go to. I'm also looking forward to spending time with my friends."

"Just be careful, FiFi," her dad said. "The fellas at work were telling me about all the drugs coming into town. I don't want you getting involved."

"Of course not." Fiona put on her sincere face.

"Your mother wanted me to ask you about volunteering at Bible school the last week of June. I told her you needed a break, but it sure would make her happy."

"Do I have to?"

"Of course not. I only said I'd ask. Maybe we can come up with a good reason to tell her no."

"Thanks, Dad." Fiona gave him a peck on the cheek.

"Do you know your friend Melissa is in the hospital?" Mrs. O'Brien asked her daughter after she unpacked and sat down for a late lunch.

Did her mom know about the abortion? "Um, no. Was she in an accident or something?"

"Mrs. Micelli, my friend the nurse, told me." Then, in a whisper, "Some kind of female trouble."

Fiona's heart was racing, but she did her best to keep cool. "Oh, wow! I didn't know. I hope she's gonna be okay. Can I borrow the Corvair and go see her?"

"Of course, dear. She's been there since Monday. I always thought she was sickly. She's so pale and thin."

"Thanks, Mom. I'm gonna call Peach and see if she wants to go with me."

Fiona and Peach met in the hospital lobby.

"What happened, Peachie?"

"They did the abortion on Monday. She lost a lot of blood, so they decided to keep her till she's stable. She's not lookin' good."

"My mom's friend knew Lissie was in the hospital. If it ever gets back to her that she had an abortion, I'm screwed," Fiona said.

"It won't. Lissie's chart says she had a D and C. That's a minor procedure for fibroids and a bunch of different things. They're keeping the abortion quiet."

"What about Mrs. P? How'd she take it?"

"She's a fucking head case, and this ain't helpin'. She's working the late shift this week, so she comes in the morning. You don't have to worry about runnin' into her," Peach said.

The girls picked up visitor passes and headed upstairs.

A tray of congealed food sat next to the bed. Fiona couldn't decide which looked worse—the food or her comatose friend. A faint stench of decay floated through the air. Fiona stood almost paralyzed, holding her breath. She turned to Peach, who motioned to meet her in the hallway.

"Is she gonna die?" Fiona was panicking.

"No, she's just drugged—legally this time," Peach replied.

"If that's legal, give me illegal any day." Fiona's attempt at humor did nothing to lift her spirits.

"C'mon. Let's see if she'll wake up."

A drop of blood on the sheet was the only color in an otherwise stark room. "They need to change her napkin," Peach explained. "That's why it stinks so bad."

"How can you stand it? I'd be puking my guts out every day if I worked here." Fiona's face was almost as pale as Melissa's.

Melissa's eyelids fluttered. "Fee, Peach," she whispered as her eyelids closed.

Seconds turned to minutes. Melissa struggled into consciousness. "The fairies took me and my baby. We were trapped in their circle. We drank nectar and ate berries and mushrooms. We danced for a thousand days before I could get away. They want me back. . ."

"Wake up, Lissie!" Peach slapped her cheek. "Come back. Get away from the fairies. *Now!*"

Melissa's eyes popped open. "Hi, guys. Where are we? What stinks?"

"You, Lissie," said Peach.

Fiona stood helpless. How could Peach joke at a time like this?

"Me, stink? No way. I've been dancing with the fairies. They're real, you know. They make themselves invisible when humans come by. They've got my baby. They're gonna get me a set of wings. I've gotta go now. . ."

Melissa faded into her pillow.

Fiona and Peach tiptoed into the hallway. "Is she really crazy?" Fiona asked her friend.

"She may be wacky, but this is from some nasty sedative. Probably too high a dose for her size," Peach said.

"I had no idea they made mistakes like this. Don't they know what they're doing?"

"I've been here less than a year. I've seen so much shit go down you wouldn't believe it. They make all kinds of mistakes. This is nothing," Peach said.

"Remind me to never get sick. If I do, don't bring me here."

It was time to go.

Fiona's tears let loose once the girls were back in the car. An abortion, fairies, her best friend bleeding, lost in a haze of prescription medication. Nobody to turn to. Nobody to care.

Peach held Fiona's hand. "She'll be okay once the pills wear off. Lissie's on welfare. They want the bed for a patient that's gonna pay. Give it a day or two. They'll clean her up, stop the meds, make sure she's stable, and send her home. The system sucks, and there's nothin' we can do about it."

"She's not going back to Mickey and that house, is she?" Fiona asked.

"Part of the deal was that Lissie promised to stay at her mother's house, at least for a few weeks. Did you know Mrs. P got herself a boyfriend?"

"No shit. At her age? She's gotta be almost forty."

"Some guy. A widower with a couple of kids. She can't handle the one kid she's got now. Anyway, Mrs. P's got marriage on the mind. At least she did till this all went down. I'm hopin' she'll leave Lissie alone and keep the guy. That'll be better for everybody, except the poor sucker she marries."

Chapter 10

Peach was right. The day after she and Fiona visited the hospital, Melissa was weaned off the narcotics. Two days later, she was sent home with her mother.

Fiona went to visit Melissa after Mrs. Patten went to work.

"Tell me everything, Lissie."

"It wasn't that bad," Melissa began. "It's kind of like it never happened."

"Do you think about the baby?"

"I'd rather forget the whole thing. I'm just glad it's over. Let's not talk about it, okay?"

"Okay, if that's what you want. You know I'm here if you change your mind," Fiona said.

"The worst part was seeing the shrink and dealing with my mother. They made me sign a bunch of crap, including a promise to stay with her until I'm back to normal."

Normal? Fiona thought, then asked, "How will they know where you're living?"

"They won't, but my mother will. She'll call the hospital if I leave. I'm scared shitless they'll lock me up for being crazy. I had to make up all kinds of stuff."

"You mean the fairies? Did you say anything about Denise and witchcraft?"

"Yeah, kinda, but I didn't mention her name. I don't remember a whole lot from when I checked in till I left yesterday."

"They had you drugged. Do you remember Peach and me visiting you? You were talking about dancing with the fairies," Fiona said.

"Nope. They even told me Mickey came the day after the operation. He's been great about everything. Even brought me flowers."

That's the least he should do, Fiona wanted to say. *He should have paid for your abortion.*

"I tried calling him yesterday and today, but there's no answer. Peach said something about the house getting condemned, so maybe they shut the phone off," Melissa said.

"Do you know what condemned means, Lissie?" Fiona asked. "It means you can't live there anymore."

"Really? I thought it meant the landlord had to fix up the place. Anyway, I'm moving to Boston with Mickey when he goes to college, so fuck it."

The phone rang. "Maybe that's Mickey now." Melissa picked up the receiver. "Oh, hi, Mommy. I'm okay, just watching TV and reading. Yeah, I ate the sandwich and drank the milk."

The TV was turned off. No books or magazines were nearby. The sandwich was dry and crusty. A dead fly floated in the milk.

"Oh wow, really, Mommy? Can Fiona come too?"

Fiona detected a hesitation on the other end of the call before Melissa said, "Groovy! I'll ask her. Hope she'll say yes. Okay, see you tonight."

"Guess what, Fee? My aunt Marge in Florida invited me down for a week! Mommy thought it would be nice for me to get away. Can you believe it? And she said you can come. We can take the train. Far fucking out!"

Fiona's thoughts tumbled faster than an Olympic gymnast. Florida? Was Lissie well enough to travel? Would she flip out on the train? What would she tell her parents? And the biggest question of all: What about Jack?

"When would we leave?"

"Not for two weeks. I have to get better first."

"That'll give me time to talk to my parents. I can't imagine them saying no." It would be the perfect excuse to get off the hook for Bible school. It was also one of the same weeks Jack would be in Virginia.

"Guess what else, Fee? Bella's is closing. I'm out of a job. Now I've got the whole summer to hang out and have fun."

Talk about crazy. You're losing your home, you've lost your job, your baby, probably your boyfriend, and you haven't got a clue.

"I think it's a splendid idea," Mrs. O'Brien said at dinner. "I know you can't go on vacation with your dad and me this summer, so this should make up for it. I'll tell Pastor Ritchey you won't be able to help at Bible school. I'm sure he'll understand."

Fiona glanced at her dad. His expression seemed to say, *You lucked out this time.* They shared a conspiratorial smile.

Jack called after dinner. Fiona bubbled over with excitement. "And it means we won't have to spend more than two weeks apart."

"That's great," Jack replied.

Fiona detected a slight hesitation in his voice. Was he losing interest in her?

What a Trip

She needn't have worried. She and Jack spent nearly every day together until he was scheduled to leave for Virginia. Their final night together, she and Jack snuggled in the front seat of the Nash.

"I'll miss you, babe," Jack said as he kissed her for the last time.

"Me too," Fiona said. Could she survive two whole weeks without him?

Chapter 11

The next week was spent arranging train tickets, shopping for bikinis, and packing. They each decided to bring one large suitcase and an overnight bag for their makeup and toiletries. Other than brief trips to the Jersey Shore, this was the first time either of them would be away from home without their parents. Excitement upstaged nervousness, at least most of the time.

Mr. and Mrs. O'Brien, accompanied by Mrs. Patten, drove the girls to the train station. It was a twenty-five-hour ride to Fort Lauderdale. Fiona worried about the long ride and what to expect when they arrived in Florida. She suspected her parents felt the same."

Please don't make a fuss at the station. And please don't wait with us till the train gets here.

They all waited, and yes, they made a fuss over their daughters.

"Keep your money close to you at all times, and whatever you do, don't forget your pocketbooks. If anything happens on the train, you go right to the conductor and tell him. And be sure to listen to everything your aunt Marge has to say. Don't go anywhere without telling her," Mrs. Patten said. "And let's see, what else—"

"Girls, be sure to call when you get to Marge's house," Mrs. O'Brien added.

"Take lots of pictures," her dad said, "and don't lose the Brownie camera."

As the girls boarded the train, Fiona whispered to Melissa, "Got the bikinis?"

"I stuck them between my panties," Melissa replied.

The girls had each bought the skimpiest bikini they could find. Fiona knew her mother rifled through her drawers, looking for contraband. Melissa's mother, with less free time, was an easier mark.

They turned and waved to their parents. They were on their way.

Walking to their assigned car, they passed open cabins with bunk beds and private baths. Those larger rooms dissolved into small private rooms with two seats that converted into beds at night. The next car had bunks with curtains on either side of a narrow aisle. Toward the back of the train was their car. No bed, no bath, nothing but a double seat. Home for the next twenty-five hours.

A bold red sign at the front of the car announced NO SMOKING. Further explanation appeared in smaller print: "Smoking permitted in club, bar, and dining cars, and the ladies' and men's lounges only."

"Looks like we won't be spending much time in this car," Melissa said.

Fiona nodded. She had a more pressing worry. "Where are our beds?"

"I didn't get us any beds," Melissa told her friend. "I figured it was only one night, so we could save some money."

Fiona was angry but didn't want to start an argument. Instead, she said, "C'mon, let's eat."

Lunch in the dining car was a disappointment. Dried-out chicken salad on stale white bread, cheap potato chips, watered-down soda, and single-layer chocolate cake reminiscent of their high school cafeteria. They ate sparingly and smoked leisurely.

The waiter escorted an older man to their table. "Mind if I take a load off?" he said as he plopped himself down next to Fiona. He reeked of cheap cologne and stale cigars. His wide maroon spotted tie wasn't broad enough to conceal an ample gut, which strained behind the plastic buttons of his sweat-stained shirt.

"Where're you gals headed?" He angled his chair closer to Fiona, providing her with a whiff of his unwashed armpits.

"Fort Lauderdale. What about you?" Melissa replied.

Big mistake, Lissie. Don't encourage this asshole.

"I'm headed to Jacksonville. Name's Murphy. Fred Murphy. Fuller Brush salesman extraordinaire. Got me a new sales territory. I'm done with the Northeast. Too much snow. I'm makin' my move south to wow the little ladies with my wares. You gals needin' any brushes?"

"No thanks," Fiona jumped in before her friend could get them in deeper.

"Whadda ya say, girls? Got any plans for later? I got me a bottle in my room. Get the porter to send up some ice and soda. Coupla highballs, maybe a game a' poker. Ya know, strip poker. I'll show ya a real good time."

"We gotta go."

Both girls stood, attempting to leave. Fred grabbed Fiona's forearm, forcing her back into her chair. Melissa caught the porter's eye.

"Sir, why don't you leave these gals alone?" the porter asked.

"Hey, just havin' a friendly chat. No harm done," Fred said as he made room for Fiona to leave the table.

"Car H, room twenty-six. I'll be waitin'."

"Stay away from him. He'll be in the bar car later, so watch out. He gives you any more trouble, you let me know. I'll personally take care of him. Name's Sam." The porter escorted the girls out of the dining car.

"Thanks, Sam," Melissa said as they headed back to their seat.

"Fuckin' A, that was a close one," Fiona said. "From now on, let's smoke in the ladies' lounge. It's gotta be safer."

To get to the ladies' lounge, the girls had to walk through the bunkhouse, as they renamed the sleeping car. Who lay behind the curtained beds, and what were they doing? Muted conversation seeped through a few drapes. The rest were silent. Did they conceal murderers, rapists, or more characters like Fred Murphy? The girls slipped into the ladies' lounge before they had a chance to find out.

A cloud of stale smoke hit them as they entered the sanctuary. Vinyl chairs and love seats, decades old, lined the walls. Formica end tables and ashtrays on floor stands accessorized the seating arrangement. Mirrors, cracked and grimy, attempted to give the impression of spaciousness. The residents, like the furnishings, had seen better days. Some read magazines. Some played cards. Others stared at the floor. All smoked.

One of the women raised her head. "Hey, girlies, have a seat. Move your behind, Clara, and let the tootsies take a load off."

Melissa and Fiona exchanged glances, as if to say, *Is this place for real?*

Melissa took the initiative and said, "Thanks. We're just here for a cigarette." They squeezed onto the love seat next to Clara, whose behind left a bowl-like indentation on the seat.

"I'm Edith, Edie for short. Been ridin' the rails nigh on to forty years. Back in the day, I use'ta ride the freights. Now I got my security check comin' in, I get t'ride in style. Them conductors look the other way mosta the time and let me an' my pals ride for nothin'. Don't hafta worry 'bout no *cinder dicks* no more."

"What are *cinder dicks*?" Fiona asked.

"Don't ya know nothin? *Cinder dicks*. The sum bitches kickin' us outta freight cars just when we's gittin' com-forble." Edie smiled an almost toothless smile. What remained of her dental work was nicotine stained and crooked. Crumbs of mascara littered her eyelashes and flaked onto her cheekbones. Two perfect circles of rouge sat on her wilted cheeks. A trace of lipstick graced her upper lip. The rest adorned one end of her unfiltered cigarette. Her greasy gray hair was twirled into pin curls.

"Where ya dolls headed?" she croaked.

This time Fiona answered. "Fort Lauderdale."

"Me, I'm headed to Miami. Got me an ol' man and a place t'sleep. When I can't take him no more, I head up north. Git my security check and do it all over agin. Ain't that right, Clara?"

Clara nodded. She wasn't much on conversation. Neither

were Melissa and Fiona. They finished their cigarettes and explored the back of the lounge. Toilets, sinks, and three stall showers reeking of mildew greeted them.

"Let's wait till we get to your aunt's house before we take our showers," Fiona said to her friend as they exited the lounge.

"Come back later, girlies. I'll sing ya a tune," Edie called to them.

"Thank you, ma'am," Melissa replied.

A little unsteady on their feet, they began the trip back to their car.

"We're not in New Jersey anymore," Fiona said in an attempt at *Wizard of Oz* humor. *But I wish I was.* She didn't complete the sentence aloud. No point in upsetting Melissa, who seemed as shaken as she.

Fiona went on, "We can't eat in the dining room, it's too weird to smoke in the lounge, and we can't take showers. What are we going to do for the rest of the evening?"

"You can stay in your seat, Miss Fiona O'Brien, but I'm not letting that sleazy salesman keep me from eating. Sam said he'd protect us. And those women, well, they were kinda fun. Face it, Fee, we'll probably never get to hang out with anybody like them again."

"Except on the way home," Fiona mumbled.

They passed the next several hours watching the scenery and discussing their plans for the week. Thoughts of dinner eventually crept into their heads and worked their way to their stomachs.

As if on cue, Sam came by. "Just thought you ladies would like to know your friend Mr. Murphy finished his supper. Looks like he'll be stayin' in the bar car for the rest o' the trip. Might be a good time to get yourselves a bite to eat. I'll walk you to the dining car."

"Thanks, Sam!" Melissa and Fiona said in unison.

"Maybe this won't be such a bad scene after all," Fiona whispered as they sat down to dinner.

After they ordered, Fiona asked her friend, "What do you think you'll do about working when you get home?"

"I think I can collect unemployment for a few months till it's time to move to Boston. Since they're making me live with my mother, I can at least spend most of my daytime with Mickey. Once we get to Boston, I'll think about school and a part-time job."

Fiona wanted to slap her friend back to reality. Instead, she said, "Peach told me they're looking for somebody to help out at the hospital gift shop a few hours a week. Might be a way to make a few bucks. Peach and I thought it might help get you out of your mother's apartment sooner."

"Are you for real, Fee? It's nothing but a bunch of old biddies at that shop. Why would I waste my time and give up my unemployment money? I need time to chill before Boston."

Fiona shrugged her shoulders. "Well, then, let's make this a summer to remember."

"Cool. Let's start right now!"

Full stomachs gave the girls a false sense of confidence, which brought them back to the ladies' lounge for an after-dinner cigarette. Edie was still holding court.

"I knew you dolls would be back. Here, take a load off. Time I gave the ol' gams a stretch. Back in the day, these gams took me places." Edie stood and lifted her skirt above the knee, showing off her legs. "Not bad for an old dame, eh?"

Fiona and Melissa exchanged glances as they squeezed next to Clara on the love seat.

"Give the ladies a smoke, huh?" Clara asked.

Cautiously, Fiona opened her pack of Kools, handed one to Clara, and offered the pack to Edie. Edie helped herself to two and handed them back.

"Thanks, toots," Edie said. "Hey, I told ya I'd sing ya a tune. Whadda ya like? I got me a repa-tory long as this train. Sang my way through the Depression, I did."

"Do you know any Janis Joplin?" Melissa asked.

"Who the hell is that? You want some lady melody, ask me ta sing ol' Billie or Bessie."

"Okay. How about 'Lover Man'?" Melissa suggested. She and Fiona adored the torch songs of Billie Holiday and Bessie Smith.

Edie let out a guttural cough. In a contralto voice that had seen better days, she began to sing. "I been feelin' kinda sad. My lover man is missin'. Where is you now?"

She gasped for breath, took a drag from her cigarette, coughed, and spit into the ashtray. "Think I may a' fergot some o' the words, but ya get the idea. Went from one speakeasy to the next singin' my way through the Depression. Sometime they gi' me a five spot. Sometime they ain't got no dough, they gi' me hooch. Speakin' a hooch, how 'bout a taste?"

Hooch? What's hooch? Fiona looked to Melissa for a translation. Melissa was as clueless as her friend.

Edie pulled a half-empty pint bottle out of her pocket, took a drink, coughed, wiped the lip, and handed it to Clara, who, in turn, handed it to Fiona. Fiona politely declined.

"More fur me then," Clara said as she brought the bottle to her mouth.

"I'll sing you girlies one more tune. D'ya know 'Nature Boy'?"

"Maybe. It sounds familiar," Fiona said.

"Nat Cole sung it. Whadda sweet soundin' voice he had."

Edie cleared her throat and began to sing. Her voice screeched as she doubled over into a coughing fit. "That's enough singin' for one night. Time ta rest the ol' bones. Stand up, dollfaces."

The girls didn't have to be asked twice. They stood, gave up their seat, and headed for the door. It would be their last visit to the ladies' lounge. They found a quiet restroom off the dining car that served their needs for the rest of the trip.

Sam brought them pillows and blankets and invited one of the girls to move to an empty seat so both could stretch out. The night passed uneventfully.

In the morning, they washed as best they could in the tiny sinks, changed their clothes, fixed their makeup, and headed to the dining car for breakfast.

Sam stopped by their table. "Your stop is next, gals. 'Bout twenty minutes. I'll be by in a bit to help you with your luggage. Are you meetin' somebody?"

"My aunt Marge," said Melissa. "We'll be staying with her for a week. Will we see you on the way home?"

"You just might. It's been a real pleasure," Sam said.

Chapter 12

The sun reflecting off the white pavement and buildings nearly blinded the girls as they exited the train. Tall palm trees framed the stucco station that flaunted a red-tiled roof. Sam wheeled their luggage into the waiting room, where Aunt Marge anxiously waited.

"Missy! Over here!"

Aunt Marge would have been a carbon copy of Melissa's mother if Mrs. Patten hadn't been beaten down by the world. She wore a skin-tight turquoise sundress, rhinestone-studded sunglasses, and a wide-brimmed straw hat, all of which complemented her deeply bronzed skin. The move from New Jersey to Florida had turned her into a real Southern belle.

"My little chipmunk! You're so pale and thin. Y'all stick with your aunt Marge, and I'll have you right as rain. And this must be Fiona. You're a real looker, hon. Better watch that pale skin of yours while you're here." Marge opened her arms. "Now, how about giving your old auntie a hug."

Melissa ran to her aunt. Fiona held back for a moment, not used to outward displays of affection from adults.

"Now, I know y'all will be heading for the beach most days,

and you don't need me butting into your comings and goings, so your uncle Hal and I will leave a key under the doormat. All we ask is that y'all visit with us today and go out to dinner with us a couple of nights. The rest of the time you're on your own. Just tell me if y'all be home for my cookin' any other night. If you'll be out past midnight, just give a call."

"Wow, thanks, Aunt Marge," Melissa said.

"I was young once. Let's just keep it between us. Your momma doesn't need to know. Come on. Hal's waiting in the Caddy." Marge offered a conspiratorial smile and winked at the girls.

Uncle Hal stood next to a baby-blue Cadillac convertible with the largest fins Fiona had ever seen. He opened the passenger door, bowed, and said, "Your chariot awaits, ladies, but first, how about a big Florida welcome."

He planted a sloppy kiss on each of their heads. Melissa hugged him, leaving an air pocket between their bodies. Fiona smiled awkwardly and climbed into the back seat.

"I brought sunglasses and kerchiefs for y'all to keep your hair in place and the sun out of your eyes." Marge passed two pink silk scarves and two pairs of sunglasses with fins nearly as big as the Cadillac's to the back seat.

I sure hope I don't see anybody I know in this getup.

They drove on a four-lane highway for about half an hour before turning at a garish pink sign: WELCOME TO FLAMINGO ESTATES. YOUR LITTLE PIECE OF HEAVEN.

After a few twists and turns, they pulled into the driveway of a yellow stucco ranch indistinguishable from dozens like it on the winding streets of the development.

"Home sweet home," Hal said as he flashed a smile into the back seat.

A blast of cold air hit them as they entered the front door.

"Your room's down here on the right. Hope a double bed is okay with you two," Marge said.

Any kind of bed was welcome after a night on the train.

"Y'all unpack, have a shower, and meet your uncle Hal and me by the pool. I'll have sweet tea and sandwiches waiting. I'm pleased as punch having you here." Marge kissed Melissa's forehead and closed the door.

"Your aunt is so cool," Fiona said. "I never met anybody like her." *Your uncle gives me the creeps*, she wanted to say but kept the thought to herself.

"I wish she was my mother instead of the one I've got." Melissa seemed energized and more upbeat than Fiona had seen her since high school.

A large platter of tea sandwiches arranged in a star pattern was garnished with blueberries and sliced strawberries. A sweaty pitcher of sweet tea sat nearby. Hal, also slightly sweaty, sat by himself on a glider. He patted the seat next to him.

"C'mere, little lady," he said to Fiona, "and let's get acquainted."

Reluctantly, she sat down, leaving plenty of space between them.

"Come a little closer. If you don't, I will. I don't bite." He winked at her, glided across the cushion, and glanced at his wife, who was busy arranging a plate of cheese and crackers.

The conversation centered on people, stories, and places Melissa had never mentioned to her friend. Fiona sat quietly eating, gradually sliding to the other side of the glider. Each time she moved, Hal followed.

"Fiona, why don't you give me a hand in the kitchen. It'll give us a chance to get to know each other. I'm sure Missy and her uncle have lots of catching up to do," Marge said.

"Have a seat, darlin'." Marge pulled out a kitchen chair for Fiona. "Now, listen to me. Hal's a great husband and a good provider, but he loves the ladies. He's got kind of a reputation around here. Most of the time I turn a blind eye. Men will be men, if you get my drift."

Fiona was beginning to feel uneasy. Did Aunt Marge think she was flirting with her husband?

"I know you're young, and you probably haven't had much experience with the opposite sex. Hal knows to keep his hands off little Missy, but y'all aren't family, so he'll see you as fair game. Be careful and do your best to keep him at arm's length. If he tries anything, you come to Aunt Marge. Okay?"

"Um, sure," Fiona replied.

"Don't be afraid, hon. He knows not to bring his philandering into this house. Let's not give him any opportunity to forget the rules. Now, put a smile on your face, give me a hug, and let's bring out the dessert. I made ambrosia, Missy's favorite."

Chapter 13

The next morning, Aunt Marge mapped out the bus route to the beach with a warning not to get too much sun the first day out.

"I think as long as we keep applying baby oil, we should be fine," Melissa said as they got off the bus.

"I brought this beach jacket in case I start to burn," Fiona added. "I want to be especially careful so we don't have to hang around your aunt's house. Your uncle Hal gives me the creeps. The last thing I need is for him to see me in my bikini."

"He's slimy. Bet you didn't know he dated my mother before he married Aunt Marge. He started cheating on her with Aunt Marge. When my mother found out, she was really pissed off and broke up with him. Aunt Marge got pregnant. She lost the baby after they got married. They never had any kids."

"No shit?" Fiona said. "How do you know all that?"

"I picked up bits and pieces. My mother and Marge didn't speak to each other for forever. A couple of years ago, he left Aunt Marge for some bimbo. I think my mother realized how lucky she was not to have married him, so they made up."

"I can't believe she took him back."

"They've got some kind of arrangement. He needs a wife,

and she needs money. I'm so glad me and Mickey aren't like that. I'd never marry a guy for security," Melissa said.

"Me neither."

A wide strip of white sand stretched on for miles. Across from the busy highway that lined the beach stood tall hotels and apartment buildings. Where was the boardwalk? Where were the amusements, the carousel, the saltwater taffy stands? To Fiona, the Fort Lauderdale beach seemed like a foreign country.

"Did you think it would be like this? It's like a beach in a city," Fiona said.

"I kind of knew. Aunt Marge sends my mother postcards and photos trying to get her to move down here. Come on. Let's grab a spot under one of the palm trees."

"Don't you think we should rent an umbrella so we don't burn?" Fiona asked.

"Fuck, no. We wanna get some color so everybody'll know we've been to Florida. And look, we've got the palm leaves for shade," Melissa replied.

Bad move, Fiona thought as she helped unfold their beach blanket.

Less than two hours later, the white-hot sun had transformed their pale skin into a dangerous shade of pink. As they ran to the water to cool off, Fiona noticed how many eyes were on them. The weekday beach crowd was mainly older couples, single men, and mothers with young children. She loved the attention her skimpy bikini created but tried to pretend she didn't care.

When they returned to their blanket, they noticed two young

guys had parked under the next tree. With their long blond wavy
hair, deeply tanned skin, chiseled abs, and skimpy suits that left
little to the imagination, Fiona found herself staring.

"Lissie, check out the hunks. Should we talk to them?"

"Fee, you're a sucker for blonds," Melissa said.

"That's why you're my best friend," Fiona said as she rumpled Melissa's long blond hair.

"Anyway, what about Jack? I thought he was your Mr. Wonderful."

"Jack and I've been going out, like, a month. Yeah, he's cute,
he's great in the sack and all, but something's missing."

"You've said that about every guy since Andy dumped you."

A cloud crossed Fiona's face when she thought of Andy,
who'd dumped her right after they graduated from high school.
"Andy has nothing to do with it. I've got this feeling about Jack.
Maybe it's ESP. Maybe it's because he talks about joining the
navy. Maybe it's the way he bullshits my parents. But we're on
vacation, and two cute guys are checking us out. I'm gonna go
for it."

"I guess it won't hurt to talk to them," Melissa said. "Maybe
they'll buy us lunch. But if they invite us to their apartment, I'm
not going."

"Suit yourself." Fiona stood, shook out her auburn hair, and
flashed a smile at their neighbors. Putting just the right amount
of sway to her hips, she made her way to the next palm.

"You chicks aren't from around here," the taller of the two
said to Fiona.

"How did you know?"

"No self-respecting Florida chick would let herself get as red
as you're getting," he said. "Take it from us. Put a hat on, cover

that luscious body of yours, and get out of the sun, or you're gonna fry."

Fiona blushed, though she was too pink for anyone to notice. She ran back to grab her things and joined the guys. Melissa followed reluctantly.

"Next time get here early morning or late afternoon and don't spend more than two hours on the beach. And if you've got the bread, rent an umbrella. Take it from us. We've been down here going on three years. I'm Mike, and my friend here is Kenny."

"Nice to meet you. I'm Fiona, and this is Melissa."

"What's the matter with your friend?" Mike asked. "Doesn't she talk?"

"Of course I talk," Melissa replied, staring at the ocean. "Just not to every strange guy I meet."

Fiona cringed. She didn't want her friend to ruin what might become the best part of their vacation.

"Kenny doesn't have a lot to say either," Mike went on. "You know, the artsy type. Thinks he's a poet."

"I am a poet," Kenny retorted. He turned to Melissa. "I had two poems published in the University of Miami literary magazine."

That got Melissa's attention. "No shit? I write poetry too. My boyfriend plays guitar and made a song out of one of my poems."

Mike turned to Fiona. "You got a boyfriend too?"

She shot Lissie a warning glance. "Not right now."

"I play guitar," Kenny said. "Maybe you could help me write a song."

Melissa was flattered. "Oh wow, really?" She moved closer to him, turning her back to the ocean and Fiona.

"Seems like everybody claims to be a poet or musician these days. Are you a poet too?" Mike asked Fiona.

"An artist. I'm studying art in college."

"Hey, me too. Majoring in art at the University of Miami. I'm making up two classes this summer at Broward so I can graduate next year," Mike said.

"What medium do you work in?"

"Pen and ink's my favorite. I'm putting a portfolio of sketches together from my Life Drawing class."

I'd pose for you any day, Fiona fantasized as she inched closer to Mike.

"I'd kinda like to get work as an illustrator after graduation, but I've gotta think about the army. No way in hell I'm goin' to Vietnam."

"Are you against the war?" Fiona asked.

"Damn straight. Kenny and I went to DC to protest at Nixon's inauguration in January. We went back in April for an antiwar demonstration. I'm not dying for Big Brother. No fuckin' way."

He thinks like I do. He's an artist and really hot. Jack? Jack who?

Mike spent the next hour regaling Fiona with his antiwar doctrine. She knew she was against the war but never had a clear understanding of the politics that led to the protests. His wasn't just a voice of complaint. He was an activist and a participant.

In addition to supporting and campaigning for the 1968 antiwar presidential candidate, Eugene McCarthy, they hitchhiked to Chicago to protest the war during the Democratic National Convention. Returning to Florida that fall, they continued their activism and, according to Mike, became some of the loudest voices in the state.

For once, Fiona stopped thinking about herself and seducing

the cutest guy in the room. Her attention was sharply focused on every word and every idea Mike presented. Lives were being lost in a violent struggle that made no sense. Political conspiracies and corruption were destroying the country and its youth, not to mention innocent Vietnamese. Corporations and politicians were profiting from death and destruction. It had to end.

"Sorry," Mike said as he paused his rhetoric. "I tend to get carried away. I'm so passionate about nonviolence and the evils of bureaucracy I sometimes forget there are other important things in life—like art, and like getting to know you. What's your story? What are you and your girlfriend doing down here?"

"There's not much to say." Fiona was at a loss for words. She felt small and insignificant.

"You can start by telling me where you're from." Mike smiled as he returned to the reality of sand and sun.

Fiona took a deep breath and began by telling Mike about their adventures on the train. The more she talked, the more attentive he became, and the more relaxed she became.

"You're one far-out chick," Mike said, "and it looks like Kenny feels the same about your friend. Do you ever think about karma? Like why we all showed up on this beach on this day and time? Almost like we were supposed to meet."

"Do you really think so?" Fiona was feeling more like herself.

"Time will tell. Hey, are you hungry? Do ya want to get some lunch? You two have used up your beach time for today. If you don't get out of the sun, you won't be coming back tomorrow."

He turned to his friend. "Hey, bud, how 'bout we treat the chicks to some lunch?"

"Huh, what?" Kenny and Melissa were deep in conversation,

oblivious to the rest of the beach. "Yeah, sure. Okay with you, Lissie?"

Melissa was momentarily transformed. Her waiflike appearance was gone. She stood, looking tall and bright, the sadness gone from her blue eyes. All signs of fatigue had vanished.

"I'm starved!" she replied.

Fiona couldn't remember Melissa ever saying she was starved. What kind of power did Kenny have over her?

"Grab your stuff and let's blow. We'll take you to our favorite joint. It's only a couple of blocks from here," Mike said as he helped Fiona to her feet.

It was a relief to leave the beach. Fiona felt burning behind her knees and on her shoulders. She knew now she should have covered up. She would be a lobster by nightfall.

They crossed A1A and walked for a few blocks, finally turning into an almost hidden door. HEALTH NUTS, the sign read.

"We like to think of ourselves as vegetarians. They make a mean soybean burger," Kenny said.

"And the carrot juice is made fresh to order," Mike added.

Fiona had thought many times about giving up meat but had never considered alternatives like soybean burgers and carrot juice. She put a smile on her face and said, "Sounds delicious!"

Melissa looked like she wanted to vomit.

The restaurant, if it could be called that, was cramped and dark. Mismatched tables and chairs appeared to be rejects from the Salvation Army. A pungent odor of sauerkraut permeated the air. Several tables were occupied by stringy older couples. They grabbed a table for four by the window.

Fiona sat facing a bulletin board littered with flyers: DOES BROCCOLI SCREAM WHEN IT'S CUT? SAMSON'S NUDIST COLONY: FREE YOUR SPIRIT. NOAH SAVED THE ANIMALS TO FREELY ROAM THE EARTH.

"Some of this is a bit extreme," Mike said. "You've got a bunch of older diehards who drink sauerkraut juice at every meal. Then there's the rest of us just trying to live a more humane existence." He stood and walked to the counter. "I'll order for us."

A waitress dehydrated from too much sun delivered their food. The carrot juice was bright orange and tasted sweet and refreshing. The soybean burgers could pass for hamburgers if the girls didn't look too closely. All in all, it wasn't a bad meal.

"Can I bring you some zucchini cake with whipped soymilk?" the waitress asked as she cleared their plates.

"Absolutely," the guys said in unison.

Fiona usually felt lethargic and slightly nauseous after eating, but for once she felt energized. She was more convinced than ever that being a vegetarian was in her future.

"Let's go for a walk. We'll show you around the neighborhood," Mike suggested. "We can leave our stuff behind the counter. It'll be safe."

A string of mom-and-pop shops lined the street. Shoe repair, TV and radio repair, pawnshop, florist, a second-hand shop claiming to sell antiques. Middle-aged proprietors sat in front of their stores waiting for customers. As they crossed into the next block, the merchandise got more interesting. Record shop, head shop, boutiques selling tie-dye everything from T-shirts to socks, Indian imports, Frye boots, and fringed leather jackets. Hippie proprietors stood in doorways smoking cigarettes, oblivious to the lack of customers.

They stopped in front of an empty storefront, its window littered with flyers, some in Day-Glo colors opposing the Vietnam War, others more subdued and written in Spanish.

"We've got a situation with the Cubans," Mike explained. "Lots of them have immigrated to South Florida. Some of our older white residents aren't happy about it. It's kind of added another dimension to our political situation."

"What do you think?" Fiona asked.

"I dig it. Castro is a dictator. Power to the people!"

Isn't that a Black Panther saying? Fiona shivered.

"We haven't had a whole lot of time to devote to the Cubans," Kenny added. "You gotta pick one cause and stick to it. Ours is the war."

"Don't think we don't support them. We do. We're just two guys trying to make a difference," Mike said.

Melissa and Fiona had nothing to add. They looked at each other. What the hell did they know? They were just a couple of chicks from New Jersey.

The next shop caught Melissa's interest. MISS SARAH, READER AND ADVISOR, TAROT AND ASTROLOGY, WALK-INS WELCOME.

"Wait!" she commanded. "What do you guys know about Miss Sarah?"

"She's cool. Part of the scene," Kenny said. "Kinda weird, but they say she's got the gift."

"Ever get a reading from her?" Melissa asked.

"Not our bag," Mike said, "but don't let us stop you."

Melissa reached for the door.

"Lissie, why don't we come back tomorrow?" Fiona's conservative Christian upbringing manifested when she least expected it. Miss Sarah would have to wait.

At the end of the block, Mike pointed to a shabby pink stucco building. "We live over there. You chicks want to come up and smoke a J?"

The girls passed looks back and forth. "Okay, but we have to catch the bus back to my aunt's in a couple of hours," Melissa said.

Fiona nodded in agreement. She liked this new Lissie.

Two rooms, a kitchenette, and a bath. Two mattresses on the floor covered in Indian cotton bedspreads and pillows. Piles of books and papers on what should have been a kitchen table. Dirty coffee cups, ceramic and Styrofoam, perched on windowsills and end tables. Grubby clothes spilling from open dresser drawers and the ubiquitous pile of dirty laundry in the corner.

This place is almost as disgusting as Melissa and Mickey's. For the first time in hours, she thought of Jack. He wasn't as hip as Mike and Kenny, but at least he was neat and clean.

"Have a seat." Mike motioned to the neater of the two mattresses. "I'll get our stash."

Melissa plopped down on one of the mattresses, lit a cigarette, and threw the match into an overflowing ashtray. Fiona remained standing.

Mike rolled two joints while Kenny opened two bottles of Mateus rosé. "This is Kenny's space," he said. "Fiona, come with me."

Fiona looked at Melissa, who seemed perfectly content. Mike took her hand, escorted her into the next room, and closed the door. The room was smaller, neater. Four Richard Avedon Beatles posters and some original pen-and-ink nudes hung on the walls. She relaxed, sat on the mattress, and gave Mike a seductive smile.

"Love the artwork," Fiona complimented him.

"Thanks. Like I said, it'd be great if you could pose for me."

She removed her cover-up and lay back on the mattress in a pose accentuating the curve of her hips.

"How's this?"

"Hold on a minute. Let's have a couple of tokes and some wine first."

He sat next to her and passed the joint and the bottle. As they began to relax, he slipped his hand between her legs and slowly trailed it from her torso to her lips. She tickled his fingertips with her tongue before his mouth joined hers. Art and sunburn were forgotten, but not for long.

It was over before Fiona knew what had happened. Mike lay on top of her, sweating and wheezing. For the second time since they entered the apartment, she longed for Jack.

The backs of her knees were on fire. Her shoulders ached. She hated Florida and longed for home. She tried extricating herself, which only aggravated her sunburn.

"That was great, Mike, but I've gotta get up. My sunburn is killing me." She pushed him off her.

"You're one sexy babe," Mike said as he rolled onto the floor. "Too bad you're only here this week. Kenny and I are heading back to Miami tonight."

Maybe there is a God. Fiona smiled.

Mike peeked into the other room, where Kenny and Melissa were deep in conversation. "Still want to pose for me? We won't be leaving for a while."

"Sure, why not?" Anything so she wouldn't have to fuck him again.

What Mike lacked in lovemaking skill, he made up for in artistic ability. His pen-and-ink sketches captured Fiona's essence. The lines flowed and brought her to life. By the time they heard activity in the other room, he had completed three drawings. He put the best one in a manila folder and gave it to Fiona.

"To remember this day." He smiled and kissed her.

"Thank you." Fiona would treasure the drawing but not the memory of the day.

They joined the others in the front room. Melissa was beaming. Fiona suspected she didn't want to leave, but the afternoon was coming to an end. The four exchanged phone numbers and addresses. Fiona knew they'd never meet again.

The girls had lots to discuss on the bus ride home.

"Weren't they the coolest guys you ever met?" Melissa asked Fiona. "If I wasn't going to Boston with Mickey, I'd move down here and be with Kenny."

"Did he say anything about you moving down here?"

"Well, no, but he dug me, and Mike dug you. We could double date all the time and maybe even get an apartment together."

"Lissie, you're dreaming. Today was just today. I've got no interest in seeing them again," Fiona said.

Melissa turned to stare at her friend. "What happened?"

What a Trip

"We got laid, if you could call it that. Thank goodness it only lasted a couple of minutes. I was so grossed out."

"But they're cute, they're smart and talented, and they've got their shit together about the war. Maybe next time it'll be better."

"Maybe." There would be no next time for Fiona. "I'm gonna send Jack a postcard. I'm really starting to miss him."

Chapter 14

By that evening their skin had transformed into a fiery shade of crimson. Movement of any kind was next to impossible.

"Y'all are redder than Satan himself," Aunt Marge exclaimed as she escorted the girls to the shower. "Keep it a little cooler than lukewarm," she instructed. "It'll take away some of the burn. I'll be back in a jiffy."

She returned with a bottle of milk and a box of rolled cotton. "Nothin' like milk to cool you off. C'mere, darlin', let Aunt Marge take the sting away."

Fiona relaxed as the pain from the day subsided. She wasn't sure what hurt more—her sunburn or her bruised emotions. Both eased with Aunt Marge's gentle touch.

The next day, Aunt Marge took them shopping on Las Olas Boulevard. For the first time in her life, Fiona enjoyed spending time with an adult. She envied Melissa and wished she had an equally hip and understanding aunt.

Even though their tender skin had begun to heal, Aunt

Marge recommended a second day out of the sun. They visited the Fort Lauderdale Art Center, after which she took them to lunch at the Elbo Room.

"Y'all can't come to town without stopping at the Elbo Room," Aunt Marge told the girls. "It's one of our most famous spots. They make super burgers. Y'all remember the movie *Where the Boys Are*? Well, it was made right here. That was about the biggest thing ever to happen in this town. I stood right across the street while they filmed. I even got Connie Francis's autograph."

The Elbo Room was a great spot for people watching. No hippies or withered vegetarians like Health Nuts, but lots of tourists and beach bums. Aunt Marge snapped their photo outside the restaurant.

"Now y'all are official Florida tourists!" she said proudly. "Come on, let's skedaddle."

They spent a leisurely late afternoon by Marge's pool, safely shaded under beach umbrellas. Uncle Hal was nowhere to be seen.

"That hubby of mine is off on another business trip. Gives us gals a chance to relax. He'll be back for your last night in town," Aunt Marge said.

Aunt Marge declared the girls fit to return to the beach the following day with a warning to stay out of the midday sun.

On the bus ride into town, Melissa brought up something that had been on her mind. "I think we need to see Miss Sarah. I felt her energy pulling me in the other day. Can we go?"

"Why not?" Fiona said. After two days in the world of adults, she was ready for some excitement.

"Maybe we'll see the guys again. We could walk past their apartment and see if they're back," Melissa said.

"I guess it wouldn't hurt to walk by. After all, we are going to Miss Sarah's." Fiona hoped Mike and Kenny had been honest when they said they were going back to Miami. She didn't know what she would do if they crossed paths.

The girls spent an hour under the palm trees and then played in the surf until the sun rose to its zenith. Packing up their belongings, they headed for the hip side of town.

Miss Sarah sat in the doorway of her studio, her raven-black hair flowing past her waist. She had olive skin and almond-shaped brown eyes that sparkled beneath a fringe of dark lashes. A paisley silk scarf draped one shoulder. The other was bare except for a crescent moon and star tattoo. She smoked leisurely, watching the tendrils of smoke float in the light breeze. The girls froze about twenty feet from her.

"She's beautiful," Fiona whispered. "I'm nervous. Maybe we shouldn't do this."

"Come on. We said we'd do it. I feel drawn to her," Melissa said.

Miss Sarah turned to face them. "Don't be afraid. You need to be here. The cards have a special message for you. Come in." She rose, gathered her green silk skirt into her hands, and stepped into the shop.

Lengths of fabric draped the walls and veiled the ceiling, making the girls feel as though they had entered a tent from *The Arabian Nights*. A stained-glass sphere overhead cast soft shadows onto the couch and tables in the room. Miss Sarah lit a stick of incense. More swirling wisps of smoke eased through the room.

"Please, sit. I'll read for each of you. But before I do, I need to know if your readings will be private or if you want to share in each other's experience."

Melissa and Fiona mouthed *share* to each other.

"I thought so. You." She pointed to Fiona. "I'll read for you first. Have a seat at my table. You." She pointed to Melissa. "Have a seat on the couch, but make sure you can see the cards. You'll be a reader one day."

Melissa perked up. "Me? A reader? Far out."

Fiona could see Melissa's wheels turning. *Don't be so gullible,* she wanted to say but kept quiet.

Fiona sat at a small round table covered in a black velvet cloth. A crystal ball sat in the center. To the side was a deck of cards wrapped in blue silk. She moved her hand to touch the cards.

"Don't touch the cards until I've cleared their energy," Miss Sarah said as she sat across from Fiona. "Be still."

She placed her hands an inch above the deck, closed her eyes, took several deep slow breaths, brought her hand into prayer position in front of her heart, and quietly chanted in a foreign tongue.

Fiona felt like she had stepped into *The Twilight Zone*.

Miss Sarah opened her eyes and reached for a small brass bowl. She ran a wooden mallet around the inside of the bowl, creating a bell-like tone that vibrated through the room. She opened the silk packet, shuffled the cards, and smiled at Fiona.

"I know this is your introduction to the tarot. Think of a question or something you wish to know, but please don't tell me. Shuffle the deck until you feel complete. Then place the cards on the table, cut the deck into three parts, and put them back together in whatever order you feel is correct."

Fiona's palms began to sweat as she held the cards. She had so many questions. What should she ask? How would she know when she was done shuffling? What if Miss Sarah gave her bad news? Why did she let Lissie talk her into a reading?

She handed the deck back to Miss Sarah.

"I'm going to lay ten cards in what's known as the Celtic Cross. It's a very ancient method of divination. You know, the mystical history of the cards goes back at least to ancient Egypt. Some say they have been with us for thirty-five thousand years. They are the keepers of ancient wisdom and universal law."

The first card Fiona drew was the Empress. "Oh, it's so beautiful! What does it mean?"

"This is you. A lovely card, but it's reversed," Miss Sarah said. "I planned to lay all the cards before beginning your reading, but this one tells me you're almost always in a state of despair. You work hard and feel as though you should prosper, but instead you experience poverty and hopelessness. You believe you were born under a bad sign. But trust me, my dear, you have much to accomplish in this lifetime. You must meditate and discover your inner self to relieve the burden you feel. Until you do, success and happiness will elude you."

Fiona pushed back tears. How could this stranger know the inner struggle she worked so hard to hide?

Miss Sarah pulled the next nine cards, studied them for a few moments, raised her head, and stared deeply into Fiona's green eyes.

"You have six cards from the Major Arcana, which indicates you're at the beginning of a spiritual quest. Most of them are in the reversed position, which means things will not come easy to you."

Miss Sarah pointed to the Chariot card. "This card tells me you often waste your energy and talent. Some of it has to do with associations with the wrong people. This doesn't mean they are evil, but they don't have your highest interest in mind.

"And here is the Knight of Wands. This indicates a fair-haired young man who is charming, impetuous, and prone to making sudden decisions. He may be taking a journey over water soon. Do you know this man?"

Jack? How could she possibly know? "Um, I think so."

"Now, this card." Miss Sarah pointed to the Lovers. "This does not necessarily have to do with physical or emotional love, though I know you wish it did. In this position, the card tells me that you must listen to your inner voice and remember you always have free will.

"You've had some challenges with an older woman. I'm seeing the letter *H*. Does this mean anything to you?"

Fiona hesitated. "My mother's name is Helen."

"She's not a malicious person but has caused you much sadness. She has a strong will and a very narrow outlook on life, which has held you back. To achieve your potential, you must become free of her and her doctrines."

"She's very religious and tries to push it on me," Fiona said. "We fight about it all the time."

"Just remember, she is on her own spiritual path, which is different from yours. She may never understand who you are or your personal journey. Until you come to terms with this, you will never be at peace.

"Here is the Knight of Swords." Miss Sarah pointed to the next card. "You don't know this man yet, but he'll be entering your life soon. He has dark hair and is very intense. He will lift you out of depression and help you grow into the next phase of your life. Remember, the souls we meet on our journey through this lifetime are here to help us. Relationships may not always be easy, but they are necessary. Most of the people we meet we've known in other lifetimes and in other roles. You and I, for example, have a strong connection. I'm not usually able to read a first-time client so deeply."

Fiona sat transfixed. How could Miss Sarah see into her soul?

"Your final card is the Wheel of Fortune. I know you don't trust in God or the universe, but this card is telling you that you must. Life will present some challenges for you in the next few years. When you are down on the wheel of life, there is nowhere to go but up. Change is part of life. Nothing is real. This world and everything in it is an illusion. Don't give up, no matter how bleak things look. You're a fighter. Please remember this and please remember our meeting. You and I may never meet again on this physical plane, but I will be with you always."

Miss Sarah gathered the cards, shuffled them, and wrapped them in the blue silk. She bent toward Fiona, looked deeply into her eyes, and whispered, "You and your friend have a shared destiny. You have much to learn from her. Remember my words. A time will come."

A time will come? Fiona felt a chill run down her spine. She started to speak, but Miss Sarah stared intensely into her eyes and softly shook her head.

"Before I read for you," Miss Sarah said, looking at Melissa, "why don't we take a moment to clear the energy in the room with a short meditation?

"Sit quietly with both feet firmly planted on the earth. Rest your palms on your thighs, facing upward so you're receptive to the positive energy in the universe. Close your eyes and breathe slowly and deeply, inhaling and exhaling through your nose."

The girls did as they were instructed. Miss Sarah chanted softly for a few minutes, then more audibly, "*Namaste.* Now, bring your energy back into your bodies and softly open your eyes."

She offered a seat at the table to Melissa and followed the same ritual with the cards as she had with Fiona.

Miss Sarah barely looked at the spread she had laid out. Instead, she stared at a spot just above Melissa's head.

"I see an orb over your head. An orb is a ball of light or energy that can only be seen or felt by those with the gift. Orbs can be angels or spirit guides, or they can be souls that are clinging to us in this lifetime. Yours is shimmering silver and very vulnerable. It's telling me you had a deep connection that has been severed. She is feeding on your energy and is unable to let go. In order for you both to move forward, you must separate. This can only be done through meditation and prayer. We'll leave her for now. After your reading, I'll prepare a prayer for you."

Melissa shook her head, as if she were trying to release herself from the orb. "I feel it," she said.

Fiona sensed an uneasiness in the room. Could the orb be the soul of Lissie's baby?

"Now for your cards. Your spirit card is the High Priestess, a beautiful card. She tells me there is much that lies under the surface. You have the gift of intuition and spiritual inspiration, but you are living behind a veil. Your purpose in this lifetime is to lift the veil for yourself and those close to you. Believe in yourself and your higher power. One way to do this is to study the tarot."

"I want to be a reader," Melissa said. "I knew it was important to come here. This is my destiny."

"One step at a time." Miss Sarah's voice carried a warning. "Stay focused, please."

Melissa sank into her chair and turned her attention to the cards.

"Your next card is the Knight of Swords. Your friend drew this card, but it represents a different person in each of your readings. For you, I see a dark-haired young man who is very prominent in your life. The card is reversed, or upside down, meaning he doesn't have your best interest at heart. He is selfish and may have an adverse effect on your future. Somehow there is a negative connection between him and your orb. Your orb is no longer shimmering."

"That couldn't be Mickey, could it?" Melissa asked.

Miss Sarah ignored the question.

"Following the Knight is the Five of Cups. You've had some challenges and some sadness recently. Have courage. What may feel like an ending could be a new beginning. A new home or workplace would be good for you at this time."

"My boyfriend and I are moving to Boston in September," Melissa said. "That's a new home. I could work as a card reader."

"As I said," Miss Sarah continued, "one step at a time. Nothing is as it appears, nor is it otherwise. Your next card, the Sun, says you must stop daydreaming and have a more realistic outlook on life. Examine all aspects of a situation before acting."

"But it's such a beautiful card. How could it be telling me something negative?" Melissa's mood had turned somber.

"When this card is reversed, it indicates a challenge. You can see challenges as negative or as opportunities for growth. The choice is yours."

The next card in the spread was the King of Swords. "This card represents an older man who will be coming into your life. He is dark and intense and may upset your balance. When you meet him, tune in to your intuition and know he is a charlatan."

"You're scaring me," Melissa whispered.

"Finally, we have the Magician, which is also reversed. It's telling me this man will abuse his power and hurt you if you allow him. I can't stress this enough. Trust in your intuition and look deeply into every situation."

Melissa had folded into herself, wisps of hair hiding her face. In spite of the heat, she trembled.

"You have a gift, yet you are often troubled by sadness," Miss Sarah explained. "Knowledge is power. Awareness is the first step toward enlightenment. Now, I promised to create a prayer for you. You'll need to come back in about an hour. Why don't you and your friend visit the occult bookstore on the next block? Ask Sandy, she's the proprietor, for a book on the tarot. You may want to buy your own cards. I recommend the Rider Waite Deck. I'm sure Sandy will tell you the same."

Miss Sarah hugged each of the girls. In Fiona's ear, she whispered, "Take care of your friend. Keep her energy positive, and remember to always walk in the light."

Fiona nodded politely. She didn't need more responsibility in her life. She had enough trouble taking care of herself.

Chapter 15

The Florida sun jolted the girls back to reality as they left Miss Sarah. Too stunned and overwhelmed to speak, they made their way to the bookstore.

"Is this the right place?" Melissa asked as they looked into the store window. Like most bookstores, the display featured current best sellers such as *The Godfather* and *Portnoy's Complaint*, greeting cards, pens, and stationery.

"I think so. Look." Fiona pointed to several books in the corner: *On Death and Dying*, by Elisabeth Kübler-Ross; *Freedom from the Known*, by Jiddu Krishnamurti; and *The Satanic Bible*, by Anton Szandor LaVey.

They stepped into the store.

"Can I help you?" a large woman in a flowered caftan asked them.

"Miss Sarah sent us. She said you sold tarot cards," Fiona said.

The woman smiled. "Miss Sarah, yes. Come with me. By the way, I'm Sandy." She led them to the back corner of the showroom. "Here's what we've got. I'm assuming she wants you to buy the Rider Waite Deck."

"Yes," Melissa said. "She said I have the gift and I should be a reader. It's my destiny!"

Sandy smiled sardonically. Fiona became instantly suspicious. She wondered if the two women were in cahoots. Did they send customers to each other, or was she mocking Lissie?

"Anyone can learn to read the cards. It's like learning to dance. We can all do the foxtrot, but to be a great ballerina takes years of practice and study. The cards can take you in many directions, but be sure to steer clear of the Thoth Tarot and Aleister Crowley. Some say they're associated with black magic."

Fiona thought about her mom, who would kill her if she knew where she was. Black magic? Satan? Fortune telling? Maybe it was time to go. She started to move toward the door.

"There's nothing to fear," Sandy continued. "If your heart and intentions are in the right place, the tarot can work miracles. Do you each want a deck? How about the accompanying book?"

"I'll take both," Melissa. said. "What about you, Fee?"

Fiona hesitated but realized her intentions would only be for good. "I guess so, but you'll have to keep them at your house till I go back to college. I can't let my mom find this stuff."

Back outside, Melissa was practically jumping up and down. "This is so cool! I can't wait to get started. I knew there was a reason we came to Florida."

"Remember what she said. Take it slow and really learn the cards," Fiona said. "I don't know your aunt all that well, but maybe we shouldn't say anything to her about this."

"Good point. Let's keep it our secret for now." Melissa put her arm around Fiona and gave her a hug. "Let's go back to Miss Sarah and get my prayer."

Miss Sarah was outside her shop, smoking and staring into space. "I see you made a purchase. You won't regret it, I promise. Now come inside."

Fiona waited on the couch while Miss Sarah spoke to Melissa. "I'm giving you a Sanskrit prayer and mantra. The sounds carry with them the sounds of creation. They are for you and you alone. Don't worry about the literal meaning. If I translated the prayer into English, it would lose its power. Don't share this with anyone, including your friend. Sit quietly, breathe deeply and slowly, and when you feel ready, recite the syllables three times. The vibration will bring peace to you and allow the orb to release itself." She stood and walked back to Fiona.

"Here's a Sanskrit mantra for both of you," Miss Sarah said, handing each of the girls a sheet of blue stationery. In flowing calligraphy were the words: *Lokah Samastah Sukhino Bhavantu.*

"In English, it means, 'May all beings everywhere be happy and free, and may the thoughts, words, and actions of my own life contribute in some way to that happiness and to that freedom for all.' Mantras speak directly to the universe—to our cells and our soul. Go in peace." Miss Sarah folded her hands in prayer and bowed her head. "*Namaste.*"

The magical peace of the blessing surrounded the girls like a warm hug as they left Miss Sarah's sanctuary.

The bus was filled with tourists, beach bums, and a group of chatty elderly women—a sharp contrast to the serenity and solitude of Miss Sarah's.

"It's like finding a whole new reality," Fiona said. "It was so peaceful in her shop. I felt really connected to her, but at the same time I'm kinda freaked out."

"I'm freaked out too, especially that part about the orb. Do you think that's my baby?"

"I don't know how it could be," Fiona replied. "I thought she was seeing some kind of light reflected over your head. It's gonna take me a while to figure this all out."

"Not me. This is the world I want to live in. There's a whole lot going on that we can't see. I want to learn everything I can. I think you feel the same way, but you're scared 'cause of your mother."

"Yeah, my mom would say Miss Sarah's doing the Devil's work. She'd start in again about how evil I am and how I have no soul." Fiona turned her face toward the window.

"No soul? What are you talking about?"

It took Fiona a moment to respond. "When I was, like, nine or ten years old, my mom started screaming at me. I must have done something wrong. Maybe I started giving her some shit about not going to church. Anyway, she started in on her religious crap. The more she preached, the more I resisted. Finally, she told me I had no soul. That somehow when God was giving out souls, he skipped over me."

"What kind of bullshit is that? Who says that to a kid?"

Fiona turned her face to the window. She didn't want anyone on the bus to see her crying. "What if it's true? What if God did skip over me? What if I don't have a soul and I'm doomed for eternity? If he forgot to give me a soul, what else did he forget?"

Melissa leaned her head on Fiona's shoulder. "Miss Sarah says I have the gift, and I say your mother is full of shit. How's that for my first prediction?"

Fiona smiled in spite of her pain. "Thanks, I guess."

"Miss Sarah didn't say anything about you not having a soul. She also said you need to get away from your mother, right?"

Fiona nodded. If she could, she would walk away from her mom, but that would mean she would have to leave her dad. She couldn't do that. She wished they had never met Miss Sarah.

"She said you've got lots of important work to do in this lifetime. I think today is gonna open up a whole new world for us," Melissa said.

"I wish we could get stoned. That always makes me feel better."

"Here, have a cigarette." Melissa handed her pack of Marlboros to Fiona.

Fiona was upset, but not so much that she would smoke a Marlboro. "Miss Sarah did say this world is an illusion. If she's right, then my mom and her bullshit aren't real. Nothing is real, not even the butter my mom puts on the table." Fiona smiled.

"That's better. Now, let's hide our cards in our beach bag and get our story straight for my aunt."

Chapter 16

"**Y**our uncle Hal and I have a special surprise for y'all. For your last night in town, we're treatin' you gals to a sunset dinner at our favorite spot. Be sure to wear your best," Aunt Marge said.

Melissa's best was an empire-waisted white cotton sundress with splashes of pink and red. Fiona's was a simple white cotton sheath with black polka dots. They admired themselves in the bedroom mirror.

"We definitely look like we've been on vacation," Fiona remarked. "I'm glad our sunburn turned to tan."

"It's a good thing we packed these dresses. I thought we'd never get to wear them," Melissa said as they walked into the living room.

Aunt Marge stood facing the window, watching as her husband backed the Cadillac out of the garage. The back of her floor-length flowered silk dress dipped below her waistline. The halter neckline revealed toned arms and shoulders. Her hair had been styled in an updo, giving her face a youthful appearance.

"Y'all look darlin'," she said, turning toward them.

Fiona didn't feel darlin'. Compared to Aunt Marge, she felt like she'd stepped out of a second-hand shop. She wondered if she would ever have the poise and sophistication of the older woman.

Uncle Hal imagined himself to be a ship's captain. He wore a navy blazer with an unidentified coat of arms on the pocket, a pale blue ascot in place of a tie, a white shirt, and white polyester trousers. White patent-leather shoes and a navy captain's hat completed the outfit.

Behind his back, the girls stifled giggles. Melissa whispered in Fiona's ear, "Kinda early for Halloween."

They drove along A1A, crossed a waterway, and turned onto a side road. Ahead was a tall building with the most unusual rooftop they had ever seen.

"This is it," Aunt Marge said. "Pier 66. Another famous spot in our lil' ol' town. Top of the Pier is where we're going. It's a revolvin' restaurant. It takes sixty-six seconds for the elevator to rise from the ground floor to the lounge. The lounge does a full rotation every sixty-six minutes! Can you imagine?"

Neither Melissa nor Fiona wore a watch, so they had no way to time the elevator ride. Arriving at the top floor, they were greeted with spectacular views of the Atlantic Ocean, Intracoastal Waterway, Port Everglades, and downtown Fort Lauderdale.

"Wow!" they said in unison.

The hostess seated them at a table for four by the window. "This is our usual table," Uncle Hal said as he took the seat next to Fiona. "Just remember, gals, if y'all leave the table to freshen up, be sure to memorize what our table looks like, 'cause when you return, it won't be in the same place."

"Betcha didn't know the legal drinkin' age in Florida is nineteen," Uncle Hal went on. "What's your pleasure, ladies? Martini? Manhattan? Highball?"

"I won't be nineteen for another two weeks," Fiona replied.

"And my birthday isn't till October," Melissa chimed in.

"Drat," said Uncle Hal. "Guess I won't be able to get y'all liquored up and take advantage of you."

Aunt Marge narrowed her eyes and glared at her husband. He immediately changed the subject. "The steaks here are the best. How about it? Porterhouses all around?"

"Let the gals take a look at the menu, dear," Aunt Marge said. "Maybe they'd like fish. I'm sure they don't get fresh fish at home."

Drink and appetizer orders were placed. A daiquiri for Aunt Marge, Dewar's scotch and soda for Uncle Hal, and Cokes for the girls. A second round of alcohol was served with their shrimp cocktails. A third scotch arrived as they finished their appetizers.

The girls followed Aunt Marge's lead and ordered the mixed seafood platter. Dinner arrived as the sun dipped below the horizon. Fiona ignored her meal, mesmerized by the light show on the water. Rays of tangerine and gold cascaded from clouds to water and back up again. It took her a moment to realize Uncle Hal had placed his hand on her leg and was sliding it up her thigh.

She froze, unsure of what to do. She glanced at Aunt Marge, whose attention was focused on her dinner, oblivious to her husband's advances. "Please excuse me. I need to use the restroom," Fiona said as she stood. The errant hand retreated.

What a letch, she thought as she headed to the safety of the ladies' lounge. She smoked an entire cigarette before she had the courage to return to the table. As she opened the door, she was met by Uncle Hal.

"I thought you got lost," he said as he pinned her against the wall. "A pretty gal like you needs lookin' after." He leaned toward

Fiona and nuzzled her neck. She tried to push him away, but he was too strong for her. A whiff of whiskey hit her nose as his face came closer.

"Please don't do this," she begged.

"What? I'm just lookin' for a little lovin'. How 'bout it? Give your uncle Hal a kiss."

"*No!*" Fiona surprised herself. Saying no was a new experience, but then again, she had never been in a situation like this with an older man.

The maître d' surprised them as he approached. "Is there a problem, miss? Is this gentleman bothering you?"

"No problem, Andre," Uncle Hal replied. "We're having dinner with my niece and her friend here. She left to freshen up and didn't come back, so I came looking for her. It's her first time in a moving restaurant. Thought she may have gotten lost."

Andre looked to Fiona for verification. She smiled and nodded.

"Well then, allow me to escort you to your table." Andre placed his hand on Fiona's back and led her back into the restaurant. "May I reheat your meal?"

"Thank you," Fiona said.

Uncle Hal didn't return to the table. Fiona saw him take a seat at the bar.

"Remember, I told you to tell me if that husband of mine starts any mischief with you," Aunt Marge said as Fiona took her seat.

"Everything's okay," Fiona mumbled as she buttered a roll.

"This isn't the first time he's pulled somethin' like this, and it won't be the last. You're safe for now. He won't be botherin' you for the rest of the evenin', but make sure y'all lock your door tonight. He's been known to wander."

Fiona wanted to ask how anybody could put up with a husband like Uncle Hal but kept quiet.

Andre returned with Fiona's dinner. "Ladies, desserts are on the house."

Uncle Hal was subdued on the ride home. The blood vessels on his cheeks and nose were nearly as red as Fiona's sunburn earlier in the week. He chain-smoked to stay alert. Back at the house, he bid a quiet goodnight to everyone and closed the door to his den.

"That's the last we'll see of him tonight," Aunt Marge said. "Now, why don't you gals get your things together. I'll be drivin' y'all to the train first thing in the a.m." She hugged each of them and shooed them into the guest room.

"What the hell happened back there?" Melissa asked as she closed the door.

"Your uncle's a big fucking creep," said Fiona. "I'll be so glad to get away from him."

"I don't know how Aunt Marge puts up with him. I'm exhausted. Let's pack our stuff and get to bed."

The girls spent a good part of the twenty-five-hour train ride home studying the tarot. They practiced reading for each other, but none of the readings had the impact of Miss Sarah's. By the time they pulled into Trenton, they felt comfortable with the Celtic Cross layout and had a general grasp of a handful of cards.

Reality hit as they switched to the Trenton Local. A forty-five-minute ride to their station, then a short car ride in Mr. O'Brien's Buick would bring the girls back home to a boring summer job for Fiona and an unknown future for her friend.

They dropped Melissa off at her mother's apartment and headed for home.

"It's too bad about that family. Wouldn't it be nice if her mother could meet a man and leave her job? I hate seeing anyone living in poverty," her dad said.

"I heard she has a boyfriend. Some guy named Mr. Giovanni," Fiona replied. "He's got a couple of kids and a big ranch house outside of town."

"Hey, that's great. Let's pray they get married. It'll make a world of difference for that family."

Fiona would pray. She'd pray the boyfriend had enough sense to stay away from Mrs. Patten.

Fiona's parents wanted to hear about the trip, but she put them off until dinner. Two letters from Jack sat on her dresser. The content was generic and vague: a few stories about his aunt, the area, and the weather. He confirmed the date of his return and said he looked forward to seeing her.

Fiona wondered if Jack had lost interest in her or was just a poor letter writer. She wished she hadn't given Lissie her tarot deck to hold. She could have done a reading to figure out what was on his mind.

Realizing there was nothing to be done, Fiona joined her parents for dinner, where she gave them an equally generic version of her Florida adventure.

Fiona settled into her favorite living room chair for an evening of TV. She enjoyed the Saturday night lineup of *Get Smart*, *My Three Sons*, *Hogan's Heroes*, and *Petticoat Junction* but was not usually at home to see them.

The O'Briens' phone rang as *Get Smart* was ending.

Fiona picked up the receiver on the kitchen phone. Hysterical screams greeted her.

"Lissie? Is that you?"

"*Get over here, now—please!*" Melissa's voice burned in Fiona's ear.

"What's the matter?"

"*Just get here!*"

Fiona hung up the phone and went back into the living room. "Can I borrow the Corvair?"

"But you just got home, FiFi. Why do you want to go back out?" her dad asked.

"Melissa needs me for something." Fiona hoped her vague response would satisfy her parents.

"That girl has one problem after another," her mom said. "Go, but don't be late."

"Thanks, Mom."

Pulling into Melissa's driveway, Fiona noticed Chana's car was gone. Mickey's parents' Mercedes sat in its place. Boxes crowded the back seat. She hoped his parents weren't in the house.

One of the cracked glass panels in the back door was covered by a tattered sign: EVICTION NOTICE, followed by rows of small print that blurred the longer she stared. At the bottom of the paper she read: FINAL NOTICE: PREMISES MUST BE VACATED BY JULY 31, 1969.

This is the big problem that couldn't wait?

Fiona opened the door and stepped across the unpainted step into the kitchen. The usual pile of dirty dishes sat in the sink and across the left side of the counter. An open box of Sugar Pops rested next to two bowls half full of milk. On the table were three large boxes partially packed with plates, mugs, and utensils.

Guess they're all leaving. End of an era.

She thought about calling out to Melissa but changed her mind. She tiptoed into the living room. Seeing nobody on the first floor, she climbed upstairs to Melissa and Mickey's bedroom. The furniture was as she remembered, but the walls were stripped bare. Her friend's clothes still hung in the closet. A pile of Mickey's T-shirts sat in the corner. Another pile of his underwear and socks lay on the bed.

"Lissie?" she whispered.

She heard a rustling in the hallway, then Melissa tiptoed into the room.

Mascara dripped down her cheeks. Her hair stuck out at unnatural angles. She held on to the wall for support as she walked into the bedroom.

"What the fuck's going on?" Fiona asked.

Melissa crawled onto the bed and kicked Mickey's underwear onto the floor.

"Is it the eviction?" Fiona asked.

"N-no—well, maybe—n-no," Melissa said between sobs.

Fiona put her arm around her friend. "You're safe now. Tell me what happened."

"Well, after your dad dropped me off at my mother's apartment, I decided to come back here. I saw the note on the back door and freaked out. I called to Mickey from downstairs, but he didn't answer."

"Maybe he's out with Rick and Chana," Fiona said.

Melissa continued as if Fiona hadn't just spoken. "I came upstairs, called again, then started to unpack. I needed to pee, so I went to the bathroom, and then . . ."

Melissa began hyperventilating.

"Have a cigarette and calm down," Fiona said.

Melissa shook her head. After a minute her breathing slowed, and she went back to her story. "I opened the bathroom door and turned on the light. Rick was standing in the tub, facing Mickey. Mickey was kneeling in front of him. He was holding Rick's ass with one hand. His other hand and his mouth were on—"

"No!" Fiona didn't know what to say. She knew Mickey cheated on Melissa, but she never expected it was with Rick.

"I screamed. Mickey stopped and they both stared at me. It was like time stopped, then Rick closed the shower curtain and turned back to Mickey. I shut the door, ran downstairs, and called you."

"Where are they now?" Fiona asked.

"When I came upstairs, they were in Rick and Chana's bedroom. I went back into the bathroom to wait for you."

"What are you gonna do?"

"Wait until he comes out, I guess," Melissa replied. "Will you stay with me?"

Fiona looked at the clock. *Petticoat Junction* would be starting in fifteen minutes.

Wait a minute. What's more important, a stupid TV show or my best friend?

"Sure, Lissie."

The girls lay back on the bed and silently stared at the ceiling.

Fiona opened her eyes with a start. Had she fallen asleep? She saw Mickey sitting on the bed, staring at her and Melissa, a towel wrapped around his hips.

"Mel, wake up," Mickey said.

Melissa's eyes fluttered open. "Mickey, what—"

"So now you know, Mel."

"What the fuck, Mickey? I'm gone a couple of weeks and suddenly you're makin' it with Rick? Do you like guys now? You couldn't wait for me to come home? I don't understand."

"Get real. Rick and I have been doin' it for months. Even before we moved in here. How could you not know? Everybody knows. Right, Fee?"

"I didn't know," Fiona mumbled.

"Bullshit. Nobody knows. Chana doesn't know. Nobody said anything to me!" Melissa screamed.

"Are you kiddin'? Of course Chana knows. The three of us get it on all the time. We dropped hints for months for you to join us, but you were so dense we gave up. The funniest part was how you thought I had somethin' goin' with Denise. Talk about clueless." Mickey grabbed his pack of Marlboros, lit two, and handed one to Melissa.

What a Trip

"Do you want me to leave?" Fiona asked.

"Stay, Fee," Melissa commanded.

"It's not like I never cared about you," Mickey went on, "but you're so needy. You want me all for yourself, and I'm not ready for that. It was fun with you, but it's more fun with Rick. Once you got pregnant, it turned into a major bummer."

"You son of a bitch!" Melissa wailed. "How can you be like this after all we've been through?"

"All we've been through . . . yeah, that's *why* I'm like this. Well, I've got news for you. Me an' Rick, we're takin' off. This house is done for. Chana's movin' to the Village. She's got someplace to crash. Thinks she can make it as a folk singer. Can you imagine? What an ass."

Melissa dragged deeply on her cigarette. Small whiffs of smoke floated from her nostrils as she exhaled from her mouth. She seemed to be at a loss for words.

The three sat in silence. Who would be the first to speak?

In a kinder voice, Mickey finally said, "Rick and I will be gone by the end of June. Nobody's payin' July's rent. You should get out too, before you gotta come up with the whole nut."

"W-w-where are you going? W-w-what about Boston?" Melissa pleaded.

"I was never gonna take you to Boston. Me and Rick are headed to Upstate New York to Dai Bosatsu Zendo. Get our heads on straight. From there, maybe college, maybe the brown robes."

"What the fuck are you talking about?" Fiona asked.

"It's a Buddhist monastery. This scene's too much for me. I'm thinkin' meditation might be the answer. Rick knows a coupla dudes who went there for a month and decided to stay. They shaved their heads and wear brown robes."

"But, Mickey, your hair's so beautiful." Melissa reached for his head.

Mickey pulled away. "Come on, Mel. Get some boxes and get packin'. You got less than a week to get your shit together." He stood, tossed his half-empty pack of Marlboros on the bed, and walked out.

Melissa smoked and stared into space. "I can't believe it's over. This whole last year. Boston, my future, everything. What did I do to deserve this?"

You don't know how lucky you are to get rid of him, but you'll never believe me. Aloud, Fiona said, "You didn't do anything wrong. Mickey's an asshole. You deserve better."

After a moment of silence, Melissa said, "Maybe Denise isn't getting Mickey, but her witchcraft's responsible for this mess. Peeing in front of her barbecue didn't do shit. Maybe I'll pee on her car."

Despite the tension in the room, the girls giggled.

Chapter 18

Fiona spent her first week back home preparing projects and a loosely structured curriculum for her teaching job at the Methodist summer camp. She wanted most of her work done ahead of schedule so she would have more time to devote to Jack once he returned from Virginia. The rest of her free time was spent helping Melissa pack her things in preparation for the move to her mother's apartment.

Melissa's life amounted to a dozen supermarket boxes and two suitcases filled with clothes, books, record albums, and memories. What took most of their time and energy was sorting through the household debris, remembering what she had brought into the house and into her relationship with Mickey. Chana would take most of the furniture. Sheets and towels that hadn't seen a washing machine in months would stay with the house. Most of the ashtrays, posters, and drug paraphernalia belonged to Rick and Chana, but Melissa saw sentimental value in each item. A few she hid under her clothing. Others she deliberately destroyed in an attempt at revenge. Fiona doubted any of it would be missed.

Mickey had moved into Rick's room. While she packed, he lay on Rick's bed, smoking and listening to music.

"What a coward," Fiona said. "Doesn't even have the courage to face you."

"It's better this way," Melissa replied. "He left me a note saying when I'm allowed in the house to pack my shit. He doesn't want to see me, and I don't know what I'd do if I saw him. I might kick him in the balls."

You're full of shit, Lissie. You'd take him back in a second. I bet you'd even go to that monastery if he asked you.

Melissa stopped packing and sat on the bed, turning her face away from Fiona. She sniffled, brushed away her tears, and lit a cigarette. "What happened? I thought we'd be together forever."

"Life happened, Lissie," Fiona replied. "As soon as things got complicated, he decided to split. I just can't believe he likes guys."

"He says he doesn't. He says he's just exploring his sexuality. I mean, he was doing it with Rick and Chana," Melissa said.

Fiona wondered who else Mickey was screwing. Maybe he had been with Denise and some other guys too.

"Better to find out now before you moved to Boston with him." Fiona wanted to finish by saying, *Like that was ever really gonna happen*, but kept quiet.

"I didn't tell you I tried calling Kenny from Florida."

Fiona had put the "Florida guys" out of her mind and thought Melissa had also.

"The operator said the number was not in service. I waited a day and tried again. That time I got some old lady who never heard of Kenny and Mike. I think he made a mistake when he wrote down the number, so I sent him a letter," Melissa said.

Fiona knew there was no mistake but innocently asked, "What did you say in the letter?"

"I told him my boyfriend and I broke up, and if he wanted me to come back to Florida and be with him, I could. I said I'm learning how to read tarot cards and I could open a place in Miami in the fall when school starts again. I gave him my mother's phone number and told him to call me."

"You spent one afternoon together and now you want to move in with him?"

"Fuck, no. I thought I could move in with Aunt Marge until I started making money, and then I'd move in with him. We had a connection."

Fiona thought it best to end the conversation. "Come on, let's get back to packing. The sooner you get out of here, the better."

Melissa's mother welcomed her daughter back home with one stipulation—she had to find a full-time job. With Mickey out of the picture, there was no advantage in taking the summer off. She also needed money. The trip to Florida had drained her savings.

"My mother says she can get me a job at Sears," Melissa told Fiona and Peach the next afternoon over coffee and cigarettes. "She said to tell them about my experience at Bella's Gift Shop. What do you guys think?"

"What a drag," Peach said. "Working in a department store sucks. It's not gonna be like Bella's, where you can help yourself to the merchandise and fuck off in the back room. Do you really wanna be part of corporate America?"

"Not really, Peachie, but what else can I do? I need the bread."

"They're hiring at the hospital. You could get a job as an aide. It's gotta pay more than Sears, and you'll get some experience," Peach suggested.

"What about my operation and them thinking I'm crazy?"

Operation? Was Melissa still in complete denial about the abortion?

"It's worth a shot," Peach said, overlooking the obvious. "Whenever they hire somebody, there's always a break-in period. They give you a coupla months to see if you like the job and they like you. And between us, I don't know if they really bought into you being crazy. It coulda just been a convenient excuse to give you the abortion, er, I mean, the operation."

"I think you should listen to Peach. You've got nothing to lose. You'll make your mother happy, and you may even like the work," Fiona added.

"Well, I guess so," Melissa said reluctantly. "My life sucks anyway, so what's one more downer?"

The hospital hired Melissa as a nurse's aide. Her starting salary was barely above minimum wage, but because she agreed to work the three-to-eleven shift, a stipend was added. The hospital put her on a probationary period while she trained.

"I vouched for you, Lissie," Peach told her, "so don't let me down."

Peach needn't have worried. Melissa was a quick learner and enjoyed the work. The workload slowed as the night progressed, giving her time to study the tarot cards. She kept to herself and made no effort to make friends with her coworkers.

What a Trip

Fiona worked from early morning until four in the afternoon. Peach worked the night shift. Their schedules left little time for socializing.

Chapter 19

*E*ven the moon landing on July twentieth did little to disrupt the tedium that had taken over the summer. Jack invited Fiona to watch the event with his grandmother. She declined, saying that she had no interest in supporting anything that had to do with the government. His reaction was less than positive. Fiona immediately regretted her words.

Another nail in the coffin. Why am I such an idiot?

One afternoon about a week later, Peach called a meeting in the park, saying she had a news flash. She, Fiona, and Melissa passed a joint and enjoyed the warm summer sun.

"Have you heard about the humongous festival in Upstate New York next month?" she began. "It's gonna be three days of peace and music. I think we all should go. Janis Joplin is gonna be there."

"Far out," Fiona said. "Tell us more."

"Tickets are seven dollars a day, or eighteen for all three days. Janis'll be there on Saturday," Peach explained.

"Maybe we could go just to see Janis," Fiona said.

"I think we should go for all three days," Melissa suggested.

"What about work?" Fiona asked

"Screw work," Melissa said. "You've had perfect attendance at your job, and Peach and I can ask for the days off. C'mon, let's do it. This summer's sucked since Florida."

"Here's the thing," Peach went on. "My brother and his friends told me about the festival and asked me to drive them, so my car's gonna be full. Fee, maybe you can borrow your mom's car."

A nervous tingle erupted in Fiona's stomach. "She'll never let me have the car overnight. Maybe Jack can drive us. I could tell my parents we were going with you, Peachie."

"Whatever. You don't have to tell them it's on a farm. They're calling it Woodstock, so tell them it's a concert at someplace in the town. They'll never find out. Take a look at who's gonna be there," Peach said, opening an advertisement for the event.

"Holy shit! Jefferson Airplane; The Band; Crosby, Stills, and Nash; Richie Havens; Joan Baez." Melissa continued reading a wish list of performers. "We've gotta do this."

Jack called Fiona after dinner. She took the call in the kitchen while her parents relaxed on the front porch.

"Did you hear about the Woodstock music festival?" Fiona asked him.

"Yeah, I heard somethin'. Supposed to be a lot of bands. Why, do you wanna go?"

"I do. Janis Joplin's gonna be there on Saturday. I'd give anything to see her," Fiona said. "Do you think you could borrow the Nash and take Lissie and me?"

A minute of silence, then crackling and crunching. Was he eating potato chips?

"Listen, babe," Jack said. "Why would ya drive all that way for a concert when you can watch it on TV?"

Who are you? Fiona asked herself, then said, "Creedence'll be there. Arlo Guthrie too. It's gonna be really great. We could take sleeping bags and camp, or we could sleep in the Nash. You've called it the bedroom since our first date."

More silence. "That'd mean losing three days of work. I also might have to go back to Virginia for a few days to see my aunt."

"That will make three trips to Virginia this summer. Just admit it—you don't want to go," Fiona said.

"I'm not gonna lie, Fee. I can't see going to all that trouble for a little music. If you and Lissie wanna go, I won't stand in your way. Have fun and tell me all about it."

Fiona didn't know whether to scream or cry. The more time she spent with Jack, the more of a mystery he became.

"Suit yourself. I don't understand why you have to go to Virginia all the time," Fiona said.

"I didn't want to tell you, but my nana wants to move in with my aunt. She's gettin' old and doesn't want to take care of the house anymore."

"What about you? Are you gonna move with her?"

"Don't worry about me, Fee. I'm not goin' anywhere."

Fiona waited until the week before the Woodstock concert to ask her parents to borrow the Corvair.

"I don't think it's a good idea," her mom said. "A rock and

roll concert? Where would you stay? I can't see you spending your hard-earned money on a motel."

"Melissa and I can take our sleeping bags. We'll go to a campground. Tickets to the concert are cheap, and we can pack our own food."

"Oh, no," her dad said. "No daughter of mine is camping without an adult. And three days of concerts? I've heard too many stories about drugs and wild teenagers doing all kinds of illegal and immoral acts. I'm sorry, honey. The answer is no."

"Could we just go for Saturday? We really want to see Janis Joplin. We could drive up in the morning and be home that night," Fiona pleaded.

"FiFi, you're young. You don't have much experience driving. That's too many miles in one day. Why don't you wait till there's a concert closer to home?"

"What if we could get a ride from somebody?" Fiona asked.

"And who would that be? Jack? Or some other boy? I forbid you to go anywhere overnight with a boy. You're asking for trouble. This discussion is over." Her mom's anger was rising to the surface.

Fiona knew the warning signs. The discussion *was* over.

Peach left for the festival around noon on Friday. It was only a three-hour drive, and even if she hit traffic, she would be sure to get there in time to see Sweetwater, the band scheduled to open the concert at five o'clock. Melissa had asked for the weekend off, just in case she and Fiona could find a last-minute ride. It was not to be.

On Friday night, they watched the news at Melissa's apartment and heard about the massive traffic jam on the New York State Thruway. The conservative news coverage focused on a generation of hippies on their way to the decadent musical event of the decade. Discouraged and depressed, they turned off the television.

"Here we are, stuck at home, while everybody who is anybody is in Woodstock," Fiona said. "When I go back to college, I'm gonna have to listen to everybody's adventures, and I'll have nothing to share. I hate my parents."

"We should've hitchhiked."

"Now you think of it," Fiona said.

What a Trip

It was a typical Saturday night for the friends. A pint bottle of Southern Comfort, a joint, and a ride to Billy Brown's Road in the Corvair. They pulled to the side of the deserted road and sang their favorite Janis Joplin songs as they alternated hits from the bottle and the joint.

"If we were in Woodstock, I know we'd have met Janis. This sucks. Once I save up some money, I'm buying a car," Melissa said.

"I should have enough money for my own car by the end of the summer. Maybe next year they'll have another festival. I won't be stupid enough to tell my parents. I'll lie and say we're going to the shore for the weekend."

"Live and learn. Right, Fee? I've got the munchies. How 'bout we head for the diner?"

They sat at the counter and ordered their standard fare—beer-battered onion rings followed by two slices of cherry cheesecake and coffee. They turned their attention to the eleven o'clock news on the overhead television.

It was a war zone: thousands of grimy hippies, some covered in filthy blankets, others huddled inside brightly painted Volkswagen vans, still others dancing in the rain. Nothing but people, abandoned cars, mud, and garbage for miles.

"Am I glad we didn't go." For the first time in days, Fiona felt relief. "And I was worried about how I'd be able to put on my makeup!"

"What about bathrooms? Not even showers. Where would you pee?"

"I hope Peach is okay. I wonder if she even got close to the stage," Fiona said. "I'd be in such deep shit with my parents. As it is now, I'm gonna have to listen to their 'I told you sos.'"

"I never said a word to my mother," Melissa added, "and there's no way I'm telling her about Peach."

Peach arrived back in New Jersey early Monday evening. She called Fiona and asked to meet her in the park.

"Well, we survived," she told Fiona. "This was the worst weekend of my life. We never got close to the stage, never saw any of the performers, never got to take a shower, and had almost nothing to eat."

"I guess you didn't get to see Janis," Fiona said.

"Fuck, no. We may have heard her but even when we could hear the music, I couldn't tell who it was. My car's a mess. Full of mud inside and out. I've hardly slept since Thursday, and now I've gotta work the night shift."

"Why don't you try and catch some Zs before work?"

"Nah, if I do that, I may never wake up. I'll go to work and hope there're no emergencies. Tomorrow I'm taking the phone off the hook and sleeping all day."

Fiona was relieved she'd stayed home. She couldn't imagine all that mud in her hair.

By midweek, Woodstock had become an international sensation and the musical event of the century. Liberal news reports told of the peaceful, loving vibe surrounding the festival.

"Now, aren't you glad you didn't go to that concert?" her dad said, looking up from his copy of the *New York Times*. The front page was covered with photos from the concert.

"I guess so," Fiona replied.

"You guess so? Who knows what might have happened to you? Thanks to our Lord, you're safe and sound," her mom added.

"Our Lord" had nothing to do with it. You just didn't give me the car.

After two nights of sound sleep, Peach told her friends, "I've gotta say, in spite of the conditions, it was the most incredible, far-out experience of my life. I wish you guys coulda been there. I feel like I'm part of history."

Melissa and Fiona remembered Peach's initial reaction. Fiona suspected if she had been there, she too would be singing the praises of Woodstock.

Chapter 21

Jack called Fiona about an hour before their date. "Hey, Fee, I've got a surprise for you. How'd you like to double with some friends of mine from out of town? They're on their way up from Virginia headin' to Maine and will be stayin' with me and my nana for the weekend."

Fiona hesitated. She wasn't in the mood to spend the evening with strangers. "We've only got one more Saturday night till I go back to school. I thought we'd hang out, just the two of us."

"Wait'll you see their car. Beats the hell outta the Nash. Come on, babe, it'll be a blast. I got a surprise for you too."

"I do love surprises. Okay, see you in a few," Fiona said reluctantly.

To avoid any suspicion from the O'Brien neighbors, Jack picked up Fiona in the Nash. From there they drove back to his grandmother's house. In the street sat a blood-red Camaro, complete with a black-and-white racing stripe down the hood.

"That's our ride for the night. Someday I'm gonna own one of these babies."

Fiona had little respect for guys who drove "greaser-mobiles," as she and Melissa called them. Not wanting to offend Jack or his friends, she said, "It's a beautiful car. I bet it cost a bundle."

"These guys are older, so they've got the bread. C'mon, let me introduce you." Jack waved as a couple in their mid-twenties stepped out of the car.

"Miss Fiona O'Brien, let me introduce you to Nick and Sandy Friender. Nick just got home from a tour in Vietnam."

Nick was dressed in a short-sleeved madras plaid shirt and khaki pants. His close-cropped hair and freshly shaved face reminded Fiona of army advertisements she'd seen on TV. He held out his hand. Fiona hesitated. "Nice to meet you," she said.

Sandy stood in the background and nodded shyly. She wore a pastel pink Villager sundress that landed just above her knees. Fiona shuffled from foot to foot. Jack's friends were dressed like preppies, while she stood there in cutoffs and a tank top. Who were these people? More importantly, who was Jack?

Jack and Fiona climbed into the back seat, Nick and Sandy into the front. The engine rumbled to life as they pulled away from the curb. Nick rolled up the windows and blasted the air conditioning.

Fiona hated air conditioning. She hated being with these people. It would be a long night.

"Hey, man, check it out. Got this after-market eight-track installed before we left," Nick said as he popped a cassette into the player under the dashboard. "Back in the USSR" from the Beatles *White Album* nearly shredded their eardrums.

Nick pushed the pedal to the metal as they headed out of town. "Hey, bud, better watch the speed limit. We don't want to get busted," Jack yelled from the back seat.

A few miles outside of town, Nick pulled to the side of the

road. "Now for the big surprise," he said, turning to Jack. "Organic mescaline."

Fiona was curious about mescaline but felt uncomfortable trying it for the first time with strange people. "I don't know if I want to do this," she whispered to Jack.

"Come on, Fee, it's organic. It's not like acid that fucks you up. It only lasts a few hours. Your parents are away for the weekend, so you've got nothin' to worry about." Jack dropped the tablet on his tongue and washed it down with Budweiser.

Fiona watched as Nick and Sandy swallowed their hits.

Jack took the fourth tab and laid it on his tongue. He pulled Fiona close to him, kissed her, and transferred the mescaline into her mouth.

What the hell. I don't want to be the only straight one.

"Good girl," Jack said, handing her the can of beer. "Down the hatch!"

They drove for about an hour, waiting for the drug to take effect. Slowly, the colors in the interior of the car began to vibrate. Fiona looked at the instrument panel on the brightly lit dashboard.

"Oh wow, Jack, I feel like I'm in *Star Trek*. Check out the dashboard."

"And there's Captain Kirk at the controls. Ready to go where no man has gone before?" Jack pulled Fiona closer. "I'm ready to go where no man has gone before." His tongue tickled her ear.

"Hey, man, this shit's starting to hit me," Nick said from the front seat. "Is there somewhere we can park and groove on the music?"

"The old quarry's not too far from here. Kids swim there in the daytime, but nobody'll be there now," Jack said.

What a Trip

They pulled down a deserted dirt driveway. Each pothole jarred them back to reality, if only for a second. The colors grew brighter and more vivid after each bump. The night had taken on a surrealistic quality.

"Havin' fun, babe?" Jack whispered.

"I think so. I feel so weird. Everything's kinda lost its edges, like I'm blending into the cosmos." Fiona surprised herself with the depth of her insight. "It's like we're all one."

"I'm ready to blend into you," Jack said as he slid his hand under her cutoffs.

For a moment, she was concerned that Jack's friends might turn around to watch them. As she moved to kiss Jack, her embarrassment evaporated.

"Cut it out, you two. You're freakin' my wife out," Nick said as he killed the engine.

Fiona wondered how Nick could know she was freaked out. Sandy hadn't said boo since they got in the car.

"Sorry," Fiona mumbled as she pulled away from Jack.

Nick turned to Jack. "Listen, me and Sandy wanna get it on in the back seat, so you guys have to split. We need about an hour. There's a blanket in the trunk. Make yourselves comfortable out there somewhere. I'll come get ya when we're done."

What an asshole. What if Nick and Sandy left without them? She wished she had never dropped the tab of mescaline.

"Come on, Fee. Let's leave these two lovebirds alone." Jack pulled her out of the car. Once outside, he said, "You kinda have to humor Nick. He had a bad time over there. Saw a lotta killin' and other weird shit. He's not gonna leave us here, but if it makes you feel any better, I'll ask him for the keys."

"That would make me feel better. Thanks, Jack."

Nick and Sandy had already climbed into the back seat. Jack opened the driver's door, turned off the ignition, grabbed the keys, and slipped them into the inside pocket of his denim jacket.

Venus sparkled below a crescent moon that lit up the night sky. The longer they stared at the heavens, the more stars appeared. An occasional cloud drifted past. Nick and Sandy were forgotten.

Jack and Fiona undressed each other, lingering after each button. The process was painfully slow, increasing their desire. They lay naked on the blanket, letting the soft breeze cool their skin.

"I've never felt like this," Fiona said as she turned toward Jack. "So free, so vulnerable, and at the same time so powerful. I love it."

Jack ran his fingers up the inside of her thighs. Fiona thought she would melt. She wanted their lovemaking to last forever and did her best to put thoughts of time out of her mind.

Was she in love with Jack, or was it the mescaline? Sex had never felt so delicious.

It could have been an hour. It could have been five minutes. Fiona lost all track of time, but it didn't matter. She lay safe and secure in Jack's embrace.

"Dig the colors," Jack said, rolling onto his back. "D'ya think it's the northern lights?"

"Maybe. This has gotta be the most beautiful night since the beginning of time. Why don't we take a walk and see what we can find?"

They stood, stretched, and after a few wobbly steps, checked out their vertical reality. An overgrown dirt trail lay in front of them. Arm in arm, they set out.

"You know that poem by Robert Frost, 'The Road Not Taken'?" Fiona asked Jack.

"Not really. I was never much into poetry. How does it go?"

"I don't know the exact words, but there's this guy who has to decide whether to take the path everybody takes or the one less traveled. It's about not following the crowd and going your own way. I feel like that's what we're doing tonight."

"Not for nothin', but this is definitely the road less traveled. C'mon. Let's see where it goes. Hope you've got a good sense of direction." Jack took her hand as they carefully made their way down the path.

Once again, time melted into space as they walked. The trail ended at a railroad crossing. To the right, the tracks passed a mountain of dirt and crushed rock. To the left, a railroad trestle appeared to cross a ravine.

"As long as we stay on the tracks, we can't get lost. Let's cross the bridge and see what's below," Jack said.

"I feel like I could float across. Ever since Florida, I've been obsessed with trains. I want to take a cross-country train trip," Fiona said.

"Me too. Maybe we could do that someday. Let's see how many times we can jump from tie to tie without missing."

Neither missed a tie until they arrived at the bridge. "Is it strong enough to support us?" Fiona asked.

"It's gotta be. If trains can cross, then so can we. Wouldn't it be somethin' if a train came by?"

"That would never happen out here. I bet there hasn't been a train here in years. But yeah, it would be cool," Fiona agreed.

In spite of its appearance, the bridge was solid and supported them as they crossed to the other side. They continued jumping the ties for a few hundred feet until the game became boring.

"Let's head back," Fiona said. "I think I'm coming down a little."

"Me too. Hey, is that a car?" Jack pointed to a speck of light farther down the tracks.

"I doubt it. What would a car be doing here?"

The light became brighter and larger. "It can't be a car. It's a single light. It's gotta be the mescaline."

"I don't know," Fiona said. "What's that noise, and why are the tracks shaking?"

"Shit! It's a fuckin' train! Let's get outta here!" Jack jerked Fiona's arm as he ran toward the bridge.

The light grew brighter and brighter. The tracks rumbled. It was a train. Their only hope was to outrun it and get to the other side of the trestle. Halfway across the bridge, they realized they weren't going to make it. Jack flattened himself against the splintered guardrail and pulled Fiona behind him. The impact nearly sent Fiona off the bridge. She grabbed on to Jack and the broken wood and held her breath.

Death had its hand out waiting to catch her. What if her mother was right about God and heaven? If she died now, she knew she would go straight to hell.

It was over in seconds. Nothing but a small engine, coal car, and caboose on their way to an unknown destination. The bridge swayed. The wind surged past Fiona and Jack. They were shaken, yet alive.

It took a few minutes for their legs to stop trembling and their heartbeats to return to normal. Hand in hand, they made their way to safety.

What a Trip

"What a fucking rush!" Jack said.

"Nobody's ever gonna believe this happened to us. I can't believe we're still alive. Where did that train come from?"

"Beats me. Let's go tell Nick and Sandy. Maybe they'll wanna come with us and wait for another train."

"Another train? You want to do this again?" Clearheaded now, Fiona strode ahead of Jack, eager to get back to the car and then to the safety of her home. She promised herself this would be the last time she'd let Jack talk her into anything foolish.

PART TWO

Chapter 22

As she reexamined her "near-death experience," as Fiona thought of the train adventure, her feelings toward Jack softened.

Life was exciting with Jack. So what if they didn't share the same worldviews? Wouldn't it make for interesting and challenging discussions? She knew he had a lot on his plate with his grandmother moving to Virginia and school starting up soon. Where would he live once his grandmother's house was sold? Maybe Fiona could convince him to transfer to her college. He could live in the men's dorm until they were able to find an apartment together.

Fiona kept these thoughts to herself in the week before returning to college for her sophomore year. She expected to discuss her idea with Jack on their final Saturday night date, but he surprised her by saying he had to make another trip to Virginia.

"Community college starts a week later than your school," Jack told her. "That'll give me another chance to get down to Virginia and get things squared away for my nana. I'll miss you, babe, but it'll only be a couple of weeks till we see each other again. You'll see. It'll go fast."

She was disappointed but understood.

After unpacking and setting up her dorm room, Fiona headed to the Student Union for a meet and greet with the Art Department. Antiwar posters and slogans decorated the walls of the building. Someone had painted peace signs in Day-Glo colors on the entrance doors. "Feel Like I'm Fixin' to Die Rag," by Country Joe and the Fish, blasted from the PA system. Skirts were shorter, hair was longer, jeans were dirtier, and everyone looked stoned. Woodstock had made its way to the college campus.

She looked for familiar faces in the maze of hippies. She recognized a few, but most were disguised behind scraggly hair and beards. Turning to her left, she spotted a group of fellow artists. They waved to her as she fought her way through the crowd to join them.

Conversation was superficial and easy: summer jobs, art projects, fall courses. Fiona hoped no one would bring up Woodstock, but of course, they did. Only one of her classmates had made it to the festival. Instead of glorifying the experience, he complained about the traffic, the crowds, and the mud but felt fortunate to have been part of history.

Fiona hoped she would have a chance to be part of history. Woodstock couldn't be the only big event to happen in her lifetime.

She sat, smoked a Kool, sipped a Coke, and stared into space until something jolted her back into the room. Looking up, she saw a striking guy take a seat at the next table. Fiona couldn't take her eyes from him. The words *tall, dark, and handsome* ran through her head. She smiled at the cliché. *Something my mother would say.*

She averted her eyes as he looked in her direction. She

blushed. He smiled. She smiled and brought her attention back to her friends.

Who was he, and why was she so nervous? She had never been attracted to any guy who wasn't a blond. She glanced at his table and blushed again. The first day back at school, and she was already making a fool of herself.

Dr. Hacking from the Art Department motioned to her table. It was time to go. Fiona secretly hoped the stranger would join them. He stayed seated.

After her meeting, she returned to the Student Union, thinking she might see him again. He was gone.

Classes started the following day. Fiona enrolled in two art classes, Life Drawing and Principles of Design. Life Drawing began with small wooden figures posed in various positions. The assignment was to draw quick sketches of each, followed by ten-, fifteen-, and thirty-minute drawings. In a few weeks, the class would move on to live models, some nude, some clothed. The professor stressed the importance of maturity and respect for the body.

Even though her other classes were not as exciting, she felt good being back in an environment of learning among her peers. She hadn't planned on going home that first weekend. Jack would be in Virginia. Melissa and Peach were both working.

Late Friday afternoon, Fiona stopped at her mailbox before riding the elevator to her room. Several flyers announced anti-war rallies, sales at the college bookstore, and a schedule of weekend events. She hoped for a letter from Jack, but there was nothing.

She was lying on her bed thinking of the long weekend ahead when she heard her name called.

"Fiona O'Brien! Phone call."

Had something happened to her parents? She ran down the hall to the public phone.

"Hello?"

Silence, then breathing, then a sigh.

"Hello?"

"Oh, yeah. Hi, Fee. It's Jack."

"Hi, Jack. Aren't you supposed to be in Virginia?"

"I'm leaving in a bit. Just wanted to talk to you first."

Fiona smiled. He missed her.

"Listen, I have to tell you somethin'," he blurted out. "I'm gettin' married."

"*What?*"

"Maybe that wasn't the best way to put it. Um, see, when I went to Virginia, I met my old girlfriend Cindy. We started hangin' out, and I realized how much I missed her. That's why I kept goin' back."

"You fucking lied to me."

"Not exactly. My nana's moving. That's the truth. I hope you're not pissed."

"*Pissed* isn't the word, Jack. I spent my whole summer with you."

"There's more," he said. "I'm joining the navy."

Fiona held on to the phone for support. "You're kidding."

"I know you're against the war, but I want to serve our country. Cindy understands. See, her family is navy, like mine. I'm goin' to boot camp in Great Lakes, Illinois, starting December fifth."

"I thought you were going back to college." Tears dripped from her eyes. She turned her face to the wall as two of her dorm-mates passed.

"Fuck college. This is my big chance."

If she opened her mouth, she would start to sob.

"Fee? Are you there?"

"Yes," she whispered.

"I just wanna say you're a nice girl. I had a lot of fun with you this summer, especially our train adventure. Okay, so bye."

She made sure no one was in the hallway before slamming down the receiver. With controlled breathing, she steadied herself and walked back to her room.

A mix of emotions flowed through her. The hurt she felt had nothing to do with lost love but with humiliation. Heat rose in her cheeks as more tears formed in her eyes. How could she have been so foolish to think Jack cared for her? How could she have missed the warning signs: the trips to Virginia, the subtle way Jack withdrew his connection to her, the differences in their outlook on life? She had known he was a get-over since he conned her parents the evening of their first date. But this?

What a piece of shit he is, and what a bigger piece of shit I am for falling for him. She should have realized she wasn't good enough for him. Was she merely auditioning for the role of girlfriend? What was wrong with her? What did Cindy have that she didn't?

Fiona fell back on her bed and sobbed as loudly as she could without being heard in the hallway.

She must have fallen asleep. When she opened her eyes, the room was dark. She stood at the window and watched a light rain falling in the streetlights. She grabbed her sketch pad to capture the scene. Jack's face appeared in the mist as though he were melting and leaving her world.

"Take a hike, asshole," she said as she threw her sketch pad on the floor. "Go join the navy and see where that gets you."

Art therapy did wonders for her psyche. She summoned the energy to change her clothes, fix her makeup, and go to the cafeteria for dinner. Last semester, she wouldn't have been caught dead having dinner in the cafeteria on a Friday night. How quickly things had changed.

On her way, she saw a crowd of people sitting in the Student Union building, singing and holding antiwar posters. Fiona was drawn inside. Someone moved to make room for her and passed her a flyer listing upcoming protests in New York, Boston, and Washington, DC.

Some posters were simple: END THE WAR IN VIETNAM. Others were more dramatic: DON'T PLAY WITH MY LIFE and WE WON'T FIGHT TO MAKE BIG BROTHER RICH.

She felt caught up in the moment. Dinner was forgotten.

Thoughts of Jack's phone call floated in and out of her mind. For the moment she was grateful for the breakup. She would have felt like a hypocrite if she were still dating Jack. She joined in the chanting.

The squeal of a microphone silenced the group. Two campus activists she remembered from last year brought the students to attention.

"Our lives are at stake. Our lives and our future. We need to rally together to fight injustice, to fight hatred, to fight killing, to fight Big Brother!"

The crowd cheered.

"Resist the draft. Burn your draft card!" The speaker pulled out what appeared to be a draft card, struck a match, and set it on fire. He held it high until it was consumed, then began singing "We Shall Overcome." Those in the audience stood, clasped hands, and joined in.

A voice sounded in Fiona's ear. "You know, burning your draft card doesn't do shit. It's symbolic."

Startled, Fiona turned to see Mr. Tall, Dark, and Handsome standing next to her.

Before she had a chance to respond, he continued. "They can still draft you. Yeah, it's an act of resistance, but you're screwed if they call you. Canada's the only answer."

"Canada?"

"That's where I'm goin' when my number's up."

"I thought you couldn't get drafted if you were in school," Fiona said.

"And what happens after you graduate? I've got two years left, and then I've gotta make a move. Sorry, I'm Reuben Goldberg. What's your name?"

"Fiona. Fiona O'Brien."

"An Irish lass. Pleased to meet you, lassie."

Fiona smiled in spite of his poor attempt at humor. "Nice to meet you too. I haven't seen you on campus before."

"That's not true. You saw me the other day. How could I miss you staring at me? Your cheeks were as fiery as your hair. Kinda like they are now."

His comment only made her cheeks redder. "I meant before this semester."

He laughed. "I knew what you meant. I'm only bustin' on you."

"Oh, okay." What was the matter with her? Why couldn't she turn on the charm?

Fiona tuned out the speakers and took a good look at her new friend. He was tall, thin, deeply tanned, with shoulder-length chestnut hair, high cheekbones, and expressive deep brown eyes. Once again, she found herself staring, this time memorizing his features so she could sketch him later that evening.

"You're staring at me again," Reuben said.

"S-sorry," Fiona stammered. "Your face is so interesting. I was trying to take it all in so I can sketch it later."

"Is that a take on 'come up and see my etchings'?" Reuben's joke about an old seduction line helped to break the ice.

Fiona laughed. "I'm an art major, actually art minor. My major is gonna be education, though I wish it was art."

"Like me. I wanted to major in journalism, but now it's my minor."

"Your parents?" Fiona asked.

"Hell, no. My parents encourage me to follow my dreams. I want to be a writer, but it's tough getting published. I decided to start out in education and go from there."

"Lucky you. My parents are paying my tuition, so I kinda have to do what they say."

"Don't be afraid to cross the line," Reuben said. "Take out a loan, do your own thing. Fuck the establishment."

If it could only be that easy. Reuben had no idea who she was or what kind of home she came from. It was time to change the subject.

"Are you a transfer student?"

"I did two years at Temple, but the bread's tight, so I decided to switch to a state school."

"Why not take out a loan?" Fiona threw his rhetoric back at him.

"Touché. Hey, did you eat yet? Can I treat you to dinner at the dining hall? I hear they've got the best Salisbury steak in town."

"Do you hate Salisbury steak as much as I do?"

"More. Come on. This rally's fading."

Friday night was fish night. Fish sticks, french fries, and coleslaw. A step up from Salisbury steak but a far cry from gourmet dining. They grabbed a table by the window and sat across from each other.

"So who are you?" Reuben asked

Where do I start? Fiona wondered. She nibbled on a french fry and stared out the window.

"Maybe that was too broad a question. Why don't you tell me about your summer?"

Fiona liked his first question better. "Well—" She proceeded to tell him about her trip to Florida, her job at summer camp, and her failed attempt to go to Woodstock. Her friend's abortion, Uncle Hal, and Jack never appeared in her story.

At the end of her monologue, she turned the question on him. "What about you? How was your summer?"

"My plan was to go to summer school, finish college in three years, go to grad school, and get my doctorate. Once I realized I'd end up getting drafted after my bachelor's, I chucked the idea and got a summer job. I feel like I'm marking time till they call me up."

"This war sucks. Maybe all the protests will help to end the war, and you won't have to worry about the draft," Fiona said.

"Maybe. I can't count on it. How 'bout we talk about something else?"

"Sounds good to me," Fiona said. All this talk of war brought her thoughts back to Jack. She couldn't believe she'd spent the summer with somebody who would be joining the military.

After a comfortable pause, Reuben continued. "You say you're an artist. If you had one grand work to complete, what would it be?"

She thought for a moment. "I'd love to create a mural for the lobby of a really important building. I could study the history of the building or the city and do some kind of abstract representational painting." *Where did* that *come from?* she asked herself.

"Good for you! Dare to dream the impossible and it might come true. I want to write a novel about my father's family and how they suffered during the Holocaust. It's gonna be an epic, which is why I thought I'd support myself with teaching until I get published."

"You're so ambitious!"

"You gotta dream big," Reuben said, "otherwise you'll end up right where you started. Here's something else I've been thinking. I think everybody's life has a theme. What's yours?"

Fiona put her fork down and looked into Reuben's brown eyes. "Um, I guess I never thought about it."

Fiona was feeling small and insignificant. Reuben was markedly different from her friends at home.

"That's your challenge for the weekend. Do whatever you planned to do but keep your theme in the back of your mind. I'll expect an answer by Sunday night."

"Wait a minute." Fiona regained her poise. "What about you? What's the theme for your life?"

Reuben smiled. "You got me. I don't have one either. I only started thinking about it during that rally. Cool, huh?"

Fiona relaxed and smiled. Reuben was trying hard to impress her with his mind. It was a different way to get in her pants. She liked it.

The conversation turned ordinary: college, the weather, movies. She found him easy to talk to, open, and friendly. They lingered over coffee and cigarettes until they saw the lights dim. Turning around, they realized they were the only two left in the dining hall.

"Guess we better make our move," he said.

"What dorm are you in?" Fiona asked as they left.

"I've got a room over the Powder Puff Salon in town. Makes it easy to get my weekly wash and set."

She laughed. "You're joking, right?"

"About the wash and set or the Puff?"

"Both?"

"Only one," Reuben replied. "The Puff is on the first floor of an old house. They rent the upstairs to guys like me. I haven't needed a wash and set yet."

Fiona couldn't believe she was laughing so much after just getting dumped.

They stopped at the entrance to her dorm. "Thanks for a fun dinner," he said.

"I'd invite you up to see my etchings, but you know the rules. No boys allowed," Fiona said, grinning.

"That's cool. I've got some studying to do." Reuben paused, then, "Hey, they're showing *Easy Rider* tomorrow in the auditorium. Would you like to meet me there? We can check on the progress of our themes."

"I'd like that," she said.

"I'll meet you in front at quarter to seven. 'Night."

That's it? What about a goodnight kiss? Confused, she stood motionless, staring into the center of the quad. As she was about to go inside, Reuben turned, waved to her, and sprinted away.

Chapter 24

The first thing she saw as she flipped on the overhead light in her room was the pile of tissues that had absorbed her tears. The contrast between her upbeat evening and her earlier mood sent her into a fit of uncharacteristic rage. She grabbed the mound, crushed it into a tiny ball, and threw it against the wall. A new round of tears exploded as she bent to pick up the crumpled mess. Feeling lightheaded, she leaned against the closet door for support.

She was in over her head. More than anything she needed to talk to Melissa.

A phone call was out of the question. Her friend was at work. She needed to find a way to survive until morning. She reached for her sketch pad, her connection to sanity.

She sketched a montage of the summer. Jack's face moved in and out of her mind's eye. Each time it surfaced, it distorted slightly until she could no longer make out his features. The final silhouette was simply an oval with a mustache floating inside. As she drew, she smudged each piece of the collage with a tear. When her tears dried, she spit on the drawing. Her shoulders relaxed; the grip on her charcoal softened. Relief washed over her as her breathing returned to normal.

Adios, asshole. Fiona added the two words in a captioned cloud to the right of Jack's final face.

A good night's sleep and a phone call to Melissa the next day helped ease her pain. As a final good-bye, she put a match to last night's used tissues. It was time to move on to somebody who shared her values. Could Reuben be that somebody?

In case it might be Reuben, Fiona carefully selected her Saturday night outfit. She crammed her body into a new pair of bell-bottom jeans, lay back on her bed, sucked in her tummy, and zipped them closed. A white gauzy peasant blouse and her favorite silver hoop earrings completed the outfit. She wanted to be sexy but not too obvious in case she was misreading him.

Reuben waited for her outside the auditorium, wearing blue jeans, a denim shirt, and Frye boots. His hair was pulled back in a ponytail.

Looking good.

Conversation was light and easy as they waited for *Easy Rider* to begin. They, along with the rest of the audience, sat in muted horror as the film concluded.

"Heavy, man," Reuben sighed. "So much for an uplifting film. Those dudes didn't deserve to die 'cause of their appearance. Too many judges, too much persecution. Seems like the whole country is on a downer."

"Do you think we'll ever be able to change the world?" Fiona asked.

"I fuckin' hope so. Come on, let's split." He placed his hand in the small of her back and escorted her out of the theatre.

The September night cooled their skin and lightened the mood.

"Coffee?" Reuben suggested.

"Sounds good."

"Let's take the long way around," he said, pulling a joint from his back pocket.

When they reached the Student Union building, he turned to her. "I've got a good buzz goin'. How 'bout you?"

"Definitely. I've gotta put my straight face on for the crowd," Fiona said as she burst into giggles. She hadn't laughed this much in a very long time.

Coffee in hand, they sank into two beanbag chairs away from the overhead fluorescents.

"So, lassie, any thoughts on your life theme?"

Fiona felt her stomach tighten thinking of the mess she had made of her life. Doing her best to stay positive, she replied, "Life hasn't been easy for me since I've been a grown-up. I kinda feel like even though I've got a lot going for me, things aren't working out."

"You're saying your life is a failure? That's your theme?"

"When you put it like that, no," Fiona said. "I was an honor student last year. I got all kinds of awards for my art in high school. It's like my friends at home are all fuckups, and I'm afraid I'm gonna end up like them." She failed to mention her greatest fear—that she would end up homeless by the time she was thirty.

"You can change, you know. Change your mind, change your life. I can help with that." Reuben reached across and clasped her hand. "You come across like a really cool chick who's got her act together. That's eighty percent of the solution. Take that outward appearance and bring it inward."

"How do you know so much?" Fiona asked.

"I worked at the town library last summer. There wasn't a whole lot to do, so I sat in the stacks reading philosophy and self-improvement books. Best job I ever had."

"Okay, enough about me. What about you? What's your theme?"

Reuben melted into his chair. "I've been handed lots of adversity in life, lots of shit keeping me from my goals, but no matter what, I'm gonna persist."

"Impressive." Maybe she could learn something from Reuben.

"Enough seriousness. Are you as stoned as I am?" He grinned at her.

"More." They laughed till the tears ran down their cheeks. She preferred these tears to those shed last night.

The building closed at midnight. Reuben walked her to the dorm, clasped her hands, and said, "I had a really good time with you tonight. Sorry about the theme pressure. I hope it didn't bum you out."

"I had fun too. Now at least I don't have to think about my theme anymore."

"Never stop thinking about your theme. We'll both work on them till we get them perfect, okay?"

"Okay." She smiled.

"See you tomorrow. Dinner at our usual place?" Reuben asked.

"You mean the dining hall?"

"Where else? See you there at seven." As he did the night before, Reuben smiled and made his way through the quad.

For the second night in a row, Fiona stood motionless. No kiss. No move to get in her pants. What was wrong with her?

Chapter **25**

Over the next several weeks, Fiona and Reuben enjoyed dinner together most evenings and attended campus events, parties, and antiwar meetings. Fiona longed for a physical relationship. Reuben seemed content to keep their friendship platonic.

Fiona had been keeping Melissa updated on her fledgling relationship through letters and phone calls but longed for a face-to-face visit with her confidante. She came home the last weekend of September and met Melissa at the diner Friday evening before they headed out to a party.

"It sounds like you and Reuben are really hitting it off. Any clue why you guys haven't gotten laid yet?" Melissa had no qualms about getting to the heart of the matter.

"No. I don't understand what's going on. I know he likes me a lot, but he hasn't even kissed me. I never had this problem before. Maybe I'm losing my looks," Fiona said.

"Hardly. You're still a hot chick."

"Thanks, Lissie." Fiona smiled. "Was that supposed to make me feel better?"

"It's the truth. Maybe he's a homosexual," Melissa said.

"I don't think so. Maybe he's got a girlfriend that I don't know about," Fiona said. The unsaid words, *like Jack*, hung in the air. "I never had to make a move with a guy except to keep him away from me. Reuben's different. What about you, Lissie? Anybody in your life?"

"I don't meet anybody at my job except sick old people. I don't want another messed-up relationship. I think I might be cursed."

"Come on, Lissie. That's bullshit. You're young, you're cute. You need to get out and start meeting people. How much longer are you gonna work the night shift?"

"Well," Melissa said, "I do have some big news that's gonna change things. Guess what? My mother's getting married to that guy she's been dating, Mr. Giovanni."

"What's that mean for you?"

"Lots. They're getting married at Christmas. My mother's renting the apartment till the end of the year, then we're moving in with him and his kids. He's got that huge ranch house out past the school."

"Couldn't you keep the apartment? Maybe get a roommate or two?"

"That'd mean I'd have to keep working. My mother made a deal with me. If I move in with them, she'll let me work part-time and start community college in January."

Could her friend be getting her life together?

"And guess what else? I'm getting a car!" Melissa said excitedly.

Jealousy crept into Fiona's heart. More than anything she wanted a car. Even though she had saved enough money for a used car, her parents refused to let her purchase one. They argued there was no need for their daughter to have a car on campus.

"Do you have enough money for a car?" Fiona asked.

"Mr. Giovanni's giving my mother a new Thunderbird as a

wedding gift, so she's gonna give me her old Rambler. I'll be able to drive to school and maybe come see you on weekends."

Maybe there was a silver lining. Her jealousy evaporated. "Far fucking out, Lissie. Then I'd never have to come home till the end of the semester. And you'd get a chance to meet Reuben. That is, if he still likes me by then. Come on, let's split."

They doused their cigarettes in their half-empty coffee cups and paid the check.

Sticking with tradition, they each took a shot of Southern Comfort on the way to the latest party scene, a dilapidated brick farmhouse on the outskirts of town. By the time the girls arrived, the celebration was in full swing. Led Zeppelin's "Babe I'm Gonna Leave You" greeted them as they walked into the back of the house.

"Of all songs to be playing," Fiona said. "Just what I don't need to hear."

"I know what you mean." Her friend sighed.

A wave of new faces drifted in and out of the shabby kitchen. Somebody passed a hash pipe to them. Melissa took a hit. Fiona refused.

"What's the matter, Fee?"

"I really don't want to be here. It's the same old shit. Get stoned, listen to music, pretend to be cool, then shack up with some strange guy."

"What's your point? I thought you dug it," Melissa said.

"I feel so old. Some of these kids just graduated high school. There's gotta be more to life. Maybe you were right. Maybe we are cursed." Fiona shrugged and lit a cigarette.

"I'm still convinced Denise put a curse on me to get Mickey, but she lost out too. Maybe the curse backfired on her, and she's really pissed at both of us."

"Why would she want to curse me?" Fiona wondered.

"Because you're my friend. Don't forget, she was kind of a loser in high school. Girls like her thought you were Miss Popularity."

"Hardly," Fiona said. "Maybe in comparison to her I was popular, but that's a real stretch. I think I was born cursed."

"Whatever. I wish there was some way to get uncursed. I'm gonna do a tarot spread when I get home tonight. I'll let you know what the cards say."

Somebody passed the hash pipe to them. This time they each took a hit.

"Two tokes of that hash and I'm buzzed. I feel better already," Melissa said.

Melissa was right. The hash was potent and the music hypnotic. The girls moved into the living room and squeezed into an oversized mohair armchair with half its stuffing exposed. The pipe came around time and time again. Each hit brought them further into the sensuality of the moment. Cigarette and hashish smoke created a surreal cloud, making everyone and everything indistinguishable. Their troubles were forgotten.

Fiona pretended they were in a raft on a river, floating through a misty fog. She wanted to share her fantasy with Melissa, but the music drowned out her voice. Instead, she closed her eyes and swayed to the rhythm of her imaginary journey. Melissa leaned her head on Fiona's shoulder, undulating in time with her friend. Every cell in Fiona's soul felt alive as though she were experiencing her body for the first time. Without thinking, she turned toward Melissa and blew in her ear. Startled, Melissa turned to face her friend, smiled, and began tickling Fiona's stomach. Fiona returned the tickles. They dissolved into laughter as their bodies melted into each other. Melissa placed a kiss on Fiona's cheek.

"That's not a real kiss," Fiona said. She turned to face her friend. Their lips met. Tongues explored each other's mouth. Soft arms embraced. The crowd and the music were forgotten.

She ran her hand down Melissa's arm. Her friend trembled and giggled. They rocked back and forth, lost in their drug-induced ecstasy. She wanted more.

Fiona stood, holding on to the chair for stability. She took Melissa's hand and guided her out of the room. Her feet barely felt the floor as they clambered over bodies in random states of consciousness. Holding on to each other, still giggling, they made their way up the stairs to explore the mysteries of the second floor.

The air was clearer, the music more distant. The hallway seemed to go on forever, doors lining the passage. Each bedroom was home to one or more couples in various states of passion. One room housed a menagerie of arms and legs. A loose arm waved for them to enter. They walked past.

At the end of the hallway were a sleeping bag, pillow, and rumpled blanket. They lay back on the disheveled pile and stared at the paint and plaster peeling from the ceiling, which shimmered in the reflection from a streetlight.

"I feel like I'm on a mountaintop in the Himalayas, and we're the last two souls on earth," Fiona whispered.

Melissa didn't answer. Long strands of hair had fallen forward, covering half her face. Fiona pushed it aside and kissed her forehead, her cheek, and her lips.

No longer giggling, Melissa returned the kiss, her lips softly open to receive Fiona's tongue. Every nerve, every taste bud came to life as their kisses deepened. Legs and arms entwined, they rocked back and forth as one body, oblivious to their surroundings and the guy who stumbled out of the bathroom and stood watching them.

Fiona drew her friend closer, moving her kisses to Melissa's cheek, her ear, her neck.

What was that? Fiona opened her eyes to the sound of clapping and a look at their voyeur.

"What's going on, Fee?" Melissa asked as she opened her eyes. "Oh, my God," she screamed. "Get the fuck out of here, you pervert!"

"I'm not the pervert," he replied, clutching his crotch. "Thanks for the show. Gotta finish myself off in the bathroom, unless you ladies want to lend a hand."

The girls sat up, no longer stoned. "Leave us alone," Fiona echoed.

He took a last look, laughed, and returned to the bathroom.

"I'd laugh if I wasn't so embarrassed," Fiona said. "Do you know him?"

"Never saw him before, and I hope I never see him again," Melissa replied.

The girls looked at each other awkwardly. "I'm feeling kind of weird about what we did," Fiona said. "It has to be the opiated hash. It was really potent."

"Definitely the hash. Listen, other than that stoner guy, nobody knows what happened," Melissa said. "Let's keep this to ourselves."

"Works for me," Fiona agreed.

"We're not lesbians, are we, Fee?"

Fiona hesitated. She thought about the party at school last year where she'd ended up in bed with a weird chick from town. She was drunk that night and told herself it didn't count.

"No way," she finally replied.

"Come on, Lissie, let's go before somebody else comes along and sees us."

They held on to the wall to steady themselves, left the party, and called it a night.

Saturday afternoon the girls met Peach at the diner for coffee. Fiona and Melissa exchanged looks as if to ask, *Are we cool?*

Peach looked at them curiously. "Everything okay with you two?"

"Yeah, why?" Melissa said, lighting a Marlboro.

Fiona was quick to change the subject. "Peachie, I feel like I never see you anymore."

"That's what a job'll do to you," Peach replied. "This work shit's gettin' to me. I can't party till eleven and be to work by midnight anymore. I'm getting too old. I'll be twenty in a coupla months. Life's passing me by."

"I dig what you're saying," Melissa agreed. "Work sucks. What are you gonna do?"

"I've got two weeks' vacation comin' up in November. I thought I'd get in my car and drive south to see what's happenin' in the rest of the country," Peach replied.

"I wish I could take off. I don't even have a fucking car," Fiona sighed.

"Hang in there, Fee. Your day will come." Peach's words did little to soothe her friend. "So what's up with you guys?"

Melissa came to the point of their meeting. "Peachie, did I tell you that Fee and I are cursed?"

"What the fuck are you talkin' about?" Peach put out her cigarette and stared at Melissa.

"No matter what we do, it turns to shit. Neither of our lives is working out, especially compared to you. We don't have boyfriends. Nothing. Right, Fee?"

Fiona shrugged. "I don't know what to think anymore."

"I don't have a boyfriend either, but you don't see me complaining," Peach said.

"Yeah, but that's never been important to you. If I don't have a boyfriend, I'm nothing," Fiona said.

"What kinda bullshit is that?" Peach asked.

Melissa interrupted before Fiona had a chance to answer. "I did a tarot reading last night. The cards said me and Fee are definitely cursed, but we can lift the curse if we find the right antidote."

Exasperated, Peach turned to Melissa. "I think you're fucking nuts. But if you really believe something's going on, I heard about this shop in Philadelphia that sells all kinds of candles, herbs, and shit to get rid of negative energy."

"Really?" Melissa practically jumped out of her seat. "Can we go now?"

"Slow down," Fiona said. "Why can't we just buy a book?"

"What if we make a mistake, and the curse gets worse? I'd rather go to an expert," Melissa said.

"I don't even know where this place is. If you've been cursed for a while, then another week won't make a difference. I'll get more info, and maybe next weekend we can all go together," Peach said.

Fiona still thought her friend was wrong about a curse, but a trip to Philly sounded like fun.

Chapter 26

Fiona's parents were surprised to see her home two weekends in a row. They were even more surprised to see her dressed to leave the house at eight o'clock in the morning.

"One of our assignments for my Principles of Design class is to visit an art museum and write something about the architecture and how it enhances the museum's collections. My professor recommended the Philadelphia Museum of Art. When I talked to Peach last week, she said she'd like to see the museum, so she volunteered to drive me," Fiona lied.

"I wish you would have asked us," her dad said. "We could have made it a family day."

"I didn't want to bother you, Dad. You always have so much to do on the weekend."

"I'm never too busy for my little girl," he replied. "Well, you and Peach have a nice time. Don't be too late."

"We won't. I doubt we'll stay till closing time."

"So where are we going, Peachie?" Fiona asked.

"The place is called Harry's Occult Shop on South Street. It's been in business since 1917. It's *the* place to go for anybody who thinks they've been cursed. They claim to get rid of any negativity in the body or spirit. Harry works with the occult, which he claims is white magic. They've got a bunch of spiritual advisors to help you with your problems. You can buy candles, incense, herbs, powders, and spells."

"How did you find out about this place?" Fiona asked.

"Some of the Black nurses were talking about it. Their grandmas came up from the South and were into something called hoodoo," Peach said.

"Don't you mean voodoo?" Melissa asked.

"Nope. When the slaves came from Africa, they brought their religion and magic with them. They called it hoodoo. Anyway, when the Black people came north after the Civil War, they went looking for a place to buy their supplies. Harry's was a regular drug store, but they kept asking him for their shit, so he started carrying it. Then I guess he started making it himself and became an expert in the occult."

"I can't believe the original Harry is still there," Fiona said.

"I don't think he is. Whoever's there knows what they're doing," Peach went on. "These nurses swear by the place."

"And you trust them?" Melissa asked.

"Hell, yeah. They're the best nurses on the floor."

The girls were consumed with edgy excitement as they headed toward South Street. Fiona relieved the tension by tapping her foot in time to an imaginary symphony playing in her head. Melissa glanced at every street sign in anticipation. Peach focused on her driving, doing her best to stay alert.

Traffic slowed as they neared Independence National Historic Park. Turning down South Third Street, they drove through Society Hill, an upscale section of the city.

"Look at these beautiful old homes," Melissa said as they passed stately brownstones on the tree-lined street. "Which one is Harry's?"

"Hang on, Lissie. We're gettin' there," Peach grumbled. She made a right onto Lombard Street, an eventual left onto South Broad, and a quick left onto South Street.

Graffiti-adorned storefronts supporting three-story tenements replaced the earlier brownstones. Scraggly sticks passing for trees lined one side of the street. Weeds peeking through sidewalk cracks added a touch of greenery.

"I never saw so many hippies in one place," Fiona said, looking at the crowds drifting down the street. "They all look like they need a cup of coffee and a shower."

"That's 'cause you didn't go to Woodstock. This is nothin'," Peach said.

Do you have to keep rubbing it in? I get it. You're cool. I'm not.

"There it is!" Fiona shouted. She pointed to an innocuous sign in red-and-green lettering, HARRY'S OCCULT AND SPIRITUAL SUPPLIES, hanging above a disintegrating building next to a vacant lot.

Peach found a parking spot nearby, and the three made their way to the shop.

"This place gives me the creeps," Fiona said as she looked at the display of religious articles in the grimy windows.

"Not me. C'mon. This is exactly where we should be." Melissa opened the door to the store. The others followed.

The first thing they noticed was a sign above the main

counter, WE AIM TO PLEASE. Shabby shelves and cabinets held candles, incense sticks and burners, charms, rosary beads, crystal balls, books, pamphlets, and cards. Jars full of loose herbs, powders, roots, and oils sat next to an ancient balance scale. A mixed metaphor of religious statues from the Virgin Mary to the Buddha rested under a layer of dust. A row of folding chairs lined one wall. The only thing missing was a salesperson.

They sat and waited. Eventually, voices sounded from the back of the store. A stooped elderly woman with a black lace shawl over her head left hurriedly without so much as a glance at the girls.

A large round man stepped to the counter. "May I help you?"

Ice-blue eyes peered out from a crumpled, pasty white face. His gray work pants were cinched at the waist with a frayed cardboard belt. A colorless oxford shirt lay beneath an olive-drab button-down sweater.

Grandpa gone bad, and we expect this guy to help us?

Again, this time louder, he said, "May I help you?"

Melissa jumped to attention. "Yes, sir. My friend and I are cursed. We heard you could help us."

He rose to full height, towering over Melissa's five-foot-one frame. His eyes bore into hers. "Who sent you?"

Peach took over. "Some of the nurses I work with said this is the place to come if you think someone has put a spell on you."

He relaxed. A hint of a smile crossed his face. "You ladies are too young to worry about spells and curses. Come with me." He swung open the gate and invited the girls into the back office.

Fiona hesitated. Was he a pervert? What were they getting themselves into?

Melissa practically ran inside. Peach whispered to Fiona, "C'mon, Fee. Safety in numbers, right?"

The back room was in even more disarray than the store itself. Boxes filled with mysteries of the occult were stacked floor to ceiling. Torn paper bags littered the countertops. Fiona was drawn to a yellowed newspaper ad hanging by a single thumbtack. LOVE ME FOREVER PERFUME, ATTRACT THE LOVE OF YOUR LIFE. ONLY $1.10. She stared at the cartoonish woman with massive cleavage and the slick man fawning over her. Signs papering the back wall touted the properties of rose quartz, ruby, tourmaline, and other stones. Each poster showed photos of the gems, mystical symbols, and nearly unintelligible script.

Stale incense fumes combined with dust, mildew, and dandruff to make breathing a challenge.

Fiona couldn't believe she was going along with Melissa's scheme. "Are you Harry?" she asked, hoping to relieve some of the tension.

"Harry retired back in forty-five. I'm Lou. Took over the shop more than twenty years ago. Now, tell me why you think you're cursed," he said, inviting the girls to sit.

"My life keeps getting worse," Melissa began. "First, I had to go for an operation, then my boyfriend left me, then we got kicked out of our house, and I had to move back with my mother. Now I have a shitty job, and I can't find a new boyfriend."

"Doesn't sound like a curse to me. Just part of finding your way," Lou said.

"There's more. You see, there's this chick. Everybody knows she's been into magic ever since that movie *Rosemary's Baby* came out. She was in love with my ex-boyfriend. When she knew she couldn't have him, she came after me."

"Hmmm, interesting and plausible." Lou stroked his chin and stared into Melissa's eyes. "What about you?" He turned to Fiona.

"I-I don't know," she stammered. "I didn't think I was cursed, but my life hasn't been going well at all. My boyfriend dumped me too. I like this other guy, but he only wants to be my friend."

"And you?" He looked at Peach.

"I'm just the driver."

"Let me think about this." Lou carefully opened a cabinet with its door hanging from the hinges. He rummaged through the rubble, pulled out two brown glass bottles, and held them to the light. "This is my special blend of oils that promote love, spiritual cleansing, power, and healing. Put ten drops in your bathwater and meditate on what you want from life."

"Is that Love Me Forever perfume?" Fiona asked.

Lou smiled. "That was one of Harry's come-ons back in the old days. I keep the ad up for a laugh. This, my dear, is the real thing. Nothing but pure essential oils from plants gathered from round the world. Here, smell." He held the bottle under Fiona's nose.

It sounded safe enough, and the oil would be good for her skin. "It smells really nice."

"That's Tahitian vanilla. Vanilla encourages love and has a soothing aroma. I also added rosemary to increase your female power. There are a few more herbs in there, but it's our secret formula."

"I want a bottle!" Melissa practically grabbed the bottle from Lou's hand.

"Hold on, young lady. We're not done yet," Lou said as he opened a locked drawer and removed two small vials. "The oils in these vials are very rare and powerful. Take a whiff but be careful."

The sensuous aroma caused Fiona to forget her surroundings. "Wow, I've never smelled anything so fantastic!" Fiona exclaimed.

"You're smelling ylang-ylang and neroli. Ylang-ylang is one of the most beautiful fragrances in the world. It soothes the soul. Neroli is a woman's oil. Take no more than two drops and rub between your breasts if you want to attract the opposite sex. If peace is what you're looking for, rub it onto your temples."

I love this. There's nothing scary here, but I'm still not telling my parents.

"Now, you said a woman has put a spell on you. Do you want something to release yourself from her evil influences?" Lou asked.

Fiona's concerns escalated. "Um, maybe not."

"Come on, Fee, that's what we came for," Melissa said. "Right, Peachie?"

Peach was at the other end of the room checking out the books. "Huh? Oh, yeah. What you said."

"Pay close attention." Lou stared into Melissa's eyes. "The ritual I'm sharing with you will drive out evil influences."

"That's what we need," Melissa said. "At least, that's what I need."

Lou continued, "Beginning on a Saturday, set up a small altar. It doesn't have to be anything special, just lay a white silk scarf on a table or on the floor. Meditate for a few minutes to prepare yourself. Light two violet candles and a stick of incense; then you'll repeat a special incantation."

"Tell me what it is," Melissa begged.

"You will receive full instructions at the end of our meeting," Lou said with an air of mystery. "After repeating the incantation, visualize a ball of white light filling the room and purifying everything and everyone in the space. Repeat the entire ritual for three days, and the spell will be broken."

"Thank you, Lou. I'll take everything," Melissa said.

"I'll take the two oils," Fiona replied cautiously.

"What's the matter, Fee?" Melissa asked her friend.

"I'm not convinced there's a spell on me. I just think my life is in the toilet," Fiona said.

"Spells and incantations aren't for everyone," Lou added. "You have to feel comfortable with the ritual. Own it for yourself. The oils are a good introduction."

Fiona smiled, relieved. "Thank you, Lou."

Lou escorted them to the front of the store. Peach followed with a handful of books. "I can read these at work when it's slow. Might as well learn something."

Lou wrapped their packages in plain brown paper and sent them on their way.

Fiona took a last look at Lou before leaving the shop. Was that worry clouding his eyes? She gave him a quick wave and joined her friends.

Back in the car, Fiona made a request. "Can we drive by the art museum so I can see what it looks like in case my parents grill me?"

"Sure, no problem," Peach replied. "So, Lissie, are you gonna tell us about the spell?"

Melissa opened a large manila envelope. Inside was a square of white silk and a sheet of instructions. She began reading. "Before beginning, soak the silk in a shallow pan of cool saltwater and let it dry in the sunshine or under an incandescent light for three hours. Spread the silk on a low table or on the floor. Place two violet candles on the cloth, one on each side, and a stick of incense in the center. If you have been given a ritual oil, anoint your body as instructed before beginning."

"Freaky," Peach interrupted.

"Next, light the incense. Take a deep breath in and out through your nose, bringing its essence into your soul."

"Are you really gonna do this?" Fiona asked.

"Shit, yeah, Fee. I have to."

"Keep reading," Peach said. "I can't wait to hear what's next."

"Okay, where was I? 'Spend a few minutes in quiet meditation, asking for the positive energy of the universe to be with you. Light the candles from left to right, remembering energy comes into the body on the left and exits on the right.'"

"It's so fucking complicated," Peach remarked. "What if you mess up?"

"I can't mess up. This is the most important thing I've ever done." Melissa continued reading. Fiona tuned out the rest. She had heard enough.

Peach broke into her daydream. "Remember, Lissie, he said to start on a Saturday. Can you do this tonight?" she asked.

"My mother will be with Mr. Giovanni tonight, so no problem. The sooner I start, the sooner the curse will be lifted."

Fiona tried to ignore the anxiety that permeated her body. She hoped her friend knew what she was getting into.

Chapter 27

"Today we have our first live model," Dr. Hacking, Fiona's Life Drawing professor, announced. "I want to introduce the models gradually, so today's subject won't be totally nude. Remember the elements of line and movement that we studied with the manikins. We'll warm up with several one-minute sketches, then two ten-minute sketches, and finally a twenty-minute drawing. I don't want any snickering, nor do I want any disrespect."

Nervous whispers floated through the air as the students set up their easels and sketch pads in a semicircle surrounding the raised platform that served as their stage. Charcoal sticks in hand, they awaited their subject.

Fiona dropped her charcoal when she saw the model was Reuben. She looked down at her ripped jeans paired with her dad's old undershirt. Could she be any less attractive right now?

Reuben, draped only in a white sheet, sauntered into the center of the classroom and took his place on the platform. He stood, unmoving, head down, holding the sheet in true Roman fashion. His face betrayed nothing, but Fiona knew he was enjoying himself.

The muscles of his arms and legs were lean and toned. A fresh scar cut diagonally across his left forearm, nearly bisecting it. Slight shadows cast by the overhead spotlight emphasized his high cheekbones and hinted at the ribcage beneath his nearly hairless torso. His olive skin complemented his dark hair and eyes, providing a Sephardic palette for the students.

Fiona thought he was the perfect model with impeccable bone structure and just the right amount of definition, unlike Jack, who was in training for a beer gut. She wondered if Reuben was a runner or perhaps a dancer. She picked up her charcoal and timidly went to work.

By the time they got to the ten-minute sketches, Fiona realized this might be her only opportunity to see him naked. She regained her composure and decided to enjoy the experience.

At the break, he slipped into the storeroom that served as the dressing room and returned in a black-and-white checkered robe and matching flip-flops.

"Surprise!" he said.

"Why didn't you tell me?" Fiona asked.

"And ruin the element of shock? You said you wanted to sketch my face, so why not my whole body?"

"Is this gonna be a regular thing for you?"

"If they like me. It's a good gig. Pays eight bucks a class, plus I get to see you blush." Reuben smiled.

This is all I need.

"I'll wait for you after class. I've got some big news. Hey, you smell great. Not patchouli like everybody and their grandma," he said as the break ended.

"Thanks." Harry's oils were doing their job.

What a Trip

They left the art room together, Reuben carrying his wardrobe in a well-worn knapsack and Fiona carrying her oversized portfolio binder.

"You know about the big antiwar demonstration next week, right?" Reuben said as they left class. "Well, I heard this morning the school's arranged a bus to New York. Classes won't be canceled that day, but kids who sign up for the bus'll be excused. I was the first one to sign up—actually, you and I are the first on the list."

What if there was trouble and she got caught up in a riot? Before responding, an image of her parents watching her on television flashed through her mind. "What about the demonstrations here on campus?"

"That's chickenshit. This is history in the making. You're with me on this, aren't you, Fiona?"

Screw her parents. This was her chance to be part of history. "Definitely. I wouldn't miss it."

Reuben wrapped his arm around her shoulders and gave her a hug. "We're a team, you and me."

She'd rather be a couple, but a team was better than nothing.

"I can't get enough of that oil. Smells like you stepped out of an orange grove and rolled in a flower bed."

"Thanks." She gave him a sincere but sexy smile. She hoped Harry's special oils would continue to work their magic.

Chapter 28

The bus left the college at eight o'clock on Wednesday morning, October fifteenth. Students would be dropped off in lower Manhattan for a noon rally on Wall Street, after which they would make their way uptown for a four thirty demonstration in Bryant Park. They could attend a memorial service in Penn or Grand Central Station, after which the bus would return them to campus. The only event they would miss was a candlelight gathering in Washington Square Park.

Fiona and Reuben took a seat near the back of the bus. As if in rehearsal for the day's events, the students joined in singing John Lennon's "Give Peace a Chance," followed by a selection of antiwar songs by Pete Seeger, Bob Dylan, Richie Havens, and more. The day's organizers had thought ahead and passed out typewritten copies of lyrics so all could sing along.

Enthusiasm waned about thirty minutes into the trip. Reuben turned to Fiona. "I'm as patriotic as the next guy, and probably want to stop the war more than any of these dudes, but enough with the singing already. We've gotta save our vocal cords."

"Do you really think today's march will do any good?" Fiona asked him.

"I sure hope so. Mayor Lindsay is on our side, and I heard a bunch of his compadres are calling for a withdrawal of troops in a year. Not exactly how I'd handle it, but it's something I think Nixon might go for. Listen, we're gonna be talkin' war all day. How 'bout we change the subject?"

"Sure, whatever."

"I really like you, lassie. I think I owe you an explanation," Reuben said as he stared into her eyes.

"I like you too, Reuben." Fiona turned a bright shade of red.

"There's stuff I didn't tell you about why I left Temple," he went on. "Money was a big part of it. There was shit at home I had to deal with too. My grandfather died last spring."

"I'm so sorry. Were you close?"

"I only met him once. He lived in Czechoslovakia. He and my father had been prisoners at Terezín during the war. My grandmother too."

"I've never heard of that. Was it a concentration camp?" Fiona asked.

"Yeah, in Czechoslovakia, not one of the more famous camps. My grandmother died, but my grandfather and father made it to the end when the camps were liberated."

Reuben's voice faltered as he went on. "I suppose they were lucky to be there rather than Auschwitz or Buchenwald. At least there wasn't as much forced labor at Terezín. They also had lots of cultural programs—"

"Culture in a concentration camp?" Fiona blurted out.

"It was a big propaganda machine, but still, it kept my grandfather alive. He was a prominent journalist and illustrator in Prague. Keeping him and my father around was in the Nazis' best interest."

"What about your grandmother?"

"My father said she starved to death," Reuben mumbled, turning toward the window.

Her heart went out to Reuben. She reached for his hand. "Nobody deserves to die like that."

"Thanks. Can you understand why I'm so against this war? It's not just that I don't want to fight. I learned from an early age the cruelties governments can impose on innocent people."

"I guess we all have our reasons. I don't believe in killing or harming any being. That's why I think about becoming a vegetarian."

A shadow crossed Reuben's face. "This is so much bigger than killing. It's a stand for freedom and human rights."

Fiona squirmed in her seat. She felt like a fool.

"Hey, I'm sorry," Reuben said after a few moments of silence. "I get carried away sometimes. The most important thing is to oppose the war whatever your reason."

She thought for a moment before responding. "You're right. I guess I never looked at things from your perspective."

"Anyway, I've got more to tell you," Reuben went on. "When my grandfather died, it brought up a whole lot of crap for my father. He never hid what happened, but we thought he had gotten past it. He kinda went off the deep end, having nightmares and all kinds of mental problems. He couldn't work for a while. That's when some of the money issues came in. I thought it would be better if I went to school closer to home, in case he needed me."

Fiona sat in silence, giving Reuben her full attention.

"There's more. I had this girlfriend at Temple. We were getting serious. We even talked about moving in together. She got really pissed at me when I said I wouldn't be coming back in the fall." He paused, waiting for a response.

Once more, Fiona was unsure of what to say. "W-what was her name?"

"Becky. I didn't blame her for being upset, but she really lost it. Right before we left for the summer, she broke most of my albums, cut up some of my clothes, and then she started on me. Came after me with a stupid pocketknife. You know that scar on my arm? That's from her. That and a cigarette burn on my leg."

Who is this guy? Fiona asked herself. *And what kind of world does he live in?*

"I wondered about your arm. I never saw your leg. You kept it covered during art class."

"You'll see it next time I model." He took a long, slow breath. "So that's my story in a nutshell. A real bummer, but I'm kinda glad it happened before Becky and I went any further in our relationship. In a way, I feel like I was saved by my grandfather dying."

"Where is she now?" Fiona asked.

"Who the fuck knows? Probably back at Temple terrorizing some new guy. Anyway, I thought maybe you were wondering why I hadn't put the moves on you."

"Yeah, I was wondering."

"I got burned—literally." A bitter smile crossed his face. "I need time. If you want to still hang with me, that'd be cool, but if you're lookin' for more, I understand."

"I'm not going anywhere." Fiona squeezed his hand in sympathy and moved closer to him on the seat.

She knew now that the oils really did work and wondered what would have happened if she had taken three baths with

Harry's oil instead of one. She imagined they would be getting laid right on this bus.

They sat without speaking, drifting past oil refineries on the New Jersey Turnpike. Reuben's confessions swirled inside Fiona's head. She wondered what would happen now. Should she ask him more questions about his family? His ex-girlfriend? Change the subject?

After a few minutes, Reuben broke the silence. "I hope I didn't freak you out, Fiona. I don't want there to be any secrets between us."

Did this mean she had to tell him everything about her life? She had too many secrets, too many insecurities.

"I'm glad you feel comfortable enough to talk about it with me," she said after a pause. "What was it like growing up, knowing about the concentration camp?"

"When you're a kid, you think your family is normal. I didn't even know my father had a foreign accent until I heard him speak in public when I was about nine. He gave a talk about his experiences in the camp. I looked around and saw women in the audience crying. That's when I started asking questions."

"What kind of stuff did he tell you?"

"He never wanted to talk about what happened at Terezín. He talked mostly about what a great life he had as a kid. Anyway, the theme of my father's life is that you can have everything and just like that, Big Brother—or in this case, Hitler—can take it all away, and you're left with nothing."

"Kind of like my dad." She went on to tell Reuben the story of her grandfather losing everything in the 1929 stock market crash, his suicide, and how her father went from a life of privilege to one of poverty.

"We've got a lot in common, don't we? Different stories but the same theme," Reuben said.

Fiona thought for a moment. "I'd never have thought so before, but you're right."

Her heart raced, and her breath quickened. She felt so close to him. Should she reveal her biggest fear?

"What's goin' on for you, lassie? You look like you're gonna cry."

"I-I never told anyone this before," she said, "but I've always felt like I'd end up homeless by the time I was thirty. I used to think I was born under a bad sign, but I think I've figured it out. It's because that almost happened to my dad, and I'm afraid history will repeat itself."

Reuben gave her a hug. "Holy shit. You've been carrying that around with you all these years?"

Tears spilled from her emerald eyes, smearing her mascara. She nodded. "I'm sorry. I didn't mean to be a bummer. We were talking about you."

"Don't apologize to me, ever."

As the bus dipped into the Holland Tunnel, the group's organizer called the students to attention. "Listen up. Here's what's happenin'."

"To be continued," Reuben said as he gently brushed a wisp of hair from her face.

Relief flowed through Fiona's veins. She had never opened her soul so deeply to anyone before. She had reached her emotional limit.

Fiona and Reuben intended to stick with the group from the bus but soon realized that was impossible. It was all they could do to stay together as they made their way to Wall Street. Thousands of protesters, mostly students wearing black armbands, peacefully jostled one another as they moved forward. Arms held high waved peace signs, while simple and elaborate posters calling for an end to war bounced to the rhythm of youth in motion. The spirit of the crowd was infectious.

They melted into the audience, each individual becoming part of a universal wave of energy as they stood waiting for the speeches to begin. Fiona found herself distracted by the chants, the songs, and the intensity of the multitudes. She looked to Reuben, who appeared fixated on what the speakers were saying.

Unable to stay focused, she turned her thoughts inward. *Finally, I'm a part of history. Being here today is probably the most important thing I've ever done.* She was so caught up in her daydreams that she didn't notice when the program ended.

Reuben gave her a gentle push as the throng began to move. "Hang on to me," he shouted in her ear. "We can't get separated."

She linked her arm in his as they moved forward. As they

made their way north, the crowd thinned, though the energy of the moratorium was still with them. When they reached the Chelsea section of Manhattan, they ducked into a deli. No seats were available. They took their tuna sandwiches and chips and sat on the stoop of a brownstone apartment building.

"Fuckin' A, what a day!" Reuben was at a loss for words. "D'ya think Nixon's watching any of this?"

"I bet he is, but will it do any good?" Fiona had her doubts. "Hey, did you see the sign that said DROP LSD, NOT BOMBS? That was my favorite."

"Yeah. It kinda pissed me off. I've got nothing against the drug scene, but I don't think we should be mixing the politics of drugs and war. Not to change the subject—did you know today is day four of the World Series? My father's rooting for the Mets. They're playing today at Shea Stadium. I heard Mayor Lindsay wanted to fly the flag at half-staff, but they won't let him. Bastards."

"My dad likes the Mets too, so I know about the Series. That's all he's been talking about. What about you? Do you follow baseball?" Fiona asked.

"Yeah, sometimes. Not this year, though. Too much else on my mind."

They sat in silence, eating their sandwiches, grateful for a respite from the frenetic pace of the day.

Bryant Park was much too small to contain the thousands of protesters who arrived long before the speeches were to begin. Fiona and Reuben crowded elbow to elbow with people of all ages. A young boy stood in a garbage can holding a simple sign that read END THE WAR NOW.

"I bet his dad is over there," Fiona shouted.

Someone handed them a leaflet announcing the day's speakers, which included Eugene McCarthy and New York mayor John Lindsay. Shirley MacLaine, Tony Randall, Eli Wallach, and Rod McKuen were also on the program.

They carved a spot for themselves at the corner of Forty-First Street and Sixth Avenue. The roar of the crowd merged with the sharp peal of car horns and police sirens. Pushcarts taunted them with the aroma of hot dogs and soft pretzels. In spite of the assault on the senses, an air of tranquility permeated the park.

"It's gonna be impossible to hear what they have to say." Reuben had to yell to be heard.

Fiona nodded, knowing it really didn't matter. The most important thing was being there to support the cause.

As the sun went down, the speeches came to a close. Arm in arm, they headed to Penn Station and the final event of the day.

"Tired, lassie?" Reuben asked.

"A little. I feel like I need to do something to get the blood flowing in my legs again."

"How 'bout we get off Sixth Avenue and run down one of the side streets? That should loosen you up."

Turning right on Thirty-Eighth Street, they broke into a run that took them to Seventh Avenue, where they were bombarded with another wave of humanity. Winded but rejuvenated, they joined the throng making its way to Penn Station.

The final event of the day at Penn Station was a memorial service and reading of the names of Americans who had died in the war. The group was small and lacked the fanfare of the day's earlier events. Without street vendors, loud protesters, and television cameras, the service left a sobering effect on those in attendance. They left in silence.

It had been a long, tiring day. No songs were sung on the ride home. Peanut butter and jelly sandwiches and cans of soda were passed around. Enthusiasm was replaced by exhaustion. Fiona leaned her head on Reuben's shoulder and closed her eyes. The next thing she knew, they were back on campus.

"I can't wait to read tomorrow's papers," Reuben said as they exited the bus. "Sleep tight, my friend. Thanks for our talk. I'll see you tomorrow at dinner."

"G'night, Reuben. Sleep well."

Almost as an afterthought, he planted a gentle kiss on her cheek.

I guess that's progress. She dragged herself into the elevator, rode to her dorm room, and collapsed on the bed.

Chapter 30

The *New York Times* reported more than a quarter million protesters had gathered in both Washington, DC, and New York City. An estimated two million marched in other cities and colleges, participating in what was the largest and most influential moratorium to date.

"We can't stop now," Reuben said at dinner the next day. "We've gotta show Nixon we mean business. He promised a gradual troop withdrawal and hasn't kept his word. I wish I was working in journalism. I'd write some kick-ass articles."

"If you were out of school, you'd be drafted. You're making a difference the best way you can right now," Fiona said.

"You're right, I guess. Listen, I want to thank you for letting me open up to you yesterday," Reuben went on. "I've been carrying that shit around with me for months. You're so easy to talk to, and you've been such a good friend. I feel like I'm ready to move on."

"Move on?" she asked.

"I was thinking maybe we could go on a real date one night."

"I'd like that."

"I've gotta go home this weekend. How 'bout we plan something after that."

"Definitely." Fiona felt the heat rise in her cheeks.

Even though she wished their date could be sooner, she was glad for the delay. It would give her a chance to go home and take two more baths with Harry's magic oil.

"You must have a lot going on at school these days, FiFi," her dad said at dinner the following Friday evening. "I miss your weekly visits. I noticed Jack hasn't been coming around. Did something happen with you two?"

"He's in Virginia with his grandmother," Fiona said, hoping to end the conversation.

"No more college?"

"He's joining the navy," Fiona replied.

"Tell you the truth, honey, I never thought he was college material," her dad confessed.

"Guess you were right, Dad."

"You can do a lot better. You're too young to get serious about a boy, right, Helen?" Mr. O'Brien turned to his wife.

"I never trusted that boy, but it's good to know he's serving our country," her mom said.

"He's a heck of a lot better than those hippies we saw on the news the other day. Imagine, disrespecting our armed forces and our president. I never thought I'd live to see so many long-haired bums," her dad said, taking the last bite of his meatloaf.

"They're not all bums, Dad. They're standing up for free speech and for a war that they believe is wrong."

"What about you, Fiona? Are you against the war?" her mom asked.

"I'm against all war and all killing." Fiona was doing her best to be diplomatic and avoid an argument.

"You're entitled to your opinion, miss, but do not, I repeat, *do not* get involved with those no-good drug addicts." Mrs. O'Brien stood, grabbed the empty dinner plates, and strode into the kitchen. She took a few deep breaths to calm herself and, in a pleasant voice, said, "Anybody for dessert? I bought a lemon meringue pie."

"No thanks, Mom." Fiona echoed her mom's cheery tone. "I'm gonna take a bath and meet Melissa."

Fiona filled the tub to the brim, aware that her parents would reprimand her for wasting water if they knew. Before stepping in, she piled her auburn curls on top of her head and carefully added ten drops of Harry's bath oil. She thought about painting a picture of herself in the tub and sending it to Lou. He could use it as an advertisement and pay her in merchandise. She smiled as she sank into her bath and fantasized about her upcoming date with Reuben.

Melissa was in an upbeat mood when Fiona arrived at her apartment. Melissa's mother, Mrs. Patten, soon to be Mrs. Giovanni, was out for the evening.

"I think Harry's spell is working," Melissa announced. "I feel more relaxed. I'm not thinking so much about Mickey and wishing things were different. And guess what? I joined a yoga class!"

"I didn't know they had yoga classes in town," Fiona said as she lit a Kool.

"Remember Peach telling us about that Indian yogi, Swami Satchidananda at Woodstock? I guess he started a whole new thing, and now his disciples are teaching yoga classes all over the place. I went to the community college for a Tuesday morning class so I could meet people before I start school in January. They have a Saturday morning class too. You should go with me tomorrow."

"I'm there," Fiona said. "Any cool guys in the class?"

"Well, there's this one dude who's kinda cute. I've been checking him out, but I don't think he's noticed me yet."

"Have you taken the baths and used the oils?" Fiona asked.

"Not yet. I only did the ritual. I thought doing it all at once might be too much. There's only one thing that's got me freaked out."

I knew it. Should I even ask? Fiona waited for her friend to continue.

"Remember that asshole from the party? The one that watched us fooling around?"

Fiona had done her best to put the events of that night out of her mind. "Yeah, Mr. Creepo. What about him?"

"He's in the yoga class. I thought I was going to die when I saw him, but I think he was probably too wasted that night to remember me. I'm afraid if I use Harry's oils, he might get turned on and realize who I am," Melissa said.

"Well, you're either gonna use the oils or quit the class. What do you know about him?"

"That's it. I'm worried he might be in school with me in January."

"It was dark in that hallway. We could see his face, but I bet you anything he wasn't looking at our faces," Fiona rationalized. "You've gotta decide if you're ready to meet Mr. Wonderful right now or just be happy Denise's curse is broken."

The doorbell rang, interrupting their decision-making process. Peach joined them. It was time to unveil Fiona's surprise.

"Check it out, ladies. Courvoisier cognac. It's been in the back of my parents' liquor cabinet forever. They'll never know it's gone." Fiona pulled the small bottle of liquid gold from her purse, dusted it off, and passed it to her friends. Melissa tuned the radio to a progressive rock show on WNEW-FM.

Fiona regaled her friends with a detailed narrative of her experiences at the New York moratorium and how proud she was to have participated in such an important event. "You guys agree that we need to do everything we can to stop the war, right?"

Even though she verbally agreed, Fiona sensed Melissa was more interested in fighting curses and evil demons than fighting for peace and justice. Peach was on board.

"Remember I told you I had vacation time coming next month?" Peach began. "Looks like my plans have changed. Read this." She passed a flyer to Fiona with the headline "Act to End the War in Vietnam," under which was a hand displaying the peace sign and the words "Join Us in Washington on November 15."

Fiona learned that the Vietnam Moratorium Committee, sponsors of the October fifteenth protest, had planned a second round of antiwar moratoriums around the world. The rally would be scheduled on November fifteenth, the day after a March Against Death, where people were asked to parade down Pennsylvania Avenue carrying signs with the names of dead American soldiers and the names of destroyed Vietnamese towns.

"Another rally!" Fiona exclaimed. "Maybe Nixon won't ignore us this time. I wish I could go."

"I'm goin'," Peach announced. "My vacation starts November tenth, so I'm gonna drive to Virginia, chill for a coupla days, then head to DC."

"Where are you gonna stay?" Fiona asked.

"I bought a tent, a sleeping bag, and some camping shit, so I figure I'll find someplace to crash. I can't be the only one there for the duration. Maybe we could meet there, Fee."

"How am I supposed to do that? I'd like to go with Reuben, but neither of us has a car. Maybe we could hitch a ride with somebody from school," Fiona said.

"We've got a month to figure it out, so don't give up yet. What about you, Lissie? Are you in?" Peach asked.

Melissa was lost in a daydream, watching wisps of cigarette smoke drift toward the ceiling, mouthing the words to the Beatles' "Norwegian Wood" playing on the radio.

Peach shrugged her shoulders as if to say, *What else is new?*

Fiona joined Melissa at the Saturday morning yoga class. They grabbed mats and set up in the back corner of the room. As the session was about to begin, Mr. Creepo from the farmhouse party arrived and took a spot in front of them.

Fiona thought she would be sick.

The teacher, an older wiry man with unruly white hair and beard, instructed the students to move into downward-facing dog. "Come to hands and knees on your mat with your knees directly below your hips. Extend your hands ahead of your shoulders. Inhale, and as you exhale, lift your knees away from the floor and your hips toward the ceiling. Focus your gaze at your thighs or, if possible, at your navel."

As Fiona moved into the pose, she glanced in front of her and noticed Mr. Creepo's face staring at her from between his legs. She was sure he recognized her. She coughed to get Melissa's attention, then tilted her head toward Mr. Creepo. Melissa's expression mimicked Fiona's emotional state. It would be a very long class.

Fiona was grateful for *savasana*, a relaxation pose signaling the end of class. As the group gathered up their belongings, their nemesis joined them.

"Do I know you chicks from somewhere?" he asked.

"I don't think so. I'm just here for the weekend," Fiona said.

"That red hair of yours. I know I've seen it before."

"Excuse me, we've gotta go." Fiona hid her face with her hair, making her words unintelligible.

"Ralph's the name. Maybe I'll see ya again."

"Okay, bye." Fiona nudged Melissa with her knee, and the two hurried out of the classroom. "Sorry, Lissie, you're on your own. No more yoga for me. If he sees us together again, he's gonna put two and two together."

The girls left in the Corvair, lit a joint, forgot their worries, and in a few minutes were laughing hysterically.

Fiona took a third bath for good luck before returning to school on Sunday afternoon, hoping the magical powers of Harry's bath oil would hold until her dinner date with Reuben the following Friday evening.

Chapter 31

For dinner, Reuben suggested The Chalet, a restaurant offering an inexpensive all-you-can-eat buffet between five and seven o'clock on Friday evenings.

Fiona's last class on Friday ended at two o'clock, which gave her several hours to fix her hair and makeup and choose her wardrobe. After showering, she considered putting a few drops of bath oil in her hair but held back, afraid of unleashing too much sexuality and frightening Reuben.

She wrapped her hair around large rollers to soften her curls and then sat under the hairdryer provided in the dormitory bathroom. As she waited for her hair to dry, she carefully applied her makeup—just a touch of light foundation and blush, a thin line of forest-green liner to accentuate her eyes, and plenty of mascara to darken her pale lashes. She thought of her face as a canvas, an artistic endeavor. Smiling in the mirror, she gave her creation the seal of approval.

Now to choose her outfit. Every dress she owned fell high on her thigh, drawing attention to her thin but firm legs. She chose a dark green V-neck cable-knit dress that accentuated her breasts. She paired it with fishnet stockings and a pair of brown suede lace-up boots.

She secured her hair behind her ears with tiny silver clips

that complemented her favorite hoop earrings. A dab of lip gloss and the final touch—two drops of Harry's essential oil between her breasts.

Her heart pounded, her stomach churned, and her shoulders tightened. She gave herself a pep talk. *Get a grip. It's only dinner. No guarantee we'll do anything else tonight, but I'm glad I'm wearing my best bra and panties—just in case.*

She took one last look in the mirror and shut her door.

She took slow, calming breaths as she rode the elevator to the lobby, where she would meet Reuben at five o'clock. The women's dorms had recently eased their curfew restrictions. Rather than requiring female students to be in their rooms by midnight, the rules now allowed them the freedom to stay out all night, provided they indicated their status on the sign-out sheet. Hopeful she would be so fortunate, Fiona checked the "return by noon" box, took a seat, and waited for Reuben.

Promptly at five, Reuben arrived wearing his fringed brown suede jacket, slightly flared brown corduroy slacks, and Frye boots. His hair was neatly tied back in a ponytail, which accentuated his cheekbones. Fiona smiled and stood. She was relieved he hadn't worn a suit.

"I dig your outfit. You look really cool!" Reuben said, giving Fiona a peck on the cheek.

"You too, Reuben. Love the jacket."

"Thanks. Let's split."

A ten-minute ride on the campus bus took them from the Student Union building to the center of town.

"I've only been downtown a couple of times. Last year, I mostly stayed on campus during the week and went home on weekends," Fiona said.

"There's not much to see. If you look down that street there"—Reuben pointed to his left—"you'll see the Powder Puff, home of yours truly. Come on. Here's our stop."

The Chalet imagined itself to be an Alpine retreat. The restaurant, which had seen better days, catered to college students and local families on a budget. Faux gabled windows were framed by dark wooden beams. Private booths with red vinyl seats lined the walls; tables for four were scattered throughout the center. They sat in a booth for two, far enough away from the buffet for privacy.

"There's no way we can score drinks in this place. They're on the lookout for college students like us," Reuben apologized.

"I'd never be able to pass for twenty-one anyway. I wish the drinking age was eighteen like it is in New York." She would have given anything for a drink or a joint to calm her nerves.

"Why is it that we're old enough to be sent to Vietnam but not old enough to vote or order a glass of wine?" Reuben shook his head and stared at the ceiling.

They ordered Cokes from the waitress and made their way to the buffet, a meat lover's paradise. Hot and cold slices of roast beef and ham, beef stroganoff, ground beef and macaroni, cheap cuts of steak, and plenty of mystery meat—more meat than Fiona had ever seen in one place.

"I know how you feel about meat, but they do have lots of vegetables and salads," Reuben said, handing her a plate.

Back at their booth, Reuben asked, "I think I know the answer, but I want to be sure. You're not dating anybody, are you?"

"No," she replied simply.

"But were you?"

A piece of scalloped potato lodged itself halfway down her throat. She coughed. "Well, I sort of was, but it's over."

"Was it serious? I told you my story, but you never told me anything."

Fiona stared at her plate. It was now or never. "I was seeing this guy from high school, Jack. We started going out last spring and broke up right around the time school started. The whole thing was a big mistake."

"Couldn't be as big a mistake as my fucked-up relationship. What happened?"

She took a breath, then began. "I kinda knew it wasn't gonna last. He was a real get-over with other people, but I didn't think he'd pull any crap with me. I was so wrong. He called me at the dorm to break up. Didn't even have the nerve to do it in person."

"I wish my breakup had happened over the phone. I could've avoided the scars. It always looks better from the other side, doesn't it?"

"I guess so. When I look back, I should've seen it coming, but I didn't. Here's the worst part—he's joining the navy. He knew how I felt about the war, and he still enlisted. I'm really better off without him." There was no way she'd tell Reuben about Jack getting married.

Reuben reached across the table and held Fiona's hand. "A guy like that's always gonna bring you down. I'm sorry you had to get hurt, but if it hadn't happened, we wouldn't be here today."

I don't deserve to be with Reuben. Wait till he gets to know me; he'll dump me too. Fiona tried pushing her thoughts aside. It was too late.

"What's on your mind? You're a million miles away," Reuben said, squeezing her hand.

"Sorry. I was just thinking how nice you are," she said.

"Trust me, I'm not that nice."

"I think you are," she said and then changed the subject. "How about dessert? I wonder if they have bacon ice cream."

Reuben reached for the check, which surprised Fiona, who'd expected them to split the bill. He escorted her out of the restaurant, resting his arm at her waist. The evening had turned into a real date. They might actually end up in bed together. Fiona regretted eating so much.

As they turned off Main Street onto a shaded residential avenue, it began to drizzle. "Here's our second dessert," Reuben said, pulling a joint from his pocket. "I thought it would be more fun to wait till after dinner to smoke this. Are you okay walking in the rain?"

He lit the joint from his cigarette and passed it to Fiona.

"Sure. It's just a light mist." She hoped it wouldn't ruin her hair. "Is it cool to smoke here?" she asked. "Won't somebody call the cops?"

"Nah, most of these are frat houses or student rentals. Nobody gives a shit." He took a hit and passed it back to Fiona. "I thought we could walk around the block a couple of times, and then if you want, I'll introduce you to the Puff."

"I'd like that," Fiona said, taking hold of Reuben's free hand.

Reuben led her through the residential neighborhood until she lost her sense of direction. Finally, she spotted a large pink-and-white hand-painted sign, POWDER PUFF SALON, under which hung a smaller, darker sign, PRIVATE ROOMS FOR GENTLEMEN. By the light of a streetlamp, she could make out a three-story, pink-and-white, gingerbread-covered Victorian mansion, complete with a wraparound porch and white wicker furniture.

"This is where you live?" Fiona asked as she started up the porch stairs.

"Hang on. There're a few rules of the house. C'mere." Reuben moved away from the streetlight. He lowered his voice to a whisper. "That's the salon entrance. The 'gentlemen's' entrance is back here." He steered her to the side of the building and a set of rickety steps leading to the second floor.

"Before we go upstairs, I gotta tell you that no girls are allowed except on Sunday afternoons, so we're gonna have to be real quiet."

Fiona remembered sneaking Jack into her dorm room. "No biggie. I'll be quiet. Anyway, who's gonna tell on us?"

"Most likely nobody." Reuben started up the stairs. "Watch out for the third step. It creaks."

They entered the second-floor hallway, lit by two dim overhead bulbs. Five-paneled wooden doors numbered one through eight stood on either side, with a bathroom at each end of the hall. Peeling floral wallpaper, probably original to the house, adorned the walls. Reuben stopped at door number seven and inserted his key. The door groaned open, and they tiptoed inside.

He lit a small lamp covered with a sheer green scarf, lending a softness to the room. She laid her purse and jacket on a dresser that looked like it came from Goodwill, and sat on the brass bed.

What a Trip

She picked at the white chenille bedspread, not knowing what to expect.

The mattress springs squeaked as he sat next to her. "I want tonight to be special. How long can you stay?"

"We either have to be back by midnight or sign out overnight. I-I didn't know what to do, so I signed out overnight."

"Far fucking out," Reuben said, leaning back on the mattress. He pulled Fiona toward him, planting soft kisses on her hair, her forehead, her cheeks, and finally her mouth. She parted her lips. Their kisses deepened.

She felt like she was floating. She hadn't made out this much without fucking since she was fourteen. *I hope there's nothing wrong with him*, she worried.

Reuben moved away, as though sensing her thoughts. "I've fantasized about having you in my room since the first day we met. Are you okay with this?"

No guy had ever asked her that before. She was more than okay. "Uh-huh. I thought about it a lot too," she said.

"Are you, um, are you on the pill?" Reuben asked.

"I am." No guy had ever asked her that before either. They just assumed.

Reuben kissed her again. "I'm glad." Reaching to the side of his bed, he said, "I almost forgot. I brought a bottle of wine from home. It's French. A Bordeaux."

Fiona was impressed. "I'd love a glass."

"No glasses, but I promise it'll taste just as good from the bottle," Reuben said, passing the bottle to her.

The wine left an earthy sweetness in her mouth as a warm sensation spread through her chest.

"Kisses always taste sweeter with wine." Reuben set the bottle on the nightstand, drawing Fiona closer. Their breath quickened as their bodies moved in rhythm. *I am so ready for this*, Fiona thought as Reuben released her and reached for the wine.

"Let's make it last," Reuben said, passing the bottle to her.

The concept of sex lasting was foreign to Fiona. You did it, then hopefully did it again once or twice more.

After a few sips of wine, he kicked off his boots. She sat on the side of the bed, unlacing her boots. Reuben lifted her hair and ran his tongue down the back of her neck. She turned to face him.

"Let me help you with that dress," he said, sliding it up past her hips and over her breasts. She lifted her arms as he pulled it from her body, revealing her pink lace bra and matching bikini panties. A white lace garter belt held her fishnet stockings.

Reuben moaned. "Lassie, you look more beautiful like this. Why do you even bother wearing clothes? Take off your stockings; then I want you to undress me."

She hesitated for a moment until Reuben guided her hand to his shirt. One by one, she undid his buttons, sliding her hand inside his shirt, fondling the chest she'd sketched only a few weeks before.

"Now, take my pants off. Do it real slow."

She loosened his belt and tossed it on the floor. As she unsnapped his pants, his pelvis arched slightly. She lowered the zipper and slid his pants to his ankles, briefly noticing the small round burn just below his right kneecap. He kicked his pants to the floor.

He coaxed her onto her back, raised her arms over her head, and wrapped her hands around the posts of the brass headboard. "Hold on and don't let go until I say so," Reuben whispered as he leaned over her.

Fiona arched her back. She wanted him to fuck her right then and there.

"You smell wonderful," he said as his fingertips slid from her neck, across her bra, to the top of her panties. He ran his middle finger around her navel.

He glided his body along hers until their lips met. They kissed. She let go of the headboard to put her arms around him.

"Don't let go, Fiona, no matter what happens," Reuben said firmly.

His tongue and fingers made their way from her throat across the top of her breasts and down to her panties. This time he slid her panties from her body and slipped his hand between her legs.

Fiona squirmed with anticipation. Her breath quickened. "I want you so much."

"Not just yet," he replied as he moved back up her body. This time he straddled her, rubbing against her, kissing her face, her neck, her ears. He pulled away, kneeled in front of her, and removed his briefs.

She started to reach for him, then remembered the rules.

"Good girl. No touching. Now take me in your mouth, but no hands." Reuben moved closer to the headboard, allowing Fiona to follow his instruction. She ran her tongue around him and felt him grow harder. He pulled away. "Not yet."

He passed the wine to her. Without the use of her hands, some spilled on her chest. Reuben was quick to lick the drops before they stained her bra. This time, as he moved down her body, he let his mouth fall between her legs.

Fiona arched her hips to meet him. Without thinking, she released her arms from the headboard. Reuben stopped what he was doing and lifted his head in warning.

"Don't stop," she moaned, moving her arms back to their assigned position.

When she thought she could take no more, he slid his body forward and entered her. He held her wrists firmly with his left hand, while his right held her hips. They moved in sync, consumed in their moment of infinity until their passion exploded and he collapsed on top of her.

Their breath came in diminishing gasps that filled the silence of the room. Slowly, Fiona returned to the outer world—a light rain falling on the trees, a car passing on the wet street, a soft breeze stroking the evergreen trees, and Reuben's damp, angular body draped over hers. She wanted to open her eyes but knew when she did, the magical aura they had created would disappear.

This had to be the best sex she'd ever had. She thought of what she had been missing in her life and wondered where he'd learned to do all he did.

She worried. Was she good enough for him? What if he didn't like it? What if he didn't want to be with her after tonight?

Reuben raised himself on his forearms and stared at her. "Hey," he said, "you still in there?" He brushed a moist curl from her face and dropped a kiss on her eyelid.

She opened her eyes. "Hey." She smiled.

"That was amazing. I really like you, Fiona."

"I like you too. It was amazing," she agreed.

"I've got one more in me. Do you?" he asked.

"I do if you do."

He rolled her onto her stomach, lifted her into a kneeling position, spread her legs, and entered her from the rear. He moved quickly this time, fondling her breasts still concealed in her bra, then sliding his hands back to her hips. Fiona turned her head to look at him. As she did, he gave her a light slap on her behind, bringing their lust to a peak.

What was that all about? she thought as she lay under Reuben. *I hope he isn't one of those guys that gets off on beating girls.*

"Fiona, I can't get enough of you. Why did I wait so long to be with you?"

"Good things are worth waiting for, I guess." She rolled onto her back, put her arms around Reuben, and kissed him on the mouth.

"And through all that, I never got to see your tits."

She reached behind her back to remove her bra.

"No, keep it on. Like you said, some things are worth waiting for."

You're a strange guy, Reuben.

They snuggled on his twin bed, covered only with a sheet, and passed the wine bottle back and forth until it was empty. He sat the bottle on the floor and spooned with Fiona, who was already lying on her side. They fell into a deep sleep. Neither remembered to brush their teeth.

Chapter 32

Sunlight flooded the room. Fiona opened her eyes to see Reuben leaning on his elbow, staring at her.

"Morning, lassie. I trust you slept well."

"Mm-hmm." She turned to kiss him, then pulled back. Her body felt like it was stuck to the sheets. Looking down, she saw she was still wearing her bra.

"What's the matter?"

"I didn't brush my teeth. My breath must be awful, and my eye makeup has gotta be all over my cheeks."

"My breath smells like dog farts, but who cares?" Reuben said, kissing her on the mouth. "Tell you what. I'll make sure the coast is clear, then we can use the bathroom—pee, shower, and brush our teeth."

"I don't have a toothbrush," Fiona said.

"I bought one for you, hoping you'd spend the night." Reuben pulled a brand-new toothbrush from his nightstand. Her name was written on a scrap of paper taped across the package. "I didn't want you to think I keep spare toothbrushes in case I get lucky."

"That's the sweetest thing anybody's ever done for me."

"Here, wrap yourself in a towel. Let's see what's happenin' in the rest of the world."

Nothing was happening in the hallway, so he motioned Fiona to join him in the bathroom. He lifted the toilet seat and dropped his towel.

"Oh! I can't stay here," she said, turning toward the door.

"Don't tell me you're shy."

"About some things, yeah, I guess I am shy." She felt her whole body turn crimson.

"Coulda fooled me last night. Can we take a shower together, at least?"

"Of course. We can even brush our teeth together. I'll wait in your room till you're done." She discreetly closed the door and walked back to Reuben's room. She was getting quite an education.

They brushed their teeth, then made love in the shower. As they dried off, Fiona said, "You're spoiling me."

"You're meant to be spoiled. And, by the way, you look gorgeous without your makeup. Let's go for breakfast, and then we've gotta get you back to the dorm before the clock strikes noon."

Back at the dorm, Fiona called Melissa. "Well, we did it, Lissie. It was incredible. I think he really likes me."

"I want all the details," Melissa said.

Fiona had been eager to share every moment with her friend but surprised herself with her reticence. Partly out of embarrassment, partly out of a newfound sense of privacy, she only wanted to reveal the most superficial memories of their night.

"I'm sure it was Harry's oils that made it happen," Fiona said.

"I wish they'd start working for me," Melissa said. "I think I have more crap to deal with than you, so I'm just gonna keep on keepin' on. I did talk to that cute guy in yoga, and the asshole hasn't been back. That's an improvement."

"Cool. I'll see you in a couple of weeks." Fiona hung up the phone and felt an enormous emptiness settle over her. With nothing to do but homework and artwork, she shrugged her shoulders and returned to her room.

Fiona spent a good part of the day staring out her window onto the quad. The autumn foliage urged her to pick up her colored pencils and record its fleeting beauty. As she created an impressionistic landscape of orange and gold, she realized it was the first time she had drawn anything resembling joy from her vantage point. *What a difference a night makes. I'm gonna give this to Reuben. But what if he takes it the wrong way?*

Self-doubt and insecurity had haunted her since childhood—never good enough, talented enough, pretty enough. When would it stop? *Live for today. Stay in the present. It's all we have.* She'd tried the positive self-talk many times, only to hear the negative chatter return. This time had to be different. She had too much at stake.

She slid the drawing inside a manila folder and scribbled "Reuben" on the outside before she could change her mind.

Her silent motivational speech was still in force on her way to dinner. The streetlamps created shadows of light and dark on the fallen leaves. As she walked, she kicked and crunched the leaves beneath her clogs, causing other students to lift their eyes and smile, as though noticing her for the first time.

She felt like she was finally maturing, finally finding her place in the world. For the first time in her life, she had experienced grown-up sex. How had Reuben learned to do what he'd done?

Lost in thought, she didn't realize she had walked past the dining hall. Reuben startled her as he came from the opposite direction. "Hey, did ya eat already?"

Fiona jumped. "No, just daydreaming. Here, this is for you." She handed him the drawing before she lost her nerve.

"Thank you. It's beautiful." He put his arm around her and kissed her cheek. "Looks like you were inspired. Speaking of inspired, I've been writing all day. I decided to dedicate my novel to you, my muse."

"I guess I could say the same about you." She smiled, realizing it was his first public show of affection.

Conversation was no different from any other evening, but Fiona felt a heady current flowing between them. She was certain other diners felt the energy as they passed. Eddie Mays, head of the Campus Chapter of the Students for a Democratic Society, or SDS, and his girlfriend, Anna, actually stopped to chat.

"You cats heard about the November fifteenth protest rally, right?" Eddie said, adjusting his wire-rimmed glasses. "No more fuckin' bus to NYC. We're makin' our own noise, havin' our own rally right here."

"What about the march in DC?" Reuben asked. "Wouldn't that be more effective? Strength in numbers and all."

"Point taken, dude. We figure the more campus protests, the

bigger the numbers. I'm playin' my axe, and Anna here's gonna sing. Right, babe?"

Anna brushed her waist-length blond hair from her face. "I've got a whole set planned. I would love for you two to be there. I'm—"

Eddie interrupted, "Gotta split. Here's a coupla flyers. Pass 'em around. Right on."

"Should I puke now or later?" Reuben said, picking up the flyer. "He's got all the connections for the bus. Unless we hitch a ride, looks like we'll be marching here."

"Did you ever hitchhike?" Fiona asked.

"Lotsa times. Never as far as New York or DC. How 'bout you?"

"Never, but I want to."

"Maybe in the spring we could go somewhere," Reuben said.

"Definitely," she replied, hoping they would still be together at that time.

Reuben poked at his thick, rubbery spaghetti and spongy meatballs, took a bite, and said, "Last night was perfect. Making love with you was fantastic."

Heat rose from Fiona's abdomen to her face.

"You don't need to say anything. Your coloring says it all. What part did you like the best?"

Fiona squirmed. "We-l-l-l, I think I liked how you made it last. I never did it like that before."

"How'd you like not using your arms? That was the best part for me," Reuben said.

"That was cool, but I kept forgetting."

"Next time bring a scarf and I'll tie your arms to the bed. Actually, I'd like to tie you to that chair and do it right now."

"Reuben!" Fiona's voice drew attention from the neighboring tables.

"Can't a guy fantasize? We writers have great imaginations."

"I guess you've watched a lot of porno movies."

"Some, but I've had a lot of experience too."

I knew he was too good to be true. How many girls has he fucked?

Reuben sensed her unease. "Don't get me wrong. I've only had a few girlfriends, but, well, you might say I had some lessons."

"Lessons? Who has lessons?"

"Here goes. When I was, like, fourteen, I made friends with this kid Jeremy. We hung out at his house every day after school except on the days he went for music lessons. One day when he was gone, his mother asked me to come over and help her with something. She answered the door in this see-through nightgown, and I mean see-through. I didn't know what was going on."

Fiona started to speak but was at a loss for what to say.

"She was my Mrs. Robinson," Reuben said, referring to *The Graduate*, in which an older Anne Bancroft seduces a younger Dustin Hoffman. "She took me upstairs and introduced me to sex for the first time. For the next year or so, I went to see her whenever Jeremy wasn't around. I got a real education."

"Did you like it?" Fiona asked.

"At first, I felt really shitty, almost like I imagine girls feel when they've been raped. I felt guilty, like I was doing something wrong, but I kept going back. She had me by the balls." He smiled at his pun.

"After a while, it got to be normal. I kinda feel I lost something by not doing it first with somebody my own age, but I can't change what happened. Like anything in life, there's pluses and minuses. Now that I met you, I hope you can enjoy some of the pluses."

"I want to—I mean I already did—I mean—"

"I know it's a lot to take in. Like I said, I want to share every part of me with you," Reuben said.

"Me too," she replied. The more she got to know Reuben, the more complex he became. What else would he reveal to her, and how would she react?

Chapter 33

The local chapter of the SDS presided over the campus mora-torium on Saturday, November fifteenth. Hundreds of students, along with several professors and townspeople, attended the event. Energy was high, voices loud, emotions heated. As promised, Eddie Mays on guitar, and Anna with her deep alto voice, led the crowd in singing "Blowin' in the Wind," "We Shall Overcome," and "Fixin' to Die Rag," ending with John Lennon's anthem "Give Peace a Chance." Philosophy professor Dr. Arm-strong and Art Department chair Dr. Hacking spoke of the atroc-ities of war and the rights of all citizens to stand up for peace.

Kevin Reilley, a Vietnam veteran student, spoke of women and children murdered by some of his squadmates, of others left maimed and crippled for life, of villages ruined, of American lives wasted. The crowd stood in silence until a jet flying to an unknown destination pierced the air. Shouts of "Peace Now!" followed him as he left the stage.

"Check out the reporters," Reuben said, pointing to cameras from CBS, NBC, and ABC, the three major news networks film-ing the demonstration.

"I doubt they'll show much from here. The big news will be in New York and Washington," Fiona said. She worried that her parents would see her on the evening news but did not express her concern to Reuben.

"Next time we've gotta plan ahead so we can go to Washington," Reuben said. "We have to be where we'll make the biggest impact."

After dinner, Fiona and Reuben headed to the Student Union to watch the evening news. They learned the moratorium in Washington had attracted over a half-million demonstrators, including performers and activists such as Pete Seeger; Peter, Paul, and Mary; John Denver; and Arlo Guthrie. Protests in New York and San Francisco had also attracted hundreds of thousands of marchers.

They watched a recording of President Nixon's reaction to the demonstrations: "Now I understand that there has been, and continues to be, opposition to the war in Vietnam on the campuses and also in the nation. As far as this kind of activity is concerned, we expect it; however, under no circumstances will I be affected whatever by it."

"Son of a bitch." Reuben shook his head. "What's it gonna take to get through to the bastard?"

"I don't know if we can get through to him. He's a monster," Fiona replied.

"Don't forget, it's not just him we have to convince. It's an entire generation. Until the silent majority pulls their support, nothing's gonna change," Reuben said, turning his attention back to the television.

The networks reviewed footage from the March Against

Death, which began on Thursday evening and continued into Friday. The march ended at the Capitol building, where placards, each containing the name of a dead American soldier or a destroyed Vietnamese village, were placed in coffins.

The majority of the protests were peaceful, but the network aired footage of a conflict at DuPont Circle where the police sprayed the crowd with tear gas. Fiona looked for Peach in the crowd and hoped she had not become an unfortunate victim of police brutality. It was impossible to identify any one person.

The broadcast ended with brief film clips of the larger campus protests in the area. Fiona and Reuben watched highlights of Kevin Reilley's speech. As the cameras swept through the crowd, Fiona recognized her fiery red mane next to Reuben's chestnut ponytail. She strained to see her face before the filming moved to another scene.

Please, Mom and Dad, don't watch the news tonight, she prayed silently.

Chapter 34

Fiona and Reuben said their good-byes on Tuesday afternoon, November twenty-fifth. The Thanksgiving recess would be their longest separation since they met in September.

"Have you told your parents about us?" Reuben asked. "Is it okay if I call you?"

"I don't tell my parents much," Fiona replied. "I thought I might say something, especially if you're gonna call. What about you?"

"I haven't said anything. They were really upset about what happened between Becky and me. I don't think they're too anxious for me to get involved in another relationship so soon."

"I'm nothing like her, am I?" Fiona hoped she was the polar opposite of Reuben's ex-girlfriend.

"Far from it, lassie. I would've never gone for her if you were in my life."

But if I'd been at Temple, you would have left me just like you left her.

As Bill, Fiona's ride home, pulled up to her dorm, she gave Reuben a gentle kiss on the mouth. Their real good-bye had taken place at the Puff the night before.

"See you Sunday." She blew another kiss as she threw her suitcase in the back of Bill's Chevy Bel Air.

What a Trip

Dinner at the O'Brien home Tuesday evening was Irish-style lasagna: ground beef cooked with onions, layered between overcooked noodles, jarred spaghetti sauce, and sliced mozzarella cheese. Her mom's standard salad of iceberg lettuce and fluorescent orange French dressing served as their vegetable. As unappealing as it was to Fiona, it was a significant improvement over the cafeteria food she had grown accustomed to.

Her dad was in an upbeat mood after his pre-dinner Manhattan, obviously glad to have his daughter home. Her mom stewed silently from her seat near the kitchen, picking at her food. Fiona suspected she had indulged in an extra martini or two.

"Helen, aren't we happy to have our little FiFi home after all this time?" her dad asked.

"That's all you have to say, George?" Her mom threw her fork onto the table and balled up her napkin on her untouched plate. "Aren't you forgetting what we discussed? November fifteenth?"

Fiona's appetite disappeared, as did the smile on her lips.

"We think we saw you on TV at the antiwar protest at your school," her dad said. "I told your mom there had to be an explanation, but she's insisting you're becoming one of those dirty hippies."

"That was Fiona. I'd know my own daughter's hair anywhere. It was you, wasn't it?" Her mom's voice and temper escalated.

Fiona had had time to concoct a plausible story in the week after the moratorium. "I was there for a while. I had to be."

"Had to be?!" her mother screamed.

"Helen—"

"Yeah, I had to be." She took a deep breath and almost

choked. "One of my profs is the chairman of the Art Department. He was the main speaker and asked us all to come and hear his speech. We discussed it in class on Monday."

"I told you she'd get in trouble with those liberal artists. It's all your fault, George. Fiona, come into the kitchen. There's more." Her mom stood, grabbing the back of her chair to keep it from toppling to the floor.

Fiona looked to her dad with panic in her eyes. "Daddy, what's going on?"

"I'm sorry, honey. Your mom's been having her migraines, and her pills aren't helping. She thinks an extra martini or two will fix things. Best to go see what she wants."

Fiona's legs shook as she walked into the kitchen. Her mom stood with one hand on the sink. In her other hand, she waved a round plastic dispenser holding Fiona's birth control pills. She threw the pills in the sink, grabbed her daughter, and slapped her across the face.

Through clenched teeth, she spat, "Do you really think I'd be this upset over seeing you at that rally? That's nothing. But this—" She picked up the packet and shoved it in Fiona's face. "I found this in your jewelry box. You're having sex, aren't you? With who? Every boy in town? With that no-good Jack? You're going to hell. And after all I've done to try and save you."

"You're drunk, Mom," Fiona cried.

"I am *not*! My headaches are back, and it's no wonder, with a daughter like you."

Mrs. O'Brien hadn't struck Fiona since she suspected her daughter of having sex when she was a sophomore in high school. That time, Fiona was innocent. Now, it was another story. She was ready with an explanation.

"Mom, I've been having all kinds of problems with my period. Don't you remember I told you that?" Fiona had fabricated the period story to get her initial prescription for birth control pills back in high school. "It's the only thing that's helped me. Otherwise, I can't get out of bed sometimes for two days a month."

Mrs. O'Brien slid to the floor as tears ran down her cheeks. "I do remember now. Isn't there something else you can take? These are immoral times. I don't want you to be tempted. God is always watching and judging. Remember that, Fiona."

Fiona left her mom on the kitchen floor and rejoined her dad in the dining room.

"I'm so sorry, FiFi," her dad said. "I try talking to her. Sometimes she just can't take the pain."

Fiona sobbed and fell into her dad's arms. He held her until she stopped crying. "Now, let me go see about your mom. I'll help her to bed, then you and I can clean up and watch some TV."

I wouldn't have to lie if she wasn't crazy. How does Dad deal with her? He's either gotta be a saint or he's lying his ass off too.

More than anything, she wanted a cigarette, a joint, anything to take her away from her problems. For her dad's sake, she decided to stay home. She flipped on the TV, tuning to *The Mod Squad*, one of his favorite shows. She would rather have watched *I Dream of Jeannie* but was too upset to care.

Fiona had no idea what to expect when she came downstairs the next morning. Her mom surprised her with a smile and a cup of coffee, as though nothing had happened the night before.

Was she so drunk she can't remember, or did Dad have a talk with her? Fiona wondered, knowing she was safe at least until that evening. She kept her mom company until she was due to meet Peach and Melissa at the diner.

"I've got so much shit to tell you guys," Peach said. "You're never gonna believe all that happened on my vacation."

"Tell us," Melissa said. "I need some good news."

"I drove down to Natural Bridge, Virginia, which is this awesome state park, figuring I'd camp there a few days before headin' to DC for the rally. I set up my tent, went for a hike, and met these hippies campin' at the other side of the park. They invited me to hang with them, so I moved my shit. Man, it was so worth it. We dropped blotter acid and stayed up all night groovin' on the trees and the cosmos. I learned the secrets of the universe. It was the most far-out experience of my life."

Fiona was happy for her friend but also envious. Why did Peach get to have all the fun? When would it be her turn? When she was thirty?

"That's so cool," Melissa said.

"What about DC?" Fiona asked.

"It was almost like another Woodstock," Peach went on, "only this time it wasn't for fun. We were there to stop the war. We walked in the March Against Death on Thursday and Friday. We were at DuPont Circle when the pigs sprayed us with tear gas. Let me tell you, that shit is nasty. Two guys in our group got arrested, but they were out the next day."

"We watched it on TV. I looked for you, but there were way too many people," Fiona said.

"About half a mil," Peach went on. "The energy of the crowd was outta sight. I know we got through to Nixon."

"Don't be so sure. You know they're probably gonna sign that draft lottery into law today," Fiona said.

Melissa sat and smoked, oblivious to the seriousness of the conversation.

"I doubt it'll pass. Here's the big news. I kinda have a thing for one of the cats I met." Peach's announcement finally got Melissa's attention.

"You met a guy, Peachie?" she asked.

"Yup. Calvin. He's a musician from St. Louis. Blues guitar. Kinda like Jimi Hendrix."

"Is he Black?" Fiona wanted to know.

"Like I said, like Jimi Hendrix. Giant Afro, tie-dye, and all."

My mom would go ballistic if I went out with a Black dude.

Peach continued. "He got tired of the music scene down there and took off in his VW van. Picked up some hitchhikers along the way and ended up at Natural Bridge. After the rally, we went back to Virginia, and I spent the rest of my vacation with him. Now, for the big news—"

"Did you get laid?" Melissa wanted to know.

"Shit, yeah. That's about all we did. I couldn't even walk afterward. Do you want the big news or not?"

"Of course, Peachie," Fiona said.

"He came back home with me and is stayin' at my brother's pad until I can quit my job."

"You're quitting?" Melissa shrieked. "You lucky chick!"

"I saved a ton of bread, so why the fuck not? Me and Calvin

are takin' off in his van for parts unknown. Maybe end up in Frisco. Being a musician, he can get a gig anywhere. Like me being a nurse. I can get a job anywhere too."

"And you're the only one who didn't buy Harry's oils," Melissa said. "I've been using the shit for weeks, and I've got nothing."

"You gotta be patient, Lissie. I was, and look what it got me," Peach said.

"We're gonna miss you, Peachie," Fiona said.

"I'll miss you guys too," Peach replied.

"Yeah, but you'll be the one having all the fun while we're stuck here." Melissa frowned.

"You chicks are my best friends. I'll write, I promise. I'm even gonna keep a journal. Maybe I'll be another Kerouac. Oh, speakin' of books, I want you to have the books I bought at Harry's. Maybe they're what brought me luck." She piled her collection on the table. "Help yourselves."

"Why don't you take them first, Lissie?" Fiona suggested. "I've got finals coming up, and I've got Reuben. You need them more than I do."

"Thanks, Fee. That's the nicest thing you've ever done for me." Melissa pulled all the books toward her and stuffed them back in Peach's bag before Fiona could change her mind.

Chapter 35

*N*ixon's draft lottery was signed into law, as expected. The fate of all males born between January 1, 1944, and December 31, 1950, would be determined Monday evening, December first, when the first draft lottery drawing since 1942 would take place at the Selective Service National Headquarters in Washington, DC. The drawing would decide the order of call for induction into the armed services beginning in 1970.

"I can't believe my future will be determined on TV tomorrow night," Reuben said at dinner Sunday evening.

"At least we'll be watching at the Student Union. We'll have plenty of company."

"Waiting is the toughest part," Reuben continued. "Not knowing if I'm gonna be number one or three hundred is really doing a number on my head."

"Mine too. It's not just the guys that are affected," Fiona said. "It's all of us. What happens to you happens to me, to your parents, your sisters, everybody."

"Yeah, but it's the guys that have to serve."

Fiona couldn't argue his point. "We've got time on our side. You've got a year and a half left of school, so maybe they'll change the rules by the time you graduate, or maybe the war'll be over. Let's think positively."

"Think positively and act proactively. Or as my parents say, 'Hope for the best and plan for the worst.' At least they're behind me. If I have to go to Canada, they'll do what they can to help."

"Me too." Fiona pulled his face to her. As she kissed him, the ends of her hair dropped into her chicken chow mein, bringing an end to their depressing conversation.

"Can you stay with me tonight?" Reuben asked.

"I dropped off my stuff at the dorm and signed out till Monday morning just in case."

"Cool. I don't want to be alone."

They walked to the Puff, grateful for the cold air and the respite from reality. Rather than their usual routine of sex, pot, and rock 'n' roll played softly, they lay on Reuben's bed and cuddled. Fiona felt Reuben's heartbeat and heard his labored breathing.

She thought of Jack, who was scheduled to begin basic training in a few days. He would never act like Reuben. He'd call Reuben a commie faggot. *You're so wrong, Jack. Reuben is the true hero.* She held him tighter until they fell asleep.

School should have been canceled on December first. Tensions were high. Most students cut classes; those who didn't were unfocused. Professors in all departments discussed the ethics of the lottery and the war. Hearts beat in time to the second hand of a universal clock, awaiting the CBS News broadcast that evening.

CBS preempted *Mayberry RFD* to air a live broadcast from Washington correspondent Roger Mudd at the Selective Service Headquarters. "Tonight, for the first time in twenty-seven years, the United States has again started a draft lottery," Mudd announced as the ceremony began.

Three hundred and sixty-six blue plastic lottery capsules, each holding a birth date, were dumped into a glass container resembling a water cooler. Someone would reach into the jar, pull out a capsule, read the date, and announce a lottery number, starting with zero-zero-one.

Fiona gripped Reuben's sweaty palm as Congressman Alexander Pirnie drew the first number. Pirnie's voice cut through the silence in the Student Union as he unrolled the paper and announced, "September fourteenth is number zero-zero-one."

A scream echoed from the back of the room. Everyone turned to see Eddie Mays raise a fist and shout, "Fuck you, Big Brother. I ain't goin'!" Anna tried to get him to sit. Instead, he marched out of the room, slamming the door as he left.

Faces were distracted only for a moment. Three hundred and sixty-five numbers still needed to be drawn.

"Talk about selfish," Reuben whispered to Fiona. "What about his friends and the rest of us? He's not the only one getting fucked here."

Congressman Pirnie stepped aside and yielded the spotlight to Selective Service Youth Advisory Council delegates who would take turns drawing five or six capsules each. Dates were posted on a large board with a slot for each birthday, including February twenty-ninth. The board was titled "Random Selection Sequence, 1970."

Capsule number eleven was drawn by the second delegate. "August thirty-first. Number eleven is August thirty-first."

All the color drained from Reuben's face. The muscles of his jaw tightened. His moist eyes stared at the television. A drop of sweat ran from his hairline past his cheek. Fiona tried hugging him closer, but his body remained rigid.

The drawing continued. Random curses erupted as young men heard their birthdays drawn. Roger Mudd explained that 850,000 young men would not have to wait to discover their fate. He told viewers that President Nixon had been unable to abolish the draft system because of the war's massive manpower demands.

"Millions of protesters between the October and November marches, and this is what happens." Reuben shook his head, the first move he had made since hearing his birth date announced.

"Do you want to leave?" Fiona asked, seeing the crowd diminish.

"No. I want to be here to support everyone right down to the last stinkin' blue capsule." He turned his attention back to the television.

Cheers rang out as the numbers moved into the two and three hundreds. "Lucky sons of bitches," Reuben muttered.

When it was over, only a few students remained. They supported those with low numbers and cheered those with high numbers until security came to lock the building.

"I suppose I should be relieved," Reuben said as they walked into the cold. "At least I know my fate, and I can start making plans. Last year I made a half-assed attempt to look into Canada, but now I'm gonna get serious. I couldn't get through this without you, lassie."

What a Trip

She wanted to answer by saying, *I love you, and I want to go to Canada with you*, but she didn't want to freak him out. In reality, she didn't want to freak herself out. She had never told a boy she loved him and wasn't ready to do it now. What if he didn't say it back? What if he didn't want her to go to Canada with him?

He stopped walking, pulled Fiona to him, clasped her head with both hands, and kissed her passionately. "Don't ever leave me. I need you so much."

"I won't. I'll always be here for you."

Hand in hand, they walked the rest of the way to Fiona's dorm.

Chapter 36

The panic of Monday evening dissipated as students returned to their schoolwork. Exams would begin in two weeks, followed by winter break. Even Reuben seemed more relaxed.

"Do you know what today is?" he asked Fiona on Thursday.

"Sure. Thursday."

"It's a lot more than that. Tonight's the first night of Hanukkah."

Fiona hadn't given a thought to Reuben's religious background since they discussed it back in October. Immersed in an entirely Christian world, she had no idea when Hanukkah was or how it was celebrated. "Is it Happy Hanukkah or Merry Hanukkah?"

"It's 'Happy,' thanks. But here's what I want to tell you. My family is doing the big Hanukkah thing tonight, even though I'm stuck here. My sisters and everybody else expect it. Anyway, I called home this morning and talked to my mother. I told her all about you, about how you're so different from Becky."

"I thought you didn't want to tell them anything," Fiona said.

"I changed my mind. My parents said they're gonna do whatever they can to help me fight the draft, so I figured I'd be honest with them. They were happy to hear I found somebody, and they want to meet you."

"They do?" Fiona had never been formally introduced to anyone's parents and wasn't sure she wanted to start now.

"They invited you to come to the house for the weekend. Hanukkah's a big deal at our house. It's eight nights long, so my mother agreed to make another batch of latkes and her famous matzoh ball soup on Saturday. She said she'll even make jelly donuts."

Fiona had no idea what Reuben was talking about. What were latkes? And what was so great about jelly donuts?

"You're looking at me like I've got two heads," Reuben said. "Latkes are potato pancakes, soup is soup, and her donuts are the fucking best on the planet."

"But the whole weekend? Where would I sleep? And what if they don't like me?" Fiona panicked.

"Don't worry, they'll love you. We'll catch the noon bus Saturday, get there in the afternoon, light the Hanukkah candles, eat dinner, and go to bed. We'll leave Sunday after breakfast."

"What about sleeping?"

"You can sleep in my twin sisters' old room. Since they started high school this year, my father fixed up the third-floor attic for them."

She felt resentment toward Reuben for the first time. *Who does he think he is, ordering me around, telling me where to go and where to sleep?*

Reuben sensed her anxiety. "Maybe I came on too strong. Ever since Monday night I feel like I'm running out of time. I apologize. I should have asked you first."

Yes, you should have, she wanted to say, but the damage was done.

"My parents are psyched to meet you. I can't tell them you're not coming. It'll be fine, I promise. You'll be with me. Have I ever let you down?"

"No. Sorry I got so upset." She wasn't really sorry but didn't want to start an argument.

"I'll make it up to you at the Puff Friday night. Bring that silk scarf. You can tie me up. This time I need to be punished."

"And I know just how to do it. I learned from the best," Fiona said as her mood lifted.

In spite of protests from Reuben, Fiona insisted on wearing one of her "parent-pleasing outfits"—a pair of lightly flared navy wool slacks, a white cable-knit sweater, and low black heels—to meet his parents. A blue paisley scarf held her unruly curls in an orderly ponytail.

"I almost don't recognize you," Reuben said as she dressed on Saturday morning.

"Is that good or bad?" she asked.

"Always good, just different. My parents'll dig it. C'mon. We don't want to miss the bus."

An uneventful hour on the bus and a two-block walk brought them to the northern New Jersey suburb that Reuben called home. Home was an early-twentieth-century white clapboard residence, complete with a wraparound porch and gabled windows on the third floor. Nothing but a single driveway and a scrawny patch of lawn separated it from the neighboring houses, all born in the same era.

Most homes on the street were decorated for Christmas. Plastic Santas and snowmen dotted the lawns. Evergreen wreaths and MERRY CHRISTMAS signs adorned the front doors. The Goldberg home was one of a few that lacked the Christmas spirit.

"I guess your family doesn't decorate for Christmas," Fiona observed.

"You better not say that to my parents," Reuben said. "Some of the Jewish families put up outdoor lights and even have Christmas trees, or Hanukkah bushes, as they like to call them. My parents call them hypocrites and, when they're really pissed, fake Jews."

"What are they gonna think about me? Will they care I'm not Jewish?" Fiona said, hesitating in front of the house.

"Shit, no. We're not religious. All this is about tradition. They're proud of our Jewish heritage. What's important to them is that we stay true to who we are."

What a switch from my parents. All they care about is appearance. They wouldn't know a tradition if it bit them in the ass.

"I don't think you know how lucky you are," she said. "My parents are the biggest phonies on earth, especially my mom." She took a deep breath. "I guess I'm ready. Let's go inside before I chicken out."

A warm smile from Mrs. Goldberg melted Fiona's fears as she welcomed them into the foyer. She was a tiny woman, just over five feet, olive-skinned like her son, with gray streaks peppering a messy brown bun. Over a nondescript blue dress, she wore an apron, actually more of a smock, sporting flecks of flour, grease, and purple jam.

"You have to forgive the mess," Mrs. Goldberg said. "Reuben told me how much you enjoy jelly donuts, so I've whipped up a bunch for ya. Got half of 'em on me, but I promise the other half'll be much more appetizing. Now put your stuff over there on the chair, and c'mon in. The girls are upstairs, and your father's in the study. What else is new?"

Fiona couldn't imagine a woman more different from her own mother. The O'Briens rarely entertained, and when they did, it was a stiff and formal occasion. Mrs. O'Brien would be dressed to the nines, every hair in place, her makeup a mask of perfection. Every piece of their Danish modern furniture, every ashtray, every vase would be arranged like the showroom their house was.

"Frank!" Mrs. Goldberg yelled up the stairs. "The kids are here. Girls, front and center!"

Reuben escorted Fiona into the living room. Overstuffed couches and chairs upholstered in maroon and royal blue invited them to sit. The *New York Times* was sprawled across the coffee table next to a half-empty coffee cup and half-full ashtray. Cream lace curtains partially concealed a brass candelabra sitting on the windowsill.

"Relax, relax. Have a seat. Hope you brought your appetites," Mrs. Goldberg said as she disappeared into the kitchen.

"Your mom is so sweet," Fiona said as she sank into the mohair sofa.

"Told you it'd be okay, and don't worry, they're not gonna overdo it. Tonight's just about family, food—and Fiona." Reuben placed a soft kiss on the back of her neck.

They turned to the sound of footsteps on the wooden stairs.

"How's it goin', Pop?" Reuben and Fiona stood as a tall man with faded ginger hair entered the living room. "This is Fiona. Fiona, my father, Frank Goldberg."

"At last. Is pleasure to meet you, my dear," Mr. Goldberg said in a noticeable Eastern European accent. "Please, sit on sofa. Tell me, how do you like my son?"

"Come on, Pop. She likes me fine. Otherwise, she wouldn't be here," Reuben said, rescuing Fiona.

"I see she does the blush. Don't worry. I am only teasing you." Mr. Goldberg smiled. "Now tell me about school. What is news?"

Fiona observed father and son as they spoke. Reuben mirrored his father's height, his prominent cheekbones, his intense brown eyes.

Reuben's twin sisters interrupted the conversation as they ran into the room. "You must be Fiona. We heard Reuben had a new girlfriend," one said.

"Sorry," Reuben said. "These are my sisters, Amy and Audrey."

"Hey," they said in unison.

The girls had inherited their father's coloring as well as his height and features. *They're gorgeous. Much prettier than I was at their age.*

"Go help your mother," Mr. Goldberg said to them. Turning to Fiona, he added, "Teenagers, right?"

Fiona daydreamed as Reuben and his father discussed school, the draft, and people unknown to her. After what seemed like an hour, the twins scurried into the room. "Pop, it's time to light the candles!"

Mrs. Goldberg rushed from the kitchen, wiping her hands on a tattered dishtowel. "František!" she called, using her husband's Czech name, "the menorah."

Mr. Goldberg pulled the curtains aside and placed the menorah on the end table that sat under the front window. Amy (or was it Audrey?) placed three candles in the nine-branched candelabra from right to left. She handed a fourth candle to her sister, lighting it with a stainless-steel cigarette lighter.

The twin held the lit candle as the family recited the Hebrew blessings. Fiona stood self-consciously watching the unfamiliar ritual. It was the first time she had heard Hebrew spoken.

After the blessings, Audrey (or was it Amy?) lit the three candles in the menorah, moving from left to right, finally placing the fourth candle in the center slot.

Mr. Goldberg returned the menorah to the window. "So all can see," he said. "Now we eat."

Reuben reached for Fiona's elbow, keeping her in the living room. "I know this is new for you. You must be feeling kinda weird."

"I am. I was doing okay until all the prayers. We probably should've talked religion before we got here," she replied.

"Like I said, we're not religious. Dinner'll be cool. My mother's a fantastic cook, so just enjoy the food. We'll have time after dinner to talk. C'mon."

Mrs. Goldberg's soup was thick and rich with big chunks of chicken and carrots and tiny matzoh balls. "Hope you like my soup, Fiona," she said. "Most people make matzoh balls the size of golf balls, but I like 'em tiny. More surface area to absorb the flavors."

"I never had homemade soup before. This is delicious." Fiona's soup history consisted of Campbell's condensed soup. Matzoh balls, large or small, were foreign territory.

"Doesn't your mother cook?" one of the twins asked.

"She cooks, but not like this."

"That's why she's got such a beautiful figure," the other twin added.

Fiona stared into her bowl, not knowing how to react.

"I usually serve brisket, but Reuben told us you don't like much meat, so I made extra latkes," his mother said. "It won't hurt any of us to go without meat, right, dear?"

"Is all good to me," Mr. Goldberg said.

Mrs. Goldberg's latkes were done to perfection—crisp on the outside and soft on the inside. She served them with sour cream and homemade applesauce, another new experience for Fiona, who had never eaten pancakes without maple syrup and butter.

Conversation was light and relaxed throughout the meal. The family encouraged Fiona to talk about her artwork and her career plans. The twins eagerly asked Fiona about makeup tips, clothing, and her preferences in music. Fiona caught Reuben staring at her, looking pleased with his family's positive reaction to her.

Mrs. Goldberg's jelly donuts were an explosion of flavor with just the right amount of sweetness, a perfect ending to the best homemade meal of Fiona's life. She offered to help clean up but was shooed out of the kitchen. Reuben suggested they go for a walk.

"You're a big hit with my family," Reuben said once they were outside. "I hope they didn't come on too strong."

"They're wonderful. You're so lucky," she said, the words catching in her throat.

"Are you okay, lassie?"

"I don't know," she sobbed. "I-I n-never knew anybody could have a good time with their family."

"Hey, it's okay. How bad could yours be? It's not like they beat you or anything."

"No, I guess not," she lied, remembering the sting of her mother's slap.

They walked in silence, tuning in to the *whoosh* of traffic on the nearby avenue.

She sighed audibly. "My dad, he's okay, just wants the best for me. My mom's crazy and the biggest phony on the planet. No matter what I do, it's wrong. She says I'm evil and that God's got it in for me. I've had religion pushed down my throat since I was little. The older I get, the more I realize it's all bullshit, at least the way she does it."

"You must have freaked out when we lit the candles," Reuben said.

"A little. I was afraid your family would hate me because I'm not Jewish."

"No way," Reuben assured her.

"I'm also afraid to bring you to my house," she went on. "My mom said I could never date anybody who wasn't a Protestant. I think she was talking about Catholics. I don't know what she'd do if I brought you home."

"No biggie. We just won't say anything."

"They're also a couple of conservative bigots. Anybody with long hair is a drug addict out to destroy the country. And forget talking about the war."

"Let's sit for a while and have a cigarette." Reuben motioned to a bench near the entrance of a small park. "You know, you don't have to show me to your parents anytime soon. I get it."

"You do?"

"Of course. My parents have their hang-ups too."

Fiona couldn't imagine Reuben's parents having hang-ups about anything. "They seem so cool."

"They are about a lot of things," Reuben said. "They're just kinda conservative when it comes to sex, so don't expect me to sneak into your room and fuck your brains out."

"It's a deal." She smiled and took a drag from her Kool.

"You've been so nice to me. Everything was perfect," Fiona said as she and Reuben prepared to leave.

Breakfast—or brunch, as the Goldbergs called it—included brewed, not instant, coffee; fresh, not frozen, bagels; an array of smoked fish; and freshly squeezed orange juice. Fiona, still full from the night before, wondered how the family could eat so much and stay so trim.

I wish I had their genes.

"You've been so nice to me. Everything was perfect," Fiona said as she and Reuben prepared to leave.

"Please come again. You are good girl for my son," Mr. Goldberg said, kissing her on both cheeks.

Walking to the bus, Reuben said, "I think you're good for my father too. This was the best I've seen him since my grandfather died."

"Other than being kinda quiet, he seemed okay."

"Depression is like that. It sits and waits, and then one day it takes over. You've gotta beat it down till it goes back into hiding. I think he's almost there; at least I hope he is."

Chapter 37

$\mathcal{N}$ational politics took a back seat for the next two weeks as students prepared for finals and winter recess. An air of excitement permeated the campus but did not extend to Fiona and Reuben, who would be separated for more than three weeks.

"My folks said you're welcome to stay with us for a few days. Maybe come for New Year's Eve," Reuben suggested.

"I don't know how I'd swing that with my parents. My mom would go nuts if she knew I was sleeping under the same roof with you. Maybe we could meet in the city or something," Fiona said.

"When do you think you'll tell your parents about me?"

She hesitated. "Here's what I'm thinking. My mom's a fucking head case, but my dad's not a bad guy in spite of his politics. I thought I'd tell him about you and ask his advice on how to deal with my mom."

"It's important to stand up for what you believe and who you are. Don't forget that, and don't be a coward. I've seen a big change in you this semester. You're more confident, braver, and not afraid to be who you are," he said.

Reuben's pep talk hit home. She stood taller, imagining her

body filled with courage. If she could maintain that attitude, she'd be home free—or home alone if she chickened out.

They said their sad good-byes as Fiona's ride home pulled up to the dorm.

"I'll call you tonight at seven." Reuben gave her a final kiss.

It's gonna be a long three weeks, Fiona thought as she waved good-bye.

An air of disarray permeated the O'Brien home when Fiona walked into the living room. Her dad's slippers sat in front of his favorite chair. Their *TV Guide* and *Good Housekeeping* magazines lay open on the coffee table next to an empty, lipstick-stained glass. The couch needed fluffing, and the pillows were out of place. A thin layer of dust masked the usual tabletop shine.

Hearing the front door open, Mr. O'Brien hurried out of the kitchen, calling, "Helen? Is that you?"

"It's me, Dad," Fiona said.

"FiFi! You're early."

"No, right on time. Where's Mom?"

Mr. O'Brien shifted his glance away from his daughter. "Have a seat, honey. We need to talk."

Fiona sat on the couch and absentmindedly straightened a pillow.

"Your mom's okay—at least, she's going to be okay," he began.

"What's going on?"

"This isn't easy. I know Mom can be unreasonable some-times, but she means well. She told me she hit you the last time you were home."

Fiona fought back tears, reminding herself to be strong and remembering her conversation with Reuben.

"That was the last straw for me. I know she drinks too much. She says it helps her pain, but I finally put my foot down. I made her see a doctor. Should have done it years ago."

"Is it serious?" Fiona asked.

"The doctor doesn't think so. They're running some tests to rule out anything physical. He told me in confidence that it's nerves—all in her head. She's taking new pills to calm her down. She thinks it's headache medication."

"Pills and alcohol? Why isn't the doctor telling her the truth?"

"Best not to upset her further, the doctor said. He was adamant about not drinking with the pills. Said it could kill her."

"Do you think she'll listen?"

"We've cleaned out the liquor cabinet. I'm not drinking at home either," Mr. O'Brien said. "If I want a drink, I can always stop with the fellas on the way home."

"What should I do?" Fiona asked.

"Nothing. Act like everything's okay."

Everything has never been okay. Could she act like everything was normal when her mom came home? She doubted it.

"It'll take a few weeks for the pills to kick in. She said she's had fewer headaches and they're less severe. I think you'll see a big change around here."

Fiona stared into space, at a loss for what to think or say. Her dad might actually be on her side. "I've got some news," she whispered.

"What? Speak up. Did you say you have news?" her dad asked.

"I made dean's list again, a 3.75 GPA for the semester."

"That's my girl."

"And I met a really nice boy."

That got her father's attention. "I hope he's not another smart aleck like Jack."

"His name's Reuben. He wants to be a journalist, but he's an education major, like me. I think you'd like him. I-I'm just afraid to tell Mom."

"You leave that to me. Now tell me more about this Reuben."

Father and daughter were deep in conversation when Mrs. O'Brien came home. They said their hellos, after which her mom drifted into the kitchen. Fiona immediately noticed a shift. Her mom was physically present, made dinner and small talk, but seemed detached, floating in and out of another dimension.

This is too weird. She's so passive. Did her dad notice, or was he as relieved as she was?

Fiona sat in her bedroom after dinner reflecting on the mother she had known for the last nineteen years and the woman she met today. She hoped the doctors wouldn't find anything physically wrong with her mom, but she didn't want her to be crazy either. Would pills make her kinder, more understanding, less judgmental? Would this be the end to the religious fanaticism, to the moral code of conduct that ruled her life? These were the questions that swirled in Fiona's mind. Questions with no answers.

It took several days for Fiona to get used to the new version of her mom. She hoped the doctor could adjust the dosage before her mom slipped over the edge. In spite of the changes, she didn't ask to spend New Year's Eve at Reuben's home, nor did she ask to invite him to theirs, but he was a positive topic of conversation on a daily basis.

Peach had left with Calvin, her new boyfriend, in early December, promising to write and call when they got settled. Fiona missed her more than she expected. Melissa was her only close friend in town, and even she was distracted.

"Only a few more days, and my mother will be Mrs. Giovanni. How strange is that?" Melissa said at lunch one day. "I can't believe she's getting married and we're moving. I'll miss that shitty apartment."

"Lots of changes, Lissie. A new home, a new decade. Can you imagine—1970?"

"And me starting school in January." Melissa lit a Marlboro. "I have a surprise for you. Remember I told you about that guy I checked out in yoga? His name's Scott, and he's taking classes at the college too. He told me about a big New Year's Eve party. Said we could meet there. I think Harry's oils are finally starting to work."

"Cool."

"The party is at that farmhouse where—well, you know—" Melissa said, referring to an evening they both would rather forget. "You and me can go together and meet Scott there. You'll like him. It's not like a date or anything. Please?"

"Sure, why not?" She would do anything to avoid staying home with her drugged mother.

Reuben called a few days before New Year's Eve. She told him about the new Mrs. O'Brien and seemed hopeful that one day soon she could bring him home to meet her family.

"Any plans for New Year's Eve?" he asked her.

"Lissie wants me to go to some stupid party. If my mom wasn't such a wacko, I'd be happier staying home."

"The invitation is still open to come here," Reuben said. "My parents are having a small party. They'd love it if you came."

"I wish I could. I'm scared to do anything that'll set off my mom."

Reuben sighed. "I guess I understand. Don't fall in love with some new guy at the party."

"C'mon, what kind of person do you think I am?"

"Only kidding. Have fun, and I'll talk to you in a coupla days."

Fiona climbed the stairs to Melissa's apartment, realizing it would be her final visit. Mrs. Patten, now Mrs. Giovanni, was on her honeymoon. All that remained of a life once lived was a mattress and several boxes in Melissa's bedroom. Books from Harry's Occult Shop spilled onto the floor. Fiona wondered if her friend was touched by nostalgia or if she was eager to move on.

"I feel like this is the end of an era," Fiona said as she moved through the emptiness. "It's been quite a year."

"More for me than you, Fee. This is my second move this year. Is this what it's like to be an adult?"

"What do I know? It kinda feels like purgatory. We're not kids anymore, but we're not quite grownups either." Fiona was surprised by her insightfulness. "C'mon, let's go before I change my mind."

The girls fell into their usual routine—a joint and superficial conversation—on the way to the party. Before going into the house, Melissa turned serious. "I've been reading those books Peach left," she said. "There's a lot to this witchcraft stuff. It's a real religion called Wicca. It's been around for thousands of years."

Fiona felt her mom's warnings of fire and brimstone circling around her. Much as she denounced religion, a certain level of fear stayed with her.

"I hope you're not getting into black magic or conjuring up demons," Fiona said, trying to keep her tone humorous.

"No way, Fee. It's all about tuning in to the energy of the earth. Y'know, herbs and stones, connecting with the moon, stuff like that. I wish they offered courses at college. I'd major in it. Maybe you and me could study together."

"I don't see how I could," she said. "Plus I want to get a part-time job so I can buy a new car next summer."

"I can come up and stay with you on the weekends I don't work. I'm getting that car next week," Melissa said.

"We'll see." She was certain Reuben would dump her in a minute if he knew how messed up her friend was.

Nothing had changed at the farmhouse since Fiona's last visit. The sweet scent of marijuana mixed with acrid sweat drifted through a thick layer of smoke. Creedence Clearwater Revival's *Green River* screamed from the stereo in the next room. Melissa grabbed her arm, pulling her from room to room, looking for Scott.

"There he is." Melissa pointed to a nondescript figure

propped against a far wall with light brown hair falling in his eyes, wire-rimmed glasses, rumpled khakis, and a denim shirt—indistinguishable from every other twenty-year-old in the room. Catching sight of her, Scott smiled and waved.

"He's got a nice smile," Fiona yelled as they crossed the room to meet him.

The three squeezed into a corner, taking hits from the pipe as it came their way. Fiona wondered if everyone felt as insecure and isolated as she did, if parties weren't a superficial escape from nothingness.

Is this all there is to life? she wondered. *I want so much more.*

She jumped as a warm body fell into her. Turning, she met an impish grin on a vaguely familiar face. In the seconds of silence as *Green River* ended and before another album fell onto the turntable, he spoke.

"Hey, I remember you. Two summers ago?"

Fiona searched her memory. *Two summers ago? I'd just graduated high school. Oh shit*, she thought, *the party down by the Delaware River.* A group of kids from Fiona's high school had spent the morning tubing down the river and met up with another group of kids. She smoked and drank a little too intensely and ended up with somebody in the bed of a pickup truck. He was that somebody. She never did learn his name but had always hoped to run into him again.

She smiled and nodded. "Sure. The river. The pickup," she said, fully aware of the double meaning.

"C'mon. Let's get re—" The rest of his words were lost. Janis Joplin's "Kozmic Blues" nearly broke the sound barrier. He held out his hand.

Before taking his hand, Fiona checked on Melissa, who was

fully engrossed in Scott. *What the hell. Anything to get out of this room.*

As he led her upstairs, she checked out her new friend from the rear. Nice butt. Not too short, not too tall. Gorgeous shoulder-length blond hair. Since being with Reuben, she had forgotten her weakness for blonds.

She hadn't thought about Reuben since she arrived at the party. Where was he tonight and what was he doing? What would he think if he saw her now? She pushed thoughts of him out of her head.

The long hallway and open doors on the second floor were all too familiar. It was early, most of the rooms not yet occupied. He led her into a room and closed the door.

"I never learned your name," she said.

"Never knew yours either. How 'bout we keep it like that? More of a turn-on." He gave her a gentle push onto the bed and climbed on top of her, nuzzling her neck.

Fiona's breath quickened as her mind raced. What was she doing here? What about Reu—?

His kisses consumed her as her body recalled their last encounter. She tuned in to the moment, taking and letting herself be taken. Who cared what his name was? This was so much more exciting. She relished his touch, his body moving in sync with hers, their lust exploding as they came together.

They were lying in the remnants of their lovemaking, still partially dressed, when they heard a knock on the door. "Hurry up in there," someone shouted. "We don't rent these rooms by the hour." Harsh laughter followed.

Fiona's head cleared. What had she done? She checked out the bed. How many couples had lain on these filthy sheets? How many more would before the night was gone? She attempted to remake the bed, then stopped, realizing the futility of her effort. She turned to her partner. "Guess we better split."

"You're a good lay," he said in an attempt at kindness. "Maybe we'll meet again sometime."

He unlocked the door and stepped into the hallway without waiting for Fiona. Another couple pushed their way in.

She smoothed her sweater and adjusted her jeans. Guilt and feelings of inadequacy bled from her heart. Was she nothing more than a quick fuck? This had to be the last time. No more parties, no more nameless sex. As she descended the stairs, her convictions wavered. Was this the end of an era, or was history doomed to repeat itself?

She pursed her lips to stop them from trembling. She needed to leave, but what about Melissa?

Melissa had moved into the kitchen with Scott and hadn't noticed Fiona's disappearance. Gathering her courage, she tapped her friend on the shoulder. "Lissie, I've got really bad cramps. I need to get out of here."

"Fee, it's early, and it's New Year's Eve. Can't you stay?"

"I feel so shitty I'm about ready to pass out. Can Scott take you home?"

Scott smiled. "Sure. I can give you a lift. Nice to meet you, Fiona. Hope we get to hang out sometime."

"Me too. Thanks." She hugged her friend and whispered in her ear, "You'll be okay, right?"

"More than okay. See ya."

Fiona checked the clock in the Corvair. Eleven thirty. Too early to go home. Her parents would wonder what happened. She sat and waited. Streams of music and laughter reached her ears, making her situation even more unbearable.

Shame, insecurity, and depression created a deadly cocktail of emotions in her mind. Nausea spilled from her stomach to her throat. She opened the car door and vomited onto the street, quickly glancing around to see if anyone had seen her. They hadn't. She wiped her mouth and eyes, using the box of tissues her mom kept in the glove box.

What a way to welcome the new year. She made a promise to herself not to tell anyone, not even Melissa, what had happened. This would be the last time she'd make it with anyone besides Reuben. It would be the last party at the farmhouse. It was the beginning of a new decade, a new opportunity to start over. She heard Reuben's words in her head, *You're more confident, braver, and not afraid to be who you are.* He believed in her. It was time she believed in herself.

For the last year, Fiona had seen herself moving away from her hometown friends. So many were stuck in a downward spiral. Peach had found a way out. Melissa had found a new guy. She was starting school, moving to a new house, getting a car, but she was drifting into the world of magic and witchcraft. The tarot was harmless enough. The rest was frightening.

Fiona didn't want to abandon her best friend, but it was time to distance herself physically, if not emotionally.

Midnight on the Corvair's clock. "Happy New Year," she said to no one but herself. She checked her makeup in the rearview mirror, started the engine, and took the long way home.

PART THREE

Fiona and Reuben grew closer through the winter of 1970, spending most of their weekends on campus. Reuben wrote for the college's literary magazine, *The Beacon*, as a volunteer and, on occasion, asked Fiona to illustrate an article or poem. They secured part-time jobs, Reuben in the library and Fiona in the office of the Art Department. For the first time in her life, Fiona felt good about herself and believed she was making a difference in the world.

She and Melissa spoke on the phone several times a week, but Fiona could feel the pull of maturity separating them. She knew Melissa felt it too. They both sensed a different vibe in the air when she went home. They continued to get stoned in her mom's Corvair and share coffee and cigarettes at the diner, but Melissa was more focused on her volunteer position with the community college newspaper, her relationship with Scott, and her study of the occult.

"Don't you think it's time I met your parents?" Reuben asked one morning in late February.

"My mom went from monster to moron," Fiona said. "The

doctor has her on some kind of pills. She thinks it's for headaches. My dad says it's for her nerves. The doctor's worried she might be headed for a nervous breakdown."

"You've told them about me, right?" Reuben asked.

"Sure. My dad wants to meet you. I don't want you to get freaked out by my mom."

"My father went through his shit last year. How much worse could it be? Why don't you see if we can visit this Saturday? Even if I can't stay overnight, I could at least come for dinner."

"My mom's cooking is one step up from cafeteria food, not like your mom's," Fiona said, shaking her head.

"It's not about the food. It's about them getting to meet me and making a statement about our relationship. Or don't you feel that's important?" His eyes narrowed for a moment as he stared into hers.

Fiona weighed her options. She could bring Reuben home or risk ruining their relationship. She had proven herself strong these last two months. Perhaps it was time to take a stand.

"Okay, let's do it," she said.

To Fiona's surprise, Reuben dressed in a blue oxford button-down shirt and a pair of gray wool slacks to meet her parents. She hoped his conservative clothing would minimize his shoulder-length chestnut hair, which he tied back with a leather thong.

"Look at you, Mr. Conservative." Fiona smiled.

"You dressed up for my parents. I want to do it for yours," he said.

"Thank you. I really appreciate it." Fiona kissed his cheek.

What a Trip

Mr. O'Brien met the couple at the town bus station.

"FiFi's told us so much about you. I feel like I know you already," her dad said.

Reuben tilted his chin, and with a grin he mouthed, *FiFi?*

Shhh! she mouthed back and smiled.

"Your mom's making a special ham dinner tonight. Hope you brought your appetites," her dad said.

Fiona knew many Jews avoided ham and other pork products. She was relieved Reuben didn't follow the tradition. It was one less thing she had to explain.

Reuben and Mr. O'Brien hit it off. Reuben spoke of his writing and his family. He encouraged her dad to talk about his work as an engineer. Politics and religion remained off the table.

Before entering the O'Brien home, Fiona's dad winked at her as if to say, *He's okay in my book.*

Now all she needed to do was convince her mom.

Mrs. O'Brien greeted them in a green-and-brown-plaid two-piece ensemble. Her makeup and hair were as neat and precise as the house, which had returned to showroom condition. Not a speck of dust was to be found. Not a chair, curtain, or magazine out of place.

Fiona suspected the doctor had adjusted her mom's medication. She hoped her mom could keep it together through the visit and avoid any controversial conversations.

Reuben was quick to praise Mrs. O'Brien on her outfit and home decor.

"I try," she said.

"You do more than try," Reuben said. "Our house is always turned upside down."

But it's so much homier. You don't know how lucky you are.

Her mom ate up the compliment. "Dinner's just about ready," she said. "Why don't you men have a seat? Fiona, help me in the kitchen."

Fiona knew Reuben would be safe with her dad. But how safe would she be?

In the kitchen, her mom said, "He seems like a nice enough boy. But that hair. If you're going to get serious with him, he has to get it cut. I don't want my daughter going around with a long-haired hippie. It will create a very bad impression here in town."

"Come on, Mom. I can't tell him to get a haircut, and neither can you."

"Well, I see you haven't toned down your snotty attitude."

"I'll bring in the salad and rolls." Fiona grabbed the food and slipped into the dining room.

Mrs. O'Brien trailed after her daughter with a pitcher of water.

"The salad is delicious," Reuben said.

Fiona shot him a sideways glance.

Black olives and chunks of orange cheese rested on top of sliced iceberg lettuce. Mrs. O'Brien had dressed the salads with Wishbone Italian dressing. Fiona assumed her mom didn't want the orange of her usual French dressing to clash with the cheese.

The ham was adorned with canned pineapple rings and whole cloves. As much as Fiona hated meat, she appreciated the extra effort her mom had taken to make the meal special. She even served real mashed potatoes and candied carrots.

"Helen, you've outdone yourself," her dad said.

The others echoed his sentiment.

When Mrs. O'Brien didn't respond immediately, Fiona turned to her mom and repeated, "Great dinner, Mom. Mom?"

Her mom stared into space with eyes as glazed as the ham.

"Helen!"

"What is it, dear?"

"We were all saying what a wonderful dinner you made," her dad said.

"Thank you. Anybody ready for dessert? I didn't have time to make something, but I did get Fiona's favorite lemon meringue pie from Turner's Bakery."

What was going on? Why was her mom going to such lengths to impress Reuben? Or was this a peace offering for her daughter?

Mrs. O'Brien became more distant over dessert and coffee. She refused Fiona's offer to help clean up and retreated to the kitchen. Fiona and Reuben joined her dad in the living room.

"We'll have to leave in a bit if we want to catch the last bus," Reuben said.

"Next time, Reuben, why don't you plan to stay overnight? We've got a nice guest room that doesn't get enough use. You could join us for church on Sunday morning and stay for lunch."

"Umm, Dad," Fiona whispered, "Reuben's family is Jewish."

Her dad squirmed in his seat. "You know, I thought maybe you were Jewish with a name like Goldberg."

"Yes, sir. My father's family suffered greatly during the Holocaust. He was lucky to stay alive and even luckier to get to America."

"Well, then, I guess church is out of the question. I'd still like you to stay longer."

Fiona's eyebrows inched closer to her scalp. Was this her dad speaking?

They thanked her mom for dinner and rode to the bus station with her dad. Before dropping them off, her dad whispered to his daughter, "Let's not tell Mom that Reuben's a Jew. We'll keep that between us for now."

"That went much better than I expected," Fiona said as they got on the bus.

"Your dad's a great guy. I'd like to get to know him better."

"Politics and religion are the only two things I've got against him. After tonight, maybe it's just politics," Fiona said.

"If he can accept me as a Jew, then maybe he'll come around on the war. Your mom, though—" Reuben didn't have to finish his sentence.

"She was on her best behavior. I don't think anything will change with her."

"Tonight was special for me. I know this wasn't easy for you. Thank you, FiFi."

Fiona nudged him in the ribs and smiled. They snuggled into one another as the bus left the station.

Chapter 39

Political unrest escalated at colleges and universities across the country after President Nixon announced the expansion of the Vietnam War into eastern Cambodia on April thirtieth. Fiona and Reuben joined in peaceful demonstrations on campus, calling for an end to the conflict.

Eddie Mays, head of the campus chapter of the SDS, monitored the news broadcasts from the Student Union building. On Saturday, May second, he announced that a group of students at Kent State University in Ohio had buried a copy of the United States Constitution, claiming that Nixon had killed it. Later that day, the Kent State ROTC building was set on fire. The Ohio governor ordered the National Guard sent to the city.

"I'm afraid of violence," Reuben confided in Fiona.

"I think it's already turned violent at Kent State," she replied.

"I mean here. I don't trust Eddie."

Fiona shivered. "Neither do I."

On Monday, May fourth, Fiona and Reuben watched in disbelief as events at Kent State unfolded in front of their eyes on the Student Union television. Shortly before noon, the National Guard used tear gas on a crowd that refused to disperse. Their action sent a volley of rocks toward the Guard from the protesters, who chanted, "Pigs off campus!"

The Guardsmen, with bayonets fixed on their rifles, advanced upon the protesters. They confronted the students, shooting and killing four and injuring nine. Two of the four students killed had participated in the protest. The other two had been walking from one class to the next at the time of their deaths.

Eddie Mays addressed the student body.

"We must join in solidarity with other colleges and universities across the country and strike," he shouted from the second-floor balcony. "Our aim is nonviolence, but be aware that things could turn violent at any minute if our demands are not met. We will not sit by and watch Nixon and his pigs take over our country."

"*No violence!*" Reuben shouted from his seat on the main floor.

His statement was met with cheers of "Right on, brother!" and hands held high waving the peace sign.

A scowl crossed Eddie's face. Rarely were his commands challenged. He and his fellow SDS members thrust closed fists in the air. "Power to the people! *Strike now!*"

Fiona turned toward Reuben. "I'm so proud of you for standing up to that asshole," she whispered in his ear.

"Violence never solves anything," he replied.

What a Trip

The Moratorium to End the War in Vietnam, begun the previous October, promoted the idea of a general strike on the fifteenth of every month until the war ended. Enthusiasm for the cause waned over the winter, but the Kent State shootings rekindled the fire. Protests and strikes were staged at more than 450 college and high school campuses across the country. A demonstration in Washington was planned for Saturday, May ninth.

"We have to go to DC," Reuben announced on Tuesday. "We did our thing in New York and here, but it's time we take a stand in a big way."

The intensity of the last few days unnerved Fiona. "How would we get there? Where would we stay? What if it turns violent?"

"It already has turned violent. Innocent people are getting killed on our soil. No more back-seat protests. Think of the stories we'll have to tell our grandchildren."

Grandchildren? Was Reuben committing to a lifelong relationship or speaking of grandchildren in general? Fiona wondered as she stared into space without responding.

Caught up in the excitement of the moment, Reuben failed to notice her silence. "Listen, lassie, we talked about hitchhiking. This is our chance. The school's on strike. We could leave Thursday morning, get to DC that night, hang out on Friday, and march on Saturday. How 'bout it?"

"Well, it would be an adventure," she said hesitantly.

"I've got it all figured out. My friend Jeremy's at Georgetown University. I called him, and he said we could crash at his pad. We could take a bus home on Sunday and be back for class on Monday. What d'ya say?"

Fiona remembered Reuben telling her about the affair he'd had with Jeremy's mother and how she had been the one who introduced him to sex. Did Jeremy know about the affair? What would he think of Fiona? How would she compare with Reuben's past girlfriends? She debated whether or not to bring it up, eventually deciding to keep it to herself.

"Hey, Fiona?"

"Oh, sorry. I was just weighing the pros and cons. Definitely more cons than pros, but what the hell. I'm in," she said with a forced smile.

He nuzzled her ear and whispered, "You're the best."

"So are you." She planted a soft kiss on his cheek, pushing her insecurities aside. She thought about saying, "I love you," but held back. She wasn't about to say it without hearing it from Reuben first.

Chapter 40

Reuben borrowed a sleeping bag and knapsack. They packed light—a change of clothes, toothbrushes, Dr. Bronner's peppermint soap that would double as toothpaste, a road map, some snacks, and a thermos of water. Fiona wanted to bring her makeup but knew the demonstration was not a place for vanity. Reuben had seen her without makeup and would have to understand.

Hitching a ride was simple enough in town. Two guys Fiona recognized from campus took them as far as the entrance to the interstate.

"Wish we could take you the whole way, but we've got jobs in town. Here, take this for luck." The guy in the passenger seat handed Reuben a joint. "Show those pigs we mean business."

"Thanks," Reuben said.

Fiona's legs wobbled as she walked along the shoulder of the entrance ramp. The situation had become all too real. What if some wacko picked them up? What if they got busted for the joint?

"Wait a minute," Reuben said, moving into the brush on the side of the road. "I don't feel right about hitchin' with a joint. Better smoke it before we get started."

Fiona had thought about throwing it away. Reuben's idea was much better.

Ten minutes later they were back on the road, giddy and ready to begin their trip.

"Hold your arm like this." Reuben held his right arm straight at his side, thumb pointing out. "We've gotta look hip, like we've done this a million times."

It wasn't long before an eighteen-wheeler pulled to the side of the road. "Let me get in first in case the driver's a pervert," Reuben said.

What have I gotten myself into? Fiona thought as she pulled herself into the cab.

He was a large man with a belly that competed for space with the steering wheel. Wisps of colorless hair poked from under a red cap that read GUARDIAN TRUCKING. Bloodshot blue eyes peered out between layers of unshaven fat. "Where you folks headin?"

"DC, man," Reuben said.

"Ain't goin' that fur, but I'll take youse ta Harrisburg. From there, ya wanna get on eighty-three south."

"Works for us," Reuben replied.

Fiona nudged Reuben, whispering, "I thought we were going down ninety-five."

Reuben mouthed, *It's okay.*

Turning to the driver, he said, "I'm Rube, and this is Fee. Have a smoke?" He passed his open pack of Marlboros to their chauffeur.

Rube? Fee? Where did that come from?

"They call me Bug," the driver said, taking a cigarette. "Suppose youse are headin' to the demonstration."

"Right on." Reuben continued to play it cool.

"Me, I served in K'rea. Can't say's I like your long-haired

polly-ticks, but this here's still America. Got the right to free speech an' all."

Fiona worried Reuben would start a political argument with their driver, but he remained as neutral as someone with Reuben's convictions could be.

"I do the east—west run ev'ry week. Gives me lotsa thinkin' time. I consider m'self a highway philosopher. Here's what I gotta say." Bug paused as he downshifted.

"Back in my day, we was proud to serve our country. We was fightin' fur freedom, fur democracy, all that malarky. T'day, I ain't so sure what the fightin's about. I don't say that ta many folks, but seein' as you's headin' ta Washington, I'm bein' honest. I didn't like them National Guards shootin' innocent kids one bit."

"That's why we're marching," Reuben said, relieved at Bug's support.

"We got a coupla hours 'fore Harrisburg. Lemme tell ya 'bout my family. Gits kinda lonesome drivin' this rig. Open the glove box. Gotta scrapbook of the wife and kiddies."

The change of subject allowed them all to relax. Bug was rough around the edges by Fiona's standards but more intelligent than she'd given him credit for at the start of their trip. The three talked about family, friends, and travel. By the time they reached Harrisburg, Fiona was sorry to say good-bye.

"I'll be thinkin' a youse on Sat'day. Stay away from them Guardsmen, an' I'll look fur ya on TV." Bug slapped Reuben on the back as they said good-bye.

They managed to score two short rides through convoluted roadways, eventually getting dropped off near the entrance to the Pennsylvania Turnpike. It was nearly five o'clock. The trip had taken longer than expected.

"We've got about a hundred twenty-five miles to go. We need to find somebody going straight to DC. Otherwise, we're screwed," Reuben said. "I don't want to be out on the road at night, do you?"

"I told you we should have left earlier. If the cops don't get us, the bears will," Fiona fumed. She imagined the headlines: "College Students Dead on Interstate," "Young Couple Found Brutally Beaten," "Bears Attack Hitchhikers."

"Don't worry, lassie. We'll be fine," Reuben said.

"And what if we're not? What if nobody picks us up?"

"Are you kidding me? There have to be thousands of people like us on their way to DC." Reuben's pep talk was as much for him as it was for Fiona.

No amount of arguing would change their situation. Instead, she began visualizing someone coming to their rescue.

After about thirty minutes, a blue-and-white Volkswagen van pulled to the side of the road. Garish geometric neon designs decorated the sides of the vehicle. A giant peace sign obscured the rear window.

"We're saved!" Reuben shouted. "C'mon!"

As they jumped into the side door of the van, they were hit with the overpowering stench of unwashed bodies laced with incense and hashish. The driver, a young, lanky guy wearing a red bandana around black frizzy hair, turned and said, "Welcome to our pad. Where you cats headin'?"

"DC, man," Reuben replied. "What about you?"

What a Trip

"Maryland Line, 'bout fifty miles. Make yourselves at home." He pulled into traffic without checking the rearview mirror.

Fiona wondered if she could endure the stench for that long.

Reuben tried breaking the ice. "I'm Reuben, and this is Fiona." Rube and Fee stayed behind in Bug's eighteen-wheeler.

The guy in the passenger seat, a carbon copy of the driver, turned to them. "Far out. Got any smokes?"

Reuben relinquished his pack of Marlboros.

Fiona checked out the rest of the passengers. Two girls looking no older than sixteen had pushed themselves into the back corner of the van, oblivious to everything happening around them. A glassy-eyed older couple leaned against the back of the front seats. Another guy lay on his side staring at the roof, which was covered with a tie-dyed sheet. Each wore a tie-dyed shirt and filthy, frayed jeans. Empty soda cans, half-eaten bags of potato chips, and plastic bags of what looked like granola provided texture to the knapsacks, sleeping bags, and blankets that littered the floor.

No one introduced themselves. No one spoke. A top-forty radio station played softly in the background. Fiona and Reuben huddled together, unsure of what to say or do.

After about fifteen minutes, the driver spoke. "Lemme tell you somethin', man. Where we're goin', there's not a whole lot happenin'. It won't be easy scorin' a ride this time a day, and you don't wanna be on the highway at night. Not safe."

Fiona felt the knot in her stomach getting larger by the minute.

Reuben glanced at her anxiously, then turned to the driver. "Got any suggestions?"

"Yeah, man. Come with us. We're headin' for a happenin'. Junior, tell 'em."

The reclining passenger, presumably Junior, sat up. "Sorry for the silence. We're savin' our energy for the weekend. You cats are cool, so I'll tell you what's happenin', and then you can decide what ya wanna do."

Fiona and Reuben relaxed for the moment.

"We're as fired up, as pissed off as you. We've got a different way of handlin' things. We're stagin' our own protest, more of a ceremony. See, we're into Wicca. Ever hear of it?"

"Sure, my best friend's into it. I read tarot cards." Fiona had read Reuben's cards many times and had discussed her concerns about Melissa's experimentation with the occult.

"We're part of a coven from Philly," Junior continued. "We're meetin' the rest of our members and cats from two other covens at this park near the Maryland border. Tonight's just a gatherin'. For the next coupla days, we're callin' on the powers o' the universe to stop the killin'."

"Heavy," Reuben said.

"If we go to DC, our energy'll be mixed with protesters, pigs, and politicians. We need to be at least fifty miles, but no more than a hundred, from the center o' things to be effective, so this Maryland Line place is perfect."

"Can we crash there for the night?" Reuben asked.

"Yeah, man, but we can't invite you to be part o' our ritual. Guess you know, a coven's limited to twelve, plus the high priest or priestess. I'm the high priest of ours," Junior explained. "What coven does your friend belong to?"

"None right now. She's just getting into Wicca. We went to Harry's Occult Shop last fall."

"Did ya meet Lou?"

"He waited on us," Fiona said. She had to be careful how

much she revealed, not wanting Reuben to know about her special oils.

"Righteous dude," Junior said before lying back down.

The van left the interstate, continued along a country road for about half an hour, and eventually pulled into a wooded picnic grove. They headed to the rear of the park and located the other members of their coven. The girls in the back of the van came to life, threw a few handfuls of granola into their mouths, and gathered up their gear.

Junior was the first to exit the vehicle. He stood at soft attention, supervising the unloading of passengers and supplies. "It don't look like you two thought about food," he said.

"We thought we'd eat once we got to DC," Reuben replied. "Never expected the trip to take two days."

"We have a bag of Fritos," Fiona said.

"Keep your Fritos," Junior replied. "We'll feed ya. Next time you meet somebody who's hungry, feed them. It's all about balance in the universe."

Fiona felt her shoulders relax as she grasped the new concept. "Thank you."

"Yeah, thanks, man. We really appreciate everything," Reuben agreed.

The coven members set up tents and built a campfire. Fiona wondered if the group would be eating any special foods, but they had brought standard picnic fare: potato and macaroni salad, burgers, hot dogs, cans of baked beans, two cases of Budweiser, and a case of Boone's Farm apple wine. To Fiona, the group appeared normal except for their lack of conversation. What were they planning for the weekend, and more importantly, what would happen that night? She couldn't wait to tell Melissa everything the next time they were together.

Reuben, too, was unusually quiet. He sat smoking on a picnic bench. Fiona finished what she was doing and joined him.

"I am so sorry I got us into this mess," he began. "I would never, ever, intentionally do anything to put you in danger. We should've taken a bus."

"Yeah, we should have." Fiona knew there was no point in continuing the argument. She still resented Reuben for talking her into hitchhiking. "But it all turned out okay."

"But what if it hadn't? What if we were still on the highway and something happened to you? I could never forgive myself."

This was a softer, gentler side of Reuben. Her anger faded as she put her arm around him and kissed his cheek.

He stared into her moist green eyes. "I-I love you, Fiona."

Fiona was speechless.

"I've never said that to anyone before."

She kissed him, softening her lips to allow the words to slide out. "I love you too."

They laughed as the remaining tension melted away. They forgot about their circumstances and decided to enjoy their special moment.

The coven scattered to several picnic tables and invited Fiona and Reuben to join them. The meal was uneventful, conversation minimal. After dinner, which included generous paper cups of wine, Junior said the group had work to do, and politely asked Fiona and Reuben to make themselves scarce.

They washed and brushed as best they could in the public restrooms. Fiona knew her hair and clothes were filthy. The night was too chilly to sleep naked, and she was concerned about sharing their small sleeping bag. Would he still love her in her present condition? She was determined there would be no sex until she could take a proper shower.

Too wound up to sleep, they sat on their sleeping bag and watched the coven from a distance. The group stood in a circle with Junior at the center. They swayed and chanted softly, the flames from the campfire reflecting off their tie-dyed shirts, creating mystical shapes of light and color.

Junior approached one of the young girls and pulled her shirt over her head. He bent to lick her breasts and ran his hands along her ribcage. He reached for the other girl and did the same. The three began dancing as one, bodies coming closer as clothing disappeared. Junior motioned for the girls to lie on a blanket near the campfire. He mounted one, then the other as the group continued their chanting.

Fiona and Reuben stared, mesmerized by the surrealistic events. They lay on top of their sleeping bag, forgetting the chill, forgetting the dirt of the road, never taking their eyes off the scene unfolding nearby. It wasn't long before they followed Junior's lead.

After Junior finished with the girls, the members of the coven removed their clothing and joined in a circle again. They danced, chanted, and two by two, made their way to the tents.

Only Junior and the girls remained standing by the fire. He smiled and nodded to Fiona and Reuben as the girls bent to lick his erection. The three sank to the ground and disappeared from view.

A cool wind brought Fiona and Reuben back to reality. They dressed quickly and climbed into their sleeping bag. The ground was hard and bumpy, the bag too small for two bodies. In spite of their discomfort, they fell into a sound sleep.

A lion roared, then another. Fiona tried pulling herself from the sleeping bag but realized the zipper was locked. She kicked and kicked again. The lions were coming closer, the roaring more urgent. They were going to eat her for breakfast, and Reuben for lunch.

Her eyes snapped open, assaulted by the morning sun. Reuben lay next to her, still asleep. She lifted her head to search for the roar that traveled with her from dream to daylight. Motorcycles!

Six motorcycles were parked in the next picnic grove with more on the way. She nudged Reuben awake.

"What the fuck?" Reuben said as he sat up.

"I think it's the rest of Junior's group," she replied. "I wonder what time it is."

"I don't know. This might be our cue to split."

Fiona agreed. They gathered their belongings and headed for the restrooms.

"What was that all about last night?" Reuben asked. "One of the weirdest things I've ever seen, but what a turn-on."

"It was like watching a live porno movie. I really got off on it," Fiona agreed. "I think it had something to do with their ritual.

When we get home, I'm gonna ask Melissa about it. If anybody would know, it'd be her."

"I can't stop thinking about those chicks sucking Junior's dick. How 'bout a quickie in one of the stalls before we leave?"

The idea that someone might walk in on them added to her excitement. "Can we leave the door open?" she asked.

"Even better." He grabbed her hand, and the two ran to the restroom.

In spite of not being seen, their lovemaking energized them. They washed quickly and made their way to the main road. Within a few minutes, a pickup truck offered them a ride to the interstate, provided they didn't mind sitting in the truck bed. They finished the bag of Fritos and graciously thanked the driver when he dropped them off.

A couple in their mid-thirties stopped for them within a few minutes. Fiona and Reuben climbed into the back seat of a late-model Ford Fairlane.

"Thank you very much," Reuben said as they got in.

"I assume you're heading for the rally in Washington," the driver said.

"Yes, sir," Fiona replied. She hoped her good manners would make up for her disheveled appearance.

"Thought so. That's where we're heading. My name is Charles, and this is my wife, Victoria."

"Call me Vicky." She turned and smiled. "I can't imagine how you two ended up in the middle of nowhere at this time of morning."

Reuben gave them a synopsis of their journey, without mentioning the campfire orgy.

"You must be exhausted—and starving. Have some fruit." Vicky passed an insulated bag to the back seat.

"Thank you." Fiona wanted to eat everything in the bag but politely held back.

"We're professors in the Chemistry Department at Penn State," Charles told them. "I'm absolutely appalled at what's been happening to our country. Kent State was the last straw. We canceled our classes and encouraged our students to join the protests on campus and in Washington. Now, tell me where exactly you're going."

"We're staying with my friend who's at Georgetown. He lives in the Adams Morgan section of the city," Reuben said.

"We know the area well. Great restaurants." Turning to her husband, Vicky said, "I think we can take these kids to their friend's place. What d'you say?"

"Yup. Anything to help the cause. You two have had enough adventures on this trip."

You have no idea, Fiona thought, relaxing into the back seat.

"We'll never forget you guys," Reuben said.

"Just so you know, we're taking the bus home," Fiona said.

Fiona and Reuben did their best to engage in conversation but soon fell asleep.

After what seemed like hours, Vicky nudged them awake. "I think your friend lives somewhere around here."

They found themselves on a hilly street lined with three-story brick row houses, each with a long cement staircase leading to the front door.

"Don't give up the cause," Charles said before dropping them off.

"We can't. Our lives depend on it," Reuben replied. "Maybe we'll see you tomorrow. Thanks again, man."

Reuben pulled out a hand-drawn map from the knapsack. "We're a coupla blocks from Jeremy's pad. We are so fuckin' lucky."

"Somebody's watching over us. Maybe Junior and his coven." Fiona laughed, secretly wondering if last night's ceremony had anything to do with today's luck.

"I hope Jeremy's home. He expected us last night, y'know."

They followed the map to a run-down five-story apartment building. A bodega, pizzeria, and florist occupied the ground floor.

The aroma of pizza blended with undertones of dirty feet and mold as they entered the building. Dust balls and paper shards littered the stairs on their way to the third floor. An envelope with "Reuben" written on it was taped to the door of apartment 3-H. Paint chips attached themselves to the tape as Reuben released it.

He read: "Hey, Rube. What the fuck happened? Thought you'd be here last night. Hope you're OK. I'm staying with my girlfriend tonight & tomorrow. Didn't think you'd mind. Use my bed. If you see my roommate, introduce yourself. Let's meet Saturday noon at the reflecting pool. Key's under the mat. J"

"Son of a bitch." Reuben shook his head as he hunted for the key. "This is so Jeremy."

Relief circulated through Fiona's body. No Jeremy today. Maybe no Jeremy tomorrow.

She kept her feelings inside, saying, "Why don't we drop our stuff off and get some pizza. I'm starving."

"Sounds good to me. Then I'm definitely taking a shower." Reuben unlocked the door.

Why are most guys such slobs? Fiona wondered as they stepped over old newspapers, textbooks, and a half-eaten box of popcorn. The place smelled like a garbage dump.

Reuben opened the window, hoping to send the odor of rotting food into the street. "Jeremy grew up with a maid. I don't think he ever learned how to clean up after himself. Why don't we get rid of this trash on our way back down?"

Pizza, a shower, and a nap did wonders for them. They spent the rest of the day and evening exploring Adams Morgan, enjoying the ethnic diversity of the area. They agreed on an early dinner at an Ethiopian restaurant, after which they returned to Jeremy's apartment for a quiet evening.

Chapter 41

It was easy enough to hitch a ride out of Adams Morgan toward the capital area, where the protests were taking place. The closer they came to the National Mall, the more congested traffic became. They thanked the driver, a young man on his way to work, and joined the thousands of marchers making their way toward the Mall, chanting, "Hell no, we won't go!" and "Peace now!"

They learned that President Nixon had made a surprise visit to the Lincoln Memorial in the early hours of the morning. No one was quite sure of the president's motives. Some said he wanted to show his Cuban valet the Lincoln Memorial at night. Others thought Nixon had too much to drink and wanted to get to know the students on a more personal level. Still others said it was an attempt to explain his recent actions on Vietnam as motivated by a desire for peace.

"Bet you anything he was drunk," Reuben said. "I would've dug seeing him, but after everything that happened in Maryland, I'm happier we had a decent place to sleep."

"Me too," Fiona said, secretly wishing they had been there for the experience.

Even though the demonstration was a spontaneous response

to the Kent State shootings earlier in the week, it was remarkably well organized. Police circled the White House with buses to block the demonstrators from getting too close. That didn't stop thousands from gathering on the Ellipse in President's Park.

The rally was like all rallies they had attended—masses of passionate young people marching for their lives, carrying standard-issue handmade posters calling for an end to war. Fiona felt a sadder theme in the air this day as the protesters remembered the killing of four and the wounding of nine innocent students on May fourth. Raised voices and signs shouted, "NEVER FORGET KENT STATE," "NATIONAL GUARD—KILLERS," "IMPEACH NIXON," and "NIXON—THE NEXT HITLER."

Fiona and Reuben were carried in a wave through the throngs, chanting and singing antiwar anthems. At the National Mall, hundreds, maybe thousands, of topless men and women cooled their emotions in the waters of the Reflecting Pool while the Washington Monument and Lincoln Memorial stood as silent observers.

"Did Jeremy really think we'd find each other in this crowd? I bet he's not even here. Some friend," Reuben said.

"Why do you think we both have such messed-up friends?" Fiona asked, thinking of Melissa. "What's that saying about us?"

Reuben thought for a moment. "That we're too nice. Too tolerant. C'mon, let's go for a swim."

Fiona worried for a moment about what the water would do to her hair. Once she flashed back to the last forty-eight hours, she laughed, ran ahead of Reuben, and jumped into the pool. She relished her newfound freedom, giving no thought to her appearance or worrying that her parents might see her on television.

Feeling exhilarated after their spontaneous swim, they grabbed two hot dogs from a pushcart and found a place to sit at the edge of the Mall away from the crowds.

Reuben turned toward Fiona with a somber expression. "This whole thing is so bizarre. What does splashing around in the Reflecting Pool have to do with stopping the war?"

"Absolutely nothing," she said, echoing his serious tone. "It also has nothing to do with the Kent State killings."

"It's kinda disrespectful, but it's even more disrespectful to kill innocent students and send guys to fight a needless war."

"Good point. I bet Nixon and my parents won't get the connection," Fiona said.

"We had some real adventures on this trip. For a while, I almost forgot why we came to DC. I'm gonna be drafted in a little over a year. I can guarantee you this shit won't be over by then." He put his arm around her and kissed her wet hair.

"When I said 'I love you' yesterday, I really meant it," Reuben said. "What's gonna happen to us if I go to Canada, or if something goes wrong and I don't get there?"

"We've got a year to plan. I'm sure we can work things out." Her outward confidence masked her inner fears and insecurities. What if he asked her to go to Canada? What if he didn't?

"Would you, I mean, d'you think you would go to Canada with me?"

The remnants of Fiona's hot dog reversed their downward direction, choking off her response.

"I know it's a lot to ask, Fiona, and I know it's a long way off, but it's something we need to think about."

His quick comeback saved her from having to answer him. Instead, she reached for his face and kissed him deeply.

"I love you," he said for the second time.

This time she was quick to respond. "I love you too. I'm sure we can work it out."

His shoulders relaxed as hers tightened. Adulthood was knocking. Would she open the door or run and hide?

Their attention shifted as a group of protesters ran past them, blowing out patriotic songs on kazoos.

"What the fuck was that?" Reuben laughed, grabbed her hand, and pulled her to stand.

"Let's see where they go." Fiona laughed too, grateful for an end to their serious conversation. They followed the musicians through the National Mall and rejoined the day's events.

Before they left the rally, they added their names to the giant Petition for Peace: WE, THE UNDERSIGNED, PROTEST THE US INVASION OF CAMBODIA AND THE RESUMPTION OF BOMBING OF NORTH VIETNAM.

Neither Jeremy nor his roommate came back to the apartment that night, much to Fiona's relief. She and Reuben chose an Indian restaurant for dinner and ordered extra naan for breakfast. They had sex in every room of the apartment, including the missing roommate's bedroom, fell into a deep sleep, and caught the bus home the following morning.

Chapter 42

Fiona called Melissa on Monday and gave her a brief run-down of her weekend adventure. She downplayed the rally in Washington, knowing her friend would be more interested in Junior and their time in the park.

"See what you can learn about sex and Wicca," Fiona asked. "I'm dying to find out what that coven was up to."

"Sure thing. Hey, I got a letter from Peach."

"Me too. How about we wait till I come home, and we can read them together," Fiona said.

"Cool. See you Saturday."

"What do you think they were up to in Maryland?" Fiona asked Melissa the following Saturday.

The girls had picked up bagels and coffee and were enjoying a morning in the park.

"Well, from what I read, it's sex magic," Melissa said.

"It didn't look like magic to me. It looked like two young chicks going down on a guy named Junior."

"Listen, it wasn't about that Junior cat using witchcraft to get laid like we did," Melissa explained.

"Speak for yourself, Lissie. All I did was use those oils from Harry's. You're the one who did the ritual."

"Whatever. You told me the coven was there to cast a spell to stop the war. The sex part was to make sure it worked. In Wicca, they believe sex is the most creative energy on earth. Sex before a ritual adds intensity. That Junior dude was the high priest of the coven, so it was important for him to be the one who did it."

"I've heard all kinds of tricks guys use to get laid, but this is a new one," Fiona said.

"C'mon, Fee. Get over your mother's bullshit. This is real. It's not about getting off on the sex. Everything in the universe has an opposite. Y'know, yin and yang, good and evil."

Fiona was beginning to understand. "So it was about uniting the mind and body by bringing the male and female together?"

"Exactly. Sex magic is a total mind-body experience. Wicca believes there's no better way to focus your mind than through sex. It elevates the spirit 'cause you're totally present. It's about planting the seeds of your thoughts into the cosmos. In one book they talked about creating the magical child."

"So when I screwed some of those creeps, I was still creating positive energy in the universe."

Fiona's remark did not sit well with Melissa. "Sex is sacred in Wicca. If it's not coming from a place of love, then it loses its power."

"I doubt Junior and those chicks were in love," Fiona said.

"You're thinking of romantic love. This is universal love."

"Why didn't the whole coven do it? Why did they just take their clothes off?" Fiona asked.

"Wicca calls it sky-clad when you take your clothes off to enhance a ritual. It's supposed to bring you closer to the power of the earth's energy. They wanted to connect with Junior but not take the attention away from him since he's the high priest."

"Geez. I had no idea," Fiona said. "You really know your shit. Do you think you'd ever join a coven?"

"I'd like to. I haven't met anybody who's into it. Scott digs it, but he says it's just from an intellectual perspective. You don't need a coven to practice Wicca."

"Aren't you worried it might backfire on you? What about black magic?" Fiona asked.

"As long as I'm practicing in the light, no harm can come to me," Melissa said.

Fiona sensed an aura of unease coming from her friend. "Are you sure? I don't know much, but I do know about black magic and the tarot."

"I didn't want to freak you out since you were right there with that coven, but yeah, there's a lot of sex in black magic."

"I knew it," Fiona said. "Whatever you do, please don't go there."

"I won't. I'm not stupid."

You may not be stupid, but you are gullible.

"Anyway, there's not a whole lot of difference with black magic. They use sex same as in Wicca. It's just that their rituals are more about gaining power or money. Sometimes it's about controlling somebody or something, like if they want to take possession of your soul."

Fiona shivered.

"Another difference is that the other person doesn't always know they're being used. Sometimes the black magician steals the other person's sexual energy. The other person might go crazy or even die."

Fiona's mother had warned her for years about the Devil. Could she have been right? Were there really evil forces in the world that would take possession of your soul? She had heard enough.

"You're freaking me out. Let's read our letters from Peach."

Peach had used a sheet of carbon paper to type the same letter to both girls.

"Talk about lazy," Fiona said. "I guess we should be glad she wrote. It's been a few months since we heard from her."

The last time Peach had written was in January. She and Calvin were in Austin, Texas, where Calvin had scored a few gigs playing guitar at local blues clubs. She promised to write once they got settled.

These letters were postmarked San Francisco but included no return address.

Dear Lissie and Fee,

Here we are in Frisco, just like we talked about. What a far out place. Nobody but hippies life here. Calvin knows this drummer and we've been crashing at his pad. The cat does lots of studio work in LA. He hooked Calvin up with his agent. Now ~~onxe~~ once a week Calvin drives to LA for studio work. Ive been going with him but now I got a job at UCSF Medical Cenbter. ITs a teaching hospital and I can get my RN.

Next week were moving to our own place. ITs a studio in a old building on Waller Street and its not too far from Buna Vista Park. We're ~~taljing~~ talking about having a kid. A little coco baby.

Peopel are cool here about white and blacks couples and hav-
ing bab~~y~~ies. They dont even care if you get married.Its my
kind of town.

Sorry about the mesy typing. I miss you chicks and I'll write
again and give ~~yoi~~ you my address.

Luv, Peach

"Wow!" both girls said in unison. As if on cue, they each reached for their pack of cigarettes, lighting up as they processed the news.

"She never had a boyfriend in high school, and now she's gonna have a kid," Fiona said.

"Yeah, but she didn't have any spells put on her like I did. She'll be a good mommy. I'd be a good mommy too, if I had the chance."

This was not the time for Fiona to remind Melissa about her abortion less than a year ago.

"I couldn't even think about a kid right now. My dad would freak if I left school. Even though my mom's strung out on her pills, she'd still kill me. And forget about Reuben. That's the last thing he wants."

"Scott never talks about kids," Melissa said. "I think about them a lot."

"You guys just got together. It's way too soon for a kid."

"Yeah, but look at Peachie," Melissa said.

"Yeah, look at her." Fiona did her best to hide her envy.

Chapter **43**

"**T**his has been an emotionally and politically charged year," Dr. Hacking, Fiona's art professor, began. "I think you all are aware of my political leanings. I'm not asking you to believe as I do. I am asking you to put your personal feelings about this past year into your final project for the semester."

Fiona snapped out of her daydream of moving to San Francisco.

"I'm challenging you to think big. Get yourself the biggest canvas you feel comfortable with and go to town. Today's events are tomorrow's history. Keep that in mind. I suggest you work in acrylic. Any questions?"

Fiona's only question was, *When can I begin?* Her creative juices were flowing faster than her mind and hand could follow. Bright, dripping swaths of color depicting the protesters in Washington, bathers in the Reflecting Pool, and an impressionistic rendering of the now-famous photo of the female student kneeling next to a Kent State victim. She imagined her work fifty years in the future, serving as a reminder of a country in mourning.

"This is my chance to make a real difference," she told Reuben at dinner. "I had the art store downtown stretch out a five-by-eight-foot canvas for me. It'll be ready tomorrow. I'm putting my heart and soul into this."

"That's my girl. I'm so proud of you. You know you're the star of the Art Department." For once, Reuben's words of encouragement weren't necessary.

She showed him her preliminary sketches and explained how she would lay out the canvas. "This is gonna be my *Mona Lisa*. You just wait."

Once she ran out of steam, Reuben shared his good news. "You know Barry's graduating next month, right?" Reuben was referring to the editor of *The Beacon*. "Well, he asked me to take over for him, starting this summer. Can you imagine? Me, editor of the school's literary magazine?"

"That's so exciting. Congratulations! You'll turn out the best magazine ever." She paused. "Are you going to summer school?"

"Yup. That's what I wanted to talk to you about. I decided to go to school this summer, and I'm thinking you might wanna go too."

"Oh, wow! I never thought about it." Fiona had anticipated a solitary summer at home. Peach was long gone. Melissa was going back to full-time work at the hospital. Her mom expected her to return to her job at the Methodist summer camp. If she was lucky, she'd have a few stolen moments with Reuben.

"I've got it all figured out. We can keep our campus jobs and take up to twelve credits. If I go to summer school, I get to be editor of *The Beacon*; otherwise, they might pick somebody else. And the best part is we get to be together."

"What do I tell my parents? They might be pissed at spending the extra money," Fiona worried.

"I got that figured out too. You tell them you can graduate a semester early if you go this summer and part of next summer."

"I guess I could," Fiona speculated. "I'd love to spend our summer together. Won't you have more credits than you need to graduate?"

"Okay, hear me out. You know I'm gonna get drafted a little over a year from now. I don't see any alternative except Canada. I've been looking into grad school at the University of Toronto. They've got a creative writing program that looks really cool. If I'm *The Beacon* editor and take some extra writing courses over the summer, I might have a shot at getting in."

Fiona's mood flattened as she thought of her life without Reuben. "But what about, what about—"

"What about us, lassie?"

She nodded.

"I can't tell you what to do, but here's what I was thinking. Toronto has a great Art History Department. I know you don't want to teach, so I thought if you took some extra art courses over the summer, you might be able to finish school up there. You'd probably lose some credits, but you'd get the degree you want, and we'd be together."

"I-I—this is a lot to take in." Her mind raced as she attempted to put this alternative reality into place. In a few minutes, their conversation had gone from mundane to monumental. He was asking her to leave her life, her remaining friends, her parents, her country, her home, and her education—all with no future guarantee.

"Maybe I dumped too much on you. I probably should've waited for another day and just left it with your artwork and my writing. I'm sorry," Reuben apologized.

"I keep pretending next year won't happen. That's no good either," Fiona said.

"You know for me there's no alternative. You've got choices. You're almost twenty years old. Time to start making your own decisions, not the ones your parents make for you. All I ask is that you think about it."

"I will," she said.

He squeezed her hand. "I love you. I just want us to be together."

"I love you too." *One of these days I'll get the nerve to say it first.*

Back in her room, she turned on the radio. "Leaving on a Jet Plane," sung by Peter, Paul, and Mary, came on after a commercial break. She had always been drawn to the lyrics of lost love, never thinking it might happen to her.

Reuben wouldn't be leaving on a jet plane, but he would be leaving. So much could happen in a year. The war could be over, the draft ended. He might change his mind about Canada. Or about her. She never had a relationship last more than a year. They were in month eight. The summer could bring an end to everything. If she didn't go to summer school, he might forget about her.

Was their relationship so unstable that she needed to be in his life for the entire summer? Was she so passive that she had to follow his every suggestion? She needed to think things through. To weigh both sides of the issue.

How mature of me, she thought, hoping she wouldn't be motivated entirely by insecurity.

Chapter 44

An envelope from Dr. Hacking sat in her mailbox. It read simply, "See me during office hours on Wednesday." He was her instructor and her boss at her job in the Art Department. Was he firing her? Failing her? What had she done wrong?

It was only Tuesday morning. Twenty-four hours until she would learn her fate.

Here goes, Fiona thought as she tentatively knocked on Dr. Hacking's door.

He welcomed her into his office. "Have a seat, Fiona," he said.

Sitting kept her knees from buckling. She clasped her hands in her lap to keep them from trembling.

"I'm sure you know you're my top student," he said.

"I-I am?"

"You mean you don't know? Just look at all you've accomplished this year. That's what I want to discuss with you."

"Thank you," she whispered.

"Don't thank me. Thank yourself. Three things—first, I see you're an education major with a minor in art. That's a big mistake. You've got too much talent to spend your life in a classroom unless it's at university level."

"My parents are making me major in education. They said it's the best career choice for a girl."

"Fiona, that's something you'll have to work out with them. I strongly suggest you think about other options. I'd like to discuss this further, but today is just about planting the seed. Second, I'm teaching three symposia over the summer that I thought might interest you," he said, handing her a flyer.

She read the course descriptions. "Chiaroscuro: The Art of Light and Dark," "Painting in the Style of Picasso," and "The Impressionistic Landscape." All courses were by invitation only.

"Wow!" was all she could get out.

"I thought you'd be especially interested in 'The Impressionistic Landscape,' which brings me to the third reason for today's meeting. I've been watching the progress on your final project. I know you've got more work to do, but I've arranged to have it hung above the fireplace in the Student Union building. I hope you don't mind."

Fiona's hand pressed against her mouth to keep from crying. She knew she should thank him. Instead, she sat and stared at a pile of papers on his desk.

"You don't mind, do you?" he asked again.

"Huh?" She snapped back to reality. "No, I don't mind. I'm just—"

He laughed. "One final word. If you do plan on summer school, we could sure use your help in the office."

Fiona stood, regaining some of her composure. "Thank you so much for everything." For once, she believed her life would work out.

After her meeting with Dr. Hacking, Fiona called her parents to let them know she wanted to enroll in summer school. She discussed the courses, the opportunity for employment, and finally the news about her painting. Before her mom had a chance to argue, her dad jumped in to congratulate her and said summer school sounded like an excellent idea.

It was almost as though her dad didn't want her to come home. Was he protecting her from her mom? Or were there other things going on that he didn't want her to know about? Ever since her mom hit her, her dad had been more understanding and more in her corner.

Not only would she and Reuben be able to spend most of their summer together, but she would also be studying topics unavailable during the regular school year and earning more money than she would have if she'd worked at the Methodist summer camp.

Chapter 45

The summer of 1970 was markedly calmer than the previous year. When Fiona came home between summer sessions, she spent time with Melissa and Scott, who were settling into a close relationship. She could see that Scott was a positive influence on her friend. The stability of a relationship and a job seemed to ground her.

Even though the girls didn't spend as much time together as they had in the past, their friendship bond was strong. They were getting older and didn't feel the need to share the minute details of their lives with one another.

In July the two decided it was time for each of them to buy a car. Fiona had saved enough money to buy a new Volkswagen Beetle. Melissa was about halfway to her goal. Her new stepfather offered to cosign a loan to help her pay for the other half. She, too, had her eye on a Beetle.

They visited the showroom together to pick out their cars. Fiona chose a medium green to match her eyes; Melissa a dark blue to match hers. Special features, including radios, were out of the question. The cars were bare-bones, but the girls didn't care. They now had reliable transportation and a greater degree of freedom.

Fiona proudly drove her Beetle to college for her third summer session. Reuben's parents had given him their old 1964 Dodge Coronet.

"Look at us," Reuben laughed. "Just like that, we're a two-car family."

Family? Is that a hint? Fiona wondered.

A few days later, Reuben asked Fiona to meet him at the Student Union, saying he had something important to show her.

"I finally got it," he began.

"Got what?" Fiona loved surprises.

"This." He handed her a thin paperback, *Manual for Draft-Age Immigrants to Canada*, by Mark Satin. "I actually got it a coupla days ago, but I wanted to read through it before I showed it to you. This Satin cat tells you everything you need to know about emigrating to Canada."

This wasn't the kind of surprise Fiona was expecting. She tentatively fanned through the book, noticing earmarked pages and highlighted paragraphs. Yesterday's future had become today's present.

"He talks about applying for immigrant status at the border. He says it's the quickest method, but I'm kinda nervous about doing that. What if they turn me down? Then what?"

"Wouldn't it be better to pretend you're a visitor? Then, once you're in, you can tell them you want to stay," Fiona suggested.

"That might be my last resort. What I really want to do is apply for a student entry certificate. The book says that graduate education is expanding and fellowship money for grad students is available after a year, especially in Ontario." Reuben flipped to an earmarked page and handed the book to Fiona.

She kept her head down and pretended to read. When she raised her head to look at Reuben, all she could say was, "This is for real, isn't it?"

"Damn straight," he replied. "Lemme tell you what I'm gonna do. When we're done with summer school, I'm gonna go to the Canadian consulate in Manhattan and talk to them about my options. I'm also going to the Princeton Draft Resisters Union and maybe to the draft counseling service in Montclair. In the meantime, I'm gonna write a letter to this war immigrant thing in Ontario."

He showed Fiona information about the agencies in his book. "Will you come with me? I want you to be a part of this process. I don't want any secrets between us."

"Sure, I'll go with you." Fiona touched his arm in a gesture of support. She was doing her best to remain calm. She told herself again that anything could happen in the next ten months.

"This is for both of us," he said. "If you're gonna come with me, you'll need to know all this shit too. Not that I'm pressuring you or anything."

"You know, Reuben, this is a lot of pressure." Fiona surprised herself by allowing her thoughts to become loud words.

Reuben, too, was surprised by Fiona's outburst. He leaned back into the couch and laughed.

She felt the urge to smack him across his mouth, another surprise reaction. Why was he laughing at her?

"Oh, I'm sorry," he managed to get out while still laughing. "It's just—it's just—"

"Just what?"

He caught his breath. With a huge smile on his face, he turned to her. "I always thought redheads were hot-tempered. You are so far from that stereotype. You never get pissed. I don't think I've ever heard you raise your voice or disagree with anything I say. This is the first time, and well, it's refreshing."

"Refreshing? You like that I got mad at you? I don't get it."

"Listen, I don't want us to fight—ever. You need to stand up for yourself and what you want. If you don't, the world's gonna walk all over you." Reuben put his arm around Fiona and drew her closer.

"We both know what a big deal this Canada thing is," Reuben went on. "I know it's not easy for you, and yeah, you should be pissed and freaked out. I've said it before. You know I don't have a choice. You do, and in a way, that's a tougher spot to be in."

"I'm glad you understand that," Fiona said, still miffed.

"All I ask is that you share the process with me. Come with me, do your own research, and if it feels right to you, I want you to join me."

"And what happens if I decide not to?" Fiona asked.

"Truthfully, I'd be heartbroken, but it's out of my control. I'd never force you to do anything you don't want to do," Reuben said.

"You know I want to be with you. Just please don't pressure me so much. Let me make up my own mind," she said.

"That's my girl." He kissed her cheek. "One way or another, we'll make it work."

Chapter 46

The early part of the fall semester proved to be as unremarkable as the summer. Fiona enrolled in her first "teaching of" course, as she referred to the courses designed for education majors. The class was an easy A and provided little substance.

Melissa, now in her second semester at the community college, was considering a major in communications. She and Scott continued to volunteer for the college newspaper, Melissa as a feature writer and Scott as a photographer.

Since they both had reliable transportation, the girls were able to make the one-hour trip between their hometown and Fiona's college on a somewhat regular basis. Their short visits gave them an opportunity to get to know each other's boyfriend. Fiona liked Scott and felt he was a stabilizing influence on Melissa. They read each other's tarot cards almost weekly, but each time Melissa tried to engage her friend in a discussion about Wicca, Fiona changed the subject.

Fiona and Reuben attended an occasional antiwar rally at the college. More and more, they felt the futility of their cause, seeing no end to the fighting. Reuben continued his research on emigrating to Canada and kept in contact with the Southern Ontario

Committee on War Immigrants and the Princeton Draft Resisters
Union. He mailed his application to the graduate program in creative writing at the University of Toronto and encouraged Fiona to
apply to the art history program. She kept the paperwork on her
desk, unable to find the courage to complete it.

"Fiona, we need to talk," Reuben said as they finished dinner one
evening the week before Thanksgiving.

She'd sensed an uneasiness in him for the past week but
hesitated to ask what was bothering him in case it had something
to do with her.

"What's up?" Fiona hoped her light tone of voice masked the
anxiety she felt.

"Not here. Let's go to one of the private study rooms at the
Student Union."

They walked in silence through the campus, the streetlights
accentuating Reuben's hardened expression. His stride was long
and determined, almost as if he wanted to lose her. She was
nearly out of breath by the time they reached their destination.

They sat across from one another in the study room. The
glare from the overhead fluorescent light reminded Fiona of a
police investigation. Was she guilty? Of what?

Reuben pulled the overflowing plastic ashtray toward him
and shook a Marlboro from his pack. He knew better than to offer one to her. She followed his lead and lit a Kool. The smoke sat
midair, clouding their view of one another. She waited.

He spoke. "Remember when we first met and talked about
our lives having themes?"

She replied, "Sure. I didn't know if you were serious or trying to pick me up."

"I was serious. I'm serious now."

She leaned away from him and crossed her arms to shield herself from the abruptness of his voice.

"One of my life themes has come back, and I don't know what to do about it." He stared into the depths of her green eyes.

She shifted in her seat and waited.

"I got my student teaching assignment yesterday."

Why was Reuben changing the subject? "Did you get the high school here in town?"

"No," Reuben said. "That's what we need to talk about."

"Oh."

"They offered me a spot in my old high school, and I decided to accept it."

"How will you commute?" Fiona asked the question and immediately knew the answer. He wasn't.

"Please, let me explain. It's gonna take money for me to go to Canada, and I'll need money for grad school if I get accepted at Toronto. If I live home for the semester, I can save the rent and food money to help me get started once I leave."

Fiona's world came crashing down on her. Their relationship was over. "What about your library job? What about *The Beacon*?" And finally, after a long hesitation, she whispered, "What about us?"

"I can't keep my job if I'm student teaching. Same with being editor, but I can still write articles." It was Reuben's turn to hesitate. "And us—more than anything I want there to be an us. Do you think we can work it out?"

Except for vacations, they had spent nearly every day together for more than a year. That would all change in less than two months. Then it dawned on her. This was the same thing that happened with his ex-girlfriend Becky at Temple when Reuben moved on and left her. Is that what he meant by his life theme coming back?

"How can we?" she asked.

"We can see each other on weekends and when I'm on campus for meetings."

"But where would we—"

"Do it?" He finished her sentence. "I thought maybe you could move off campus. Y'know, share an apartment or something. Then you wouldn't have to sneak me into the dorm."

Fiona felt anger simmering in her gut, working its way to a boil. Was this how it had ended with Becky?

She was determined not to become another Becky. She had held her emotions in at home for twenty years. She could do it now. After a few slow breaths, she said, "Why didn't you talk this over with me?"

"I don't know. I probably should have. Guess I wasn't thinking," he said.

"Yeah, you should have. I thought we were a team. I knew I might lose you after graduation. I just never thought it would happen sooner."

Reuben motioned for Fiona to sit on his lap. "You're not losing me, and I don't want to lose you. Not January, not June, not ever. I know I'm asking a lot, but these are weird times. So much shit is out of our control."

"I don't want to lose you either." She melted into him, her tears staining his jacket. Eventually, her tears abated, and her anger returned.

It took all her courage to speak. "I'm not Becky. I'm not going to get violent, but is this the way you end relationships? A dramatic exit and on to the next one?"

He pulled away from her. "I don't know how to convince you that this—us—we're different. Becky was my girlfriend, but she was a mistake. Don't tell me you haven't made mistakes in relationships."

Fiona thought of her relationship last year with Jack. Talk about mistakes. Was Reuben telling her the truth?

"I only said that about an apartment 'cause I want to be with you so much. If it doesn't happen, we can still be together. It's only a few months."

A few months felt like an eternity. How could she guarantee he wouldn't meet someone else once she wasn't in his life every day? "What about after you graduate?"

"We've talked about this, lassie."

He hadn't called her lassie in months. Hearing the nickname brought her anger back to the surface. Was she a pet dog that would follow her master anywhere?

"Let's take it one day at a time. All I ask is that you trust me. I know we can work things out."

"Things don't work out for me. I'm cursed," Fiona blurted out.

"What the fuck?" Reuben pulled away from her. "Get over it. You're smart. Beautiful. Talented. Your painting's hanging in the Student Union. You've got everything going for you. You listen to your crazy mother and her fire and fucking brimstone."

Reuben's words tore through her. Maybe he was right. Everyone else except Melissa and her mom supported his opinion. Even her dad. She felt a surge of positive energy flowing through her core.

"Maybe you're right," Fiona said with new resolve. "Okay. If it's meant to be, it'll work out."

"It is meant to be. You'll see. I love you."

"I love you too." She was never the first to say it.

Chapter 47

Before returning home for Thanksgiving break, Fiona stopped at the newspaper office at the community college. She knew Melissa and Scott would be putting the finishing touches on the latest edition. The office was located in a former construction trailer, so even the smallest group of students created a crowd.

She had gone to high school with some of the volunteers; others she knew from previous visits. They welcomed her and made her feel comfortable.

"Check out the front page, Fee, and let me know what you think." Scott skipped the hellos and went right to business.

"Nice layout. You did a great job with the photos," Fiona said.

"Check out my article on page two," Melissa said proudly as she hugged her friend.

Fiona sat at the only table in the trailer and read Melissa's article on vegetarianism, followed by a recipe for pumpkin bread. As she read, she felt someone standing behind her, reading over her shoulder.

"Not a bad piece of writing, don't you think?" a deep male voice asked.

Fiona turned. An older man with black shoulder-length hair and full mustache smiled at her.

"Fee, meet Vincent," Melissa said. "He joined the staff this fall. He's got all kinds of experience with writing. He's really bringing the paper together."

"She flatters me," Vincent said as he sat next to Fiona. His almond-shaped eyes stared directly into hers.

"Nice to meet you. How come I've never seen you before?" Fiona felt uncomfortable vibes coming from him, which she desperately tried to ignore.

"Bad timing, I guess. Just started here this semester. I've been away, writing and traveling. Now it's time to get my act together and get an education. I dig this school and the paper. I especially dig Miss Melissa. We've got a lot in common."

Melissa beamed. Compliments didn't come often to her.

Fiona hoped he wasn't planning to move in on Scott. Melissa's life had become relatively sane. She didn't need anyone messing things up for her.

"Come on, gang. Let's put this baby to bed." Vincent sounded like an old newspaperman.

The entire staff followed his lead as though he were the editor, not a new volunteer.

Charisma, Fiona thought as she poured herself a cup of coffee and moved out of everybody's way. *Guess I've never been around anybody with so much of it. Maybe I've got to get used to him. The rest of them seem to like him.*

After about an hour, Fiona said her good-byes, hugged Melissa, and made plans to meet after dinner.

The girls headed out for a short ride in Fiona's Volkswagen, passed a joint, and took a few moments to catch up.

"Who's this Vincent?" Fiona asked. "I felt some strange energy coming from him."

"He's really cool. He showed up at the newspaper office one day, and it was like he'd always been there. He knew just what to do. He senses everybody's talents and how to get the most from them. The paper looks fantastic, and we're getting lots of interest."

"Yeah, but he's so much older and kinda vague about where he's been. Was he in the service? Or maybe prison?"

"He's not really that old, definitely not thirty," Melissa said. "As for where he's been, he's traveled around a lot. You don't just get an education from school."

Fiona sensed Melissa was infatuated once again. "You're not gonna dump Scott for him, are you?"

"No way. He's not interested in me that way—or anybody, as far as I can tell. We've gone out for coffee a few times, but he never mentions sex or dating. It's like he wants to know all about what I'm interested in. I even read his cards."

Fiona perked up at the mention of the tarot. "Do you remember what you saw?"

"Lots of his cards were reversed, like the Magician."

"Doesn't that mean something about abusing power and manipulating events and people?" Fiona asked.

"That's what I said to him, but he knows the cards way better than I do. He explained that for him it was more about not applying himself and lacking willpower. He said that card represented the past, not who he is now."

"What else?"

"He drew a reversed Tower card. I told him that meant change and not to resist his karma," Melissa went on. "He agreed with me on that one. The one thing I thought was kinda spooky was that he drew the Lovers and the Devil right next to each other. I didn't know what to say about that."

Fiona shivered nervously. She couldn't explain it either.

Melissa went on. "Vincent said that the Lovers card is about taking responsibility for the choices we make and how it's important to listen to your inner voice to gain higher guidance. The Devil is all about using your powers correctly and to respect the good and the evil in the universe."

"Heavy. How do you remember everything, and how does he know how to read the cards so well?"

"I wrote it all down," Melissa said. "He wouldn't tell me about how he learned the tarot. He kinda just sat and stared at me with those dark eyes of his."

"I'm not feeling so good about this guy. Just be careful," Fiona said.

Melissa turned to Fiona. "Why don't you hang out with us tomorrow? We're having a little pre-Thanksgiving party. Maybe you can get Vincent to read your cards."

Fiona hesitated.

"What's the matter, Fee? Vincent's cool, and you might learn something."

"Okay, why not?"

At the party the next afternoon, Fiona cornered Scott. "What do you think about Vincent?"

"I've decided to reserve judgment," Scott said. "I'm pretty good at reading people, but he's got me baffled. On the surface, he seems like an okay guy. He's smart and knows more about the newspaper business than the rest of us. I can't help thinking he's hiding something."

"Lissie seems taken by him," Fiona said.

"You know Lissie. She doesn't have the best human-monitoring system." He laughed. "Why do you think she's with me?"

"Stop." Fiona smiled. "You know you're the best thing that's ever happened to her."

"Enough mush. Let's join the group. Maybe between us we can get the scoop on Vincent."

They joined the crowd by the food table. Vincent was in the middle of a story, which had everyone's attention.

"Back in Frisco, I was a regular at the Drinking Gourd, where I met Paul Kantner from Jefferson Airplane. That's back when folk was just hitting the charts. He and I wrote some tunes before he moved to LA in sixty-four. Even after he left, that was the place to be. Jerry Garcia, David Crosby, and Janis Joplin were all part of the scene." Vincent stood while the rest of the group sat, forcing everyone to look up at him.

"You knew Janis?" Melissa jumped up and ran to him.

"Shit, yeah. She was cool. An artist, a poet, a real lady. It's an absolute bummer what happened to her," Vincent said.

The room grew quiet, remembering Janis's untimely death in October. Melissa's eyes filled with tears. Vincent put his arm around her and drew her to him. Scott squirmed in his seat and gave Fiona a sideways glance.

"We can't escape our destiny," Vincent said, looking directly at Melissa. "Karma gets us all in the end. Let's be glad we had her for the time we did. Now come on. This is a party. A toast to Janis!"

He raised his Coke, encouraging others to do the same. "To Janis," everyone said in unison.

The party split into small groups. Vincent and Melissa joined Scott and Fiona.

"Vincent said he'll read your cards, Fee," Melissa said.

"Now?"

"No time like the present," Vincent said. "We can do it in the editor's office. I'm sure he won't mind."

"Melissa tells me you're quite the reader," Vincent said, closing the door.

"I just kinda fool around with the cards. Nothing serious. I like the artwork more than anything," Fiona said.

Vincent pulled a tarot deck wrapped in black velvet from his jacket pocket. He held his right hand over the cards, drawing symbols in the air with his left, as he mumbled unintelligibly. He removed the cards from the cloth, held them to his third eye at the center of his forehead, inhaled deeply, exhaled, and placed the deck on the table.

Fiona realized she wasn't breathing as she looked at the unfamiliar illustrations. "These don't look like any cards I've seen before."

"I thought not," he said as he shuffled. "This is the Thoth deck, the most powerful tarot in the world. Anything less and you can't get a true reading."

Where had she heard about the Thoth deck? A memory floated from her subconscious to her conscious mind. *That's the deck Miss Sarah's friend at the bookstore warned us about back in Florida. Black magic something or other. Al Something. Al—* She gasped audibly as she remembered Aleister Crowley.

"Is something wrong?" Vincent asked.

"Umm, no. I sort of have to go." Fiona stumbled on her words.

"Sort of, or you do have to go? Which is it, Miss Fiona?"

"We-ll, maybe I can stay for a few minutes."

"Tell you what, we'll do a short reading." He focused on her eyes as he fanned the cards out. "Pick five cards."

Fiona paused, then selected five cards from the deck. One by one, she handed them to Vincent.

"The Ace of Pentacles. How appropriate for your first card. Winter. A new beginning. Looks like you're in for some big changes in the next few months. That's not so scary now, is it?"

"No, but I see it's reversed," Fiona said.

"You're getting ahead of me," he replied sharply. "You chose the Tower, the Knight of Swords, the Fool, and Justice. Interesting. Three Major Arcana cards. Everything speaks of change and karma. Time to release the old and welcome the new. Listen to your inner voice. Learn from past mistakes. You're about to go through a difficult period, and I sense much of it has to do with a dark-haired man who has a great deal of influence in your life."

Fiona guessed Melissa had told Vincent about her relationship with Reuben. She suspected he knew more about reading people than reading cards.

Fiona smiled and stood. "Thank you so much, Vincent. Lots to think about."

"There's more, but I don't think you're ready to hear it," Vincent said.

"Not now. I promised my mom I'd be home to help with Thanksgiving." She felt his eyes ripping into her back as she left the office. Fiona grabbed her coat and purse and practically ran out of the trailer.

Melissa followed her friend. "What's going on? What happened with Vincent?"

"He scares the shit out of me," Fiona replied. "There's something about him I don't trust. He did a short reading for me, but he didn't say much. And those cards. You know he's got the Thoth deck."

"He's kind of intense when you first meet him. I think he's been hurt, and that's the way he hides his true self. Those women in Florida were wrong about the Thoth. Vincent really knows what he's talking about," Melissa explained.

"Maybe I overreacted. I'm freaking out about Reuben and what's gonna happen after January."

"Anything new to tell me?" Melissa asked.

"Yeah, and it's not looking good. I'll talk to you tomorrow." Fiona hugged her friend and left for home.

Chapter 48

Thanksgiving Day was a rerun of the past twenty years. Turkey stuffed with Pepperidge Farm herbed dressing, jellied cranberry sauce, frozen peas, and mashed sweet and white potatoes were all prepared by Fiona's mom. Her dad's two brothers and their families usually provided appetizers, dessert, and wine. This year they left the wine at home.

She couldn't believe it had been almost a year since her mom had stopped drinking and started her medication regime. By now, she was used to her mom's glassy-eyed stare and her occasional drift into a hidden reality. Mrs. O'Brien's angry outbursts were less frequent, although her religious fervor still dominated her life.

After dinner, Fiona and her cousins retreated to the family room in the basement, the women to the kitchen to clean up, and the men to the living room to watch football. By seven o'clock, everyone was ready to move on. Once her dad's family was gone, Fiona felt comfortable making her exit. To her surprise, her dad mumbled an excuse and left her mom alone with the Thursday night lineup on TV.

Fiona wanted to follow her dad, but she had made plans to meet Melissa for a serious discussion.

"I feel like we need an agenda. There's so much to talk about," Fiona said as they lit their cigarettes. "Where should we begin?"

"Why don't you tell me what's going on with Reuben?" Melissa suggested.

Fiona told Melissa about Reuben's student teaching assignment. "I think he might be using student teaching as a way to get away from me."

"What a bastard. Why would he do that?"

"The sooner he gets away from me, the easier it'll be for him to go to Canada." Fiona brushed a tear from her cheek.

Melissa hugged Fiona but had no words of comfort. Both girls knew fate and the government were taking over their lives.

"I don't see how I could go with him anyway. I don't want to be a fugitive. I wouldn't mind leaving my mom, but I couldn't do that to my dad, or you." Fiona stubbed out her cigarette and immediately lit another.

"Scott's draft number is three-eighteen. I doubt he'll ever go, especially if he transfers to a four-year college next year. He's one of the lucky ones," Melissa said.

"All the marches and all the protests haven't done shit to stop the war."

"You never know, Fee," Melissa went on. "Life can change in an instant. Reuben could be 4-F for some reason. Did you make that amulet we talked about?"

"I still have to do more research, but I will."

"I gave you all the information on how to make it, what colors to use, what time of day to do the incantation, all that stuff," Melissa said.

"I'm really not comfortable with magic. I don't know that I believe it, or if it will work," Fiona replied.

"It's worked for us before, and it's worked for me a bunch of times. It's how I got my life together."

Every time I think you might have your act together, you start talking witchcraft and spells.

"Listen, Fee. You've got nothing to lose. Reuben's life is on the line. It's white magic. Think of it like wishing on a star. Now here's what you need to do." Melissa pulled a crumpled sheet of paper with a list of instructions from her purse and handed it to her friend.

"I can't do all this. I'd be too nervous."

"Suit yourself. How 'bout you just do the meditation?" Melissa said.

"Well, maybe." She handed the paper back.

Melissa crossed off a few paragraphs. "It's really nothing more than creating an altar and meditating into the candlelight. Nothing to be scared of. Trust me."

"I trust you. I better wait till I get back to school. I don't want my mom knowing. She'll start in about me being the Devil's child again."

"Do it for seven days, and make sure you do it first thing in the morning," Melissa said.

"How d'you know all this, Lissie?" Fiona asked.

"Vincent helped me. He's a cool dude, really, Fee. He wrote one of these up for a chick whose boyfriend's draft number is forty. It was different colors and a different day. When I told him about Reuben, he redid it."

Fiona felt violated by her friend. How dare she discuss her personal life with Vincent? No wonder he was so adept at reading her cards. At best he was a bullshit artist. At worst—she couldn't imagine.

"I guess you're right. I've got nothing to lose." Fiona put the paper in her purse, where it would stay until she returned to school and could dispose of it without her mom finding out.

Chapter 49

On Friday morning Fiona called Melissa.

"Hey, Fee, what's happenin'?" Fiona still wasn't used to Melissa's new upbeat personality.

"Just wondering what you're doing today. I'm feeling kinda lost and depressed," Fiona said.

"Me and Scott are meeting at the diner for coffee. Do you wanna come too?"

"As long as I'm not being a pain in the ass."

"Come on, Fee. See you in an hour, okay?"

Fiona spotted Melissa as soon as she entered the diner. Scott sat next to her. They were engrossed in conversation, their heads tilted toward one another. She sighed and pasted a smile onto her face as she walked to the booth.

A cup of coffee sat on Fiona's side of the booth. "Thanks for ordering for me," she said.

"That's not yours. Vincent's here. He went to the men's room," Scott explained.

Before Fiona could say anything or make a quick exit, Vincent came up behind her. "Miss Fiona! What a pleasant surprise. Can I get you a coffee?"

"You don't have to do that."

"I think I owe you an apology for the other day," Vincent said.

"No problem. I've been kinda stressed out and wasn't ready to have my cards read."

"Truce?" Vincent held out his hand.

Fiona felt a thick gold band on his ring finger. The ring's face was turned to his palm.

"I see you've located your missing ring," Scott said. "Where was it?"

Vincent twirled the ring, leaving it facing inward. Fiona noticed intricate engraving before Vincent dropped his hand in his lap.

"It was in a box of books I hadn't unpacked," Vincent said, then turned to Fiona. "An old friend gave it to me. Someone who hasn't been in my life for a while. Someone I'm hoping to meet again soon."

"Can I see it?" she asked.

"Some other time, maybe. It's very personal, and I need to reclaim its energy before I share it."

"Sounds so mysterious!" Melissa said.

Vincent diverted their attention to a local antiwar rally that would take place before the new year. He wanted the paper to devote its entire front page to the event. He engaged Melissa and Scott in a lively discussion about layout, photos, and distribution.

Fiona stared out the window, lost in thought. She couldn't stop thinking about Vincent and the role he was playing in Melissa's life.

"*Fee!*" Melissa shook Fiona's shoulder.

"Sorry, guess I was daydreaming." She turned her attention back to the table.

"As I was saying, I thought for the next edition we could do a feature on the tarot," Vincent said. "Miss Melissa can write the article, and I thought you might like to do an illustration for us."

"But I'm not a student."

"Doesn't matter. I've seen some of your sketches, and you know the cards. It would add so much to the paper. How about it, Fiona?"

Fiona squirmed in her seat. "I guess I could."

Vincent clasped his hands around hers. He stood, bringing Fiona with him. "Until we meet again," he said, caressing her cheek.

"What the fuck was that all about?" Fiona asked as she sat back down.

"I call him the drama king." Scott smiled. "He puts off some of the chicks on campus. They think he's trying to get laid. You've gotta get used to him. I think he's an older guy who missed out on college and is trying to make an impression."

"I think he's a cool dude but nobody I want to go out with," Melissa said as she snuggled next to Scott.

"Even better for me." Scott kissed the top of Melissa's blond head.

Before leaving for college, Fiona created a pen-and-ink sketch reminiscent of Miss Sarah, the reader who introduced her to the tarot. Swirls of incense rose around Miss Sarah's face as she pondered a spread of cards on a table in front of her. She photo copied the drawing, taking the original back to school with her.

She began to think of Vincent as a catalyst, one of those people who comes into your life and changes everything.

WANTED: ROOMMATE. The notice, tacked to the Art Department bulletin board, continued: "Female roommate wanted for spring semester, 1971. Three-bedroom apartment near campus. Art students preferred. Call Katie or Pat." Hanging at the bottom were tear-off strips with a phone number.

Fiona didn't hesitate. She ripped the first strip from the ad.

She knew the girls from a distance. Both seniors. Neither a prominent figure on campus but a constant presence around the department. How would they feel about her, a politically active junior with a boyfriend who wanted to sleep over?

What about Reuben? If she moved off campus, would it look like she was giving in to his wishes? Or would it be a sign of her love and trust?

And the biggest question of all: What about her parents? She would have to tell them since they would be writing the check.

It's only a phone call. I've got nothing to lose. Fiona repeated these words in her head over and over as she walked to the nearest phone booth and dialed. Katie answered.

"Sure, I know who you are," Katie said. "No, it's not rented yet. When can you come over?"

The apartment was only a few blocks off campus. It had been a one-family home, now chopped into three apartments. Fiona stared at the gray asbestos-shingled building with its sagging front porch and rusted fire escape weaving its way to the attic. She thought affectionately of her spotless dorm room, the clean sheets delivered weekly and the mildew-free showers. Could she exchange cleanliness for freedom?

Katie, a short, chunky brunette, welcomed her. "We're on the second floor. C'mon up."

The elaborate, curved oak staircase retained a piece of elegance long gone from the rest of the place. Paint peeled from the ceiling, but the second-floor hallway was freshly painted in bright geometric designs.

"I dig the walls," Fiona said, feeling more comfortable.

"Pat and I did that. Dr. Wilckins owns the place. This was our final project for his class last spring." Katie was referring to Dr. Wilckins, assistant chair of the Art Department.

"This is us." Katie opened a splintered wooden door into the living room.

Orange walls reflected the late afternoon sun streaming from floor-to-ceiling windows that looked onto the street. In place of furniture were cushions—cushions from old sofas, cushions from long-forgotten chairs, cushions that looked like they came from her grandparents' back porch. An elaborate hookah stood in one corner.

"It comes furnished." Katie laughed.

"Pat and I have rooms over here. They used to be sun porches. Great light for painting." Katie pointed to two small rooms, one on either side of the living room. Each had two walls surrounded by windows.

"Far out," Fiona said.

"Your room is down the hall," Katie said, leading Fiona to the back of the apartment.

The third bedroom was on the left side of the hallway across from the bathroom. Its one window looked at the naked wall of the house next door. Not inspiring but much larger than the front rooms. A double mattress lay on the floor next to a nightstand from the 1920s. A dresser covered in chipped veneer sat next to a small closet.

"Not much on inspiration, but it's the biggest bedroom and close to the bathroom," Katie said.

To Fiona's relief, the bathroom was spacious and clean. The clawfoot tub was rigged with a shower. A pedestal sink and a toilet with an ancient pull chain completed the ensemble.

A canary-yellow kitchen was located at the rear of the apartment. The appliances dated from the 1940s, as did the enamel-topped kitchen table. A walk-in pantry housed food and art supplies. Through the rear window Fiona noticed a small porch.

Katie poured a cup of stale coffee for Fiona as they discussed details. The rent was significantly cheaper than Fiona's private room at the dorm. Her dad would like that.

"I have to get the okay from my dad," Fiona said. "He's paying the bill."

"Not a problem. Dr. Wilckins prefers to rent to art students. I know he'll approve you. You're a rising star in the department," she told Fiona, who blushed visibly.

Katie and Pat would continue to interview potential tenants but assured Fiona that she'd be their first choice.

Fiona called her parents that evening. Her dad hesitated until she told him the house was owned by one of her professors. "He lives next door and follows the same rules and curfew as the dorms," Fiona lied.

"Sounds safe enough, and I like the price," her dad said. "But I want you to continue to get your meals on campus. You don't need to think about cooking and shopping on top of everything else."

The cafeteria food was substandard but definitely a step up from any meals Fiona knew how to prepare.

"And one more thing, honey. Let's keep this between us. Your mom doesn't need to know."

"It's a deal, Dad. You're the best." Her dad had been taking Fiona's side more and more in the last year. He also was spending less and less time at home.

Dr. Wilckins approached Fiona the following day in the Art Department office. "Fiona, I hear you're moving in with Katie and Pat."

His comment startled her. "Um, well, I hope I can. Don't I have to fill out some kind of application or something?"

"That's just a formality. I couldn't think of a better tenant than you. All I ask is no wild parties and no loud noise after ten at night. Overnight guests are cool as long as they don't move in. Oh, and keep the place clean."

"Thank you so much." This had to be one of the best days of Fiona's young life. "I won't let you down."

What a Trip

Fiona wanted to share her news with Reuben, but he was working at the library until seven that evening. Instead, she called Melissa when she got back to the dorm.

"That's so cool, Fee. Your own apartment. I can't wait to see it."

"I can't believe how lucky I was to get it," Fiona said. "It's like the place was there waiting for me."

"It was waiting for you," Melissa said.

"What d'you mean?"

"After we talked over Thanksgiving, I knew you needed something, so I went to Vincent. He and I created a spell to help you."

Fiona stared at the silver and black of the payphone. What do you say when your best friend practices witchcraft on you without your knowledge or permission? What do you say when she betrays your trust? And what do you say to her when you think she's gone off the deep end?

"How could you?" was all she managed to squeeze out.

"I did it for you, Fee. You're my best friend in the whole world, and you were desperate. You were there for me last year. I want to be here for you now."

"But Vincent? And witchcraft?"

"Not witchcraft, white magic. Y'know, Wicca. Our intentions were all good. Please don't be mad." Melissa was on the verge of tears.

Fiona's anger softened. Nothing bad had happened. She had gotten the apartment she wanted. "Thank you, I guess. It's just, well, I feel weird about you telling Vincent about my problems."

"He and I are getting really close," Melissa said.

"What about Scott? Please don't blow it with him."

"Don't worry. Vincent was really into Wicca a couple of years ago, and when he found out I was interested, he opened up to me. Told me how he wants to start a coven and make me the high priestess."

"You're asking for trouble," Fiona said.

"I'm not jumping into anything. You can't start a coven overnight. It takes lots of planning, and we've gotta find members. I thought you might be interested."

"That's not who I am," Fiona replied.

"I thought so. When are you gonna get past your mom's bullshit?"

"This isn't about my mom's bullshit. This is me. Are you mad at me?" Fiona was feeling guilty about judging her friend.

"No, I'm not mad, just disappointed. We'll talk more when you get home for Christmas. Still best friends?" Melissa didn't want an argument either.

"Still best friends." *But for how long?*

Fiona spent the rest of the afternoon doing research for her art history paper. By the time she met Reuben for dinner, she had all but forgotten her conversation with Melissa.

"And I don't have to sneak you in," she told Reuben at dinner. "I think things are gonna work out."

"One day at a time. You gotta have faith," Reuben said.

"Faith? Please don't remind me of my mom. I'm feeling too good."

"There's your mom's fear-based faith, and then there's faith that the universe provides. That's what I'm talking about."

Fiona's view of the world was expanding day by day. It was much greater than the guilt-based heaven and hell with which she grew up.

"We're meant to be together," Reuben said. "This proves it. Now that next semester is a done deal, we can focus on Canada."

Fiona offered a weak smile and said nothing.

"C'mon. Let's celebrate. I scored some dynamite pot over Thanksgiving. We can do a doobie on the way to the Puff. Then I'll show you a new book I got called the *Kamasutra*."

"Sounds Indian. What's it about? Meditation?"

"Kind of. It's the ultimate ancient Indian guide to sex. It's got, like, a million different positions and ways to get it on."

"No shit? What are we waiting for?" She jumped from her seat, nearly toppling their table.

"Hey, it's not just about fucking. It's got all kinds of wisdom about philosophy and the world," he said.

"Don't worry, we'll get to that. First things first."

She paused, then said, "I love you." It had taken all her courage to say it without being prompted. It felt good.

"That's the first time you've ever said it without me saying it first. That's the second-best thing that happened today," Reuben said.

Chapter 51

"I was hoping we could spend our New Year's Eve together, but something's come up," Reuben said about a week before their winter break.

"Bummer," Fiona said. "I really wanted to come to your house. What happened?"

"It's my grandma's eightieth birthday. She and my grandpa invited the whole family up for a party. Everybody's gonna be there. My aunts, uncles, cousins, everybody."

Fiona did her best to hide her disappointment. "Where do they live?"

"Rochester, New York. That's where my mother grew up. I wish I could invite you, but it's a small house and, well, y'know."

She did know. It meant three weeks at home. No Reuben. Another lonely New Year's Eve.

"It's only for a few days. I think we're leaving on the twenty-ninth. We've gotta be back that Sunday so my sisters can go back to school. We'll see each other before and after, so it won't be a big deal."

To Fiona, it was a big deal. Her thoughts drifted back to the year before. The farmhouse. The guy with no name. The filthy bed. The last time she had sex with someone besides Reuben.

She had kept her promise and steered clear of the place. What if
the only New Year's party was at that house? Would she go, or
would she stay home and watch Guy Lombardo and his orchestra
with her parents? One choice was worse than the other.

Fiona snapped back to the conversation.

"Rochester's not far from Canada," Reuben said. "I thought
I'd take a drive to the border and check things out. I'm also gonna
feel out my relatives and see what they think about me evading
the draft." Reuben avoided the label "draft dodger," saying it was
derogatory.

She didn't need to think about Canada on top of a lonely New
Year's Eve.

Back in the dorm, Fiona did her best to rationalize the situation.
Reuben was right. It was nothing more than a short visit. It
wasn't as though he would be spending the holiday with another
girl. What was so special about New Year's Eve anyway? What
made it different from any other night?

"Plenty!" She surprised herself by saying the word out loud.
It was the most important party night of the year. If a girl didn't
have a date on New Year's Eve, she was nothing. Fiona also believed that how she spent New Year's Eve was how the next year
would unfold.

*But that's not true. Look how fucked up last New Year's Eve was
and how good this year turned out.*

"Fiona O'Brien! Phone call." The words pushed through the
fog of her thoughts. She ran down the hallway to the public
phone.

"Hello?" she asked tentatively.

"Fee, it's me." Melissa's voice was a welcome surprise.

"What's up, Lissie?"

"I just wanted to see when you're coming home and if you and Reuben were gonna hang out on New Year's."

"I'll be home on Friday, but no Reuben. I'm so bummed—"

"Far fucking out," Melissa interrupted.

"No, it's not. I—"

"Listen, there's a big New Year's Eve party that we have to go to."

"You'll be with Scott, which is cool. I'm not going to any party by myself," Fiona said.

"You don't have to. That's why I'm calling. I wanted to tell you about Vincent."

"Yeah—"

"Well, he doesn't have anybody to go with either. We thought maybe you could go with him."

One alarm after another went off in Fiona's head. She thought back to the spell Melissa and Vincent had supposedly worked on her. What would a date with him look like? What would she tell Reuben?

"I don't want to cheat on Reuben," Fiona said after a long pause.

"C'mon, Fee. It's not really a date. You, me, and Scott will meet Vincent at the party. I promise he won't leave with us."

It all sounded safe enough. "Why would he want to be with me? He knows about Reuben."

"It's people from the college, mostly newspaper staff," Melissa said. "Vincent said it's really important for him to be there. Something about the night being special for him. He's older than most of the kids. He said he feels uncomfortable being there by himself."

Fiona couldn't imagine Vincent feeling uncomfortable in any situation.

"He feels a connection to you 'cause of the tarot."

"Really?" Fiona was flattered that someone with Vincent's experience with the tarot would be interested in her.

"What do you think? New Year's Eve with your parents, or a party with us?" Melissa's offer was getting harder and harder to refuse.

"There's no way I'm screwing the guy. He's gotta know that right up front."

"He just wants somebody to hang with at the party."

"Well, maybe," Fiona said.

"Cool. I'll let Vincent know," Melissa said before Fiona could change her mind.

"Make sure you tell him what the deal is," Fiona said.

"You can trust me," Melissa replied.

But can I trust myself? Fiona wondered as she hung up the phone.

Chapter 52

"Lissie and Scott invited me to a New Year's Eve party." Fiona decided to be honest with Reuben about the party but thought it best not to mention Vincent. It wasn't a date, she told herself. She would arrive and leave with Melissa and Scott. Vincent would just be one of the people who happened to be there. The party was at the duplex apartment of a married couple, not the farmhouse with a floor full of bedrooms open for sex.

"I'm glad you'll have someplace to go. I know how much you don't want to hang with your parents," Reuben said.

"You're okay with me going?" she asked.

"As long as you don't leave with some long-haired hippie." Reuben pulled Fiona close.

"Other than Lissie, you mean, right?"

"Unless you've got a thing for her," he laughed.

If you only knew. "C'mon, let's go to dinner."

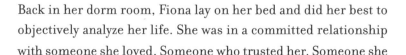

Back in her dorm room, Fiona lay on her bed and did her best to objectively analyze her life. She was in a committed relationship with someone she loved. Someone who trusted her. Someone she didn't want to disappoint. She recited the now-familiar self-talk. She was older, wiser, stronger. She had outgrown the superficial party crowd at home. She believed in herself and her personal power and was confident she would remain faithful to Reuben.

Melissa was noticeably distant during the holiday week, presumably busy with Scott and her family. They finally met at the diner for breakfast three days after Christmas.

When Fiona spotted Melissa in the booth, she noticed her friend's face was pale, accentuating the dusty smudges under her eyes. She took drag after drag on her cigarette with barely a pause for clean air. It took her a moment to lift her eyes as Fiona sat down.

"What's happenin', Lissie? You look tired."

Melissa mumbled into her coffee cup and stubbed out her cigarette.

Fiona took a hard look at her friend's red-rimmed, bloodshot eyes devoid of makeup, strings of unwashed hair falling in her face, and coffee stains on her pilled gray sweater. It was a version of Melissa she had not seen since her abortion.

"Did you and Scott break up?"

"No."

"Then what's going on?"

"I can't talk here." Melissa's voice trembled.

Fiona's frustration was building. She wanted to say, *Why is everything such a crisis? You're a fucking drama queen.* Instead, she calmly suggested, "How 'bout we go to your car?"

Melissa threw some money on the table and headed for the

door without looking at Fiona. Fiona followed, tripping over her feet as she tried to keep up.

The moment Melissa closed the door of her midnight-blue Beetle, an ear-piercing scream flew from her mouth. She beat the steering wheel, shrieking, "No! No! *No!*"

Fiona's immediate reaction was to run from the insanity of the moment, to run from this friendship that took so much and gave little in return. Instead, she put her arm around Melissa's shoulder, kissed her cheek, and said, "C'mon, how bad could it be?"

Melissa hyperventilated between screams, buried in a panic attack that wouldn't stop.

"Calm down, Lissie." Fiona's voice was smothered by her friend's cries. "Lissie! I'm going inside to get you some water. Don't move."

By the time she returned with a Styrofoam cup of water, Melissa had regained her composure. She took a sip, turned her ragged face to Fiona, and said her first intelligible words. "I've made a terrible mistake. It's the end."

"The end of what? Please. Tell me what happened."

"V-Vincent. He's evil. He's been using me."

Fiona realized her instincts about Vincent had been right. He was trouble, and now he had hurt Melissa. Maybe she wouldn't have to be with him at the New Year's Eve party. She wouldn't have to keep anything from Reuben.

"So just get away from him. It's not like you're dating," Fiona said.

"Okay, here goes. I'll tell you everything," Melissa began. "Remember I told you that Vincent had experience in Wicca?"

Fiona had heard more than enough of Wicca, magic, and

spells, but she couldn't abandon Melissa when her friend needed her.

"He told me he was into white magic and only used spells for good. Last week he told me that was a lie. He's really into black magic. Satanism."

Satanism? Fiona thought of her mother's warnings about the Devil. According to Mrs. O'Brien, there was a constant struggle in heaven and on earth between good and evil, between God and the Devil. Accepting Jesus was the only way to safeguard against Satan. The primal fear instilled by her mother returned.

"You know that ring he has? He showed it to me. It's a reversed pentagram." Melissa shivered. "Y'know, when the five-pointed star has two points at the top? That's the sign of black magic."

Fiona had seen the band of Vincent's ring when she was home for Thanksgiving and remembered how he wouldn't let anyone see the emblem on the front. Was this the reason?

"Are you sure he didn't just turn it upside down to mess with you?" she asked.

"No, he was serious. I'm gonna tell you the whole story. You can judge for yourself." Melissa paused to light a cigarette. "Back when he was in California, he sold his soul to the Devil."

Fiona questioned the existence of the soul as well as the Devil. She wondered how it was possible to sell something that may not exist to a mythical being.

"How do you begin to do that?" she asked.

"Vincent said he was looking for ultimate power. He wanted to be famous like some of those musicians he hung with in San Francisco. Somebody told him the easiest and fastest way to get there was to sell his soul to Satan," Melissa said.

"How do you even contact Satan?"

"He explained the whole ritual to me, how he did all this bathing and fasting, how he stood in a circle with an inverted pentagram inside, how he cut his hand to draw blood and used it to write the contract."

Performing magic for love or to stop the war was one thing. This was going to a place darker than Fiona wanted to visit.

"What does any of this have to do with now?" Fiona asked.

Melissa paused to light another cigarette, then took a sip of water. She continued. "After he did the ritual, things were going really good for him. But then something happened that he wouldn't tell me about. Something freaked him out. He said he wanted to cancel the deal with Satan."

"If Satan is so powerful, how could Vincent expect to get out of the contract?"

"I think he went to a priest, and they did some kind of exorcism," Melissa said. "Vincent said it worked and he promised never to mess around with black magic again."

"And now he changed his mind?"

"Yeah. He said when he met me, he felt witchcraft pulling him back in. He listened to what I knew about white magic and decided that was where he wanted to go. Then, about a month ago, Satan came to him and reminded him about the contract," Melissa said.

Staying home and watching Guy Lombardo with her parents on New Year's Eve was getting more and more appealing to Fiona. "I don't know what I believe, Lissie. I think he's crazy. I'm not going to that party with him."

"*You have to!*" Melissa shouted.

"I don't have to do anything. This is bullshit," Fiona said.

"No, it's not." Melissa squirmed in her seat. Her anxiety was escalating.

Fiona wanted to get away from Melissa and from the miserable life she had led in this town. Her hand rested on the door handle, ready to escape.

"*Listen to me, Fee!* This is the worst thing that's ever happened. Whatever you do, don't leave."

Fiona froze. She had been through more downs than ups with Melissa but had never seen anything like this.

Melissa held on to the steering wheel and took slow, deep breaths. "Vincent said the planets will be perfectly aligned on New Year's Eve for him to renew his pact with the Devil. He needs to begin the ceremony at midnight so that it can be completed by three in the morning."

"So he won't be at the party. We've got nothing to worry about," Fiona said.

"We have everything to worry about. Vincent insists he's coming to the party. He told Scott he needs a sacrifice. Since he broke the contract once, Satan wants more than Vincent's blood. I'm afraid it's gonna involve sex." Melissa stared out the windshield.

Fiona shivered, remembering Junior and the sex ritual she had witnessed on her way to the Kent State rally. That was consensual and done to stop the war. Would Vincent's sacrifice involve sex? Would it be with Melissa, or with her? Neither of them would willingly have sex with him.

"You're getting it now, aren't you, Fee?" Melissa turned her tear-stained face to her friend. "He wants one of us. Me, because I'm into white magic, or you because you're his date."

"But I'm not his date. You promised. You said we'd just hang out with him at the party." Fiona's agitation was beginning to mirror Melissa's.

"Does that mean you want me to be his sacrifice?" Melissa screamed.

"What are you accusing me of?" Fiona screamed back.

The girls sat without speaking for several minutes, watching customers entering and leaving the diner.

Fiona was the first to break the silence. "I don't see what the big deal is. We just won't go to the party."

"We have to go. If we don't, he'll see that as defying him," Melissa said. "I've been doing some research into white magic spells to counteract anything he might do."

"More witchcraft? When are you gonna stop?"

"Good is supposed to triumph over evil. I keep reading that. This is our chance to prove it," Melissa replied.

"*Our* chance? I never agreed to any of this. How could you get me involved?"

Melissa sobbed. "I never meant to. I only wanted to do good. I'm s-s-sorry."

More silence filled the car while unstoppable chatter crowded Fiona's mind. She needed time to think, to sort things out. She wished she could call Peach, who was always a grounding force in their lives. All she had was an address in San Francisco. It would take days to write and get a response. By that time . . .

Melissa's voice entered the void. "We've got Scott on our side. Vincent respects Scott. I told him to try and talk Vincent out of doing anything on New Year's Eve. He might listen."

"And if he doesn't?"

"It's our best chance. Me and Scott are working on it," Melissa said.

What a Trip

"I've got nothing more to say. I need time to think. I'll call you later." Fiona took a last look at her friend and slammed the door. The shrill wail of Melissa's car horn sounded a final good-bye.

Fiona spent the rest of the day in self-examination. She wanted someone to talk to, to help process the new information. If her mother were Catholic, she could ask her about protection from the church. She could have a priest harbor her in the sanctuary and conduct an exorcism. Things like that didn't happen in the Methodist community. Her mother in her religious fervor would confirm that Fiona was the Devil's child and melt into a mumble of meditations and prayers. Her dad would be helpless. He didn't need more problems in his life.

She had drifted away from the rest of her high school friends and had only developed superficial friendships at college. That left one person—Reuben.

Reuben was the last person she could talk to. He knew about Melissa's fascination with Wicca and supported Fiona's decision to keep her distance from anything occult, the tarot being the one exception.

If only she had brought her tarot cards home from college, she could do a reading. Had Melissa consulted her deck? She thought about asking her but was still too angry to make the call.

If she told Reuben about Vincent, he'd simply tell her to stay home. How could she tell him that she'd agreed to hang with Vincent at the party? Reuben would think she was cheating on him. He would lose his trust in her. She had been faithful to Reuben for a year and had no intention of breaking her commitment to him. Was her mother right that sex outside of marriage was a sin? Was this God's punishment for the life she had lived? For the lies she had told? For her sin of omission about Vincent?

What if there was something to Vincent and his pact with Satan? If his planned ritual involved sex, would she, as his supposed date, be the one he chose? If she refused to participate in the ritual and have sex with him, what would he do to her? Would he rape her? Send the Devil's minions to destroy her? If she agreed to have sex with him, would she be complicit in his evil?

If she didn't show up at the party, Vincent might see that as defiance. Would that incur the same punishment? Would he forget her and choose Melissa? The more Fiona thought about the situation, the more she realized she was helpless.

Her feelings toward Melissa were hovering on hate. She had never truly hated anyone before, but she remembered reading that you couldn't hate someone unless you loved them first. And she had loved Melissa. They had been there for each other since high school. She couldn't abandon her friend now.

"You're awfully quiet, FiFi," her dad said that evening at dinner.

"Am I?"

"You're miles away. What's on your mind, honey?" her dad asked.

"Just stuff," Fiona said.

Mrs. O'Brien eyed her daughter suspiciously. "What are you up to, miss?"

"Up to? Nothing, Mom. I'm just bummed that Reuben won't

be around on New Year's Eve." Fiona was becoming an expert at half-truths.

"You've been spending too much time with that boy. I don't like it."

"Helen—"

To avoid an argument, Fiona focused on her dinner. Meatloaf, frozen peas, and instant mashed potatoes had been a weekly staple for as long as she could remember. Each bite lodged in her throat, fighting its way past guilt and anger. Guilt for how she treated Lissie. Anger for how Lissie treated her.

By the time her plate was clean, Fiona resolved to make peace with her friend. Mistakes had been made, but there was nothing they couldn't work out.

She called Melissa with brief words of apology. "I'll go to the party, but there's no way I'm doing anything with Vincent. No sex, not even a kiss."

Melissa spoke between sobs. "I thought you hated me."

"I could never hate you. I was just upset. Friends?"

"Best friends."

Chapter 53

The next day Fiona turned down an invitation from Melissa to meet with her and Scott at the town library to discuss their strategy for New Year's Eve.

"This is between you two and Vincent," Fiona said. "I'm too upset, and my energy might bring negativity into what you're doing."

"Are you sure, Fee?" Melissa asked.

"Positive."

Fiona's plan was to keep her distance from the insanity unfolding around her. Not only would she feel safer; she would also feel less guilty when she saw Reuben again.

Melissa called Fiona the afternoon of December thirty-first. "Would it be okay if we got ready for the party at your house?"

Since her mid-teens, Fiona rarely had friends at her house. She was more comfortable keeping her personal life away from her parents. "We always do stuff at your house. Why the switch?"

"My mother and Mr. Giovanni are celebrating their one-year

wedding anniversary tonight. It's gonna be a zoo here. Your house is like a morgue. I need quiet time to focus on our plans for the party," Melissa said.

"Okay, but please don't arouse any suspicion with my mom."

"I promise. We can do our makeup and get dressed, and then I'll tell you what me and Scott have planned."

"I told you I don't want to get involved in your spells," Fiona said.

"You won't. I only want you to relax about tonight."

"Okay, see you later." There was no way in hell Fiona could relax about anything.

Melissa arrived at the O'Brien home carrying a blue Samsonite overnight case and a plastic garment bag.

"What's all this, Lissie? Are you moving in?" Fiona's attempt at humor fell flat.

"Just stuff to get ready and for later. Let's go to your room." Melissa waved to Mr. and Mrs. O'Brien in the living room and headed upstairs.

Inside the garment bag was a pair of white wool bell-bottom slacks and a white satin shirt. She removed a pair of low white heels from the overnight case. It was the same outfit Melissa had worn to her mother's wedding the year before.

"I knew we were dressing up, but what the fuck? I've just got this dress." Fiona pulled a short A-line dress from her closet. The knit fabric was printed with a bright wash of purple, red, and royal-blue flowers.

"You'll be fine. That's the kind of stuff most chicks'll be

wearing," Melissa said. "Me and Scott are dressing totally in white to protect us from Vincent's black magic."

"You look beautiful, Lissie." Fiona was surprised at how radiant her friend looked in her outfit. The disheveled, down-trodden Melissa of a few days ago had vanished. In her place was a stunning young woman. "Check yourself out in the big mirror."

Melissa walked toward the full-length mirror on the back of Fiona's closet door. Her smile faded as she turned wide-eyed toward Fiona. "Oh, my God. The whole room just filled up with flames." She clamped her hands over her mouth and lay on the bed.

Fiona froze. No sound or movement came from either of them for several moments.

Melissa broke the silence. "I looked at myself in the mirror. All of a sudden everything behind me burst into flames. It's gone now."

"What—what do you think it means?" Fiona's terror was mounting by the second.

"It means that tonight is the most important night of my life. That me and Scott have an obligation to stand up to Vincent and counteract whatever he plans to do. C'mon. We've gotta pick up Scott and get to that party."

Scott had transformed himself from a nondescript college student into a vision in white. He stood tall in his white pants, shirt, suit jacket, and tie. His white sneakers did nothing to detract from his commanding appearance.

He squeezed into the back seat of the Volkswagen and checked Melissa's overnight case.

"I see you've got everything, Lissie," he said.

"Just like we planned," she replied, then said to Fiona, "We started our spell on Saturday, since that's the most powerful day to drive out evil influences. It's been complicated, because the party and Vincent's ceremony are happening on Thursday and into Friday. We've got blue candles for tonight since that's the color for Thursday."

"I really don't need to know all this. I'm sure whatever you do will be just fine." Fiona's discomfort was escalating.

"Are you sure? We worked really hard on this. Vincent's a Scorpio, so we had to coordinate all the elements of his sign with the day of the week and what he's trying to do. Check it out. Garnet's the stone for Scorpio, red's the color, and iron's the metal." Scott held up a garnet necklace, a red scarf, and a cast-iron trivet.

"Do you really believe this will protect you?" Fiona's confidence in Scott was gone.

"It's not the stuff so much as the elements and colors, and what we do and say during the ritual," Scott said.

"Tell her our plan," Melissa said.

"At eleven thirty, Lissie and I will go into the bedroom. We'll set up our stuff and do our thing so we can be done by midnight. Vincent won't begin his ritual until midnight. By that time, he'll be powerless," Scott continued.

"And what am I supposed to do while you're in there? You're gonna leave me with Vincent?" Fiona asked.

"C'mon, Fee. Do your part."

Melissa parked the car in front of a brown-and-white-shingled duplex in a quiet neighborhood. "We're here," she said.

The apartment was a step up from the usual party house, as were the guests. About twenty-five people congregated in the living room, with a few spilling over into the kitchen. The furniture was cast off from somebody's grandparents: shabby but relatively clean. Conversations were intelligent, light, and cheerful, only pausing when a joint passed by. A Moody Blues album, *To Our Children's Children's Children*, played softly in the background. Fiona recognized a number of faces from the community college. None belonged to Vincent. Had he changed his mind about the party?

She turned with a start when she heard a toilet flush and a door open. Vincent walked out of the bathroom and into the living room.

At first, Fiona didn't recognize him. Vincent had grown a goatee and trimmed his mustache pencil thin, giving him a sinister, Satanic appearance. His dark hair had been slicked back, accentuating his piercing, demonic eyes. His black silk shirt and expensive, well-fitting pair of black trousers gave him a towering appearance.

He made a beeline for Fiona. "Miss Fiona. Melissa told me you'd be attending tonight. It's a pleasure to see you."

He bent to kiss Fiona's cheek before she had a chance to turn away. She felt a burning sensation run from her face to her heart. Was this the beginning of his seduction?

"Nice to see you, Vincent," Fiona replied politely. She glanced around the room, anxious for her friends to rescue her.

"Did Miss Melissa tell you what an important night this is for me?" he asked.

"Um, I'm not sure. What do you mean?"

"Why are you fidgeting? It's New Year's Eve. Nothing to be nervous about," Vincent said, putting his arm around Fiona's waist. "If anything, I'm the one who needs to be nervous. I'm meeting an old friend tonight."

"R-really? Does Lissie know your friend?"

"Not yet. I hope they'll get to meet very soon. Can I get you something to drink?"

"No, no thanks. It's kind of early. Maybe later," Fiona said.

"A glass of wine would help you relax. I'll be right back." Vincent headed for the kitchen.

Fiona had no intention of drinking anything served by Vincent. She searched for her friends. Why had they disappeared and left her alone with a lunatic?

Fiona recognized a couple from the newspaper office passing a joint in the corner of the living room. She joined them and made small talk while continuing to look for her friends.

Melissa and Scott came in the front door carrying the Samsonite case. They whispered something to their host, who motioned toward the bedroom. They returned a moment later without the suitcase and joined Fiona.

"Have you seen Vincent?" Fiona asked. "He's the polar opposite of you two. Dressed completely in black. He freaked me out."

"We warned you, Fee," Scott said. "Be friendly and don't arouse suspicion."

"He said he was getting me something to drink, but there's no way I'm drinking anything he gives me. I'm afraid he's gonna drug me."

"I never considered poison," Scott said. "I was sure we thought of everything."

I knew you didn't have your shit together.

The three stood helpless in the center of the room.

Fiona was the first to break their silence. "He's been gone a while, so maybe he forgot."

"Vincent doesn't forget anything," Melissa said.

"Speak of the Devil," Scott said as Vincent walked toward them carrying two glasses of white wine.

"That wasn't funny." Fiona glared at Scott. Was this some kind of joke to him?

"My apologies, Fiona," Vincent said, handing her a glass. "Newspaper business, you know. Now that we're all together, let's have a seat. I've been looking forward to this evening for quite some time."

They sat in a circle on the floor. Fiona placed her wine behind her, hoping Vincent wouldn't notice she wasn't drinking. Every few moments she felt his hand on her back. Each time she shifted away from him, pretending to get more comfortable. A sideways menacing glance from Vincent told her he didn't buy into her charade.

Instead of talk about Satan, Vincent diverted the conversation to Fiona's artwork. She didn't like being the focus of his attention, but it was better than a discussion of black magic. She glanced at the wall clock every few minutes. Time had never crept so slowly.

A few minutes after eleven, Vincent stretched his legs and stood. "I need some fresh air. Anybody care to join me?"

"We're good," Scott said.

After Vincent left, Fiona asked, "What am I gonna do when you two leave to do your ritual? What are you gonna say to Vincent?"

Melissa looked at Scott. "We never thought about that."

"What the fuck, Lissie? You just expect to leave me here?"

Scott thought for a moment. "I guess we could say we want to be alone. Maybe he'll think we're getting it on in the bedroom."

That excuse might have worked at the farmhouse where they spent last New Year's Eve. Fiona knew it wouldn't fly here.

"You know some of these people, Fee. Try joining a conversation or something while we're gone," Melissa said.

"I just wanna go home." Fiona was practically in tears. "This is so much worse than I ever thought it would be. What—"

"Ladies, Scott, I had no idea it was so late," Vincent said as he rejoined them. "I have some work to do before midnight. My friend is expecting me. He must not be disappointed."

He took Fiona's hand in his and brought her to stand. "It's been a pleasure." He stared seductively into her eyes and kissed her hand.

Fiona managed a smile. Vincent was leaving. She would be safe for the rest of the evening.

"Will we see you later?" Scott asked.

Shut up, Scott. Don't encourage him to come back.

"I'm afraid not. My friend and I have a ritual that must be completed between midnight and three. He is quite demanding." Vincent turned to Melissa. "My dear, you have been most important to me. Tonight would not have happened if not for you. We'll meet again. That I promise."

Vincent took Melissa's hand and stood next to her. His dark eyes stared intently at her as he lifted her chin and kissed her on the mouth. "This is your night. Do not forget what we've spoken of."

Melissa stood mutely as Vincent turned away from her and left the party.

"Snap out of it, Lissie," Scott said. "We need to get to work. Will you be okay out here by yourself, Fee?"

Fiona sighed audibly. She felt her composure returning. "I think so."

Melissa whispered something to their host, who quietly led Scott and Melissa into one of the bedrooms.

Fiona was unable to focus on anything except what might be happening behind the closed door. Vincent was gone. Why risk concocting a spell that might backfire? She couldn't imagine how a garnet necklace, red scarf, and cast-iron trivet could protect them from Satan.

With nothing else to do, she turned her attention to the television to watch the ball descend in Times Square. Fiona joined the other party guests in the countdown to midnight.

"Ten! Nine! Eight! Seven! Six! Five! Four! Three! Two! One! *Happy New Year!*" The crowd cheered. Someone popped the cork on a bottle of Asti Spumante, which was passed from mouth to mouth to mark the beginning of 1971.

Melissa and Scott slunk back into the living room and stashed the suitcase by the front door. Fiona made her way to them, missing her ritual sip of what passed for champagne.

"It worked," Melissa whispered in Fiona's ear. "I could feel the power in what we were doing. Those flames I saw in your bedroom were flames of power. We're safe. Vincent won't harm us now."

Fiona had her doubts about Vincent as well as Melissa's supposed power. If Vincent was concocting his pact with Satan at this moment, he had probably found a better place and a better victim.

Several more bottles of Asti were opened, joints and pipes were lit, and holiday cookies were passed around. As the conversations grew louder, so did the music. The party was in full swing.

Eventually, Fiona relaxed and began to have a good time.

Melissa surprised her by saying, "Hey, did you know it's after two? What time did you tell your parents you'd be home?"

"I had no idea it was so late. I told my dad I'd be home by three. What about you?"

"Me too, though I doubt my mother will be paying any attention. She's probably out cold after her party," Melissa said.

"We should think about going. We've gotta take Scott home first," Fiona said.

It was close to two thirty before they said good-bye. The night was crisp and clear. The only sound was the faint murmur of music seeping from the apartment.

Scott was the first to speak once they got into the car. "Son of a bitch. He never came back. I bet the bastard was just fucking with you, Lissie."

"Are you kidding? You know he was for real. You saw the ring. You heard what he said. Tonight was the night. I think he either did what he had to do in his car or somewhere outside," Melissa said.

"But what about his sacrifice?" Fiona asked. "Didn't he have to have sex with somebody? And didn't you think that somebody might be you or me?"

"Maybe he found some chick who was willing to do it with him, or maybe he found another kind of sacrifice," Melissa said. "I'm just glad we're off the hook."

"I've read about all kinds of sacrifices. He could've used a small animal or done some spilling of blood. It doesn't always have to be about sex," Scott said.

"I hope you're done with him, Lissie." Fiona was anxious for the discussion to be over. All she wanted to do was snuggle into her childhood bed and forget this night ever happened. She sensed that Scott felt the same.

They said good-bye to Scott at two forty-five. He promised to call Melissa the next afternoon.

"He looked so handsome in those white duds," Fiona said, trying to change the subject. "You two make a cool couple."

"Thanks." Melissa was distracted. "You know, Fee, I pretended like it's over to Scott, but I know different."

"I'm really tired. Can we please talk about something else?"

"Like what?" Melissa asked.

"Like nothing. How about we just check out the stars? It's a beautiful night."

Fiona wanted their silence to be peaceful, but the energy in the vehicle was vibrating at too high a frequency.

Melissa broke the stillness. "I really learned something tonight."

Fiona turned to her. "What?"

Melissa stopped for a red light. She looked straight ahead, unfocused.

"What did you say, Lissie?"

"I said I really learned something tonight."

Another moment of stillness. Melissa stared at nothing.

Fiona looked up and saw the light had turned. "It's green," she said.

Fiona opened her eyes, conscious of pulling paint chips out of her mouth. She looked down. One of her shoes was missing. She looked to her left. Melissa was missing. She looked past the driver's seat. The car door was open. She looked ahead. The windshield was smashed. She looked to her right. Her door was open. She looked on the ground. She saw her shoe.

She unfastened her seat belt and reached for her shoe. She put it on. That was better. It was cold. She looked at her coat. It was covered with sparkling pieces of glass and paint. She sneezed and buttoned her coat.

Where was she? Definitely not on the highway. Where had they gone? Where was Lissie?

She heard voices. A man and a woman.

The man spoke. "Are you all right?"

"Look at my coat, how it sparkles," Fiona said.

"She's in shock," the woman said.

Fiona looked at the couple. They wanted to help her. Help her do what?

"Come on, honey. Can you walk?"

Of course she could walk. What a stupid question. As she stood, she felt her legs give out.

"Oh," she said, grabbing on to the woman's coat.

"Careful," the woman said.

"I think I'm okay." Fiona's head began to clear. "Where's Melissa?"

Neither the man nor the woman spoke. Fiona shook off the woman's hand and began walking.

Melissa's Volkswagen sat on an embankment on the side of the road. The front end rested against a telephone pole. It was destroyed. Fiona looked behind her. She found the highway. She looked across the intersection at another car. A large sedan with fins. Was it a Cadillac? A group of people dressed in evening wear was hovering around a man who sat on the ground and appeared disoriented. It looked like that car had been in an accident.

An accident. They had been in an accident. All she remembered was sitting at the light. Melissa said she had learned something but never said what. What had she learned? Fiona had said, "It's green." And now. Where was she?

She looked at the highway. Cars were stopping. People were gathering. She needed to know what happened. Maybe someone could tell her. She started walking toward the highway.

The man and woman were back. They held her arms. "Stay with us until the police get here," the man said.

"The police? Did somebody do something? Where's my friend?" Fiona asked.

"You were in an accident. You're okay, but the police need to talk to you."

Flashing red, blue, and white lights. A loud noise. Two men in blue uniforms. More flashing lights. Fiona's eyes cleared. A second police car arrived. She panicked. Did she have any joints on her? Were there any in the car? She didn't think so. They weren't here to bust her. They were here for the accident.

The accident. They had been in an accident. Two policemen were talking to the people from the Cadillac while two more approached her. She flinched. She hated cops. Pigs.

"I'm Officer Salinas, and this is Officer Murdoch. Can you tell us your name?"

Her eyes were beginning to focus. They weren't pigs. They were being nice to her. "Um, I think it's Fiona."

"Fiona what?"

She thought for a moment. "Fiona O'Brien. Yes, that's my name. Where's Melissa?"

"Come sit in the patrol car. It's warm. We have a few questions."

She didn't want to leave the man and woman. She reached for them. "*No!*"

"It's okay, honey. The police are here to help. You go with them now." The woman released her hand from Fiona's arm and nudged her toward the officers.

The light and warmth in the police car brought Fiona's mind into focus. They explained she had been in a serious accident and asked her to tell them what she remembered.

"It's green. That's the last thing I remember saying. Melissa put the car in gear, and the next thing I knew I was pulling paint chips from my mouth. Where's Melissa?"

Officer Murdoch turned to Fiona and asked, "You were in an accident. How do you feel, Miss O'Brien?"

"I'm cold, and my head hurts, but I think I'm okay. Where's Melissa?" How many times did she have to ask about her friend? She began to get frantic.

The officers exchanged a look. "Your friend was thrown from the vehicle. She wasn't wearing her seat belt. An ambulance will be here in a few minutes to take both of you to the hospital. We'll know more then."

Fiona's head clouded again. She tried speaking, but the words stuck in her throat. She sat and stared at the dashboard. Garbled noise spiked from the police intercom.

"The ambulance is here. We'll follow you to the hospital and continue our investigation once they examine you," Officer Salinas said as he helped Fiona into the back of the ambulance.

One medic examined her. The other attended to a wrapped blanket lying at the rear of the vehicle. Was that Melissa?

Fiona's thoughts wandered. Did she take her birth control pill that night? She looked for her purse to check but couldn't figure out what day it was. Then she remembered. January 1, 1971. New Year's Day. That meant last night was New Year's Eve. Vincent! His spell. His sacrifice. It was to be completed by three o'clock. What time did they leave Scott's house? Two forty-five. What time did they reach the intersection?

"Three o'clock!" she screamed. "The witches did it!"

The medics stared at her as though she were still in shock. For the first time since she said, "It's green," she was in her right mind. Melissa was Vincent's sacrifice. It had nothing to do with her. She meant nothing to him.

Melissa. His nemesis. His black magic against her white. The powers of evil over good. An innocent, gullible victim. Who better to give to Satan? The timing was perfect. The flames Lissie had seen in the mirror. The fear. The rituals. It was all too real. The one question remained: What had she learned that night? Maybe once her friend recovered, they could discuss it.

The next thing she knew, she was in a hospital bed. People in white were prodding and poking her.

"Just some bruising and a cut on her hand," one said. "She'll be okay. May catch a cold from the shock."

One of the police officers approached her bed and spoke briefly to the people in white. They left. The officer spoke. "Miss O'Brien?"

She looked at him. He had a nice face.

"I'm sorry to tell you that your friend Melissa passed away in the ambulance on the way here. She was thrown from the vehicle and broke her neck. The medics did what they could to save her, but the damage was too great."

"The witches did it! The witches did it!" Fiona screamed.

"She's still in shock," the doctor said to the officer. "We're administering a sedative."

"I'm not in shock. You have to believe me. The witches did it!" Fiona quieted as the nurse slid a needle into her vein. What was the use in talking? No one would believe her. To them, it was another car accident. She disappeared into a drug-induced fog.

Chapter 54

A soft frost caught the rays of the early afternoon sun as Fiona opened her eyes. How long had she been asleep? She heard the phone ring. Her mom's voice. She tuned in to the words.

"She's still asleep, Reuben," her mom said.

Wait, I'm awake. Fiona realized she only imagined the words taking shape. She sat up too quickly and immediately lay back down. This had to be the worst hangover of her life. *Must be that cheap-ass champagne from last night.*

Her mind drifted back to the party. She had no memory of how she got home, into her pajamas, and into bed.

The volume of her mom's voice increased. She heard the words "Serious accident. She's fine. Yes, later."

Was Reuben in an accident? He must be okay since her mom was talking to him. Who was fine? She attempted to sit up, only to crash into her pillow for a second time. She raised her hand and saw a large bandage, splattered with blood on its borders. *Did I cut myself? Did I fall?* A cloud covered her thoughts each time she tried to clear her mind. What was going on?

The sunlight twinkled like tiny diamonds on her window. Hadn't she seen sparkles like these not long ago? She searched her mind for an answer. Her coat had sparkled like that recently, hadn't it?

She reached for the glass of water on her nightstand. Before drinking, she put her finger to her tongue as though she needed to dislodge something small and sharp.

The cloud cleared as the memory of last night poured into her. She stared at the ceiling. Out of every tiny crack in the plaster came a memory. She was alive. Melissa was dead. Dead!

She thought back to the party and the events leading up to it, especially the flames Melissa had seen in her bedroom. Was that a sign of things to come? What happened with Vincent and Satan? Was Melissa his sacrifice, or was it purely coincidental?

She needed to talk to Scott. And Reuben. Who should she call first?

She heard a light tapping on her door and her dad's voice. "FiFi, are you awake?"

"Yes. Come in."

The entirety of what happened revealed itself on Mr. O'Brien's face. He had aged at least ten years since last night. Tears glistened in his blue eyes.

"How are you feeling?" he asked.

"My head hurts. I'm exhausted, and I'm freezing." Fiona sneezed. "How did I get home? What happened?"

Her dad turned away from her. "We got a call from the hospital around four o'clock this morning. They said you had been in an accident, but you were okay. They told us to come right away. When we got to the emergency room, you were screaming something about witches. The doctor said you were in shock, so they gave you a sedative. He said you had a slight fever but nothing serious. We brought you home and put you to bed. Can I hug you?"

Fiona sat halfway up and reached out. Father and daughter held on to each other.

"God was looking out for you," he said.

"But not for Lissie, right?"

"It was her time. God has plans we will never understand."

Was God's plan to sacrifice her to Satan? Fiona kept her thoughts to herself. Her dad was doing his best to comfort her. She hadn't felt this close to him since she was a little girl. For a few moments, she felt safe, warm, protected.

"The doctor said to give you aspirin every four hours to keep your fever down. He also prescribed some tranquilizers." He reached into his shirt pocket for the pills.

"No tranquilizers, Dad, but I'll take the aspirin."

"They'll make you feel better and help you forget," he said.

"I never want to forget," Fiona replied.

"People have been calling all morning. All our friends from church. They sent you God's love and said how lucky you are."

Fiona didn't feel lucky. Her best friend was dead. She was the one forced to deal with the phony well-wishers, the trauma, the sadness, and the funeral.

"Will—I mean, when is the f-funeral?" Fiona's sobs returned.

"We'll talk about that later," her dad said. "Right now I need to know if you're hungry. Your mom can make you a cup of bouillon. Do you want to get up?"

"In a bit."

"Oh, I almost forgot. Reuben called. He left a number." Her dad stood. It was time for him to leave.

The aspirin helped clear her brain fog. She willed herself to get out of bed and get dressed. It would take all her courage and strength to walk downstairs and greet her new reality, a reality without Melissa.

Fiona joined her mom in the kitchen.

"Well, it's about time you were up and about," her mom said with forced cheeriness. "It's after two. You missed breakfast *and* lunch. Oh, and you've gotten a number of phone calls from our friends at church. I'll give you the list, but no need to call them back."

"Anybody else?"

"Reuben, some of your old friends from high school, and a boy named Scott. Wasn't he Melissa's boyfriend?"

"Um, yeah. I think I'll use the upstairs phone." Fiona turned to leave the room.

"Fiona, I saved you a piece of New Year's coffee cake. I'll make you some bouillon." Mrs. O'Brien continued to make small talk, never once mentioning the accident or offering consolation to her daughter.

Fortified with a hot cup of brown salty water, Fiona headed back upstairs.

She called Scott first. She told him what she remembered about the accident but wasn't sure how much he heard through his sobs. He wanted to see her and said he'd be over in an hour.

Reuben was still at his grandparents' home in Rochester. It would be an expensive long-distance call. She needed to gather her thoughts before dialing.

Reuben picked up after the first ring. "Fiona, why wasn't I there to save you? If I had stayed home, you and I would have spent New Year's Eve together, and the accident would never have happened."

"It was fate. I know it," Fiona said. She proceeded to relate the details to Reuben, leaving out her connection to Vincent. Each time she told the story, it became more bizarre.

"My family is leaving here Sunday morning. I can take a bus tomorrow and be there with you by Saturday night."

"I'd like that," she replied. "I love you very much."

"You have no idea how much I love you. I'll see you late tomorrow."

Fiona escorted Scott to the basement family room so they could talk in private. Like her dad, Scott had aged overnight. She flipped on the radio to muffle their conversation.

"I thought good was supposed to triumph over evil," Scott began. "We worked so hard to fight Vincent's magic, but he was stronger."

"Don't you think it might be a coincidence? Vincent wasn't there. How could he send those people to kill her?" Fiona asked.

"Y'know, they say God works in mysterious ways. Looks like Satan does too. This was deliberate. I'm gonna do everything in my power to figure this out and save her soul. I owe it to her." Scott broke down again, bringing Fiona with him.

"How much do other people know?" Fiona asked after their tears dried.

"Nothing, really. They knew Lissie and Vincent were interested in the occult, but they kept things private. I was the only one who knew anything. I want to keep it that way," Scott said.

"Have you talked to her mother?"

"I called, but her husband said she was hysterical and didn't want to talk to anybody. He did tell me about the funeral. The viewing will be Monday and the funeral on Tuesday." Scott covered his eyes with his hands and took a few slow, deliberate breaths. "Funerals are for old people. This is so wrong."

Fiona had attended a few funerals of older relatives. She remembered the horror she experienced staring at their dead bodies. How would she cope with seeing Melissa for the last time? How would she say the final good-bye to her friend?

"Reuben will be here tomorrow night. Maybe the three of us can go to the viewing together," Fiona said.

"Let's make a promise to be there for each other, okay?" Scott asked.

"Of course." Fiona gave his hand a squeeze.

Fiona picked at her pot roast at the dinner table. Her parents tried making superficial conversation to avoid the proverbial elephant in the room.

"Mom, before I forget, Reuben's taking a bus from Rochester and will be here tomorrow night. I asked him to stay till the funeral and everything is over."

Mrs. O'Brien clenched her fists and pursed her lips. "What do you mean inviting him without asking me first? Haven't I been through enough? If he wants to come to the funeral, he can drive here like everyone else."

"Stop, Helen," her husband commanded. "This isn't about you. Reuben is always welcome." He turned to his wife. "Come into the kitchen. Now."

Fiona tried listening through the door but was only able to

detect inflection and emotion. Her dad was furious. For once her mom was quiet.

A few minutes later her parents joined her in the dining room. Her mom spoke. "Fiona, Reuben can stay here, but you're going to have to help me."

"Helen," her dad warned.

"We'll manage," her mom said as she left the table.

Chapter
55

Reuben called Saturday to say he'd be arriving at the bus station around nine o'clock that evening. The thought of being alone until then, with nothing to think about except Melissa and the accident, was terrifying. She hadn't expected the incessant ringing of the phone—friends she hadn't seen since high school, friends of her parents, all offering their sympathy and wanting to learn every detail of the tragedy. The accident even made the front page of the local paper. She glanced briefly at the headline, "Tragedy Strikes on New Year's Eve," before shoving the paper into her dad's desk drawer.

In between phone calls, she composed a letter to Peach, who still had no telephone. Writing the details helped her put the events into perspective. She imagined Peach opening the envelope, never anticipating the words hidden inside.

She tried calling Melissa's mother but continually got a busy signal. The family must have taken the phone off the hook. She called Scott, who joined her for the afternoon. He was the only person she could relate to. Hopefully, that would change once Reuben arrived.

Fiona didn't expect the wave of sadness that hit her as she got into her car to pick up Reuben. She remembered the day she and Melissa had gone to the Volkswagen dealer to pick out their cars.

The salesman said it was the first time two friends had bought cars from him at the same time. "You two must be really close," he said.

They looked at each other and giggled. "Best friends since high school," Melissa replied.

Can you stay best friends with someone after they're dead? Fiona asked herself.

Reuben was waiting under a streetlamp. She had never been so grateful to see anyone. She forced a smile as she pulled up to the curb. He, too, had aged since she last saw him.

They held each other tightly as a new round of tears found their way to the surface. Fiona let them flow, feeling relief for the first time in two days. Now that Reuben was with her, everything would be all right.

Fiona's parents welcomed Reuben, knowing he was a tonic for their daughter. For once, her mom didn't object to them spending time alone in the basement family room. The couple talked until after two in the morning. Fiona wanted to know all the details of Reuben's trip and what he had learned about emigrating to Canada. He gently told her all that could wait for another day.

She recounted every detail of New Year's Eve: from Melissa

and Scott's plans to the flames in the mirror, the party, the accident, and its aftermath. Reuben wanted to believe the accident was a coincidence, but like Fiona, he was skeptical.

"I have my doubts about Satan and black magic, just like I have my doubts about God," Reuben said. "What I do know is there is much more to this universe than we will ever comprehend."

"Right now I need to stop being afraid that something else terrible will happen," Fiona said.

"I think it's natural to feel that way," Reuben said. "It's gonna take some time to get over this. We'll get through it together, right?"

"I guess." She thought about the empty days after he would leave her and before classes resumed. Then she remembered his student teaching assignment and that he wouldn't be on campus for the entire semester. Loneliness overwhelmed her.

Viewing hours at the McCleary Funeral Home were scheduled for Monday evening from four until seven. Fiona, Reuben, and Scott arrived at the funeral home shortly after four o'clock, not knowing what to expect. Would they stay the entire time or pay their respects and leave? What they didn't expect was the crowd of mourners who filled the home.

"I think a lot of these people are from Mr. Giovanni's family," Scott said.

"Who?" Reuben asked.

"Lissie's mother remarried last year. I guess she got more than a husband," Scott explained.

They were directed to a room at the end of the hall but held back, knowing that they would be seeing Melissa, or what remained of her, for the last time.

A group of students from the community college arrived and distracted them for a few minutes. All were quick to offer their condolences to Scott and ignored Fiona. She hoped he wouldn't introduce her as the passenger. The less she had to interact with people, the better.

As the crowd in the hallway grew larger, one of the ushers guided them toward the viewing room. Fiona held on to Reuben and Scott. Scott's hands were trembling, and his steps faltered as they walked toward the inevitable.

"I don't think I can go in there," Scott said, turning toward the wall. "I promised myself I'd be strong, but it's all too much." He lowered his head and broke down.

After a few moments, Scott wiped his eyes and stood tall. "Sorry. I'm ready now. Are you, Fee?"

She would never be ready.

Rows of chairs were arranged as though they were there for a school play. The seats near the front were occupied by Melissa's mother and her immediate family. A line of mourners and standing floral arrangements masked the purpose of the visit— the opportunity to pay their last respects to a lifeless body.

It was Fiona's turn to hesitate. She pressed herself into the back wall and froze. She wanted to run, to escape from the nightmare that kept building upon itself.

Scott nudged her forward. "Come on, Fee. We've gotta pay our respects." He swallowed, took a deep breath, and wiped away lingering tears.

She looked at Reuben, who said, "You're not alone."

What a Trip

They walked to the end of the line. Fiona watched as each person paused in front of the open coffin, knelt, made the sign of the cross, and moved on.

"Do we have to kneel?" she whispered to Scott.

"It's a way of saying good-good-bye." Scott tripped over his words.

"You do whatever makes you feel comfortable," Reuben said. "I'm not kneeling."

Someone had gone to a lot of expense. Gold letters reading BELOVED DAUGHTER wove their way through a large spray of red roses that lay on the lower half of the highly polished casket. Fiona got her first glimpse of something or someone resting inside. She closed her eyes and bowed her head.

When she looked up, Melissa's mother's eyes bored into her. As Fiona took a step toward her, Mrs. Giovanni turned away. It was obvious she wanted no contact with Fiona.

"I think Melissa's mother wishes I was the one who died," Fiona whispered to Reuben.

"Don't worry what she thinks. None of this is your fault. Let her be," Reuben said.

Before she had a second to prepare herself, Fiona was face-to-face with Melissa. A morbid curiosity kept her from looking away. Melissa's lifeless form was comforted on either side by mounds of white satin. Her eyes were closed. Her hands held a crucifix and rested on her lap. Fiona recognized her friend, but whoever had dressed her and prepared the body had destroyed her true essence.

Melissa was dressed in a sky-blue polished cotton dress with a high lace collar that hid her broken neck. Her long blond hair had been washed and arranged in a C curl that crept across her shoulder and below the collar. Someone had applied thick foundation and blush to her face to hide the bruises. A hint of bubblegum-pink lipstick covered her lips.

Fiona was not aware of how long she stood and stared, nor was she aware of the tears that ran down her cheeks. Reuben took her hand and escorted her out of the room.

"How could they do that to her? That's not Lissie. Her body's gonna rot in the ground in that fucking dress." Fiona wanted to scream.

"C'mon, let's sit over here." Reuben led her and Scott to a bench in the center hallway, away from the crowds.

"She was the best thing that ever happened to me." Scott's shoulders vibrated as his sobs returned. "How could Vincent take her life?"

"You don't have any proof he did." Reuben replied.

"I'll find proof. I won't stop till I figure this out," Scott said.

Fiona tuned out the rest of the conversation. All she could think about was the desecration of Melissa's dead body and how she could do nothing about it.

She felt a certain amount of safety on the bench. Friends from high school, Melissa's classmates from college, and members of the community stopped to offer their condolences.

By six forty-five, the crowd had thinned. A tall man dressed completely in red pushed his way into the building as others left.

"Vincent!" Scott whispered. "What the fuck is he doing here?"

Fiona stared straight ahead. She didn't want to confront the man who may have killed her best friend.

"Fiona. Look at him!" Scott commanded.

Fiona shot a sideways glance at the entrance where Vincent

stood. In his red trousers and shirt, he looked more Satanic than he had on New Year's Eve. A large brass medallion hung from his neck, resting at his solar plexus. A chunk of gold shone from his left ring finger.

"Are you going to say something?" Reuben asked.

"I-I can't," Fiona whimpered.

Reuben turned to Scott. "You?"

Scott shook his head. "What good would it do? He took everything from me."

Vincent stared through them as though they didn't exist. Without speaking to anyone, he strode into the viewing room. Only a few stragglers remained in the seats. They stood to leave as he entered. It was as though he had taken control of the room and the mourners.

Fiona watched from the hallway as Vincent stood by the casket, staring at Melissa. She could see his mouth rhythmically moving as though he were chanting. He removed the medallion, bent over, and reached into the casket as though he was touching the body. When he stood, she saw he no longer held the medallion. A glint of gold remained on his hand.

He continued to stand and chant until one of the ushers cleared his throat, indicating it was time to leave. Vincent nodded, took a final look at the body, and left the room. Without glancing behind him, he left the building. The few remaining guests looked at one another as if to say, *What was that all about?*

Scott and Fiona knew what it was all about. Vincent had claimed what was his.

Chapter 56

The funeral was held at the Catholic church the following morning at eleven. A closed casket had been carried to the front of the sanctuary, where it sat waiting for the priest to complete the mass. As the pallbearers carried the remains to the waiting hearse, the priest announced that the burial would be a private family affair at a cemetery in the western part of the state. He invited the congregation to a short reception in the church basement.

Mr. O'Brien encouraged his daughter to attend the reception. "It'll help with closure, FiFi. Fellowship is important after a tragedy. I'd like to stay, but I have to get back to the office."

Mrs. O'Brien avoided eye contact with her daughter when she spoke. "Your father's right. I'll see you at home this afternoon."

"Thanks," Fiona mumbled.

Church ladies in frilly aprons served coffee and pastries that guests carried to banquet tables covered in white paper tablecloths. The scene reminded Fiona of fellowship hour at the Methodist church, which she had managed to avoid for over a year. She couldn't understand how a few cheap desserts and weak coffee could help her with closure.

"You don't look so good," Reuben said to Fiona after they sat down.

"It's really hot in here," she replied.

"Actually, it's not," Reuben said. "You look kinda flushed, and your eyes look like you smoked too much pot. C'mere, let me feel your forehead."

She sneezed before moving closer to him.

"You've got a fever," Reuben said.

"Bullshit."

"Scott, back me up here."

Scott felt her forehead. "Yup. It's a fever."

"How could I be sick?"

"With all you've been through? I'm not surprised. C'mon, let's get you home." Reuben stood to leave.

"Please don't tell my parents."

"I won't have to. All they need to do is look at you."

The trauma of the last several days had caught up to Fiona. She spent the next two days in bed nursing a low-grade fever.

Reuben took a bus home the morning after the funeral. He called every morning and evening to let Fiona know he was thinking of her.

By Thursday she was well enough to grab her sketch pad and colored pencils and create the drawing that had been drifting through her head since the funeral. On the left she drew the back of Melissa's blond head, realizing her friend's face was already fading from memory. In the center she created an image of Melissa in her pale blue dress, resting in her satin-lined casket, the vision she feared would live with her forever. On the right she sketched a picture of herself in her flannel pajamas lying under a patchwork quilt. She felt relief once her thoughts were on paper.

Fiona hid the picture under her mattress. She finally felt ready to get out of bed and join her mom in the kitchen for a late breakfast.

"You've had a lot of phone calls. Most were well-wishers. I kept a list for you. I don't think you need to return any of them."

"Thanks, Mom." Fiona read through the list while she ate her Frosted Flakes.

"There's one other thing. The two police officers who were at the accident want to talk to you. I told them you were sick, but now that you're better, you need to call them," her mom said, handing her another piece of paper.

Fiona read the names. Who were Officer Murdoch and Officer Salinas? Her memory of them had been wiped clean.

"Finish your breakfast and call them," her mom said. "They've been waiting since Tuesday."

"Gimme a break." Fiona surprised herself by letting her thoughts become words.

"I try to be nice. I try to help. And this is how you speak to me?" Her mom pushed the note toward her daughter and left the room.

Fuck you, bitch! Fiona knew to keep those words to herself.

The police officers offered to meet Fiona at her home, but she said she felt more comfortable speaking to them at the station.

She didn't want her mom listening in on the conversation or giving her opinion about anything.

Fiona drove to the police station and met the two officers.

"We're sorry for your loss. Are you comfortable talking with us about the other night?" Officer Murdoch said, offering Fiona a seat in a private office.

Fiona hesitated for a moment. "Yes, I think so."

"Can you tell us what you remember about the accident?" Officer Salinas asked.

Fiona's memory was still empty. She recounted the little she remembered, leaving out anything having to do with Vincent and black magic.

"Shock and loss of memory are normal reactions, Miss O'Brien. We'll fill you in on what we know," Officer Salinas continued. "It appears that the other vehicle was speeding and didn't see you at the light. The driver claimed he saw the green light and did not expect a stopped vehicle in his path. The impact of the collision sent Miss Patten's car through the intersection, onto the embankment, and into a telephone pole. Miss Patten wasn't wearing her seat belt and was thrown from the vehicle. Had you not been wearing yours, you would most likely not be here today."

Fiona held her body rigid. She did not want to break down in front of these men.

"We strongly suspect the other driver was intoxicated. A sobriety test was administered at the hospital, but because some time had elapsed, his blood alcohol level was only slightly elevated," Officer Salinas said.

"Why did they wait to test him?" Fiona asked.

"Possible injuries were the main concern at the scene. All

parties were taken to the hospital. Once it was determined that the driver had not sustained any life-threatening injuries, the investigation was continued and the test was administered," Officer Murdoch said.

"So you're telling me that my friend was killed by a drunk driver?" Fiona's emotions were beginning to escalate.

"The police are conducting an investigation," Officer Murdoch continued. "The insurance companies will get involved. There'll be a hearing in municipal court in a few months that you may or may not want to attend. We'll notify you of the date. Do you have an attorney?"

"Um, no. Do I need an attorney?" she asked.

"Since you weren't injured and it wasn't your vehicle, it's not necessary unless you plan to bring suit against the other driver. You may want to talk to your parents," Officer Salinas explained.

Fiona had no intention of discussing the situation with her parents. Why would she want to sue the other driver? She had lost her best friend. No amount of money would bring Melissa back.

The officers asked her a few more questions and told her to contact them if she remembered anything else about the accident.

Fiona gave her parents a brief description of her time at the police station. She mentioned the hearing in municipal court but said nothing about hiring an attorney. If her dad wanted to pursue that, he'd have to think of it himself. She was fairly certain he wouldn't.

What a Trip

Scott stopped by her house later that day. She expected him to be outraged when he learned about the drunk driver. Instead, he lowered his head so Fiona couldn't see his tears. "Isn't it amazing how the universe works? That car could've been anywhere, but it was at the right place at the right time for Vincent's sacrifice. It just proves he has a strong bond with Satan."

Fiona had almost accepted the accident was simply bad luck —being in the wrong place at the wrong time. Listening to Scott changed her mind. With everything that had happened in the last two weeks, it seemed unlikely the accident was a random event.

"Where do we go from here?" she asked him.

"I know you're going back to school on Sunday, but I want to stay in touch. I'm gonna continue to do my research and get to the bottom of this. Would it be okay if I drive up to see you every once in a while?"

"Of course," she said.

Fiona needed to distance herself from the accident, from her hometown, and from Vincent. But she also needed support from someone who understood. Scott could be that someone.

Chapter 57

$\mathcal{A}$lthough the trauma of the accident never left her, Fiona's off-campus apartment provided a much-needed distraction. Her roommates, Katie and Pat, were welcoming and friendly without being intrusive. She loved the artistic vibe of the house, the freedom, and the extra space.

She told Katie and Pat about the accident and losing her friend to a drunk driver. They offered their sympathy and let Fiona know they would be there for her if she needed to cry or share her feelings. While she appreciated their offer of support, she preferred to grieve in isolation.

Both roommates had boyfriends who stayed overnight on a regular basis. They let Fiona know Reuben was welcome to spend the night whenever he was on campus.

Reuben spent the first week of school on campus in preparation for student teaching. For the first two days, he treated Fiona like a piece of her mom's china.

"Y'know, Reuben, I appreciate how kind and gentle you're being, but I'm not gonna break," she said.

"I'm sorry. It's like every time I look at you, I remember what you went through and how messed up you were after the accident."

"In a way, it seems like it happened a long time ago, especially now that I'm back here. Part of me wants to forget and move on, but I know that'll never happen."

"Now I wish that I'd taken that student teaching assignment here in town so I could be with you every day. This whole thing was really selfish of me."

"You had no way of knowing. Nobody did," she said.

Except for Melissa. She knew. Fiona kept her thoughts to herself.

Fiona settled into a routine. Reuben had an on-campus meeting every Thursday afternoon. He spent the night with Fiona, leaving early Friday morning for his student teaching position. Most weekends he spent Friday, Saturday, and Sunday evening at her apartment. Occasionally, she drove to his parents' house and stayed over Saturday night. Even though his parents knew they were sleeping together at her apartment, they didn't allow it under their roof.

Fiona and Reuben enjoyed hanging out with Katie, Pat, and their boyfriends, who were both music majors. For the first time in her life, Fiona was spending time with a group of like-minded, creative people. She wondered if her life would have turned out differently if she had had friends like this at home.

She and her roommates shared stories of their lives, their hopes, and their ambitions. Even though she felt a bond with the girls, something was missing. Maybe she didn't want to get too close, as she knew Katie and Pat would be graduating in May. Maybe Fiona needed to keep some distance since they lived under one roof.

"Or maybe I'll never be able to get close to another chick," she said to Reuben one Thursday afternoon.

"It's still kinda soon. Don't be so hard on yourself. I think you're doing great."

"I feel like I'm getting better, and then I get a call or a visit from Scott," she said.

Scott came to see Fiona at school nearly every Tuesday. If he didn't visit, he called. Her feelings about him and his visits were mixed. She knew he needed her and sometimes thought she needed him. His obsession with Vincent and the events of Melissa's death had taken over his life. Each week she read his tarot cards, and he shared his research into the occult and astrology.

"Why don't you tell him you're busy? Or be truthful and tell him you need to move on?" Reuben asked.

"I don't want to hurt his feelings," she said.

"And what about your feelings? What about the nightmares you have after he's been here?"

Vincent was the main character in Fiona's nightmares. He appeared as himself, as Satan, or even as her lover. Each dream followed the same sequence. Fiona would be going somewhere or doing something when she'd run into Vincent. He'd charm her, seduce her, and ask her for help. Once she accepted his offer, he'd take on the form of a demon. She'd scream and wake up in a cold sweat.

"Vincent's gone," Scott told Fiona in mid-January. "One of the guys from the paper said he saw Vincent in town a few days after the funeral, but that's it. He never came back to school. Every coupla days I drive by the house where he lived. No car. No nothing. It's like he never existed."

Fiona shivered. "You're saying he got what he wanted or needed and then split?"

"That's exactly what I'm saying. One more way of proving he was behind the accident."

It took almost a month for Fiona to get a letter from Peach.

Dear Fee,

I have not stopped crying since I got your letter. Our little Lissie is gone forever and I never got to say goodbye. Life isnt fare. Evil people live to be 90 and the good ones die young. You know I dont believe in god or anything, but maybe there is ~~reinacrnation~~ reincarnation and she will come back to us one day. Maybe one of my babies will be Lissie. Did I tell you Im pregant? Im six months along and Im having twins. We can only hope.

Calvin and me have moved which is why I didnt get your letter right away. Now we are living in a bigger apartment so we will have more room for the babies. Our address is on the envelope. We dont have a phone. Sorry.

Life has been good except now I know Lissie is gone. Maybe you and I will meet again one day. Lets stay in touch.

Luv, Peach

Peach's letter brought a deep sadness into Fiona's heart. No telephone. No way to talk to the only person who knew Lissie like she did. Despite Peach's words, Fiona felt her friend had moved on to a new life, new friends, and soon—new babies. She would keep up a correspondence with Peach but knew their relationship was forever altered.

By late February, Scott considered himself an expert in astrology.

"I did Lissie's astrology chart. Everything confirms she was gonna die that night," he told Fiona.

"Really?" Fiona didn't know much about astrology, but she knew Scott was far from an expert. She also knew that Scott was grasping at anything to make sense of what happened.

"I only had Vincent's birthday, November 15, 1942, but that was enough for me to get some information. Turns out he's got some bad shit in his chart. Put his chart and Melissa's together, add Satan, and it's death waiting to happen."

Fiona sensed she was at a breaking point. "Y'know, Scott, I'm trying really hard to get my life back on track, but all this keeps bringing me down."

Scott leaned away from her. "What're you saying? That you don't want to learn what happened? That you don't care about your best friend? That you don't wanna help me get at the truth?"

Fiona was somewhere between screaming and crying. "I don't know what I'm saying. All I know is I need a break."

Scott was visibly hurt. He stood, slump-shouldered, and walked toward the stack of canvases leaning against the wall.

"You need a break? Look at what you've accomplished. Tell

me your artwork hasn't exploded since the accident." Scott spread out six of Fiona's paintings.

She was aware that her art had morphed from soft and impressionistic to dark and surrealistic. Her professors, not aware of the accident, praised the depth and maturity of her work. More than ever, they encouraged her to abandon her education courses and pursue a degree in art history.

Scott exposed her most dramatic work. A yellow DEAD END sign in the center of the canvas stood above a bed of decaying weeds and flowers. A blond angel floated in the midnight sky above. Instead of stars, the sky was punctuated with drops of blood and tears. It was the first piece she attempted after the accident. Now, nearly two months later, Fiona wished she had destroyed the canvas.

"I'm just painting what I feel," she said, turning her head away.

"Don't ever give up on Lissie and the truth," Scott said. "You know she wouldn't give up on you if things were reversed."

Fiona wasn't so sure of Scott's words, but she was sorry for what she had said earlier. They were working through the tragedy, each in their own way. She apologized and agreed to continue their visits.

Chapter 58

Reuben received his order to report for his armed forces physical examination in late February. Fiona wished she had made the amulet Melissa had suggested he wear for protection. Reuben had no worries.

"What difference does it make whether I wear an amulet or not? I'm going for the physical like a good American citizen. It's only when I receive my notice to report that they'll realize I've left the country," he said.

"But maybe they'd find something wrong with you if you had it on."

"Do you think a bag of herbs can protect me from the army doctors? Do you really want me to have some kind of health problem?"

"I guess not."

Fiona secretly wished the army had found a minor health issue that would have kept him from serving, but Reuben was in fine health and classified 1-A, fully eligible, and available for military service after graduation.

"One more sign that Canada is the right choice," he said.

Fiona saw no point in arguing. One by one, their options were being eliminated.

In early March, Officer Murdoch informed Fiona that a hearing was scheduled for Wednesday evening, March twenty-fourth, right in the middle of spring break.

Would she have the courage to attend? To meet the murderer? Was he indeed the murderer and not Vincent? She discussed it with Reuben, with Scott, and with her roommates. Everyone encouraged her to go.

"Easy enough for you to say," she told Reuben. "You're not the one who actually has to do it."

"If you don't, you'll always regret it," he said. "The old Fiona would hide in her room. I see the new Fiona striding confidently into the courtroom."

She knew he was right. "I don't know about striding confidently, but I've made up my mind. I will go."

"That's my girl."

Was she still his girl? Was she even close to the person he met eighteen months ago?

Spring break was Fiona's first visit to her parents since the accident. She told her dad about the hearing.

"You don't have to go, you know," he said. "They've got your statement."

"I've been thinking a lot about it. I think I need to go," Fiona said.

"Do you want me to go with you, FiFi?" her dad asked.

"I'll be okay. Thanks."

Fiona's visit to the courtroom was nothing like the *Perry Mason* episodes she had watched growing up. The room was small and utilitarian, unlike the grand courtrooms on television. An empty jury box sat on the right, the judge's bench at the front. She was escorted to a seat on the left, several rows behind the bar. Other than a group of about a dozen people hovering near a man across from her, only a few people were in attendance.

Everyone rose as the judge entered. The proceedings began. Officers Murdoch and Salinas and others testified. Fiona's mind wandered until they called Stefan Arapolis to the stand.

The driver. The murderer.

His attorney stood. "My client speaks no English, your honor. We have a translator."

That's bullshit. I heard him speaking English when I first got here.

The judge addressed his questions to the translator, who then whispered to Arapolis. Arapolis whispered his answers in Greek, which were then translated for the court. Fiona strained to hear.

She stared at him, hoping to make eye contact. As he left the witness stand, he saw her. A flash of recognition crossed his face as he stared back. A mocking smirk tilted his lips upward. He turned from her and sat down.

Fiona couldn't take her gaze away from the man. She wanted her eyes to drill through his slicked-back gray hair. She wanted him to burn in hell with Vincent at his side while Satan stirred the flames.

All rose as the judge entered his chambers to decide on a ruling. Officers Murdoch and Salinas greeted Fiona.

"It's not looking good for our side," Officer Murdoch said. "They may issue a fine. That's about it."

"What do you mean?" Fiona spoke loudly enough that Arapolis and his entourage turned to look at her.

"It happens sometimes," he said.

The judge returned. "Mr. Arapolis, you were ticketed for drunk driving and careless driving. Since the hospital records indicate your blood alcohol content was within the legal limit, I have to dismiss the drunk driving charge, although I suspect you were intoxicated at the time of the accident. I find you guilty of the careless driving charge and impose a $250 fine, the maximum allowed by law. Next time, sir, and there better not be a next time, you may not be so lucky. Case closed."

"We're very sorry, Miss O'Brien," Officer Salinas said.

"That's it?" Fiona asked.

"Until the laws change, yes, that's it. Best to get on with your life and forget this ever happened," Officer Murdoch said.

"I'll never forget," she said through tear-glazed eyes.

Fiona remained seated in the courtroom as the next several cases were called. It was over. Justice had not been served. Arapolis would go on with his life, possibly to kill again. Had he been part of Vincent's plan? Is that why he was able to walk away with a fine and a slap on the wrist?

Was Melissa's life worth only $250? She thought of the flowers on her friend's casket. Those alone cost more than the fine. At the very least, Mr. Arapolis should have paid for her funeral.

The judge's gavel brought her back to the present. It was time to leave. On the way to her car, she glanced at an American flag flying at half-staff. Wasn't America supposed to be the greatest country in the world? Had she been fed lies her entire life? A drunk murderer ticketed for careless driving, civil and political unrest, racial inequality, women treated like second-class citizens, a needless war, a draft lottery. When would it stop? Maybe Reuben had the right idea about Canada.

Chapter 59

$\mathcal{A}$s soon as Fiona returned to her apartment on Sunday, she pulled out the application to the University of Toronto, which had lain on her desk for months. She filled out what information she could and decided to discuss the rest with Dr. Hacking.

She met with her professor during his office hours on Monday.

"I've told you many times that you'd be wasting your time as a teacher. You don't need to go all the way to Toronto. We've got a great art history program here," Dr. Hacking said.

"I know, but it's complicated," she said.

"I'd hate to lose you as a student, but if you decide to go, I've heard Toronto's Art History Department is top-notch," Dr. Hacking said.

"I'm so confused about everything. Lots has happened to me this past year, and I kinda think I need a change."

She suspected Dr. Hacking had an inkling of her motives.

"Tell you what," he said. "Why don't you send in your application, see if you get accepted, and take it from there? If you change your mind, all you've wasted is a little time and the application fee."

Fiona took a deep breath and relaxed for the first time in

weeks. A decision didn't need to be made immediately. Her world wasn't black and white.

"I never thought about it that way," she said.

"In the meantime, you'll need two letters of recommendation. I'll write one, and I know Dr. Wilckins will too. We'll have them for you later this week," Dr. Hacking said.

"Thank you so much." She practically skipped out of his office.

Fiona didn't mention the application to Reuben.

Since the accident, Canada hadn't been the focus of their conversation, though it was never far from their thoughts. She appreciated the respite but wondered if Reuben had changed his mind about going. Or about her.

Three days later Reuben came charging up the stairs to her apartment, waving an envelope. "I'm in! I'm in!"

He picked her up and spun her around. Outwardly, she shared his enthusiasm. Inwardly, she panicked. She knew it had something to do with Canada.

"I got accepted to grad school at Toronto! Now I don't have to worry about how I'm gonna get into the country. C'mon, we've gotta celebrate. I scored some opiated hash." He pulled out a pipe and a packet of tinfoil from his denim jacket pocket.

Fiona had never seen Reuben happier. She decided to put her worries on hold and share his joy and his stash. Several tokes later, wisps of smoke carried them into her bedroom.

"I want you so much," he whispered as he unbuttoned her shirt. He slid it from her body and turned to lay it on her nightstand. Instead of coming back to her, he paused. "What's this?" he asked, picking up an envelope.

Fiona was no longer stoned or horny. She had been found out.

"You're applying to Toronto!" he practically screamed. "Oh, Fiona, does this mean you're coming with me?"

"I don't know for sure. I have to get accepted first, and it's kinda late to apply, especially for foreign students." She failed to mention Dr. Wilckins's colleague in Toronto who would fast-track Fiona's paperwork.

"Just the fact that you're applying means more to me than anything. This is the best day of my life—well, second best. The best was the day I met you," he said.

Reuben's enthusiasm was contagious. Maybe the worst was over. Maybe they would live happily ever after in Canada.

I've got nothing to lose. I've got nothing to lose. Fiona repeated the mantra to herself on her way to the post office. After handing the envelope to the postal clerk, she froze.

The next customer waited patiently until the clerk's voice brought her back. "*Miss!* Please move along." Embarrassed, she stepped aside.

Now that the application was in the mail, Fiona was faced with the possibility that she might be accepted and actually move to Canada. Until this moment, she had visualized herself packing an overnight bag, getting into her Beetle, and making the long drive north. She had looked no further than seeing Reuben's joyous reaction upon her arrival.

Feelings of insecurity crept into her heart. What if he wasn't overjoyed to see her? What if this had all been a game to him? Was Reuben stringing her along, using her for sex and companionship until it was time to leave? Even though they had been faithful to one another for over a year, they had never discussed commitment or marriage. If he was asking her to give up her education, her home, and her country, shouldn't he be offering her some stability?

If Reuben broached the subject of commitment, what would she say? She knew she loved him and believed he felt the same toward her, but she wasn't ready for marriage.

Fiona assumed they would live together once they arrived in Canada. They were spending four nights a week with each other. Once he left, her freedom returned. That would disappear once they shared an apartment. What if they didn't get along? Ending a relationship on campus was easier than ending a relationship in a foreign country. That would present a new world of problems.

She asked herself, *What's the worst that could happen?*

She thought for a moment. If things didn't work out, she could pick up the pieces and come home. She could get back into school and finish her education. Her parents would be hurt and angry, but she knew at least her dad would take her back.

More than anything she longed for the closeness of Peach and Melissa. She could write a letter to Peach, but her friend was far away in time and in life. And Lissie—Fiona knew if she could talk to Lissie, they would find a solution.

Fiona had watched movies in which people visited cemeteries to talk to their loved ones. She had no idea where her friend was buried. Perhaps through meditation, she could connect with Melissa's spirit.

She lay on her bed and calmed herself with slow, regular breathing. She visualized Melissa sitting on the bed next to her and began a conversation in her mind.

Her friend's voice came to her clearly. "You've got nothing to lose, Fee. Life is about taking chances. Don't be afraid. I'm your guardian angel now. I'll never leave you."

Fiona sat up with a start. What happened? Did she channel Lissie, or was it her imagination?

"It's me, Fee, not your imagination. Take it one step at a time. That's all you need to know," Melissa's spirit whispered.

Fiona brought herself back to the present. Whether the voice in her head was Lissie or her mind playing tricks, one step at a time was sound advice.

It was a Friday in early April. Reuben was spending the weekend at her apartment. She knew Canada would be their main topic of conversation. She also knew not to mention her conversation with Melissa.

"Focus on the positive," Reuben said that evening. "Assume your application gets accepted. Let's make a list of everything you'll need to do."

Fiona reached for a pen and paper.

"It helps to start with the simple stuff first, like what clothes you need to bring. It's cold up there. You're gonna need lots of winter clothes."

"How do you propose I get the stuff out of my parents' house?" she asked.

"Next weekend is Easter, so you'll be going home. Your

parents won't expect you to be in the attic packing your winter coats. Your dad's never around, so wait till your mom's busy or sleeping and load up your trunk. Pack as much as'll fit. Just don't put anything inside the car that they might see."

"I guess I could do that," she said.

"Wait till it gets closer to when we'll be leaving to take stuff from your bedroom. That way you won't arouse suspicion. And while we're on the subject, when do you plan to tell your parents?"

"I thought I'd write them a letter and mail it right before I leave," she said.

If I actually do leave. Fiona's anxiety was building again.

"You're stressing out, Fee. Let's get stoned and finish the lists," Reuben said, pulling out a joint.

After a few hits, nothing seemed as urgent. Fiona decided to trust Melissa, her guardian angel.

Chapter
60

May arrived in all its spring colors, along with a letter from the University of Toronto.

"This is it," she said to the now-empty mailbox. Her heart pounded as her sweaty hands ripped open the envelope.

"Holy shit. I'm in!"

"Congratulations!"

She turned to see an elderly man walking down the street. They exchanged smiles.

"You're the first to know. I got accepted to the University of Toronto," she said to him.

"That's wonderful, young lady. Why would you want to go all the way to Canada when there's a fine school right here in town?" he replied.

"It's complicated."

"Life doesn't have to be complicated. That's one thing you young folks never understand." He smiled, tipped his hat, and moved on.

Maybe his life hadn't been complicated, or maybe he had forgotten. Or maybe Melissa had sent him.

Fiona wouldn't see Reuben for two days. Before sharing the news with him, she needed to discuss her options with Dr. Wilckins, her landlord and instructor.

"I've been accepted at Toronto," she began.

"I knew you would. I had a conversation with Dr. Osmun, my colleague up there. I told her all about you, saying you'd be a real asset to their department. You know you're going to lose some credits with the transfer," Dr. Wilckins said.

"That's the least of my worries. I'm still not a hundred percent sure I'm going. That's what I wanted to talk to you about."

"You know, Fiona, it's not my place to interfere in your personal life, but I know your boyfriend had a big influence in your decision to apply," he said.

Fiona sat back in her chair. "You—you do? How, I mean—"

"How do I know? Come on, Fiona, your boyfriend's a loud voice on campus. He's made no secret of his views on the war. Just last month he published an article in *The Beacon* about evading the draft. It's easy enough to put two and two together."

Fiona's face burned scarlet. She squirmed in her seat. So much for keeping a low profile.

Please don't judge me, Dr. Wilckins, she prayed silently.

"You've got some big decisions to make. Are you sure you want to follow him to Canada?"

"I think so, but I'm scared," she admitted.

"You realize your boyfriend won't ever be able to come back to the States. You, of course, can come and go. If you two get married, you understand you'll be living in Canada away from family and friends."

"We're not getting married," she said.

"I see. Well, that's not such a big deal these days," Dr. Wilckins replied.

What would I do if Reuben proposed? She visualized Reuben getting on one knee, taking her hand, and popping the question.

"Fiona?"

She snapped out of her daydream before she had a chance to give Reuben an answer.

"Sorry. I've got a lot on my mind." She felt the blood rise in her cheeks again.

"Understandably."

"The other thing is my parents. I don't want to tell them till after I'm gone," Fiona said.

"That's between you and your parents. All I can do is offer my assistance with your education and, of course, your apartment."

"The apartment is something I wanted to ask you about," she went on.

"I might be able to help you out," he said. "Katie and Pat are graduating in May. I planned to keep the apartment empty over the summer for painting and maintenance. If you need some time to think after the semester's over, you can stay a couple of weeks. I'll just need to know by the middle of June if you're planning on renting in the fall."

"That would be amazing. Thank you." Fiona wasn't sure an extra two weeks would make her decision any easier, but she was grateful for his kindness and understanding.

"Remember, Fiona. One door closes, another one opens. It's a cliché, I know, but there are no dead ends."

Except for Lissie. No more doors for her, Fiona thought as she left his office.

"I've got something for you to read." Fiona handed Reuben a sealed white envelope.

"You're in!" Reuben dropped the envelope on the floor and hugged her.

"I'm in, but we need to talk," she said, moving away from him.

"You are going, aren't you?" he asked.

"I want to, but I'm really nervous," she said.

"Well, Fee, I've had this speech planned for months. Guess it's time." He paused. "Have a seat."

"Are you—breaking up with me?"

He cocked his head and stared at her. "Are you crazy? My life doesn't mean anything without you. Don't you feel that way?"

She sat without speaking.

"Fiona?" Reuben was ready to cry.

"Yes. Yes, I do. I've been so freaked out this year. I lost Lissie, then I thought I was losing you. So much was up in the air, but I think things are falling into place." She curled up on the bed next to Reuben and relaxed in his embrace.

They lay next to each other, feeling the tension of the last months melt away. Eventually, they fell asleep. Reuben's speech would have to wait.

"We've gotta do some major planning," Reuben said the next morning before he left for school.

"We've got all weekend. I'll see you tonight."

For the first time in months, Fiona knew the direction her life would take. She had something to live for.

What a Trip

"Check it out, Fee." It was Reuben's turn to give Fiona a sealed white envelope. Inside was his order to report for induction into the armed forces.

"Geez, they don't give you much time," Fiona said.

Graduation was scheduled for Tuesday, June first. Reuben was scheduled to report the following Monday.

"At least I'll be able to go to graduation. I've heard some cats don't even get that."

"When are you leaving?" Fiona was surprisingly calm.

"I thought we could leave on Wednesday, maybe stop and see my grandparents in Rochester, and get to Toronto by Friday."

Her serenity vanished. "I-I can't be ready by then."

"But I have to be. You gotta understand that," Reuben said.

"I know, but listen to me. I've got an idea." Fiona had spent most of the day hatching a plan.

Reuben leaned toward her with his chin in his hands. "Shoot."

"I thought I'd tell my parents I'm going to the first session of summer school. That starts June tenth. I'll tell my dad it's some kind of special symposium so I'm not sure how to make out the check. That way he'll give me a check made out to me for tuition and rent. I'll cash the check and use the money, along with my savings, to get me started in Canada."

"Why don't you tell your parents the truth? You know I don't like deception."

"But you're deceiving your country by running away to Canada. How is that any different?" A few months ago, Fiona would never have had the courage to speak those words aloud.

"C'mon. You know it's different," he said.

"I just can't do it. My mom would go off the deep end, and my dad would be furious. It's only a few hundred dollars. I'm gonna pay them back."

"You're just postponing the inevitable," Reuben said.

"Please let me do it my way. I didn't grow up with support from my family like you did. I'll write them a letter and mail it once I get across the border. Then I'll call and explain everything."

Reuben shook his head. "I know this isn't easy for you. In a way, you've got more on the line than I do. I'm just so glad you're coming with me."

"Me too," she said, snuggling next to him. *I hope I don't chicken out.*

By the end of the weekend, their plan was complete. Fiona would stay on campus until June second, then spend several days with her parents before returning to her apartment to pack her belongings. She would leave New Jersey on June ninth, spend the night at a Holiday Inn near Rochester, and arrive in Toronto the next day.

"You could spend the night with my grandparents instead of a motel," he offered.

"I'd feel kinda funny without you there," she said.

"At least let me make reservations for you. I'll give you my grandparents' phone number if you change your mind."

"It's a deal." Things were finally falling into place.

Fiona sat with Reuben's family during the graduation ceremony. They had grown fond of Fiona and she of them. In many
ways, she felt closer to his parents than her own. She studied
their facial expressions as they watched their son receive his
diploma. She wondered what they were feeling, knowing in two
days Reuben would be out of their lives forever.

"You must be very proud of Reuben," she said to Mrs. Goldberg.

"We sure are. I wish we had more time to spend with him
before he leaves," Mrs. Goldberg said.

Fiona stared into space. How could his mother remain so
calm?

"Of course, we're worried about him," his mother went on,
"but knowing you'll be with him makes his father and me feel so
much better."

"R-really?"

Mrs. Goldberg turned to Fiona. "Honey, don't you know what
you mean to our son? All he talks about is you. He'd never have
done so well in school if you hadn't been there for him. And now
that you'll be with him in Canada, well, that just makes everything okay."

Fiona was speechless. She and Reuben had said "I love you" countless times, but she had never guessed the intensity of his feelings. She looked back on the last year and all they had shared. He had always been there for her, especially after the accident. Was she really more than someone he marked time with? She needed time to process this new information.

Mrs. Goldberg had packed a picnic lunch, which the family shared after the ceremony. Homemade potato knishes, *kasha varnishkes*, a green salad, and apple strudel. As always, the food was superb. Fiona would miss the delicious meals as well as the easy companionship of Reuben's family.

She and Reuben reviewed their plan one more time before he left with his parents. He would call her when he got to his grandparents' house on Thursday. When he arrived in Toronto, he would place a collect call, which she would refuse, saving the expense of an international call. Reuben gave her the address of the building where they would be staying. If something went wrong, she was to call the Toronto Anti-Draft Programme office, and they would relay a message to him.

Back at her apartment, Fiona relived her conversation with Mrs. Goldberg. She never realized she could mean everything to someone.

Twenty years of listening to her mother had convinced Fiona she was unworthy of love. She was flawed, evil, God's mistake. She harbored the fear that once Reuben learned the truth about her, he would move on.

She reflected on their time together, back to the day she first

saw him in the Student Union building. She was instantly drawn
to him. Perhaps it was chemistry or fate. Perhaps it was nothing
more than timing—a relationship of convenience.

She knew she used sex to mask her vulnerability. She also
knew their relationship went beyond sex. They shared an intellectual and creative curiosity and a passion for nonviolence.
Once sex took a back seat, as it inevitably would, the inner Fiona
would be revealed. It was at that point she suspected Reuben
would leave her in spite of their commonalities. Would it be better to break things off now and avoid future pain, or trust Mrs.
Goldberg's words?

Fiona needed a distraction. Janis Joplin's *Pearl* album sat
next to her bed, waiting to be packed. The album had been released in January, after both Janis and Melissa had left the earth.
For a moment she imagined the two of them in heaven, waiting
for her to join them.

Don't be crazy, she thought, snapping back to reality. *There is
no heaven, and even if there was, I doubt Janis would be there.*

She flipped the album to side two, slipped it onto the turntable, moved the needle to the second track on the album, "Me
and Bobby McGee," and sang along with Janis. When she got to
the chorus, Fiona ripped the needle across the album, deeply
scarring the vinyl.

"Fuck you, Janis!" she screamed as she broke the album in
two. Black shards lingered in the air for a moment before littering the floor.

Just like Janis, I've got nothing left to lose, not even my beloved
Pearl *album*, she thought, tossing the broken pieces into the
garbage.

She questioned her motivation for moving to Canada. Was it

love and an opportunity for adventure? Or was it more about insecurity and hopelessness? As she had done so many times since losing Melissa, she lay back on her bed, closed her eyes, slowed her breathing, and asked for her friend's guidance.

Melissa's voice came in clearly. "Take a chance, Fee."

Fiona replied, "On love? On Canada? On school?"

"On everything," her friend whispered. "Life might start to work out for you."

"But what if it's all a big mistake?" Fiona asked.

"There are no mistakes. Trust me, Fee."

Could she actually trust a voice in her head? Was she going crazy?

"You're not crazy, Fee."

"You can read my mind?"

"Of course. Don't leave this world with regrets like I did," Melissa said. "It's too late for me but not for you."

Fiona sat up with a start. The conversation was so vivid she almost expected to see Melissa sitting next to her.

"Lissie? Are you here?"

A breeze drifted through her open window and blew a piece of paper onto the floor. It was her acceptance letter from Toronto.

Chapter 62

Reuben arrived safely in Toronto on Friday. After spending a few days with her parents, Fiona returned to her apartment the following Tuesday. She spent the day packing and repacking her car and cleaning the apartment. All she had left to do was write a letter to her parents, which she planned to mail once she crossed the border on Thursday.

Dear Mom and Dad,

By the time you read this, I will be in Canada with Reuben. He and I are against the war, and this is our way of expressing our feelings.

I got accepted into the Art History program at the University of Toronto and will be transferring there in the fall. I never wanted to be a teacher like you wanted, so I will find a way to pay for the rest of my education.

I am very sorry I lied to you about summer school. I was afraid to tell you the truth. I will get a summer job, and I promise to pay back the money as soon as I can. It might take a while.

I know you will be mad at me, and I don't blame you. I hope one day you will understand and forgive me.

Reuben won't be able to come back to the States, but I can. I hope you will welcome me home when I come to visit.

I will call you once I get settled.

Love, Fiona

Fiona spotted Reuben walking down the street. He stopped and stared as she pulled her Volkswagen to the curb. She waved. He turned away. She called to him.

"What are you doing here?" he asked.

"I've come to be with you," she replied.

"Go home, Fiona."

She woke, drenched in sweat.

She told herself it was nothing more than an anxiety-induced dream, but it was enough to keep her awake for the rest of the night. She got up at five o'clock, took a shower, and grabbed a thermos of coffee, some snacks, and a few last-minute items. She closed the door to her apartment for the last time.

It was the longest drive Fiona had ever taken. She was comfortable with the traffic and urban sprawl through northern New Jersey, but she was not prepared for the hypnotic green of the Pennsylvania interstate highways. Without a radio, she had nothing to distract her. She caught herself nodding off and pulled to the side of the road. Ahead, she saw a sign, NO STOPPING OR STANDING.

"Shit," she said to no one except herself. She got off at the next exit, ate a Snickers bar, and filled up on coffee.

What a Trip

The coffee break revived her. She promised herself she would make more frequent stops. It would delay her arrival at the Holiday Inn near Rochester, but at least she would arrive in one piece.

Singing helped break up the monotony. She sang every Bob Dylan song she could remember, then switched to Janis Joplin. The music brought Melissa's essence into the car. She remembered their nights in her mom's Corvair, sharing joints and cigarettes, sharing secrets reserved for best friends.

If she kept her eyes focused straight ahead, she could pretend Melissa was sitting next to her, twirling a strand of blond hair, taking a drag from her cigarette. She thought of conversations they had taken for granted, conversations they'd never have. Friends were supposed to last a lifetime. Hers had been taken when she was only twenty. She doubted she would ever be open to another close friendship.

Thoughts of Melissa reminded her of the accident, of Vincent and the dark forces he'd planned to release that night. Was he really responsible for Melissa's death like Scott claimed, or was it an unexplained coincidence?

Fiona remembered the police talking about the debris left from the accident. She wondered if any of it remained in the bushes on the side of the road. One day, a thousand years from now, an explorer might discover a scrap of metal, a bolt, a screw, never guessing its history. Was she more debris left from the accident?

And then it hit her. Maybe Vincent really wasn't at fault. Maybe he wasn't Satan in human form but a master manipulator. A sociopath. Someone who took advantage of a beautiful, slightly unbalanced young woman who believed in fairies and the power of magic.

If he were as powerful as he claimed, he wouldn't have been

wasting his time hanging around a community college newspaper office.

Fiona suspected she had been the victim of a hoax. She had allowed a mystery man posing as Satan to control her life. The timing of events had to be purely coincidental. People were killed by drunk drivers every day, especially on New Year's Eve, when half the drivers on the road were intoxicated.

"Life is about choice," she said aloud. Then to herself, *I chose not to believe my mom and her fanatical religion. I can choose not to believe Vincent and his Satanic bullshit.*

Fiona relaxed her grip on the steering wheel. Life didn't have to be complicated, like the old man at her mailbox had said. Moving to Canada would give her a chance to start over, to leave Scott and his theories, to leave her hometown and its tragic memories. She drove on feeling free and sure of herself.

Twenty minutes later her resolve disappeared. She thought once again about Lissie and the events leading up to the accident. The question that remained unanswered continued to haunt her. What was it that Melissa had learned the night she left the earth?

She had heard that some people predict the time of their death. They receive signs, dreams, or visions that portend their future. Fiona suspected the flames Melissa saw in her bedroom the night of the accident signaled the end of her life. Could that be what Melissa meant when she said she had learned something?

Fiona stopped for gas outside Syracuse. The gift shop attached to the gas station sold a variety of New York State souvenirs. She looked for something to buy for Reuben, then hesitated. Souvenirs were mementos of vacations, of pleasant experiences. This trip was neither.

With less than two hours left to drive, Fiona sat on the rear bumper of her Beetle and snacked on a tuna sandwich and a Coke. Three fluffy clouds adorned the blinding blue sky. If she ignored the rumble of eighteen-wheelers on the interstate, she could pretend she was eating a picnic lunch on the side of a country road.

"You're deep in thought," a scratchy male voice sounded.

Fiona sat upright. Behind her stood a trucker in faded blue jeans and a blue plaid shirt frayed at the shoulders where sleeves had been cut away. A Buffalo Bisons baseball cap shaded his eyes.

Don't talk to strangers. Her mom's voice hovered nearby.

"Just taking a break," Fiona replied.

"Where ya headed?"

"To see my grandparents." She knew enough not to say the Holiday Inn.

"A cute young thing like you alone on the road. It ain't safe," he said.

"I can take care of myself."

"I'm sure y'can."

Fiona took a bite of her sandwich and looked around. She could see people in the shop but no one else in the parking lot. If he grabbed her, no one would hear her scream.

"Well, make sure y'got plenty o' gas and that car o' yours is tuned up. You don't wanna be stuck on the highway. Some dirty ol' man might take advantage. Know what I'm sayin'?"

"I'm fine, thank you," Fiona said, standing. She knew better than to get in her car. She started walking toward the shop.

"Don't be rude. C'mon. Hop in my cab. I got a bottle o' rye.

We can have a li'l drink and get to know each other. Whadda ya say?"

"*No thank you!*" Fiona quickened her steps, turned, and bumped into a scruffy gray-haired man coming out of the shop.

"He-e-ey, not so fast, dearie," the man said. "What's the rush?"

"Sorry. I—"

He hiked up his overalls and looked across the parking lot. Seeing the trucker, he quickly assessed the situation.

"Leave the little gal alone, buster," he said.

"Just bein' friendly, right, hon?" the trucker said.

Fiona glared at him.

"Git. You got yer gas."

To Fiona's surprise, the trucker turned and got into his cab.

Fiona's heart pounded in her ears. It was hard to take a breath. "Thank you, sir," she squeaked.

"Glad to help. Listen, it ain't none of my beeswax, but what's a young gal like you doin' all by yourself?"

"I'm going to my grandparents in Rochester."

"C'mon inside and wait till that trucker's long gone. And next time, don't make the trip alone."

"I won't." Fiona doubted there would ever be a next time.

Back on the interstate, Fiona questioned what she was doing alone, hundreds of miles from home, chasing a phantom to a foreign country. Besides the promise of admission into the University of Toronto, she had nothing. Reuben had professed his love for her many times but had made no promises, no words of commitment or marriage. If he had proposed, she imagined it wouldn't have made a difference. She wasn't ready for marriage—to anyone.

Reuben should have insisted they drive together. *What a thoughtless son of a bitch. He had to know how dangerous it was for me to make this trip alone.*

For the umpteenth time, she asked herself if she was running from the accident and the specter of Vincent or running to Reuben. Did she really have nothing left to lose like Janis sang? It wasn't too late to change her mind. She could turn her car around and go back home, make up a story for her parents about summer school being canceled.

What the fuck is the matter with me? One minute I'm ready to cross the border to a new life, and the next I'm backing out and going home. Fiona worried she was losing her mind.

One thing she did know for certain: she didn't have the mental or physical energy to turn back today. She would spend the night at the Holiday Inn and make a decision in the morning.

It was Fiona's first night alone in a hotel. She was grateful for the unfamiliar room with nothing to remind her of home or Reuben. She lay naked on the cool white sheets, ate a second tuna sandwich, and watched hour after hour of mindless TV.

She awoke at two in the morning. A black-and-white test pattern on the television shed an eerie light onto the bed. After turning off the set, she used the bathroom, climbed back into bed, and stared at a dim circle of light on the ceiling.

In one of her art classes, the instructor had the students

soften their eyes to get a new perspective on an object. Blurring the edges altered colors and shapes, allowing the artist to work with essence rather than content. With nothing else to do, Fiona practiced the exercise on the ceiling. A golden halo surrounded the light as the inner circle dimmed. She diverted her eyes for a second. When she returned her gaze, she saw Melissa's face looking down at her.

She had to be dreaming.

"You're not dreaming, Fee."

"Lissie?"

"Why are you surprised? I told you I'm your guardian angel."

"I'm so confused. I need you." Fiona hoped no one in the hallway could hear her.

"What's the big deal, Fee? Tomorrow you'll be in Canada with Reuben. Isn't that what you want?"

"I-I thought so, but he left me to make the stupid trip alone."

"No," Lissie said. "He asked you to ride with him. You're the one who made that decision. You're looking for any excuse to turn around and go home."

"Maybe I should go home."

"To what? Your parents? A teaching job? Peach left. I left. Scott's gonna leave soon too."

"You had no choice," Fiona said.

"You don't know that," Melissa replied.

"What—"

"Never mind, Fee. Reuben loves you. You know you love him. Live your life. Move forward and remember I'll always be with you. . ."

Melissa's voice faded, as did the orb on the ceiling.

What a Trip

Sunlight flooded the room. Fiona opened her eyes, glanced at the clock, and saw it was eight thirty. Toronto was less than a four-hour drive. Driving back to New Jersey would take the entire day. She jumped out of bed and into the shower. Her conversation with Lissie twisted itself around the voice of common sense.

Canada offered adventure, risk, a step into the unknown. Home promised security, stability, a return to safety. Either choice would leave her with regrets. She asked herself which regrets would be harder to endure.

An hour later she was in her car, armed with a thermos of coffee and an egg sandwich. She reflected on the night before. Was it a dream, or did her guardian angel visit her?

It was less than a mile to the interstate. The traffic light turned red before she had a chance to drive onto the entrance ramp. A left turn would take her back to New Jersey and a life she knew. A right turn would take her to Canada and Reuben.

She flipped her directional to the right, then to the left, and finally to the off position.

The light turned green. "It's green," she said, touching her foot to the gas pedal.

WHAT A TRIP
Playlist

On Spotify.com
https://open.spotify.com/playlist/1ctiaZjLJmPxUCyLTRmBh4

Enjoy these songs referenced in the story and get transported
back in time. Listening is free!

Janis Joplin, "Summertime"
Rolling Stones, "Sympathy for the Devil"
Moody Blues, "Nights in White Satin"
Billie Holiday, "Lover Man"
Nat King Cole, "Nature Boy"
Beatles, "Back in the USSR"
Country Joe and the Fish, "I Feel Like I'm Fixin' to Die Rag"
Joan Baez, "We Shall Overcome"
Led Zeppelin, "Babe I'm Gonna Leave You"
John Lennon, "Give Peace a Chance"
Beatles, "Norwegian Wood"
Bob Dylan, "Blowin' in the Wind"
Peter, Paul, and Mary, "Leaving on a Jet Plane"
Janis Joplin, "Kozmic Blues"
Moody Blues, "Higher and Higher"
Janis Joplin, "Me and Bobby McGee"

Here are a few suggested albums. Happy listening!

Big Brother and the Holding Company, *Cheap Thrills*
Rolling Stones, *Beggars Banquet*
Moody Blues, *Days of Future Passed*
Janis Joplin, *I Got Dem Ol' Kozmic Blues Again Mama!*
Moody Blues, *To Our Children's Children's Children*
Janis Joplin, *Pearl*

And of course, the triple album, *Woodstock: Music from the Original Soundtrack and More*

ACKNOWLEDGMENTS

In spite of the image of a writer as a solitary being, it takes a village to bring a book to fruition. I'd like to thank all those who inspired me and offered their ideas and suggestions.

I would especially like to thank the Watchung Writers, fearlessly led by Pat Rydberg. Thank you all for your patience, insight, and friendship. *What a Trip* would not exist without your support.

To Vivian Fransen, thank you for referring me to She Writes Press and for encouraging me to submit my manuscript.

Thank you to everyone at She Writes Press—especially Brooke Warner; Samantha Strom, my project manager; Jennifer Caven and Krissa Lagos, my editors; Stacey Aaronson, my book designer; and my fellow authors.

And finally, to my husband, Bob, thank you for giving me the space to write, for the hours you spent listening to draft after draft, and for your firsthand knowledge of what it was like to live through Woodstock. I love you today and always.

ABOUT THE AUTHOR

SUSEN EDWARDS is the founder and former director of Somerset School of Massage Therapy, New Jersey's first state-approved and nationally accredited postsecondary school for massage therapy. During her tenure she was nominated by Merrill Lynch for *Inc. Magazine*'s Entrepreneur of the Year Award. After the successful sale of the business, she became an administrator at her local community college. She is currently secretary for the board of trustees for her town library and a full-time writer.

Susen graduated from East Stroudsburg University with a degree in education and a minor in English. She earned a master's degree in professional studies and twelve graduate credits in online teaching and learning from Thomas Edison University.

Her passions are yoga, cooking, reading, and, of course, writing.

Susen lives in Central New Jersey with her husband, Bob, and her two fuzzy feline babies, Harold and Maude.

She is the author of *Doctor Whisper and Nurse Willow*, a children's fantasy. *What a Trip* is her first adult novel.